Ivory Lust

Colin T. Nelson

Rumpole Press of Minneapolis, MN

Copyright @ 2019 by Colin T. Nelson

All rights reserved

ISBN: 978-1-7923-0663-1

This is a work of fiction. Names, characters, places, and incidents are the product of the author's imagination and are used fictitiously. Any resemblance to actual events or persons, living or dead, is entirely coincidental.

First Edition: April 2019

Rumpole Press of Minneapolis, MN

Dedication

To my brother, Craig Alan Nelson

Also by Colin T. Nelson

Reprisal
Fallout
Flashover
The Amygdala Hijack
Up Like Thunder
The Inca Code

Short Stories

Taste of Temptation

Acknowledgements

A writer can never claim to have created a story all alone. In reality, there are many people who contribute—some by intention and some by suggestion. In my case, so many people have helped me now and in the past. For this story, I am thankful to our guides in South Africa and Zimbabwe: Warren, Isaac, Frimby, and Robert. All were intelligent, informative, generous, and loved their countries. To my wife, Pam, for all her encouragement and advice during the writing of this story. My readers, critical and essential, George Morrison, Reid Nelson, and Marilynn Curtis, helped shape the final product. I owe them a lot for their time and willingness to be critical. Cover art design from Vila Design and the best editor a writer could have, Jennifer Adkins. Thanks to all of you.

Now, looking back on my life in Africa, I feel like it might altogether be described as the existence of a person who had come from a rushed and noisy world, into a still country. So lovely, as if the contemplation of it could itself be enough to make you happy all your life.

—Karen Blixen (Isak Dinesen)

One should return to old watering holes for more than water: friends and dreams are there to meet you.

—African proverb

Ivory Lust

Map of Southern Africa

Prologue

In many parts of the world, the practice of traditional medicine still prevails. This style of medicine makes use of ancient formulas of herbs, animal parts, and various renditions of natural plants. One of the most prized of these medicines is the ground-up horn of the Western black rhino. It is thought to have supernatural healing properties, in addition to being an aphrodisiac. The timid but huge animal weighed up to 3,000 pounds. More importantly, the front horn could grow as long as four and a half feet—which made them targets.

In 1970 the price of rhino horn had soared to over $1,900 an ounce. Poachers descended on Southern Africa, the rhino's habitat, in an effort to procure as many of the horns as possible. By 1995, ninety-eight percent of the Western black rhinos had been killed.

In 2004, a non-governmental organization, Symbiose, found evidence of thirty-one rhinos in Cameroon. Anecdotes from local people said this "crash" of rhinos was headed toward South Africa.

Naturalists searched for the crash but didn't find it. Since then, no researchers or biologists have spotted any of the rhinos. In 2011 the species was officially declared extinct. (White rhinos remain in good numbers in Southern Africa and are holding their own. A small crash of black rhinos—not Western black rhinos—is also growing at Kruger National Park.)

However, stories of sightings still come out of the bush—primarily from the Zulu and Tswana tribes in South Africa—about the mystical Western black rhino. These are all undocumented, and Western naturalists distrust these tales as a result of the tribes' adherence to magic — for instance, their belief that even spotting the rare beast will cause healing. But the tribes have lived on the land for centuries and know its secrets better than anyone.

Chapter One

Dawn came early in South Africa, the orange ball on the horizon creating long, pointed shadows as if the sun were blowing them across the veld. A tall black man looked toward the morning and felt the strength of the glow on his face. Isaac was from Zimbabwe and worked as a ranger at the Sirilima Game Reserve. There were game parks in Zimbabwe, of course, but the parks in South Africa paid better.

His brother, Frimby, had followed him to the same game park and also worked as a ranger. They were highly trained, and their responsibilities were to preserve the game, help deter poachers, and guide the tourists who came in droves to photograph the magnificent animals that roamed over the reserve. Sirilima was a Swahili word that meant "mountains of mystery."

With dawn breaking, the animals stirred to find water, hunt, and play in their freedom before it became too hot. At the watering hole down the slope in front of Isaac, blue cranes walked stiff-legged as they stalked fish. A warthog lapped at the water, looked up often, and then scurried off to the protection of a mountain pear tree.

Isaac had driven from the administrative center of the reserve on the plain up through a cut in the mountains to get to this plateau. He had told his boss, Trevor Smith, that he was on the plateau to check the perimeter of the northeast quadrant. The reserve used a new security system, but some of the animals perforated the borders anyway. Isaac would investigate to see if any had strayed during the night.

Isaac had hidden the real reason he was at the northeast corner.

The straps of his backpack cut into his shoulders. In the Toyota Land Rover behind him, Isaac had a liter of fresh water. He had brought a nine-millimeter Glock automatic pistol with him, strapped into a holster on his hip. A two-way radio connected him to headquarters, but he had turned it off and left it in the truck.

With a pair of Zeiss binoculars he scanned the field in front of him. Isaac saw a stand of willow trees in the distance and two zebras with their heads down, feeding. He watched the wind lift a puff of dust off the

"I've wanted to see the big game for a long time. I've done a lot of research."

"You gotta go, dude."

Pete stood up. It would be a way to escape the anger, sorrow, and memories that weighed him down. He still lived and worked in the Twin Cities, where he and Barbara had done so many things. They'd had fun times, and she had followed her New Age craziness. Pete had thought she was nuts; now it seemed a quaint and harmless search that he should have supported. This was where Karen had been born. He needed to support her now, even if it was too late to help Barbara. Maybe they could both find peace of mind.

"I'm not worried about myself, but are these safaris safe? Are the rangers dependable and trained?" Pete asked.

Kendra laughed. "It's dangerous only if you stick your head in a lion's mouth. After all, what could go wrong in a game park?"

"Didn't you see the film *Jurassic Park?*"

"Just make sure you can run fast." Kendra laughed again and stood up.

Graves spoke softly. Pete leaned over and smelled Martin's coffee breath. Graves said, "With something as serious as this murder in the park, Washington is sufficiently concerned to have alerted all of us at the E17 security level and above. I don't get a GSD 27-3 form very often."

"What's that mean?"

"They see a possible international security issue. I'm in the cross-hairs as much as Ian. *Very* serious. To prove how much I want you to go, do you know how much paperwork I'll have to fill out? There's Form GD 8933 and that bastard, EIIO 23. That one alone is twenty pages."

"Okay. I'll talk to Karen tonight." He felt exhausted and turned to leave the office.

Graves called, "Wait." He reached behind his desk to a narrow shelf of books, arranged in order and colored like crayons in a box. His finger hooked the top edge of one, and he slid it out to hand to Pete. "Ever read Graham Greene's spy novels? This one's different." It was a copy of Greene's book *Ways of Escape.*

Pete turned it over in his hand. "Thanks. I'll read it on the flight to South Africa."

* * *

With no pending investigative assignments, Pete decided to go home. He left the office tower and crossed the Nicollet Mall on his way to the parking lot. Although he wore a long down winter coat, the wind blew up from underneath and chilled him into his bones.

He owed Martin Graves a lot. When Pete's own career was on the line, Graves had come through for him. Pete would help.

The leather seats of his old BMW convertible creaked when he sat in them. His breath puffed out in a cloud as he listened to the engine grinding, catching, and starting in a reassuring roar.

Pete had sold his small suburban home a few years back to buy a Somerset 55 houseboat. He liked the isolation of the boating community—no one bothered anyone else. And since they all lived in a marina off the Mississippi River, there were no shopping malls, sports bars, or office buildings near them. But with Barbara's death, the marina reminded Pete of a cemetery. The cold weather kept people trapped inside, so the entire basin was quiet, dotted with the gray hulks of boats that appeared like tombstones in the morning fog from the river.

He texted Karen, asking if she could meet him at the boat tonight. Would she be interested in going to South Africa? She agreed to meet but nothing else.

Pete drove east from Minneapolis toward St. Paul, dropping down from Shepard Road through the Crosby Farm Regional Park and into a stand of bare oak trees. Black, twisted limbs covered with humps of snow still gave him the feeling of descending through a magical tunnel that opened onto a secret place unknown to 99% of the people in the city.

Normally, the water in the marina would freeze solid—which could easily crush the hull of even a large boat. So, Pete had installed a special bubbler system around the perimeter of his boat. That was enough to keep the water from freezing. Besides that, Pete had electric connections to land to power his heat and light.

In a few minutes, the interior was warm. He made a small sandwich and settled back in the booth in the galley. Of all the dangers he'd faced around the world, the meeting with Karen still worried him the most.

By seven o'clock, Pete had come out on the deck. He wore his down coat, thermal gloves, and a stocking cap. Wind blew off the Mississippi hard enough to lift spray into the air like a misting rain. It froze on most surfaces the minute it hit. He sheltered his face with his hand and spotted Karen's Prius as it came into the parking lot.

When she reached his boat, Karen smiled up at Pete and climbed over the gunwale. She had black, straight hair and a hint of Asian features in her face—an inheritance from Pete's mother, who was Vietnamese. "Hey, Dad," she called and gave him a quick, padded hug since both wore heavy coats.

"Come inside; it's freezing out here."

Pete slid the glass door open, and Karen stepped across the raised transom into the warm galley. The light glowed like butter where it reflected off the wooden cabinets around them. She shucked off her coat and lifted the hair off her shoulders with both hands.

Pete wanted to say *How are you?* but hesitated.

"Anything warm to drink?" she asked.

"How about hot cocoa?" He knew she would say yes, so Pete walked two steps to the cupboard to remove a cup and fill it with water.

"I've always wanted to go on a photo safari. What's this trip about?" she asked.

"Uh, Martin gave me a job in Cape Town. He's got a friend in some trouble and wants me to help the guy. I'm going for that, and I thought you might want to come along to look at the game after I'm finished with my work." He had his back to her and didn't turn around, instead taking elaborate efforts to make the cocoa.

"Maybe." She slid past him into the booth at the side of the galley, smelling slightly of marijuana. "I guess I'm not too busy."

Pete set the timer on the microwave oven and turned around. He wanted to be honest with her. "South Africa is about as far away as we can get. Besides, the weather there will be warm. No snow. December is the dry season, so many of the leaves are down and it's easier to spot the game."

She looked away. "I don't know, Dad. I appreciate the help you gave to Tim and me for the restaurant, but you haven't been there for me a lot of times."

"I know."

"I don't know that I can just forget all that and spend time with you twenty-four seven. And you didn't treat Mom well at the end." Her dark eyes flicked up to meet his for an instant.

"I understand. I just didn't believe she would go. I mean, she was so damn obstinate, I thought she'd beat it. And you have to admit, she rejected me at times." The microwave binged and Pete retrieved the cup for Karen, setting it in front of her. He slid into the other side of the booth. The smell of the hot cocoa filled the space quickly. "You can say no to this idea."

She tilted her head back and shook the hair out of her face before sipping at the cup. "I'm doing some temp accounting work at a non-profit. I don't even think they'd miss me if I left. And I'd love to get away from town. Everywhere I go, I see Mom. But we'd have to set ground rules, Dad." Karen studied his eyes.

Pete saw her eyes were slightly wet. Red circles surrounded each one, and the skin was puffy. Too much crying.

"We haven't spent much time with each other. I don't know how it would work," she said.

"I don't know either, but let's try."

"You've said that before and then you don't follow through."

"Guilty. I don't know what to tell you except that I'll try harder."

"Umm."

"Hey, this parent/child, er, adult, thing is a two-way street, you know. You've got some responsibility in this also."

"I suppose." Her eyes widened, and she opened her mouth but nothing came out. Relaxing her shoulders, Karen said, "Uh, I don't have much money right now. I could pay you back."

Pete bobbed his head to one side to dismiss her concern. "Sure. We'll work it out. The bank will pay my way for the investigation work."

"Perfect." Karen pushed the cup to one side and drew her finger across the table. "This is my basic rule. If things get really bad between us, I can bail on the whole thing. Go on safari myself. No questions asked."

"Fair."

and tourists. His cover as a painter worked well even down to his paint-splotched hands, with different colors that he applied each day.

The apartment had been chosen specifically. It offered cover, a wide range of shooting lanes, accessibility, and several escape routes. Swart's employer had identified a snitch who needed to disappear. Surprisingly, Swart's request for the employer to pay the exorbitant rent had been granted without question, as had his fee. Swart had also insisted on purchasing top-quality equipment. Agreed. The target must present a huge threat to the employer.

His choice for equipment had been the McMillan Tac 50-A1-R2 rifle. He liked it because it reduced the peak recoil from a 50 BMG cartridge by 90%, and it had a twenty-nine-inch barrel for better accuracy. It broke down into five easy-to-conceal parts, including the bipod support for a steadier aim.

Swart had taken his time to shepherd each piece, one at a time, into the apartment. They were all hidden there now. His job today was to scout the escape routes one more time. Successful missions were the result of meticulous planning for any contingency that might occur.

He circled around Dock Road among the busy traffic and skirted the new amphitheater. The tourists were always heavy in this area—something Swart might need later to provide cover and distraction in the event of an escape.

Swart came out on the southwestern side of the harbor. Ahead of him, two long docks jutted into the bay before it emptied into the larger Table Bay and, eventually, to the Atlantic Ocean. He followed the dock that ran beside a two-story warehouse. It had a green roof, and rust streaks ran down the sides of the steel walls. On the top floor, old shipping offices had been converted to lofts and studios charging outlandish rents. He had rented the one on the end for over 50,000 rand per month—or about 4,000 U.S. dollars.

Swart climbed the iron stairs to the second floor, turned into a hallway that ran the length of the warehouse, and walked to his room. He had insisted the landlord change the two locks, which had been done. Swart unlocked them and stepped inside. At the corner, paned windows looked out on a magnificent sight.

The square harbor accommodated ships of all sizes from hundreds of countries, shouldered together to trade and do business with Cape Town. They came in colors that identified each one. The gaudiest one was from Qatar in the Middle East. From the high prow backward along the length of the boat, wide layers of green and red paint shone in the sun but were outdone by the shining gold-covered trappings on the deck.

Cranes lifted pallets out of the ships' holds. Cables creaked as the cranes bent to their work. Gulls swooped among them, playing with the wind.

Swart pulled up a chair facing backward to the window. He kneeled in the seat and lifted his head. Blonde hair fell over his forehead. The boat was still there. Large, black hull with white toppings. Red stacks. North side of first dock. Next to Swart was the iPad. It contained the photos he'd been supplied identifying the target, taken from several angles. Every afternoon the target would leave his post at the same time, using three ladders to climb down from the upper decks.

Swart reached over to lift the McMillan off the sofa. He nestled the stock next to his face. It felt cool and smelled faintly of gun oil. Through the scope, he lined up the red stacks on the boat. He lifted the barrel a millimeter to look past them to a set of steel ladders that connected the second deck to the third. He could make out the peeling paint on the handles. But there was a problem.

From this angle, Swart had one of the toughest shots of his career. It was like a three-point shot in basketball, only over a much longer distance. He had to get the bullet up over the stacks, drop it down to the deck quickly at the level of the second ladder, then get it into the target's back as he climbed down. Of course, gravity would pull the bullet down after it cleared the stacks. The scope was adjusted to compensate for that fact. But Swart needed gravity to help more than usual. He clicked up the scope's level and hoped to hell the bullet had enough velocity to clear the obstacles before dropping into the target. Swart couldn't fail. It wasn't the money; it was his pride.

He set the rifle on the sofa and stood up and arched backward to stretch.

Looking at his watch, Swart realized by tomorrow at this time he'd be done. He squinted up through the windows. Sun would be a slight issue. He took time to disassemble the rifle, nestle it into the velvet of the case, and slide it under the sofa. Swart backed up and studied the angles again. He could pull it off.

Think positive, he thought. *Chip shot for you, old man.*

Swart forced a smile, stepped to the door, and glanced around the room. Yellow light came through the windows in bright squares that slid lower against the far wall as the sun set.

Chapter Four

On a snowy day, Pete and Karen left JFK airport in New York for an overnight flight to Johannesburg, South Africa. From there, a short connecting flight would bring them to Cape Town. But in between New York and Cape Town, they faced twenty-two hours of flying with a layover in Ghana. All Pete wanted was to get to Cape Town, start the investigation, and try to start a new chapter with Karen.

With a little wine and some Valium, Pete was able to sleep for almost seven hours. Sometime during the night, he felt the plane settle on a runway and come to a stop. It must be Accra, the main city in Ghana on the western coast of Africa, he remembered. Outside the window, he saw a plane, without wheels, settled in the grass next to the runway as if it were dead.

The flight attendant announced their first stop in Africa and said, "Passengers may disembark. No one should jump out of the open doors." Damp heat, like a wet glove, penetrated the plane and made Pete's face feel greasy. He fell back into a slumber.

Sometime later, he felt the plane surge forward on the runway, shake from side to side, and lift into the air. The air conditioning kicked in, and the plane climbed to its cruising altitude of 35,000 feet above sea level, where the temperature was minus sixty degrees outside the aluminum tube he rode in.

While the flight attendants served breakfast, Karen asked Pete about the animals they'd look for. "I've seen the PBS series about all the poaching going on. Do you think there are any animals left?"

He faced her. "Luckily, there's still a lot of game. But you're right, the situation is worse. People in the Far East are crazy for ivory and horn. But because it's illegal to take those items out of the country, a black market has developed. The prices have skyrocketed."

"Which makes it more attractive to the smugglers, 'cause they make more money."

"The criminal syndicates can out-spend government law enforcement. They also have the technological advantage—infrared sensors and helicopters to spot game. I read that some poachers are using rocket-propelled grenades—usually used against tanks—to kill elephants."

"It's worse than I thought." She tried to turn away, but the space between the seats was too tight. "What's being done?"

Pete shrugged. He'd reached the back end of his knowledge of poaching. "Like the drug trade in America, you've got to find the kingpins. A tough thing to do, because you have to travel back along the transit routes to Vietnam or China."

They transferred planes in Johannesburg and flew two hours to the west coast of South Africa. Sheltered in a bay from the rough seas of the South Atlantic, Cape Town huddled under the iconic flat mountain called Table Mountain.

Pete planned to check into the Export/Import Bank office in the morning to meet the director, Ian Donahue. Pete would follow his usual work pattern: check forensics, witnesses, the crime scene. Hopefully, it would be a quick investigation, and he and Karen could have fun. He read the background literature about Africa the bank had provided.

In 1488 the Portuguese had rounded this point of Africa on their way to the riches of India. They called it the Cape of Storms or the Cape of the Devil because it was the point where the icy waters of the South Atlantic crashed against the warm waters of the Indian Ocean —causing ferocious storms.

Later settlers, trying desperately to attract more Europeans, decided the name wasn't the best marketing tool. They renamed it the Cape of Good Hope. The people came and trade increased. Clipper ships, racing to the Far East to pick up cargos of nutmeg, pepper, and cloves, and also tea, stopped to re-provision before they rounded the Cape. When they weighed anchor for the ports in India and Indonesia, the ships left passengers in their wake to start farms and vineyards.

The new people created one of the most beautiful and unique cities in Africa. Part European and part ancient Africa, white and black people mixed—like the crashing of two oceans off the coast—in troubled and tragic ways that would lead to cataclysmic events.

Pete and Karen were anxious to leave the plane when it landed at Cape Town International Airport. They staggered off, trying to get their legs to work again after so many hours of cramped flight.

"This is stunning, Dad," Karen said as they entered the huge, open interior. The roof sloped from the corners of the building down to the middle and resembled the wings of a bird in flight. Inside, there were few walls, the roof rose four stories tall, and it was immaculately clean. Images of animals in the floor tile stretched out before them. It took several minutes to cross the length of a giraffe. Karen made a game of keeping her feet within the outlines of the animal's neck.

After collecting their luggage, they came outside to meet the shuttle from their hotel. Beyond the far end of the runway was a low mountain that looked as if someone had sliced off the peak. Clouds slid over the top, and the steep sides looked purple in the distance.

"Must be Table Mountain," Pete said. "It's called that because the flat top looks like a table—"

"Got it, Dad." Karen wrinkled her face and turned away from him. "Of course."

The air smelled fresh, and the sky had a blue tint that was more intense than the skies over Minnesota. Pete found the shuttle for the Pilgrim Hotel, and they dumped their luggage in the back end of the van.

They cruised on clean, fast highways, passing signs that read Stellenbosch, Paarl, Kraaifontein, Blue Downs, and Western Cape. They also passed suburbs of small, tidy houses that looked like American suburbs.

"Sir, are you from Canada?" The driver looked into the rearview mirror and spoke with a British accent.

"No, the United States," Pete said.

"I am Oliver. Welcome to my country." A white smile took up a third of his black face.

"Thanks. We're looking forward to a great vacation."

"We have much to show you."

"Like what?" Karen asked.

Oliver laughed. "How much time do you have? There are beaches, hiking on Table Mountain, wineries, seafood, sports of all kinds, history and monuments, music, and the biggest animals on the planet."

"Are there any animals left?" she said.

Oliver frowned. "They are in trouble, but you come at a good time to see them." He looked forward and turned up the music on the radio.

It was a group of women singing in harmony with the bubbling beat of multiple drums behind them. It sounded like a Paul Simon song from his CD, *Graceland.*

"I like that," Pete told him.

"Paul Simon was here in 1985 to record the music for that album. He played with a favorite group here called Ladysmith Black Mambazo." When his eyes rose to the mirror again, Oliver shook his head. "But we have something that can beat you in the U.S."

"What?"

"Our former president, Jacob Zuma, was worse than your president, Donald Trump." Oliver laughed.

"No way," Karen said.

"I will prove it. Mr. Zuma is married but has several girlfriends. When one said she was HIV positive and that Mr. Zuma didn't use protection, he said, 'No problem; I took a shower.'" Oliver laughed so hard the van swerved on the freeway. "He is in the same party as Nelson Mandela was, but Mr. Zuma is a corruption of the great man's legacy."

"The African National Congress?" Pete said.

"Yes. The ruling party. Well, I should say the ruling clowns. It is an international disgrace."

"We know how you feel." Karen leaned forward and patted him on the shoulder.

They followed the N1 freeway for another twenty minutes. The land flattened and housing became dense as they drove west toward the center of Cape Town.

Oliver made a few turns off the freeway and slowed as he approached the center of the city, crowded with high rises and office buildings. To their left, the city opened suddenly in a flat, vacant space that stretched for blocks.

"How come nothing is built there?" Pete asked.

"District Six," Oliver said. "It was home to one of the more interesting sections of Cape Town. Since it was near the docks, most of the residents were workers. They were black and what we call 'Cape Malays.' Those are people who came over as slaves from Malaysia a century ago. Under apartheid, the laws were set up to keep coloreds and whites separate. District Six was called a slum, and in 1968 the government started to force people to move."

"Were they bothering anyone?" Karen asked.

"No. It was a thriving community, but the real reason involved money. The land was considered too valuable for coloreds and blacks to own. The whites wanted it. Too bad, because after they pushed out sixty thousand people, no one ever developed it—as you can see."

Oliver turned onto Strand Street, drove around a square that contained a marketplace covered by colorful tents, and followed narrow streets until they came to the old harbor named Victoria and Alfred Harbor. Oliver stopped before the Pilgrim Hotel and helped them unload. He was careful not to dirty his black suit and white shirt.

"Call me anytime for a ride," Oliver offered. "The hotel can find me." He waved and ducked into the cab of the van.

Pete tipped him well and turned to go inside. Gulls cawed from the water behind him, and he saw a steel crane lifting cargo into the hold of a ship in the distance.

Inside, a black woman greeted them and offered bottled water and a porter to carry the luggage. "Would you like to join our Pilgrim Hotel Preferred Member club?" she asked.

"Uh, what does it cost?" Pete said.

"Nothing. It gives you free upgrades to find the best rooms available."

"Okay." He was tired and wanted to take a nap as soon as he could. Karen was quiet and probably tired also. They stumbled up the steps to their rooms and collapsed into a sound sleep.

In the morning, they met at the hotel's dining room on a shaded terrace that overlooked a section of the harbor. The mournful call of a boat's horn echoed along the docks, and a faint mist remained at the water level. Besides two other guests, Pete and Karen were the only white people in the dining room. Coming from Minnesota, it was an unusual experience to be white and in the minority.

"What do you want to do?" Pete asked Karen.

"Trip Advisor suggested going down to the point of land called the Cape Peninsula to the Cape of Good Hope. I'd like to see that."

"Okay. Great idea. I have to make a quick stop at the bank to meet the director, and then we can go. I'm sure the hotel can line up a driver."

Karen frowned. "Why do we need a driver? I'll drive."

"They drive on the left side of the road."

"Oh, to hell with you. I'm going to do it." She turned away to stop further fighting. In a few minutes, she twisted her head and asked, "Did you say the bank lent money to some game reserves?"

"Yeah. I'll talk to the director about it. I'm still hoping to catch sight of a Western black rhino." He finished the last of his coffee.

The Pilgrim Hotel was next to a campus of Cape Town University. Several students from the school flooded the room to eat breakfast. Most were black. Several smiled at Pete—an obvious tourist.

Karen left and came back to the table. "I can't believe it."

"What?"

"They call this place a 'first world country,' but I can't even get a latte. This is not a good start," she complained.

At the hotel lobby, Pete asked for Oliver. In ten minutes, he arrived in a black Mercedes. Pete and Karen stepped outside. The sun felt hot along Pete's back and reflected off the white sides of the hotel in a bright glare.

Oliver jumped out and ran up to them. "Good morning, my friends. How did you sleep in Cape Town?"

Pete nodded. "Great. Still some jet lag, but I feel good. Can you get us to the U.S. Export/Import bank? It's on Adderly Street."

"Of course." He opened the door for Karen.

"Perfect. I'll sit up front with you. I want to see what it's like to drive on the left side."

"I never say no to a beautiful lady." Oliver smiled broadly and moved around to the other side to let Karen sit next to him.

Chapter Five

They drove off in the silence of the big car. Pete opened his window, and a warm breeze flowed in. It smelled like the ocean with a faint whiff of fish.

In fifteen minutes, they entered the traffic of downtown Cape Town. Palm trees sprouted at intersections, softening the effects of high-rise buildings. Modern offices rose next to ancient churches and English-style gardens next to them with arches of ivy as entry points. Cape Town had a moderate climate, so the growing season was long and productive.

Oliver made a tight turn around a short block. On one side of the street, a colonial hotel rose three stories. Across the street, a granite block church occupied the entire corner. It looked old and solid, with a short steeple.

"That's St. George's Cathedral. It was Desmond Tutu's church when he was the Archbishop of the Anglican Church of South Africa. From there, he devised the idea for the Truth and Reconciliation Commission."

"What's that?" Karen asked.

"After we defeated apartheid, there was much anger and age-old resentment, as you can imagine. Many people wanted violent retribution that threatened a peaceful transition to democracy. Bishop Tutu and others established the Truth and Reconciliation hearings like a restorative justice court process. If anyone had committed acts of violence or discrimination against others, they went before the tribunal, where they confessed their crimes and asked for forgiveness. If the tribunal felt the person was sincere, they were absolved of punishment. It included everyone: blacks, whites, and colored."

"What was the result?" Karen said.

"Very good. It gave everyone a chance to vent their anger without violence."

"What do you mean by 'colored' people?" Pete said.

"It is a term we use for mixed race people."

"Then who are the Afrikaners?"

"They are white, but descended from the Dutch rather than the British." Oliver turned in his seat and continued, "You Americans say you have a 'melting pot' in your country, but we have one too."

They drove up Adderly Street through a phalanx of tall office towers. At the far end of the street, green mountains rose steeply into the clouds. The tops were perfectly flat—part of Table Mountain. People crossed the street. The whites tended to dress in slacks and blouses of muted colors. Many of the blacks wore traditional tribal robes and dresses—all in bright colors.

Oliver stopped in front of the building where the bank was located. He jumped out to open the door for Karen. "Please call for me when you need to go back." He handed her his card and smiled again.

Inside the steel and glass tower, they rode to the tenth floor. At the office of the bank, they were greeted by a small black woman who wore a tight blue suit. Her white blouse reminded Pete of snow in Minnesota.

She spoke with a British accent. "So nice of you to visit with us. Mr. Donahue is finishing a call and will be right out. Tea? Coffee?"

Before she could deliver their orders, a stout man came into the lobby. He had blond hair combed straight back and blond eyebrows. A sun-reddened forehead above blue eyes gave the impression of outdoor vitality.

"Donahue," he said. "Ian." He pumped each of their hands. "Welcome to Cape Town. I last encountered Martin at a conference in Washington. Bloody good man. He told me you would be coming."

"Maybe I can help." Pete would get this over quickly.

"Yes, yes, mate. I'm using some of our own investigative resources. A good private investigator named Janette Koos. But sometimes an outside pair of eyes is preferable." He winked at Pete to remind him how a man was usually better in the business. "On holiday with your daughter?" Ian looked at Karen.

"I want to see some of the big game," she said.

"We can certainly help with that. The bank has close associations with several game reserves, and we can get you discounted tickets into the national parks, also."

"Perfect. By the way, any chance I could score a latte?"

"Certainly." Donahue pulled back the cuff of his blazer to look at his watch. "The Sirilima Game Reserve is where our problem starts, I'm afraid to say. But I have an idea. Why don't we go to the harbor area and walk around? I could show you the sights while I tell you the parameters of the tragedy and the information I have to date. Then we could have lunch. Some of our best seafood restaurants are there." He smelled of too much cologne. "And you can get your latte," he told Karen.

"Whatever you suggest," Pete said.

Ian spoke to the receptionist and said, "Adaeze, would you be a dear and take my calls?" He lifted an umbrella off a hat tree behind the door and led the way out. "Old habit from all the years of school I attended at Oxford. Horrible climate there, eh? Can't seem to shake it, although the weather here is close to perfect all year long."

They rode down to street level, where Ian caught a taxi and they all climbed in. The driver pulled out and drove toward the ocean.

On street corners, pods of young black men slouched against the walls of buildings. Ian noticed it and said, "They're doing the 'E Street Shuffle.'" He grinned. "After your New Jersey rock star, Springsteen. Those young lads are gangsters."

"How do you know that?" Karen asked.

"Look how they're dressed. 'Preppie,' as you Americans call it. Khaki pants, button-down shirts, and the worst part—the leather loafers. They don't even have to tie them." He grunted. "They took the name 'Americans' as their gang name."

Pete said, "Ah, maybe they're just trying to impress girls."

The taxi sped between the office towers to a wide freeway that skirted the edge of the city with the ocean on the right side. The ocean gave way to train tracks and freight yards, built years ago to serve the harbor area.

Once past that, they turned into a densely populated area with heavy traffic. The streets were narrow, lined with high walls that hid businesses and homes behind them. Palm trees swayed in the wind, and Pete smelled the ocean even though he couldn't see it. The taxi took a sharp left, and Ian pointed out the window to their right.

A huge harbor spread out below them. Dozens of ships of all sizes were moored around the concrete docks. Buildings fronting the water rose four stories and were painted in pastel colors of blue and yellow and grass green. Beyond the harbor, the ocean stretched out to the horizon until it merged with the sky.

"Victoria and Alfred Waterfront," Ian said. "It was built in the 1800s and is still a working harbor. Mostly fishing boats today, but the larger container ships you see have to be towed in by tugboats now. This area has also attracted artists and restaurants. There are over 450 retail shops here." He pointed past the harbor. "And that flat smudge out there is Robben Island."

"Where Nelson Mandela was in prison?" Karen asked.

Donahue bobbed his head. "He once said, 'It was a long holiday —for twenty-seven years.' Eh?"

"Wow. I bet he could hear the sounds of the harbor out there. It must have been really hard," she said.

The taxi took a right turn, drove past a Ferris wheel, and stopped in front of a modern shopping mall. The three got out, and Ian led the way along a boardwalk. They passed a band playing African music for tips. Small kiosks sold gelato and slices of shepherd's pie. Several artists sat along the walk with white canvases propped on easels as they painted views of the harbor.

"Tell me about the murder," Pete asked.

Ian leaned closer to him. "Terrible business. Normally, the bank wouldn't be involved."

"What's different?"

"We've lent money to several private game reserves. Of course, there are many national parks, but the private reserves have a different purpose. They create ecosystems that can sustain a variety of big game."

Asian tourists passed on either side of them. The Chinese were dressed formally, and the women all wore very high heels. They stopped at every kiosk while they took turns photographing each other.

Cooking smells floated on the breeze, mixed with fresh fish and the diesel smells of the big ships. Forklifts rolled back and forth between the ramps coming down from ships that lined the docks.

Ian walked with long, confident steps. He leaned closer to Pete's ear to avoid Karen's hearing. "Our deputy director at the Sirilima Game

Reserve was found dead last week. Mate named Isaac. I had hired him, secretly, to be a spy in the park. I found some, uh, irregularities."

"Anyone arrested?"

"Not even a suspect," Donahue whispered.

"Police?"

"Not too effective, particularly in the bush. Most are corrupt and not to be trusted. I'm hoping Koos can find something, but I haven't received her report yet. She's always very effective."

"So, what do you want me to do?"

Ian took a deep breath. "Find out what's really going on in the park and who killed him."

"How do you know it was murder?"

"He was shot. But you see, the strangest part of the man's death was what they discovered in his pack."

Pete frowned.

"The director had a lead box about the size of a smartphone. Inside were two kilos of cesium-137."

"What the hell is that?"

"Nuclear waste. Nasty stuff."

"Why would he have that?"

Ian shrugged. "As I told you, there are also the irregularities in the park's accounting ledgers."

A crowd of tourists from Australia surrounded them, boisterous and loud. Ian stopped while his finger brushed his lips and he said, "Later."

"What irregularities—?"

Donahue's eyes flashed at Pete as Donahue turned away. He led them through a large building that housed artists' studios and retail offerings. Many of the works of art were tribal African: colorful clothing hung on racks, artistic models of game animals standing as tall as the real animals, and furniture made out of local wood like red elm, zebra wood, and bubinga.

Around eleven thirty Karen said, "Trip Advisor recommended a Portuguese restaurant called Bacalao. The map shows we're there now. I'm starved."

"It's upstairs, but it's not my favorite," Ian said.

Pete stood up for Karen. "I'd like to try it, too. Come on."

Pete and Karen followed Donahue upstairs to the end of the hall. The restaurant door was flanked by two enormous wood carvings of jumping fish. The wood grain, from head to tail, looked like water cascading off the flanks of the fish, so real Pete glanced at the floor to see if it was wet. Bacalao was open-air. Within a minute, they were seated in the corner, overlooking the harbor and the ships below.

Ian recommended a local wine. "It's from our wine region called Stellenbosch. This wine is from the Spier Wine Farm. It's a light red that is smashing." He ordered a bottle, and the waiter brought bread. "You may not know this, but our wine industry is older than your Napa Valley in California. The Boers—the Dutch—hired French vintners to come from Europe to start the industry. Actually, it's so good, we don't export much of the product."

Pete looked down to watch men in blue one-piece work outfits pushing wheelbarrows along the dock. They wore hard hats and must have been building something. Most of them were black. A hundred feet from where he sat, a huge ship was loading. It had a black hull and two red stacks. Occasionally, a puff of smoke rose from one of the stacks. Gulls and frigate birds swooped along the decks of the boat.

The warmth of the sun and the incessant calls of the birds lulled Pete into a relaxed state—for the first time since Barbara's death. Was this a hint of what peace felt like? He wondered if he would ever find it again.

Chapter Six

Behind the open window, Swart fixed himself comfortably across the chair, wrapped the carrying strap of the McMillan around his support arm, and peered into the scope. Even after all the years he'd done this, the sudden magnification impressed him. He zeroed on the second ladder and found a brown wren perched on the horizontal step. Its head twitched back and forth, watching for danger from predators.

Keeping his shoulders and body immobile, Swart moved his own head an inch to look at his watch, propped on the arm of the sofa next to him. He'd fire the shot in a few minutes.

He opened and closed his right hand several times to loosen it. He slowed his breathing down, relaxing the muscles in his neck. The bipod attached to the end of the barrel would keep the rifle steady while Swart did his work.

His mind cleared of everything except the purpose of the mission. Swart felt dreamy, like he was turning to liquid, relaxed, everything in slow motion. He settled his eye to the end of the scope and felt a slight pressure as he pressed against it. He smelled the gun oil. The sight before him opened up in incredible clarity. Better than the human eye could see close up.

He waited.

Any time now. The snitch would begin his lumbering climb down the ladder. He always stepped down each rung, leading with his right foot, then the right foot again. Never right, left, right, left. That would help Swart as the target paused on each rung for his left foot to catch up.

He saw it first as a shadow—or was it Swart's instincts? Then a square-toed shoe filled the scope. A leg covered by blue jeans dipped into the circle. Swart waited. The man's hip swung down, his arm dropped along the handle, and he stopped to let the left leg plant itself on the horizontal. He wore a one-piece denim work suit. Now his back filled the circle of Swart's scope.

Without rushing, Swart took a big breath and let it out slowly in a controlled fashion. His right hand began the slow, steady process of squeezing the trigger, not jerking it.

He hated to use a silencer because it threw off the accuracy. Instead, Swart relied on the fact that a single crack of the rifle firing would not attract much attention in the crowds below. Particularly if there wasn't a second shot, people would shrug and continue on their way. And Swart never needed to take a second shot.

His finger curled completely, the McMillan bucked, and the crack from the explosion of the bullet leaving the muzzle stretched out into the space beyond the window and was gone. Swart watched for success through the scope.

Just as he pulled the trigger, the ship gave a blast of exhaust smoke from one of the red stacks. The minute Swart saw that, he knew he'd failed. It wasn't smoke that caused the trouble; it was hot air, which rose because it was lighter than the surrounding cooler air. That, in turn, would lift the bullet, causing its trajectory to skew upward above the target. It would probably sail right over the entire ship.

* * *

The waiter at Bacalao returned to the table, uncorked the bottle of wine, and poured three glasses. Donahue sniffed the wine and raised his glass. "Cheerio. Here's to solving the mystery," he said as he took a sip.

Pete heard the sound of breaking glass. He looked up to see Karen holding the decapitated stem of her wine glass. Red wine had splashed over the tablecloth. Pete turned to Ian. A vacant expression was fixed on his face, and his chest was covered with spilled wine. Then Pete realized it wasn't wine on his chest; it was blood.

His training kicked in, and Pete twisted to the left to look out over the harbor. Where was the shooter? He couldn't see anyone. Then Pete leaped around the table and tackled Karen. Down on the floor. She screamed.

Underneath the table, Pete yelled at her to keep down. He waited for more shots, but none came. With a gasp of breath, Ian tumbled out of his chair and landed on his side, facing Karen. Blonde hair fell over his open eyes, but he was quite dead. She screamed again.

Chapter Seven

Other diners in the restaurant reacted in stages as they figured out what had happened. Two jumped up, their chairs clattering over behind them. Waiters dashed into the room. "Ambulance, ambulance," one yelled. The noise exploded as people crashed their way to the doors to get out. Several screamed.

In five minutes, Pete heard the familiar European ambulance siren: *hee, haw, hee haw*, like the braying of a donkey. A man and a woman burst into the restaurant. They came over to Donahue. Pete let Karen get up, and he followed.

An EMT rolled Ian over, and within a few minutes, the tech shook his head. He spoke something in Afrikaans into his shoulder mic.

Karen stood with her body slumped forward. She was shaking. Staring.

"Let's get out of here," Pete said.

"Shouldn't we wait for the police?"

"In my experience in foreign countries, I don't think we want to get involved right now." He gave Karen a slight shove toward the door.

Her arm swung around but missed him. "Leave me alone."

Pete's shoulders tightened. "I want to go to the probable location of the shooter."

"What?" Karen's head snapped up.

"Come on. The bullet almost hit you." Pete pulled on her arm. She stumbled after him.

They took the escalator to the first floor and turned out into the street. Pete hurried along the boardwalk to the far end of the dock. He half-carried Karen until she dropped onto the wooden deck and sat with her knees up and her head dipped between them. Her shoulders quivered. Pete had seen this before in the Middle East when he was in a war zone. Shock.

"It's not safe to sit here," he said softly to Karen.

She looked up and tried to stand. Pete helped her up, and they stumbled forward.

The dock turned left to parallel a row of warehouses. On the second level, Pete saw dozens of windows facing the harbor—and the restaurant. He pulled Karen after him. His professional instincts drove him, but also the fact that the shot had almost hit his daughter. He couldn't let that pass.

When they rounded the corner of the dock, Pete saw two squad cars with blue and yellow striping and revolving blue lights. Signs on the side said "South African Police Services." Four uniforms in helmets were already out of the car, studying the windows on the second floor, their weapons drawn. Two officers ducked into the closest door carrying R1 semi-automatic rifles.

Pete ran toward them, identified himself, said he worked for the bank, and pushed Karen behind him as if to protect her. The officer nearest them shrugged and said to stand back. Pete pushed forward until warned a second time. From his right, a woman stepped out of the shadow of the building and came up to him.

"Did I hear you say you work for the Export/Import bank?" she asked Pete.

He turned and saw a woman about his age, light brown hair that hid her forehead, an athletic build, and eyes hidden by sunglasses. She was dressed in jeans and a blue blazer.

"Yeah. We're here from the U.S. on vacation. There was a problem I planned to help the bank solve."

She came closer and removed her sunglasses. She had a square face with wrinkles that had started their inevitable journey from the eyes to the sides of her face. She nodded and extended her hand to shake. "Janette Koos. Coincidentally, I work for the bank also." Her grip was as firm as her posture.

Pete didn't introduce Karen at first. Both of them being at the same place struck him as more than coincidental. "We were having lunch with Ian Donohue. Why are you here?"

"I heard the ID of Donahue from the EMT radio communications that drew in the police."

Pete didn't respond.

She smiled quickly; then it was gone. "I'm a private investigator and freelance mostly corporate gigs. The bank has been a new client for several months. Frankly, I didn't think Ian appreciated the gravity of the problem, so I was following him."

"He told me about you. What are you investigating?"

"Can't say right now. Security, you know." She spoke with a slight accent that came from Afrikaner.

"Well, I can't say what I'm doing here, either. But my daughter was almost killed." Karen leaned against him, her arms wrapped tightly around her chest.

Janette shifted her weight to the right leg and squinted as she looked across the harbor and the huge ship docked next to them. "I'm sure you're upset. I have children also. My son is in England with his father, and my daughter is at university here. I tell people I'm working so *she* can live the 'good life.'" She laughed, and although Koos had good teeth, she covered her mouth with her hand for a moment.

He didn't care about this stranger's life. But she might be able to give him information about Donahue and the bank. Pete asked her, "Why would anyone want to kill Ian?"

Janette glanced to the right, toward the police squads. She looked back at Pete. "The answer is, no one would. He's a minor bank official in a small American agency. I doubt anyone but a handful of people knew who he was—unless it was somehow connected to the death in the Sirilima Game Reserve."

Pete frowned. "But—"

"Did Donahue tell you about that?"

He hesitated to reveal any information to her.

"I know that's why you're here."

Karen interrupted. "I don't feel good. I want to get out of here."

"You're his daughter?"

Karen leaned on Pete and faced Koos. "Yes. We're supposed to be on vacation. We've come to see the big game parks." Her face darkened. "And now—Well, I know my father; he won't let this go without finding out what happened and why."

"Impressive," Koos replied. She had deep-set brown eyes that shifted from side to side.

"So, what do you know about the death in the game reserve?" Pete asked.

She waved her hand in front of her face as if she were swatting away mosquitos. "Let's focus on the shooting first. Tell me what happened."

Pete didn't think that information would compromise anything. He explained meeting Donahue at the bank office, the tour of the harbor, and how he'd urged Donahue to have lunch at that restaurant. Pete looked up at the second-story row of windows above them. "If the shot came from there, it would be almost impossible to hit Ian in the restaurant." Pete turned back toward the restaurant. The slice of open space between roof and outer wall that extended over the table tops' height was narrow. "He'd have to be pretty damn good to thread a bullet into that space and hit him directly in the chest. And, by the way, there's a huge ship in between."

Janette turned her head as she studied the angles Pete had pointed out. After a few minutes, she agreed. "You say the three of you walked around the harbor before lunch?"

Pete nodded.

"If we suspect a sniper, why wouldn't he take the shot then? It'd be so much easier."

"Right."

No one spoke for a long time. Each of them shuffled back and forth in a small space on the dock.

Karen said, "I can't take this anymore. I'm going back to the hotel, Dad."

"In a minute. If this was in any way intended for you or me, I can't let it go."

They all turned when a commotion erupted from the door leading to the second floor. Two police burst out, one carrying a long rifle. The cop's hand, covered by a blue latex glove, held the weapon. Pete guessed it was a McMillan Tac 50. He could tell by the way the pistol grip was carved out of the stock like a bone protruding from the muscles of a thigh. Not a sportsman's weapon. A professional's choice. His stomach twitched.

He watched Karen's eyes as they saw the cops tag the weapon with a paper ID and lay it in the rear of the van, its lights still flashing a warning. The sight of the gun upset her. After all, it was the weapon that had killed Donahue in front of her. Pete wanted to dismiss it as unimportant to relieve her fears, but he knew she was too smart for that. Instead, he chose honesty. "Dangerous piece of work," he muttered.

Karen turned to him and in rapid words said, "I'm out of here. I didn't come all this way to be killed." Her eyes moistened. "I'm going to the hotel. As soon as I can, I'm getting out of here to that game park." She looked at Janette. "Do you know how I can get to it?"

"It's called Sirilima Game Reserve, and you can get a flight to Johannesburg. From there take a taxi north for a few hours," Janette offered.

Karen collapsed onto the ground and sat with her knees pulled up around her face again. She mumbled, "I can't stay here—"

"I know people at the game reserve. I'll call ahead to get a room ready for you. You'll enjoy the viewing."

Without saying anything, Karen nodded but didn't stand.

Pete looked back at Koos and saw pinched eyebrows and a frown. She said, "That weapon takes this to a new, more dangerous level. More complicated, unfortunately."

"Against Ian?" Pete said.

Janette shook her head. "I told you, I don't think anyone cared much about him. Something bigger is behind this."

"Then why was Donahue shot?"

Janette looked up at puffs of clouds sailing across the deep blue sky. She waited. Finally, she said, "I'm going to talk with the detectives over there. I know the tall black guy." She left in a brisk stride toward the huddle of law enforcement. In ten minutes, she returned.

"They found the shooter's nest on the second floor, corner room. The sight lines were perfect to shoot across the harbor. Someone took a lot of time and effort to set this up. I think the detective will keep me in the loop—unofficially, of course."

Pete nodded as he absorbed the new information and thought about it. "If that's all true, how would the shooter know that Donahue would be at the restaurant?"

Janette's shoulders slouched for the first time since they'd been talking. "Okay, I'll share something with you."

"What do you mean?" Pete crossed his arms over his chest.

"I'm not sure Donahue was the target. The substance found in the deputy director's backpack was cesium-137. It's nuclear waste and, if combined with other explosives, could create a dirty bomb."

"Terrorists?"

Janette shook her head. "Could be, but I think it was going to be used as payment for something more far-reaching and complicated."

"What's that?" Pete asked.

Janette side-stepped along the dock in a direction away from the police. "Trafficking. The two most common products are rhino horn and elephant ivory."

"Donahue didn't mention that at all."

"He suspected something like that, but I hadn't been able to fully prepare the report of my investigations. I started following the trail of the cesium and found it was intended to be sold to finance the trafficking. Of course, there are other methods of financing, but that was the door that opened for me onto the larger crime."

"I've read about the illegal trade," Pete said, "in *National Geographic* magazine."

"Tip of the iceberg, as you Americans say. Are you aware of the international treaty called the Convention on International Trade in Endangered Species of Wild Fauna and Flora?"

"Who?" Pete said.

"It's an international treaty signed by 182 countries that became effective in 1975. Its short name is CITES." She pronounced it like *site-eez*. "It works by listing many animals and plants on an endangered list. The countries in the treaty agree to regulate trade in anything on the list. For most, that means it's illegal to buy, sell, or transport animals found on the list."

Karen yelled at them. "What the hell are you two doing? Ian was murdered. I'm not waiting any longer." She unfolded her legs, stood, and started to walk toward a row of yellow taxis. "See you at the hotel," she called to Pete from over her shoulder.

Pete watched her stumble away. He should go with her, comfort her, but this was a crime scene, and if he left it, he might miss something. He turned back to Janette.

"If anyone is caught in those countries, there are penalties. Some worse than others."

"Wait a minute," Pete interrupted. "You say Donahue didn't know anything about this, and yet he was just shot by an expert—and my daughter was almost hit. Why?"

Janette blinked. "Can't say." She walked away but spun back to face him. "Let's take this from a different direction. What if Donahue was not the intended target?"

"Okay, but you said there could be a connection between the bank's game park investments and Donahue's death. I'm here to investigate Isaac Simeon's death."

Looking up, Janette said, "I think we can walk up to the second floor if we stay away from the crime scene. Up there." She pointed to a gap in the façade of the windows. "If there's a hall behind them, we may be able to get the same view as the shooter."

She led the way around the end of the building and up some polished wooden stairs to turn onto a narrow catwalk that led along the back side of the building. Starting forward, they passed several apartments and a few small offices. Most were closed, but a few people came out and edged past them. After walking fifty feet, Janette stopped at an opening between the apartments. Pete followed her around the corner to the left and saw the entire harbor view open before them. At the second story level, a new perspective appeared in a three-dimensional framework—not only left to right, but also down.

At this level, Pete was able to see out across the harbor and spot several ships of different sizes and shapes. Some were cargo ships, tugboats, tankers, and even pleasure craft sailboats, their sails rattling like flags in the wind. The most obvious was the large cargo ship docked right in front of the apartments. Black hull, white uppers, and red stacks. Workers crawled up and down steel ladders between several decks.

The clock tower bell rang three times, the sound echoing among the ships in deep tones. Frigate birds soared, riding thermal currents from the heated work below. Pete looked at Koos standing in front of him. On the surface, she acted competent and tough, but he sensed something desperate underneath. She wanted something more than simply solving a case.

Janette stared out at the harbor for several minutes while standing with her legs spread in a military stance. Finally, she said, "What if someone on that ship was the shooter's target?" She pointed at the closest ship.

"Okay," Pete said. "But why would he hit Donahue instead of someone else?"

"He missed."

Pete shook his head. "Did you see the weapon? No one misses with that kind of hardware. I served during the Iraq war in the U.S. Army Criminal Investigation Division. I learned a lot about every weapon imaginable."

Janette shrugged. "Maybe." Her eyes shifted left to right as she thought. "Come on. I'm going to talk to my friends in the police service. Let's see what they think."

Pete followed her around the corner, down the steps, and along the dock to reach the yellow-edged crime scene. Koos dipped under the fluttering tape and talked for a long time to the same detective as earlier. She gestured toward Pete a few times. In another five minutes, Janette called to him, "Come on."

Two officers and Janette started walking around the dock to the right, toward the large ship. Pete scrambled behind.

"I've got these two officers curious enough to check out the ship. You've got permission to come along, but stay out of the way," Koos told him.

The party approached the steel gangplank that angled up from the dock to an open door in the side of the ship. As the detectives reached the door, a man in a one-piece denim work suit stopped them. A cigarette smoldered in the corner of his mouth. Without removing it, he grunted, "That's far enough, mates. We're about to weigh anchor."

The first detective, a tall black man, spoke slowly. "We can always get a court order to prevent your departure. After all, you are in the jurisdiction of the Cape Town municipal police district, and we are investigating a murder."

The sailor leaned against the door frame. He tossed his cigarette into the water far below like he was throwing away a dead fish. His face flushed red. "Aww. What the hell you want to see?" He moved back into the dark cavity, and the detective disappeared behind him.

Pete followed Janette up the ramp and entered the steel belly of the ship. It smelled faintly of oil and onions. Above them, chains clanked against steel. The party ascended a bare metal stairway through a series of switchbacks that led to the upper decks. It was hot work. Shouted orders echoed off the walls.

They all entered an open bay that was cooler. The walls were painted white and chipped in several places from tons of cargo previously loaded and unloaded over the years. As they all stepped into the open space, a pale Asian man on the far side jerked around to face them. He must have seen the police uniforms, because he darted into an open door.

"Who's that?" the lead detective shouted. "Stop him!"

The second officer ran through the door but returned in a few minutes. "Gone. Sorry, sir."

The detective turned to the sailor, who bumped his shoulders up and down. "I can't know every bloke on the ship. New guy, I think."

"Who are you?"

"Uh, I'm called the Captain—although I'm not the real skipper. Nickname for me."

The detective radioed his team on shore to seal off the ship and to not let anyone disembark. He looked at the sailor again. "Where was that man working?"

"Third deck, fourth hold aft." He pointed with his thumb.

"What's in there?"

Pulling a smartphone from his side pocket, the Captain scrolled through several screens. "I'll check the block chain records. Oranges. From Pretoria. Bound for—" He scrolled further. "Bill of lading says it's bound for Hong Kong." He raised his face, greasy with sweat.

"Let's take a look."

In twenty minutes, the group had assembled in a cavernous steel room filled with wooden boxes of various sizes and shapes. Two crew members were recruited to help and, driving a rubber-tired forklift, they rolled silently across the deck. The blades slid under the top box, lifted it slowly, and backed up to lower the cargo onto the deck. The detective ordered it opened. With two crowbars and a hammer, the crew managed to get the wooden top pried off. Underneath, shredded cardboard puffed out and fell over the sides. No one spoke, so the crew kept working. Flat crates of oranges started to pile up on the floor as the men worked their way down in the box. They leaned an aluminum ladder against the side so they could dig deeper.

In a few minutes, they announced there were no more oranges, yet the box wasn't empty. They urged the police to look for themselves.

When the lead detective looked over the edge of the box, he fell back, almost losing his balance on the ladder. "We need help," he shouted to his partner and gestured toward the direction of the dock. The Captain went up the ladder next and took several shots of the cargo with his smartphone. Back on the deck, he surveyed the group and shot everyone's face. The flash bounced off the walls so brightly it almost snapped with sound.

After that, Janette climbed up, returned with a flushed face, and let Pete climb. He took three steps up, grasped the wooden edge, and looked down. Hundreds of elephant tusks lay like corpses side by side in the box. They were tinted brown and gold, and many had numbers painted on their sides. And even in the dusky light, the ivory glowed like treasure.

Chapter Eight

The police led the way out to the porthole and down the long steel ramp to the dock. All the officers talked fast on their shoulder-fixed radios.

At the far end of the dock, two squad cars had parked under the Bacalao restaurant.

Janette pulled Pete to the side and commanded, "Follow me." She walked quickly along the dock, glancing back at the police once in a while. When she reached the corner, Janette broke off toward a side street. It was narrow and cluttered with artists' shops. She ducked into a corner occupied by a gelato shop.

"We've got to hurry," she said.

"What?" Pete asked.

"Donahue's office."

He frowned. "I thought we decided his death has nothing to do with the ivory and rhino horns."

"We don't know anything at this point."

Pete hesitated. In his experience, there wasn't a connection, but Janette was a local. She probably knew more than he did. Besides, there was the murder at the game reserve that Pete had come here to investigate in the first place. Donahue had been unable to finish the story. Maybe there was something in his office that would help. "Okay. Good idea."

*   *   *

They marched two blocks farther until they came to Janette's car. Once inside, Janette started it and rushed into the heavy traffic heading to the east.

They traveled along the expressway back toward the center of the city. Glass high-rise buildings stood in a line, facing the harbor and reflecting the sky and clouds along their exteriors. Janette raced into the right lane and pushed her car. In ten minutes, she turned onto a ramp that led down into the center of the city, called the "city bowl." They entered Adderly Street and tangled with more traffic.

Pete found the city charming. There were open green spaces, farmer's markets, and preserved colonial buildings that reminded him of London. They passed a long, two-story building. Windows on both floors marched in a line along the length of the building. A white façade stood out for its intricate and elegant carvings. "What's that?" he asked Janette.

"The Iziko Slave Lodge. It's a museum now, but it was used for years as a trading market for slaves. Ironic. It's such a pretty building that held unspeakable horrors."

Traffic came to a halt, so Janette turned the corner and came back up Adderly from the opposite direction. At the corner was a garden that covered several blocks. Surrounded by a low, red brick wall, it had blooming roses, Cape May, blue salvia, and climbing vines over white trellises. Gravel paths intersected in the middle. The signal light changed, and she gunned the car forward.

"The Company's Garden," Janette offered. "Built in 1650 to supply food for the Dutch company that founded the city."

"It's beautiful," Pete said. "Like an English garden."

Janette found a parking ramp and drove up into it. She walked them back onto the street to the offices of the bank. Pete watched her long but smooth stride. The attractive shape of her legs. The walk of an athlete.

They rode to the tenth floor. Adaeze recognized Janette. She started to smile until Janette told her about Ian. Adaeze fell backward and huddled in a corner. Her shoulders shook, and Pete could hear the sound of her sobbing. Hearing of the death, two other employees stumbled around the office. They also knew Janette, and a few people hugged her. The employees nodded and kept wandering between the rooms.

"Let's get moving," Janette told Pete.

She led the way into Donahue's office. From his window, Pete looked down on the Company's Garden. In the center of the office was a big desk, Danish modern style, and two similar file cabinets in the corner.

"Hurry," Janette whispered. "Before anyone else gets here."

She yanked open the right side drawer, pawed through its contents, dropped down to the next drawer, and did the same.

"What are you looking for?"

"Don't know." She started on the left side drawers. One after another. Methodical. Then she moved to the first file cabinet and pulled open the wooden drawer as her fingers crawled over old paper files. "Check those drawers over there for anything relating to the Sirilima Game Reserve. Oh, and grab his laptop."

He did as Janette suggested. Pete found a paper file on the game park. Like Janette's, his fingers inched through the files until he pulled out a file on Janette Koos. He glanced back at her. Janette was preoccupied with the desktop. Pete stuffed her file under his arm and took the laptop off the desk.

Janette turned over artwork on the window sill. Ebony statues of African women carrying bead baskets on their heads. Large breasts and big stomachs protruded from their middles. She searched behind them.

"Aren't we violating a law here about taking possible evidence?"

Janette laughed with a hand in front of her mouth. "Of course, but I don't trust the police to do a thorough job. Especially with an unimportant victim like Donahue. Put those things you found in my bag."

"Remember, I'm not a citizen here—"

"Don't worry. It's how I've been successful as a private investigator in this stew of a country. You must improvise outside the law at times."

The front door of the lobby burst open. Four officers from the South Africa Police Services. Pete recognized two of the men from the waterfront. They fanned out to occupy all the offices. The same detective who had allowed them to get on the ship stood in the lobby. A frown clouded his face.

"What could you two be doing here?" he asked.

Pete stammered, "I work for the bank. I'm here with my daughter on an assignment."

"I think it is more than suspicious that you were at the murder scene and went into the ship with us. What are you really doing here?" He removed his hat to reveal his shaved black head that glistened in the sun coming through the windows.

"Uh—"

"Maybe we should talk about this at the station."

"No, we're here on vacation. We were just getting ready to leave," Pete said. He edged closer to Adaeze.

"Back off, Devon," Janette shouted from the far office as she came into the lobby. She stopped in front of the detective and looked up at him. "Are you kicking us out?"

"This is now a crime scene."

"For your information, I also am on contract to the bank. I told you that at the harbor."

Devon waved his hand. "Okay. Just get out of my crime scene before you screw it up."

"I'm as innocent as a lamb." Janette gave Devon a crooked smile and stepped around him. She nodded toward Pete.

The two left, rode down the elevator, and stepped out into the clean sunshine on the street. Pete admired the way Janette had handled things.

When they reached her car in the ramp, Janette got in the front seat and grunted as she set down her shoulder bag. Pete sat in the passenger seat. "What are you waiting for?" he asked.

Janette looked around to the left and right. Satisfied they were alone, she reached into her bag. She held a black leather notebook tied with a leather strap. "We'll keep this between us. I don't think the police will miss it for a while." She grinned and handed it to Pete.

The corners were worn. "What is this?"

"It looks like Donahue's notebook—with all his passwords written in it."

Chapter Nine

After the police had seized the crate and left the ship, the Captain found a plastic chair in a hidden place on a lower deck. His legs felt rubbery, and he had to sit. A few ounces of Glenlivet scotch would sure help right now. By some miracle, he'd missed being shot.

He was the real target, no doubt. Ever since he'd agreed to help Albert Noonan as an embedded asset in a key government directorate, Frikkie Koekemoer—the Captain's real name—had thought about the risks. Captain was an honorary name which he preferred.

As a minor shipping owner in South Africa, he had become concerned that the excessive fraud and corruption were bringing the country to its knees, thus making it susceptible to being preyed upon by hostile countries and creditors. All of which was bad for his business. When Albert had approached him, Koekemoer recognized someone who might be able to change things. The assignment had been to audit financial data, looking for anomalies in spending that could mean unlawful income. But when he'd heard rumors of an illegal shipment loaded in one of his own ships, Koekemoer went undercover on the ship, posing as a working sailor.

After ten minutes in the chair, he felt better and sent a text to Albert with all the photos Koekemoer had taken of the crate and the people investigating it.

The photos came through clearly to Albert Noonan. Viewing them on his cell phone caused him to slump into the office chair. Made cheaply of black metal, it hurt his back. Albert brushed his hair, worn in a bushy Afro, with a pick. He studied all the shots for the third time. His confidence in the success of the mission evaporated like a watering hole at high noon.

"Dammit," he yelled to the techs who had worked next to him in the airless cubicle for the past two months. "God dammit."

"Dude," Cecil responded from over the low, moveable wall. "What've you got?"

"Not good."

Cecil shoved back his chair; the wheels squealed. He came around the divider and leaned forward to try and see the cell phone. Albert handed it to him. When his fingers had slid through all of the pages, he handed it back. "What does it mean, Albert?"

He stood and kicked away the chair. "All the planning, the cost, and the risk—it may all be compromised. What the hell do you think it means?" he yelled at Cecil and circled the cubicle in three steps.

"You know you always over-react. At least our informant is alive and providing accurate intel. Chill."

"Chill? You don't get it, do you?" Noonan put on his hiking boots and started toward the outer door. "Come on, you moron." Cecil hurried to catch up. He moved with a bobbing motion, like a stork trying to run.

They walked down a hall of tan concrete blocks, reached the door at the end, and pushed against the metal bar. It clanked and opened. Albert burst out into the bright sun. Their command center was hidden in an area of small factories and warehouses in Johannesburg. He and Cecil found shade under a lone fever tree that blushed in red spots between openings in the gray bark.

Cecil's hair was stringy—unusual for a black man. With his long arm propped on his hip, he waited, knowing the best way to deal with his boss' tirades was to let him process the data until it had all slotted into his brain. Cecil could watch the progress through the muscles of Albert's jaw, as if he were chewing on the information. "Albert . . . you okay?"

"I don't know. This could be a Pandora's box. We war gamed this, but our intel only goes so far. We haven't got the resources to contain everything."

"It'll be okay. Think of your training."

Albert waved in the air with his hand to dismiss Cecil.

"Didn't you serve in the South African Defense Force?"

"Yes. Counter insurgency tactics and training. I was a major."

"Did you see combat?"

"Limited. The genesis of our movement was born in both the anti-apartheid effort and the border war with Angola."

Cecil nodded and reached into the side pocket of his photojournalist's vest. "My father fought in that war. I remember he really hated the Cubans who came over to fight for Angola." He pulled out a bag of Cheetos and began munching on the orange pieces.

"I'm too young to have fought there, but the tactics we use today were developed as a result of that conflict."

"Hand-to-hand combat, I suppose."

He chuckled. "No, sorry to disappoint you. We developed intelligence for counter-insurgencies."

"So, why'd you quit the military?"

"Nowhere to go. The military makes a public relations effort about how modern they are and free of corruption. Not true. They're no different than the tired old men running this country. This opportunity came along, and it will give me a chance to change things."

"You're gonna kick someone's ass?"

"Shut up, Cecil."

"At least it's more than I've done. For years, I've sat behind a computer in that concrete cocoon. I may metamorphosize into an African Cape butterfly someday." He chewed on more Cheetos that sounded like the crunch of Styrofoam. "I can learn from you."

That hook caught Albert, and he turned to face Cecil. Albert had been mentored right from the start at the Saldanha Academy in the South Africa Army Training Formation. He wanted to return the favor to someone—even if a guy like Cecil would never see Special Forces training nor be deployed into the hot zones of combat. Besides, when Albert's generation took over, a guy with Cecil's skills would be valuable.

"Look at this." Albert flicked a fingertip across his phone screen until he retrieved the photos from the Captain in Cape Town. "We've got two breaches here."

"I suppose one is the ivory."

"You're brilliant. Yes, the ivory—it's the special shipment."

"That's odd."

"That's bad. The police stumbled onto the crate during an investigation of a shooting incident. I don't know what these other guys are doing in the ship. No matter how many tangents you input to mission game planning, how can the software anticipate something improbable like this?"

Cecil licked his lips.

"We don't want the low-level cops involved at this point."

"Top secret?"

"Almost." Albert stepped into the sun from under the fever tree. Clouds that had loaded up with moisture over the Indian Ocean trundled across the sky, still carrying their loads like pregnant women. He had forgotten his red beret in the rush to get outside, and the sun reflected off his face. Although he was considered a black man, his skin was brown, like the back of a Thomson's gazelle.

He looked around to make sure no one was outside with them. Even so, Albert lowered his voice. "You're aware of the Lord's Resistance Army?"

"That terrorist group out of Sudan?"

"Right. The LRA is in the Democratic Republic of the Congo to buy weapons in an effort to take control of isolated areas and destabilize South Africa."

"I know all this shit."

"But you were not briefed about the entire mission. The terrorists are using poached ivory as payment for military equipment. That's why I'm so interested in the shipment. I want to find out if it ends up with the terrorists. Which means someone in South Africa, at very high levels, is supplying the contraband. If I can expose those people, I'm golden. Can't stop me."

"I get it."

Albert had come a long way from the townships of Johannesburg. His mother and father were professors at the Soweto campus of Vista University—a primarily black school during apartheid. By the early 2000s, the government had combined the Rand Afrikaans University with Vista. Albert had attended one of the first "rainbow nation" efforts in South Africa, where he studied computer science. After college, he rebelled and enlisted in the Defense Force. Beyond that, he volunteered for the Special Forces and intelligence work. The military, like the civilian world, was discovering the power of big data and high-tech warfare. The military used it to analyze intelligence on individuals and organizations identified as tactical and strategic threats. For someone with knowledge in the area, at the right time in the right place, it had been the perfect opportunity for Albert.

"What's the second breach?"

Although Albert was a "spit and polish" soldier, he could overlook lack of discipline in others if necessary—like Cecil. It would be a challenge to clean him up. "The new people there. The woman and a guy."

"Who are they?"

Albert shrugged.

"What's our response?" Cecil brushed his hands against one another. The remains of the Cheetos fell like orange snow.

"I'm not too concerned about the police. We can contain them with money if we need to. But we have to act fast before they expand their investigation. I want you to contact the deputy interior minister immediately."

Cecil tapped on his cell phone to make notes.

"The bigger threat is the civilians. Who the hell are they, and what will they do now?"

"I'll check 'em out. Should take about two minutes with our databases. Can we assume they have nothing to do with the bogie and they'll forget about it? Accidental encounter?"

"We can't take the risk. Can't make assumptions. Until the facts show us the opposite, we have to prepare for the worst."

"What's that?"

"These civilians will expose things. After all, how many times does someone find a load of illegal ivory?" Albert looked into Cecil's eyes to reinforce his point. "If they talk, too many unauthorized people will get involved. Everything we've worked for—gone."

"Yeah." He swallowed.

"We're off the books, remember? My biggest fear is that it's too late. I may have failed already."

"So, what are we gonna do?"

"Capture their identities and then make covert contact. As soon as possible. They must be interdicted—by any means."

"You're serious?"

"This operation is my chance to get credibility with the right people. It's time for our generation. The old men are lazy and corrupt. We can create a 'new' Africa. But I need this win to launch my own career. I'm not going to fail." Albert slapped his hands along his thighs and stomped toward the door. "Cecil, sometimes you're so stupid."

Chapter Ten

Janette raced back to the harbor. "It's possible the crate from the ship is still being unloaded and we can find out where it's going." The traffic opened, and they reached the ship by the restaurant in less than a half hour. By that time, the police had organized the off-loading of the crate.

Pete watched as two police officers from the Service entered the ship to get the wooden box and its contents of elephant tusks and rhino horns. The ship's crane quivered as it lifted the crate and swung it over the edge above the top deck. A steel cable dropped down with yellow webbed straps at the end to secure the load.

"They'll probably take it to their property room, next to the central police station," Janette said. "I may be able to get a look at it if my contacts are working there. The facility is a sieve, and we might get lucky."

"Why are you telling me this?" Pete said.

Koos smiled. "Because you're an investigator, and I think you're interested."

"No, I'm done here. Looks like the cops have this under control."

"What about Donahue?"

Pete stopped. "My assignment is the murder at the game park. I want to get out there. I should go with Karen." He looked at Janette. "What are you going to do next?"

"If I were the police and had the jurisdiction to do so, I'd check the ship's crew. If we assume the shooter targeted someone on the ship, that would be the first thing to investigate."

"But you can't do that."

Janette's mouth tightened. "No. Not like being an investigator in the military and getting access to everything, right?"

"How did you know I was in the military?"

"You said so, and when Donahue mentioned you were coming, I did a little background on you. Pretty impressive. As to the murder, the police will undoubtedly look for the shooter. Do forensics on the weapon, the usual stuff."

"Is there any chance we could look at their investigation?" Pete asked. "My boss in Minneapolis will be shocked by this."

"Probably not. But we might be able to follow the ivory. Of course, the murder will be investigated thoroughly. As for the contraband—well, it's a big problem here, but the police resources are strained, and they don't spend much time on trafficking of ivory. That could help us."

"How is that?"

"I told you they will take the evidence to a central property room in Cape Town. I may be able to get access to it. It wouldn't be completely legal, of course."

"So you're, like, Wonder Woman?" Pete said.

Koos smiled, brought up her hand, and laughed. "I do things they don't teach you in school."

That reminded Pete of his way of operating. When Koos looked to the side, Pete studied her. Under the blazer, he could make out a firm, full figure. She seemed unemotional and direct. But her willingness to break rules attracted him. He asked, "What are you looking for?"

"Don't know for certain, but it's the only clue I can follow right now." Janette left him and talked with the detective again.

The sun flooded the dock area but didn't feel hot because of the fresh breeze coming across the harbor. Pete thought of how Martin Graves would respond to Donahue's death and how Martin would insist on answers. His job had suddenly expanded into two investigations, two deaths.

Dozens of cawing gulls swooped down on a patch of water next to them. Pieces of discarded food sloshed back and forth. The gulls swarmed and fought with each other to eat, wings flapping against wings.

He also considered Karen. One part of Pete wanted to drop everything and go with her to the game park to enjoy their vacation. But he owed Martin Graves a lot. And Pete had agreed to finish the investigation of Isaac's murder. The case had become a lot more than a possible scandal.

He walked across the dock to find Janette. Pete chatted with her briefly and realized he wanted to see her again, soon. "So, if I go with you to check out the shipment, what's in it for me?"

Janette smiled slowly. "You're an investigator. It's in your personality to solve puzzles."

"Do you want help?"

"I could always use it."

"I'm willing to work on this aspect if you help with the killing at the game reserve."

"Sure. I have a hunch they're connected, anyway."

They got into Janette's car and drove back through the city toward the Pilgrim Hotel. Janette swung to the edge of the city and climbed up the side of Table Mountain. They passed schools, cafés, and villas perched on the steep ground. Some homes had palm trees in the front yards, and a few had camphor bush trees with multiple trunks larger in diameter than the SUVs parked next to them. They looked out of place, like alien growths from underneath the mountain.

Pete looked to his left and saw the city spread out below him, stretching toward the harbor and the glistening water beyond. Then they descended into a crowded area. Bougainvillea grew in dense clumps from the front of houses and fences. Purple flowers covered the structures like colorful mold on rocks.

Janette came to a stop in a neighborhood. "This is called the 'Bo-Kaap' area. Settled by slaves imported from Malaysia and Indonesia. Muslims, mostly. It's a safe and trendy area now, with young people moving in."

The houses were painted in multiple hues—saffron, celery, raspberry, and lime green.

In twenty minutes they reached the hotel. Pete gripped her hand, said goodbye, and hurried into the hotel to find Karen. He and Janette had agreed to meet later that night. Janette would give him directions and the time. "Be ready to move quickly. If I can get us inside the police station, the window will be very small."

Chapter Eleven

He was a large man whose face was the same shape as his body, both of which looked like an African gourd: narrow at the top, spreading out at the bottom. Matimba Phatudi hadn't always looked like that. In his early years, he was an athlete and fit, but time and responsibilities had weighed on him.

His three wives caused him endless problems. Sabella was recognized by the government as his "official" wife. The other two were tribal wives who gave him pleasure and children, but also headaches. Matimba was a member of the Tswana tribe that lived in eastern South Africa and Botswana, which was named after his tribe. Further, he was a member of the Hurutshe, a subdivision of the larger tribe.

His landline phone rang in Union Building in Pretoria, where Matimba worked by day. It was his second wife, Abimbola, which meant "born with honor."

She spoke to him in Bantu, the native language. "Matimba, you are in trouble, and I will not help you this time."

His cell phone, lying on the desk, buzzed and jiggled like a dying cockroach. He ignored it. "What is the problem?" It was her fourth call of the day.

"You have lost your headdress and your spear. You are so careless. I'm tired of picking up after you."

These items formed part of his ceremonial garb for meetings of the ward. Although they weren't necessary, Matimba liked to preserve the traditions, especially against the young bulls who challenged him constantly for leadership. He sighed. "I will find them when I get time. I have problems here at the office I must attend to." While Abimbola continued to talk, he hung up.

Although Matimba lived in Pretoria with Sabella, Abimbola lived in one of the oldest black townships in Cape Town, called Langa. Originally forced into the area by apartheid, hundreds of families had chosen to remain living there. His third wife lived in a village near the small town of Mafikeng, still in South Africa, where he had been raised. The village edged against the bush, and their culture preserved many of the ancient tribal customs. Like every Tswana, he was affiliated with a patrilineal grouping of families called a ward. His full name contained the names of several generations of men in his genealogical line, and the ward was composed of descendants of the male lines of previous Tswana. As a senior male, Matimba was also a chief, responsible for many of the administrative and judicial aspects of the tribe. For most black Africans, the culture of the tribe and its teachings were as important as the rules of the civil society in which they lived.

Matimba worked full time with the South African National Defense Force, which had jurisdiction for border patrol. He commanded a company with fifteen new Toyota Land Cruisers. They had been modified for border patrol to carry more fuel and water. In addition, the configuration allowed a "stick" of soldiers (five people) and at least one ranger or police officer in the event of an interdepartmental patrol.

He looked at his cell phone. His wife Sabella had called twice. He returned the call. They spoke English. "What do you want?"

"Do not be so curt. I am your wife, not some subordinate."

"Sorry."

"It is the children. You know soccer practice starts in one week, and they do not have equipment or uniforms. When I looked at the bank statement, it is empty. Matimba, you promised we would have enough to buy these things. We do not want the children to lack them."

"I know, I know. My government pay—"

"That has already been spent for the mortgage and the Mercedes."

"Ah, yes. Well, I have another source that is scheduled to pay me in three days."

Sabella groaned. "I can try to squeeze it on the card, but it is almost full. I will be embarrassed when our children show up for practice without uniforms. You know I do not like that." Her voice trailed off with the ominous threat.

"I will work on it today. I promise."

"Can you pick up some spices on your way home? I need cardamom, nutmeg, and fenugreek. Oh, and some preserved lemons. I am making a surprise for you."

"I could use something good."

"I am sorry to be upset. You always have been a good husband. When I worked on my master's degree, you were there for me." Sabella's voice softened. "Good bye, my little warthog." She laughed at their private joke—the warthog was a small, grubbing animal that moved like a dog and was so ugly it was almost cute.

Just as Matimba hung up, Lieutenant Ibrahim Kenyatta swung into his office, his uniform crisp and spotless. Matimba had a technique for intimidating subordinates. He'd open his eyes wide to expose the whites, which stood out against his coal black skin. It worked all the time. That, and a large Roman nose, gave him an imperial look, Matimba always thought. He reminded people constantly that his name meant "gift of God."

"I am busy," Matimba shouted.

"Sorry, sir." The adjutant stopped sharply at the door.

"I don't want to be bothered."

"Yes, sir, but there is an issue."

"Not now."

"Sir, there is a problem. There's been an infiltration from Zambia."

"Have James look into it." Matimba tried to hand off the problem to his second-in-command.

"But you said to bring all—"

"Get out," Matimba bellowed like a Cape buffalo. The force of his voice blew the lieutenant out the door.

Matimba hefted himself out of the chair and walked into an adjacent room. A fridge stood in the corner with a hot pot next to it on the counter. A tray of European pastries had been ravaged earlier by the staff, but a few remained. Matimba heated water for tea and munched on a chocolate-filled croissant while he waited. Between emails and phone calls, he might go crazy, he worried.

He thought of the financial needs that his families pressed on him. His government salary was far too small to pay for everything. Like many Africans, he had set up a business—as he liked to call it—that provided extra cash flow. But because of the nature of the business, the cash flow was sporadic. He'd been assured of a lump sum in three days. At least it was tax free.

His cell phone rattled on the desk. Matimba ambled back to his office and saw it was his tribal wife, Dakini. He answered her.

"Matimba, I am furious with you."

He held the phone away from his ear. "Now what?"

"I saw Abimbola visiting in the village with a new *dashiki*. A beautiful cotton one with black and orange print. You know my favorite colors are black and orange. Why did she get one and not me?"

"You work. You can buy your own."

"You give her gifts, and I get nothing. I should not be treated that poorly."

"Sorry. I will come to visit you as soon as I can and buy you new clothes."

"I do not believe you; that is a promise you break all the time. I will have the *sangoma* cast an evil spell on you."

"Do not joke about such matters."

"Well, I am mad."

Before hanging up, Matimba agreed to meet at the one-story house in the tribal village near Mafikeng. Behind it was a storage shed next to the *shamba*, or vegetable garden, covered in a thatched roof, in which he had once found a black strongbox. Dakini wouldn't tell him what was in it, but he was certain she stashed money there. Still, he had his responsibilities, and she took good care of their children.

James, his second-in-command, pushed open the door to Matimba's office. He couldn't intimidate James as they had worked together for years.

"Matimba, you must pay attention to the reports from the border. Near the intersection of the Zambia and Botswana borders, there has been an infiltration. Our soldiers are on the spot now with three prisoners."

Matimba took a deep breath. "Do we know where they came from?"

"Probably Chobi National Park."

"Then it is Botswana's problem, not ours."

"They were apprehended in our jurisdiction."

"What's the evidence?"

James sat in the curved wooden chair before Matimba's desk. Opening a cell phone, James scrolled through his notes. "Two old Ford trucks with enclosed beds were seen as they crossed into South Africa. Our soldiers had intelligence that poaching was occurring in Chobi. When we attempted to stop them, the trucks tried to escape."

"What did they find?"

"Four AK-47s, two old shotguns, a chain saw that was still warm, a liter of whiskey, and the horns of seven white rhinos. Freshly cut. Amateurs, probably."

Matimba stood and walked in a circle behind his desk. In spite of his size, he moved like a panther. Finally, he said, "Where are the prisoners now?"

"We have them secured in our detention center."

"Minimal staff there?"

"Yes. You know we can't afford to assign personnel there. It's just lucky our team got the intel to stop these thieves. What do you want to do?"

Matimba's heavy lips turned down. "Shoot them."

"But—"

"You said yourself we don't have the manpower. That means we don't have the men or the time to bring these criminals back to Cape Town to the courts." He remembered his tea and picked up the cup to take a sip. English Breakfast tea, his favorite. One croissant remained on the tray until Matimba grabbed it. "It will take months to process the cases while my officers must come back and forth to court. No, we won't do that."

James shifted from one side of the chair to the other. He looked up at the ceiling. "I am not comfortable with this order."

Matimba brushed crumbs off his chest. "This is Africa. Life comes and goes."

"I know we have a job to do, but these men—" James stood up. "Deep down, I know you're not opposed to killing some of these animals."

Matimba shrugged. "Of course. In my opinion, the worst animals are the damn leopards. I'd like to see them all killed. I remember one dragged a sleeping baby from my village. We found the dead child the next morning hanging in a tree."

"I think the elephants are the worst. Eating everything and ruining crops for the poor farmers. They also can easily kill. My cousin was in his field and wasn't even threatening the elephants when one charged and stomped him to death."

"The truth is, after years of Western-promoted conservation of the animals, our people have received nothing from all the money and effort."

"But Matimba, we can't let our opinions of this interfere with the justice system for these poachers. The law is the law."

"Justice system?" Matimba snorted. "*We* are the justice system. The rest of them are corrupt and as worthless as the leopard." His cell phone rang. Assuming it was one of his wives, Matimba ignored it. He pocketed it and came around the desk. Putting his arm over James' shoulders, Matimba said, "Come, my friend. Let us take a walk."

"I do not feel good about this."

"Think about it: we are not much different than the animals all around us. Like them, we live and we die. But we are paid to do a job here—stop poachers. We must perform our duties in spite of what we feel."

"As you are my commander, I will do what you order me to." James straightened as if he were going to salute Matimba but stopped short of that. "But—"

Matimba's government phone rang, and he answered it.

His secretary said, "Freddy has been trying to reach you. He's called your cell phone."

A twitch went through Matimba's chest. "I am taking a walk. Tell him to meet me as soon as possible in the park." He hung up quickly.

He and James hurried through the long marble hallways of Union Building. Built by the Europeans at the turn of the 20th century, the extensive complex housed a big part of the South African government, including the president's office.

They came out in the front and waited to cross Government Street. An overloaded bus rocked from side to side as it passed them. People clung to the roof and stood on the back bumper, wearing worn-out flip flops. A man on the back carried a burlap bag stuffed with two chickens that squawked in confusion.

Across the street, a tall statue of Nelson Mandela looked up into the sky, where he stood in the middle of an English garden that sloped down toward the central city. Jacaranda trees ringed the park, some still flowering in clouds of pink and lavender. The city had more jacaranda trees than any other in the world.

They started down the stone steps that led into the garden. Matimba walked gracefully. He looked to the left and right several times and then stopped James beside a fountain. Two kingfishers perched on the side, bobbing their heads occasionally for a drink. "I have an important meeting soon," he told James. "In the meantime, you know what to do."

James' face froze. "It will be done."

"It is political. For Africans, we have grown up with big game close by, so we understand there is death and new life all around us. We both know anti-poaching policies are agreed to by African politicians who want to get rich from the tourist dollars they steal." He hunched his shoulders. "So, we are paid our salaries to stop poachers."

"Tourists who come for a few days to stare at the game do not understand."

"Yes, of course. But they—" Matimba looked up the steps and spotted a lone figure hurrying down toward them. He wore a striped *dashiki* that billowed out behind him in flashes of emerald as he jumped from step to step.

With a push on the back, Matimba dismissed James and told him to take care of the problem at the border. "You are a good soldier," he told James, who left to climb the steps back to Union Building. He passed the man coming down, but they didn't know each other.

When the man in the *dashiki* reached Matimba, they huddled together. Freddy smelled like smoke; he must have been at the township recently. Matimba glanced around to make sure no one was listening. His voice cracked with anger. "Freddy, I do not want to be seen with you—ever. It is too dangerous."

"I am sorry." The man had buck teeth that made it look like he was smiling all the time. "But there is an emergency."

"What could be so serious as to break cover?"

The man took a moment to catch his breath. "Cape Town. The police service there have confiscated a shipment of elephant ivory and rhino horns."

"Where?"

"I do not have the details yet, but I'm sure it is one of ours. As usual, they will be numbered so we can confirm their origin."

Matimba's eyelids dropped halfway over his eyes. Cogged wheels turned in his head, one wheel engaging the next one as he imagined the possible dangers that could happen to them. It made his stomach churn. He had to act. An old African proverb taught: *Even the lion, the king of the forest, protects himself from flies.* "Where is it now?"

"The police service has moved it to an evidence storage facility."

Matimba's eyes flicked open. "That is a break for us. We will take control of the ivory and override their jurisdiction. Tell them it is evidence for an investigation we are conducting into an extensive network of poachers. How soon can we get a team in there to scoop the load?"

The man smiled. "Within forty-eight hours. Maybe sooner, depending on which men are available."

Matimba also smiled. He looked up at Nelson Mandela, watching the kingfishers perch on the statue's huge brass finger. With quick action, Matimba hoped this operation could still be saved—to get the money to pay for his wives as he had promised.

Chapter Twelve

After agreeing to meet later, Janette dropped off Pete at the Pilgrim Hotel. He found Karen in the lobby, sipping tea. He sat beside her and put his arm around her shoulders.

She hunched over as her body trembled. "Can't believe—"

"It was horrible."

"Is this a typical job for you? Come to Africa and get killed?"

Pete sighed. "Sometimes, in my work, bad things happen. I'm sorry."

"I'm leaving for the game reserve tomorrow. Found a flight to Johannesburg at ten."

"Okay. I'll meet you there as soon as a few things are completed here."

She looked up at him, her face wet with tears. "You don't get it, do you? I've lost all the meaningful people in my life. I don't want to lose you."

"I do get it," Pete said. "And as soon as I can get away from Cape Town, I'll join you."

"But then you'll get sucked into the murder investigation there. I'll never have a vacation with my father, my only remaining family."

His voice raspy, he said, "I have a job, Karen. You knew that before we came here."

She waved him away. "Of course. Same old story."

"That's not fair."

"Oliver will pick me up. I'll see you at the reserve." Karen stood and stumbled toward the elevator.

Pete leaned back into the soft cushions. She might not realize it, but they did share something close—both of them were suffering from intense grief.

Later that night, before dusk descended, Pete said good night to Karen and walked out to the parking lot of the hotel. The rental company had delivered a Chevy Spark for him. He climbed in and took a circle in the lot to refresh himself about using a stick to shift. He eased onto the street, careful to look the opposite direction he would in the U.S. Pete turned into the left lane and shifted up to speed.

It felt awkward for about ten minutes, and then Pete relaxed. He drove onto M4, which took him into central Cape Town. Most of the buildings were two-story with occasional open lots of sand. Following the GPS directions, he turned onto Albertus Street. It was one-way. Several blocks ahead, the road narrowed and looked like it entered a shadowed tunnel of overhanging trees.

Pete slowed as he came closer to the intersection. A sign announced the District Six Museum. He was two blocks from the intersection with Buitenkant Street, so he pulled to the curb and stopped.

Pete called Janette. She responded and gave him careful instructions. He was to cross the Buitenkant intersection and park on Albertus. Four doors down from that was a tea shop named Blenheim Palace. She instructed him to meet her there for tea.

Pete pulled out into traffic. On his left was a two-story white structure built in the colonial style. It stretched for two blocks. At the corner, a palm tree partially obscured the sign that read "Cape Town Police Service." He drove through the intersection and into the dark tunnel of overhanging trees. Pete slid the Spark into a spot on the left side.

He walked across Albertus, turned left, and found the tea shop. Inside, it smelled good, like a bakery and ground coffee beans. Lace curtains hung at the windows, while imitation gas lights were mounted between them. A large portrait of Nelson Mandela occupied a center spot on the far wall. In a smaller frame, Queen Victoria, dressed in black, looked across the room in stern condemnation.

Pete spotted Janette sitting in the back. She was alone. As he walked toward her, the wooden floor squeaked. Koos stood up and shook his hand. She laughed. "We're actually too late for high tea. But you can still have some with a scone, if you'd like. The blueberry ones are fabulous—with clotted cream." Her hand brushed across her mouth. She wore blue running shoes, athletic pants, and a cotton hoodie. Her hair, pulled back in a ponytail, showed off her clear skin.

Pete ordered coffee from the waitress and waited for Janette to speak.

"Did you tell your boss in Minneapolis about Ian?" she asked.

"Yes. Tough conversation. Now things get messy."

Janette nodded and waited a few minutes, then said, "Did you notice that big white building along Albertus Street?"

"I passed it," Pete said.

"That's the police station. On the back side is one of their property rooms, where they store evidence during an investigation or in preparation for a trial."

"And this is where the elephant ivory went?"

"Right."

"In my experience, these facilities are locked and guarded to protect the evidence."

"Of course, but we have some help. For one thing, Donahue's murder will occupy most of their attention. Ivory is a lower priority. And I know the officer who will be there tonight. But he's only there for a few hours since he's not the usual duty officer."

Pete frowned. "So, you want to go in there against procedure? Do you know what you're talking about? And, by the way, what the hell are you going to do with the tusks once we steal them?"

Janette reached across the table and grabbed Pete's forearm. "Not so loud. We've got a small window of time when we can get the tusks out and transport them to an expert I know who will analyze them, then return them before we're discovered."

Pete questioned the plan. "Janette, this doesn't sound—"

"This is the only clue we have to follow." The urgency in her voice sounded convincing.

"But what if we're caught? A foreigner stealing police evidence? I've done many things outside the law, but it's different in a foreign country."

Janette lifted her tea and drank it.

"And the bank won't be able to help us get out of that kind of trouble," Pete added.

"Money goes a long way here," Janette said. "and we'll use some to convince my friend to help us. Since Donahue was killed, the bank has given me instructions to continue the investigation and, if possible, find his killer. This is how we will accomplish that."

Pete pushed back his chair. It scraped in protest against the floor. "Okay, I get that. Let's assume I'll help."

Janette looked him in the face. "I knew you would."

"Huh?"

"You're so transparent, Pete. You want to protect your daughter, of course, but you also want to solve the mystery. It's a sense of justice, right?"

"Well—"

Her phone rang. A short, heated conversation started. Janette moved away from the table. In a few minutes, she was back. Her eyes were damp and she breathed heavily.

"Okay?" Pete asked.

"Nothing." She cleared her throat, put her hand on his forearm, and left it there.

"Why me?"

She raised her eyebrows. "You've got a good reputation, and I need someone good with me."

"You don't even know me."

"I'm an investigator. I can read people well, and you seem honest and capable to me."

Her eyes lingered on him for a long moment. He also read people well, and Janette was interested in something more. Once again, Pete sensed her desperation—hidden deeply, but still there. What did she really want out of this? He thought of his boss and wanted to protect him.

At the hotel, Pete had done some investigation of Janette Koos. Between the bank's resources, records, and good old Google, he'd discovered a lot. She had a shady background that involved some alleged theft while in college with her future husband. He was the older one and seemed to be the mastermind, but Janette had offered to take the blame to shelter him. Eventually, they were both released with no charges because of their young ages. She went on to marry the man, had two kids, and then divorced him. Maybe it had taken her awhile to figure him out.

The paper file from Donahue's office also revealed Janette had a daughter who was paralyzed from the waist down. The daughter, Jane, had been in an accident. Ian's written notes on the file said: "JK motivated, above all, to help her child."

Her job history was checkered: manager in a vineyard, part time college instructor, and even a brief time with the Stellenbosch police department as a "cultural liaison," whatever that meant.

At this point, Pete would give her the benefit of the doubt. Besides, he hoped to use her expertise and connections for his own investigation of Isaac's murder. "What's the backup plan?"

Janette blinked a few times and sipped more of her tea. "There is none."

"What?"

"Pete, there's only a short time when things could be dicey—the actual transfer," Janette said. "As a licensed investigator, I can get legal access to the police station. Beyond that, I can't get into the property room. Thankfully, my friend comes on duty after dark. That gives us some cover."

Darkness descended an hour later.

Janette led him out of the Blenheim Palace and down the street to her Chery Tiggo SUV. With Pete's help, she folded down the back seats. Janette pulled from the curb and made several turns to get back to Albertus Street. She came up to the police station and stopped at the corner. "I'll go in first to see if my friend is on duty. You'll follow afterward." Janette reached across Pete and removed a tan envelope from the glove compartment. It bulged in the middle.

Pete remained in the car as Janette got out, cradling the envelope beside her chest. She hurried along the sidewalk and disappeared into a door on the side of the building. In a few minutes, she was back out, waving for him to follow her. The envelope was gone.

Janette led Pete through a door into a small lobby with marble floors. Pete's boots echoed off the walls and made him feel even more nervous. He tried to tiptoe forward but felt stupid. At the second door on the left, Janette stopped and pushed through it. They entered a small office area. A second door with frosted glass stood at the back wall below a domed security camera that hung from the ceiling like a black bubble. Pete thought it was probably a Bosch—cheap but very good.

69

In a few minutes, a black man in uniform came through the door. He didn't smile but nodded at Koos.

Janette said, "This is Moses."

No one shook his hand. "You have two hours," he said to Janette while he handed her a plastic card.

"Right. Meet us at the door."

Janette led Pete back out into the lobby. "Come on," she urged him. "This is going to be a close game."

Outside, they ran for her SUV and jumped in it, and Janette swung around in a wide circle. She angled for the narrow alley next to the back wall of the station. It was unlit, and Janette kept her lights off. In one half block, she came to a wide double door and stopped. "Pete, open the back hatch, then follow me inside."

Pete got out and saw the snout of another security camera staring down at them. He pointed to it as he opened the hatch.

"Don't worry. Moses has caused it to malfunction for seven minutes. Any longer will be noticed. We've got to hurry." She led the way inside to a steel door. In Old English script it read "Cape Town Police Service Property Room." Underneath that: "No Admittance. Maximum Sanctions for Infractions."

Koos swiped the card through the reader next to the door. It buzzed, and she pushed on the handle. Pete followed her.

Inside, they reached a cavernous room with faint lighting. In front of them, tall steel shelving ran forward to disappear into the darkness beyond. Each row was labeled with two letters and three numbers. The shelves were filled with boxes of various sizes, some cardboard and others plastic. Many were sealed shut with blue tape.

Pete looked at his watch. "Where the hell are we supposed to go?"

"Moses will show us." Janette darted from one side to the other. Only an intermittent beeping sound from somewhere interrupted the silence. Small red lights near the ceiling, like animal eyes in the night, indicated either smoke alarms or more cameras.

It felt chilly, and Pete wanted to bail. At this point, other than making an unauthorized entry, they'd done nothing wrong.

A door opened and shut in the gloom at the far end of the room. It sounded far away. Footsteps clopped closer to them, and Moses ducked out from around the far row of shelving. "Over here," he hissed.

They hurried to a large open bay, where the crate they'd seen in the ship rested on the ground. Next to it, a forklift stood with its tongs lifted halfway up into the air. Janette nodded at Moses and pulled a flashlight out of the side pocket of her pants. She shone it at the crate. "We need a ladder."

Moses looked around. "Don't see any." He stood still, trying to decide what to do.

"How about the forklift?" Pete suggested. "Lift the forks and we can climb on them."

Moses agreed and took two steps up into the machine. With a rumble, it started. He maneuvered it backward and to the side, approaching the crate. He inched the forks closer until they touched the wooden side of the crate; then he shut off the engine. It smelled like propane gas.

"Okay, let's go," Janette ordered. "Can you leave the forklift there?"

"Yeah. Make sure you're back in time." He pointed a crooked finger in her face.

"Of course. I've never let you down, Officer Mahlangu."

Janette lifted her foot, caught the edge of the steel fork, and grunted as she heaved herself up. She curved her leg over the top of the crate and disappeared inside up to her shoulders. "Need some help," she reminded Pete. He followed her lead.

Inside the crate, Koos brushed aside curlicue wood packing and folded cardboard. Her flashlight wavered back and forth over the cargo as she uncovered it. In a few minutes, the dull gold of the tusks was revealed. Janette stood up.

For a moment, both of them didn't move, mesmerized by the beauty, the size, and the knowledge of how the tusks had been harvested.

"Damn," Janette said as she kneeled down and brushed aside more packing material. "Doesn't surprise me."

"What?"

"Rhino horns. Mixed in with the elephant ivory. God dammit. Look at how much there is. Makes me sick."

"We don't have time."

"Okay, help me. We need three of the tusks. They're heavy."

She levered the pointed end up while Pete reach for the end that was cut off. He cupped his hands around it and lifted. The stump looked like a severed tree, and in the dim light, he saw the marks of a chainsaw. Black smudges covered one side of the tusk. Written in black ink on the ivory, Pete read *Circ/base = 28.5*.

They hoisted the tusk over the edge of the crate and eased it down to the floor. Back in the crate, Janette pushed the tusks aside to dig out one near the bottom. The third one came from the edge of the load.

"Don't you want some of the rhino horns?" Pete asked.

Janette shook her head. "They're too common, unfortunately. Asians think they can cure diseases like cancer or work as aphrodisiacs. Most of these illegal shipments are headed for Vietnam or directly to China."

Pete lifted a horn. Big. Almost three feet long. He knew that rhino horn wasn't really a horn but more like a human fingernail, only a lot harder. "Is this from a Western black rhino?"

Janette leaned over to him, her shoulder touching his, and lifted the horn. She pointed her flashlight at it. "Don't think so. Probably a white rhino. They're common in South Africa." She flicked off the light and hoisted herself out of the crate. On the floor, she asked Pete, "Can you carry two?"

Pete picked up the pointed end, grabbed the stump, and shouldered the tusk. "No prob." With his free hand, he cradled a second smaller tusk under his arm.

They hurried to the back door. Janette stopped long enough to peek outside before they slipped out to the SUV. The tusks went into the open hatch. Closing it, Janette got in and drove down the alley to Albertus Street. She gunned the car into the tunnel of trees that had now gone completely black with night. Two blocks later, she turned left and drove toward the harbor.

"Where are we going?" Pete said.

"I've got a contact with a staff member at the Ditsong National Museum of Natural History. He's waiting for us at one of his labs. He's able to test ivory and hopefully give us an idea of where it came from."

"Can we follow that to the poachers?"

"Not so easy, but it's our only play right now," Janette said.

Pete twisted in his seat and looked out into the dark. Was he wasting his time on this? He needed to complete his work on the game reserve killing and get back to Karen.

Janette glanced at him. "I know what you're thinking. I'm thinking the same, but let's see this through."

Twenty minutes later they arrived at a low warehouse near the harbor. Janette drove through a gate in a chain-link fence. The warehouse was dark except for the far end, where the windows glowed in a blue-white light. Janette pulled up to a door next to the windows. She got out and knocked on the door, and a heavy-set man stepped out. The light from inside cast a halo around him, leaving his body black. Janette hurried back to the SUV and opened the hatch. "The game is on. David is ready for us."

They carried the tusks inside, through two more doors, and set them on a stainless steel table under an overhead light as bright as any in a surgical room. Janette introduced David Stirton. He wore a white lab coat and had pink skin and a mane of yellow hair that crowned over his head to end at his shoulders.

He explained that the Ditsong National Museum had been founded in 1892. "Since then, we have worked as the custodian and documentation center for South Africa's natural history."

"David, we're on a tight schedule here." Janette rolled her hand in the air to move him along.

"You used to have plenty of time for me—" He tilted his head forward and looked at her from under his eyebrows.

"And that goes back to about the time of the Great Trek," Janette told him.

Stirton grunted and got to work. He hefted one end of the tusk in both hands and bounced it up and down. Lowering it to the lab table, he ran his fingers over the surface. "Real ivory feels heavy. Think of a billiard ball. Heavy and cool. It's also smooth to the touch." He peered at the surface through a magnifying glass. After several minutes, David walked to the corner of the table, lit a burner, and inserted a long needle into the heat. He rolled over the tusk and stuck it with the point of the needle, then leaned over to smell it "Good. No smell of burning. Another sign this is real ivory."

Pete moved closer to the examination table.

"Look at this." Pointing with his finger, Stirton said, "These are crosshatched lines. They run the length of the tusk. And these perpendicular V-shapes are Schreger lines. All indicate this is real. That's what I'm testing here." He glanced up. "These." He lifted the tusk to expose the stump. "Elephants go through two sets of tusks during their lives. This is the second set. I can roughly determine age by the size, but there are more accurate scientific tests, called bomb-curve 14c dating. It refers to the radioactive decay in ivory."

"Look at the patina. It's lustrous and beautiful." He explained, "Different parades of elephants from different geographical regions exhibit slightly different types of tusks. For instance, elephants from Namibia have thick but short tusks, while the elephants from the eastern side of South Africa near the Zambezi River have long, thin tusks."

"Can you say where these tusks are from?" Janette asked.

"I can't give you an opinion to a scientific level of certainty, but these are probably from the eastern part of the country."

"Sirilima Game Reserve is in the eastern part, closer to the Zambezi River," Janette told Pete.

Stirton bent over the tusks so that his face was inches away. "Of course, if I had more time, I could perform the chemical tests to confirm my initial findings." His eyes rose without lifting his head. He sighed. "You understand we're really dealing with an investment in extinction."

"What do you mean?" Pete asked.

"The criminal networks that smuggle the illegal ivory view it as an investment for the future. If they can keep killing enough elephants to finally make the species extinct, the ivory they've stockpiled becomes as valuable as Picasso paintings—there's no more being created."

Pete looked at Janette. A line of muscles in her lower jaw tightened. He turned back to Stirton.

"Are you serious?" Pete asked.

Stirton looked at him. "Do you have any idea what this represents?" He pointed at the tusks on the table.

"Well—" Pete backed away from him.

"Smuggling is a twenty-billion-dollar industry that is controlled by organized crime, armies, and terrorists."

Without saying another word, he turned his attention to the second tusk. He poured some liquid onto a soft cloth and buffed the side of one of the tusks until it was clean of dirt and grime. "This bothers me."

"What?" Janette said.

"The shine. Ivory has a special shine; this one does not. Hmm. I'm going to X-ray it and use spectrographic analysis for final confirmation. I'll need a few milligrams of the specimen."

They helped him carry all three pieces to another table in a sealed room. He rolled a narrow machine next to the table—the X-ray equipment—and told them to step out.

Stirton returned in ten minutes. "Janette, you've been cheated." He sat on a steel stool next to the examining table. He brushed back a swath of hair from his face. "I hope you didn't pay much for these."

"Just tell me what's the problem."

"One of these—" Stirton pointed to the second tusk "—is a fake. Someone did a beautiful job in creating it. Even the Schreger lines are accurate. The other two are real."

Pete stepped forward. "Why—?"

"That's not my job," the scientist said. "But there's more. I found a custom-made GPS tracking device embedded in the fake one."

Back in the SUV, Janette gunned it through the gate in the fence and squealed around the corner to get back on the road that led into the city. She looked at the clock on the dashboard. "It's going to be dicey."

The streets were deserted when they got to the police station. Only a few lights were on at the front entrance. Janette made three right-hand turns to get onto Albertus Street. Four blocks ahead, the station looked empty. "Quiet time of night," she said. "Before the pubs close."

She rocked to a halt at the curb. She texted Moses. He didn't respond. She texted again.

"Is everything okay?" Pete asked. In the glow from the dashboard, he could see her face was damp.

"He always answers." She looked at the clock. Two hours exactly. "Maybe we're too late. What the hell, we've got to get these back." She lurched away from the curb, drove four blocks, and turned into the alley at the back end of the station. She stopped at the door.

They jumped out. Pete started to pop open the hatch, but Janette stopped him. She texted Moses. No response. Pete stared down the alley. In the darkness, something moved at the far end, but he couldn't make it out.

"Did he shut off the cameras?" Pete said.

Janette shook her head. "I don't know."

They waited for a few minutes but still didn't get a response from Moses.

"We have to get this done," Janette said.

Pete pulled her by the arm toward the door. "Wait a minute. Before we commit ourselves, let's check out the warehouse."

He led them through the door. The interior was dimly lit, but with enough light to allow them to avoid bumping into the steel shelves. They walked around them, and Pete switched on the light from his cell phone.

In the silence, Janette's gasp was as loud as a gunshot.

The crate was gone.

Chapter Thirteen

Pete could see the tire tracks of the forklift in the dust as they curved away from the spot where the crate had been placed.

Out of the darkness beyond them, three uniformed officers came forward. They fanned out to the sides, blocking any chance of escape through the back door. They had automatic pistols drawn and pointed at them.

"We're unarmed," Janette said and raised both open palms into the air.

Pete did the same.

"Where's Officer Mahlangu?" she demanded.

None of the police spoke. Everyone waited silently for several minutes. Pete searched their uniforms to identify who they were. He saw shoulder patches that read "South African National Defense Force." That was bad. These guys were not the local police. Where had they come from and why?

From somewhere to the right, a steel door scraped over concrete. The thud of footsteps came closer, and two more police in plain clothes appeared. One old man, his face lined and as dark as the space beyond the group, seemed to be the leader.

"What the fuck you doing?" he shouted.

Pete edged closer to Janette.

When no one answered him, the leader screamed, "You know what I can do?" White saliva gathered at the corners of his mouth.

Janette lowered her hands and said, "Where's Officer Mahlangu?"

The man's shoulders relaxed and he faced her. "The police? He's been dealt with and will be disciplined. None of your goddamn business. But I have a bigger problem. Where is the fucking crate?" When no one answered, the leader turned to the other men and jerked his head toward the back of the room.

Pete's chest tightened. He didn't want to go further from the door —the way out. He tried to stall. "We couldn't possibly move the crate. We're innocent."

The leader planted his foot and spun around. He gave a thin laugh. "Oh, that's only one problem for you."

Pete studied him. Broad shoulders, biceps straining the material of his shirt, but a thin neck. With his taekwondo training, Pete was confident he could take this guy. Probably even two more of the cops. But with five of them, it would be suicide. Instead, Pete tried to talk their way out.

"Sorry to have violated any rules, but I'm from the United States where things are different. We didn't understand—"

"Shut up. Besides breaking into a secure area of the police department, bribing an officer, and stealing evidence of a crime, you are correct about one thing."

"Huh?"

"You do not have any rights here. This is South Africa, not Hollywood. You belong to me." He reached forward to grab Pete's arm.

Without thinking, he twisted to the side in preparation for a taekwondo blocking move known as *makgi*. Up on the balls of his feet, he cocked his legs and started a palm block. He raised his open palm to shoulder height and chopped it down to meet the cop's arm where it extended. The toughest part was the timing. The heel of Pete's hand slammed into the forearm of the leader before he could pull it back. Pete heard a crunch and hoped the bone was broken.

The leader screamed. He bent over and clutched his arm to his chest. He swore so loudly it echoed off the concrete. Two officers attacked Pete and smashed into his chest. He fell backward and remembered to curl his back to avoid his head slamming onto the floor.

Within seconds, it was settled. Pete, flanked by the two officers who had knocked him down, followed Janette. The older leader hobbled ahead of the group. Pete regretted his move. Another stupid reaction—something that had often gotten him into trouble in the past.

Janette whispered, "You've probably made things a lot worse."

The group moved deeper into the darkness until they reached a steel door and filed through. Beyond that, a hall ran to the left and right. A fluorescent light stretched across the ceiling that gave the white people a ghostly pallor. In single file, they marched to the right to a wooden door with a frosted glass insert in the top half. A brass plate identified it as Room 24.

Inside, four plastic chairs sat in a tight circle in the middle of the room.

"Musical chairs, anyone?" Pete tried to joke.

The officers threw them into the chairs and left. Janette leaned closer to Pete. "Don't tell them about the ivory in the car."

"We should give it to them and get the hell out."

"No." Her eyes narrowed. "These thugs aren't the locals. They're national border patrol. That means we've stumbled into something a lot bigger, like I suspected."

"What do you mean?"

Her head turned from side to side. "There's lots of illegal ivory moving through this country. For them to be this interested tells me the crate we saw is just the tip of the iceberg."

"Why bother with us?"

"Not sure. Maybe they think we took it. Or we're a loose end to be tied up. They don't want any part of the shipment getting out and into the hands of the legitimate authorities."

Pete drew a deep breath. His plan seemed so obvious. "We give up our tusks in return for our freedom. Maybe I'd fight, but that would be stupid."

"No, you've done enough damage already. You don't understand these guys. They're corrupt and brutal. We could be at the edge of something worth millions of rand. Our only bargaining chips, for now, are the tusks we have. Remember, they don't know the ivory is outside in the car." She slumped into the back of the chair. "From now on, let me do the talking. You don't understand."

In ten minutes, the leader returned with two other officers. His complexion looked dusty, and Pete knew the man was still in pain. His eyes were rimmed in red. "We have a room downstairs. You are very lucky I don't shoot your brains out there. As a foreigner, your disappearance would not be noticed by anyone. But, as I told you, I have a problem that is bigger than you."

The room was silent except for the ticking of an overhead fan.

"In spite of all the statutes you've violated, I will 'make a deal,' as you Americans say."

"What's that?" Janette asked.

"In our duties to protect our borders and stop the illegal poaching of our resources, we are interested in recovering all of the ivory and horns that were stored here."

"That makes sense."

"It is part of an ongoing investigation across the country. The president himself is determined to solve the case. Now it seems you two have knowledge of the shipment that I want." He leaned forward so his face was inches from Janette's.

"What if we have it?" she said. "What is it worth to you?"

"Your freedom—for the ivory."

Pete scraped his chair on the floor to try to get Janette's attention. She ignored him.

He had to do something, but Janette remained quiet. It took all his self-control to remain still.

Finally, Janette said, "We have the ivory."

The leader's shoulders relaxed. "I thought so. Where is it?"

"What's your name?"

"Colonel Okafor. I command the Defense Force, Cape Town Station. Now, where is my crate?"

She chuckled. "That's not so easy. See, I don't trust you. Both of us must walk out of here, unharmed, before I tell you anything."

He circled the chairs, humming quietly. When he returned to face Janette, he said, "You do not have bargaining power." From the leather holster on his hip, Okafor pulled out a .45 caliber automatic and waved it in front of Janette.

Her back stiffened and Pete noticed the blood vessel in her temple pulsating, but Janette didn't give in to Okafor.

"Your friend—I can torture him in front of you. How much would it take to obtain the information?"

Janette didn't answer.

Pete assessed the odds in the room. Besides Okafor, there were only two officers present. Undoubtedly, the others were nearby, but Pete thought it could be possible for him to take on these three. He assumed Janette could do some damage also. Then they'd have to find their way to the evidence warehouse and get to the back door. It would be a close thing.

Okafor straightened up. He pulled back the cuff of his shirt and looked at his watch. "Five minutes. Then you will tell me. Otherwise, we begin the torture of your friend in the basement for your viewing pleasure." He spun on his foot and left, followed by the other two.

When the door slammed shut, Pete waited a few seconds. "Janette, we're not even secured to the chairs. Now is the time." He stood up.

She glared at him. "Shut up. Who do you think is standing outside the door?"

"Well—" He looked at his watch and saw they had three minutes left before Okafor returned.

Janette shook her head. "I don't trust Okafor. He may have seized the crate before we got here and is playing like he's ignorant, or he doesn't have it and thinks we have all or part of the shipment. The key is, he doesn't know exactly what we have. That's our only card to play to stay alive."

Pete said, "We've only got a few minutes to come up with a plan. I've got a background in this kind of thing. Here's what we're going to do. Can you fight? I can probably take down two or three of them. Once I get them down, you grab all the weapons you find. I'll lead the way out."

"Are you crazy?" Janette shouted. "This is a fuckin' police station. You think you can shoot your way out? We'll end up like Butch Cassidy and the Sundance Kid."

Pete looked at her without speaking.

"I watch American films, too. I think Okafor is bluffing about the torture."

"What if he isn't?" Pete said. He crossed his arms over his chest.

"We negotiate. He wants our information."

"We fight," Pete insisted.

They looked around as the door shot open. Pete raised his arms and spread his legs in a practiced stance.

A black face poked around the open door.

"Moses," Janette yelled.

"Come on." Moses waved them toward himself.

They followed him into the deserted hallway. Single file, they ran, their shoes clattering on the linoleum floor.

"Moses, what's going on?" Janette called to him.

He didn't answer but led them around two turns to the steel door. It scraped over the concrete as he shoved it open. Loudly. It echoed down the hall, back into the station.

Across the evidence warehouse, Moses led them with a narrow flashlight beam. It jiggled across the floor in a cone of white light.

At the back door, they all stopped. Moses said, "They came here just before you returned. Told me they were taking jurisdiction over the case."

Pete said, "They can do that?"

Moses nodded. "They told me to go home. I knew you were coming back and I wanted to warn you, but by the time you arrived, they were already here. I am sorry you went through this."

"That's okay," Janette assured him. "Did they take the crate?"

"I do not know since they forced me to remain in my office."

"You should disappear before they catch you."

Pete led Janette outside to the car. They jumped in, she fired the engine, and the tires squealed on the pavement of the alley as they escaped into the night.

Chapter Fourteen

The next morning, Karen called Pete.

"Hey, Dad. I made it to Sirilima Game Reserve. It was an easy flight to Jo-burg—I'm already talking like a native. The drive to the game park was beautiful, but the land is drier than I thought it would be. When I got to the entrance—wow. Looked like military camp. Guards with guns and jeeps. But they were nice to me and gave me a ride up to the lodge, which is awesome."

She talked faster. "My room is simple but on the edge of a lake. The manager, Carl, warned me of hippos at night. 'Don't go out of room,' he said. Imagine what my friends in Minnesota will think when I text them! Oh, and I met nice ranger named Frimby."

Pete replied, "Be careful."

"I'm so afraid—"

"Ok, sorry. Are you feeling better?"

"Sort of. Not every day a person gets shot at. But it's so beautiful here, I'll recover quickly."

"Good."

"I can't help but think how much Mom would have loved this place. It gives me such a feeling of freedom, so close to nature, without all that crap of humans anywhere to be seen."

"That's a rare feeling in today's world. Savor it."

"Turns out Frimby is the brother of the guy killed. So sad. I like Frimby. He's from Zimbabwe. Maybe I can get some info from him about the killing and give it to you secretly."

"Don't go playing investigator."

"I like the idea of being undercover—mission impossible."

"This is serious business."

"Oh, Dad, don't worry. I'm excited because Frimby will take me out for a game drive tomorrow. We go out early morning right after sunrise and late afternoon just before sunset because the animals are more active then. I can't wait!"

"I'll get up there as soon as I can."

"The park has some Land Rovers especially designed for game viewing. What I've seen of the park so far is awesome---rivers, plains, mountains, forests, and savannah. Even on the drive up to the lodge, we saw so many animals."

"Can't wait to see for myself."

"You can't believe how big they are when you get up close."

"Not too close."

"Anything interesting there?"

"The usual, dull activities of an investigator." His voice was flat.

"How soon are you coming?"

"I'm looking into some details here. I've agreed to help Janette so she'll help me with the murder investigation at the park. We'll stop at Janette's house today to get her stuff, then drive her car, so it may take us a day or two."

"Do you trust her? Usually you work on your own."

"I've done some background checks on her already. Between Google and the information the bank has about her, I found she has two kids, divorced, and has good reputation as an investigator. Her daughter has some physical problems that I'll ask Janette about when it's appropriate."

"Okay. Love you, Dad, and be careful." Her voice trailed off like retreating wind.

Pete paused to let the last words sink in. It felt good. More than ever, he was anxious to get on with Isaac's investigation and be with his daughter.

Chapter Fifteen

Cecil almost knocked over the sheet rock cubicle wall as he hurried to give Albert Noonan the information he wanted. "Found 'em. Both trackers are still transmitting." Cecil stabbed the air with his upraised finger to emphasize his success.

"What I need to know is *who* has the shipment. It can't fall into the wrong hands or our mission is over, because no one is supposed to be doing what we're doing."

Cecil looked at the ceiling and exposed his long neck. "Hey, I've got some other intel. Did an extensive Google search, and our new facial recognition software isn't as primitive as I thought. The people who discovered the shipment—they seem harmless to me." Cecil set an open laptop in front of his boss.

Albert scrolled down through the screens. "Let's see . . ." He talked to himself as much as to Cecil. "One person is a man named Pete Chandler. Originally entered South Africa with his daughter, Karen. Minnesota residents. She owned a restaurant. Here's their email addresses." He studied the data for another ten minutes. "Oh, no. Shit! This is worse than bad luck."

"What did you find?"

"Chandler is an investigator for the U.S. Export/Import Bank. Military service in the Middle East. Why the hell couldn't he have been a life insurance salesman on vacation? There must be a reason an expert like him is in South Africa. Questions is, what's his connection with the ivory?" Dressed in a camo t-shirt, Albert's arms bulged with muscles.

"Maybe he's only visiting and the discovery was an accident."

"Don't be stupid. He's an investigator. Check on the bank and see if they've got connections with ivory, game parks, NGOs, or government contracts. And look at the third one. Janette Koos, another investigator hired as a contractor for the same bank. Cecil, this is bad voodoo." He pushed back his chair and brushed the top of his hair while he thought. "This can't be an accidental occurrence."

"Well—"

"Cecil, do most tourists board freighters, go down in the holds, open crates, and find a cache of illegal ivory and rhino horns? We've got to act immediately and with full resources."

"Told you I found the trackers."

"Lovely. Let's see where they are."

They both moved from the cubicle, walked down a narrow hall, and turned into a larger room. A conference table with a loose leg stood in the middle, hemmed in by three chairs. A wall of computer screens hung from the east wall. Cecil slid into a stool before a keyboard. He tapped quickly and then looked up at Albert. "I'm getting some data."

"How dependable are these things?"

Cecil's face glowed. "You tasked me to develop a tracking device capable of transmitting exact locations without any dead zones. Remember? It needed to be durable and small enough to fit inside the cavity of the manufactured tusk."

"Wasn't there an expert in California?"

"Yes. Dr. Condon. He designed a GPS tracker that the U.S. Geological Survey embedded in Burmese pythons to monitor the invasive snakes in the Florida Everglades. For our project, he took months but finally came up with a battery capable of lasting more than a year, a GPS receiver, an iridium satellite transceiver, and a temperature sensor."

"Right. I remember."

"Here's the Google map right now." Cecil shifted aside so Albert could move forward and look at the screen.

Albert leaned in and saw a pair of tear-shaped blue dots superimposed over a map of Cape Town. The dots were separated by several miles, but stationary. As he watched, one of the dots twitched, like a fish nibbling at a lure. Then it started to move in a square pattern from the central area of Cape Town.

They both stared at the screen as the dot moved, stopped at corners—probably street lights—and moved again, working its way east of the city.

"Which one should we follow?" Cecil asked.

Albert perched on the edge of the stool. "Don't know. But I do know we're not getting anything done waiting here." He jumped up and hurried out of the conference room. "Come on, Cecil. We need to get a government transport to Cape Town as soon as we can. And take all your equipment. We have to find those trackers." He fitted his red beret tightly over his head.

It took several hours, but finally they commandeered a private plane for the short flight. They landed at the section of Cape Town International Airport reserved for military, government, and private jets. A taxi drove them into the city to a small hotel that fronted DeWaal Park in the City Bowl area.

They carried minimal luggage to make room for the technical equipment they needed. The driver, dressed in a blue suit and white shirt, helped them lift everything out of the boot of the car. "Been here before?" he asked.

"Dude. 'Course, but we're operational in Jo-burg," Cecil said.

"I suggest you take a walk through the park."

"We're in a hurry," Albert said as he hefted the laptops onto his shoulder. With his free hand, he grabbed the black leather case with the armaments.

"Look at the fountain," the driver insisted. "Victorian. And the view—" He swung his arm out to the side.

Albert glanced up and stopped. It was magnificent. Across from them, Table Mountain stretched across the sky to cover the entire horizon. Green at its base, it towered straight up, etched by lines in the gray stone, until the top flattened as if some giant had sliced off a mountain peak.

"We've got to go." Albert spun toward the door of the hotel.

Their work was top secret. If discovered, it would be, at least, an embarrassment, the death of many careers, and probably prison for Albert and Cecil. As a result, an anonymous hotel was their best cover.

In the room, they cleared a large space on two desks set under the windows and ordered a car for their use.

Albert paced across the room while Cecil plugged in cords and tested the equipment. He barked at Cecil, "We've already lost several hours. If we don't find the shipment, we'll be fucked. Hurry!"

Albert was a member of the Zulu tribe, one of the oldest in Africa. They were warriors who had fought the British to a standstill until the British began to use machine guns. The Zulu religion believes everything results from evil sorcery—which is why they interact with the spirits. Prior to the British, the Zulus had conquered most of the smaller tribes around them. Today, they still feel superior to those other tribes.

Cecil, on the other hand, was a member of a smaller tribe, the Venda, who have secret rituals and have a special relationship with the crocodile. Bodies of water are sacred sites at which they interact with their ancestors. They also practice polygamy, as do many other tribes.

Moisture prickled across Cecil's forehead. "Can you get me some Cheetos?"

"What?"

"Room service. I work better."

"Oh, for God's sake. All right." Albert found the hotel phone and ordered four bags but quickly added, "They're for my associate."

Cecil perched on the chair while his knees protruded and bumped against the edge of the table. He keyed one laptop, then moved to the second one. He looked from one monitor to the other. "Got 'em."

Albert darted in to view the screens. There they were: the two blue teardrops. One was still stationary near the edge of the city. The other moved a few inches on the Google Earth map. "Where—?"

Cecil toggled the cursor to the side, rotated the map, and finally pulled back. "It's headed toward the southeastern suburb of Stellenbosch."

"I would expect it to go towards a port on the coast or north to the closest border. Get in closer."

Cecil burrowed down from the satellite, through the atmosphere, and into a green expanse until individual buildings and cars came into focus. "Here." Cecil pointed at the screen. "I can't tell for sure, but I bet it's located inside that SUV. Unless they've removed the tracker from the tusk, it's probably in the boot."

"Great work, Cecil." Albert stood back. "God dammit." His stomach grumbled. "Check the other tracker." He stopped behind Cecil and watched him pull back the map to include all of Cape Town.

"It's on the edge of the city. A suburb?"

"Get in there, dammit."

Cecil zeroed in on the pulsing blue teardrop. "Shit!" He slumped in the chair.

"What?"

"Can't see much. Tree cover has obscured whatever's below."

"Rotate to street level."

"Too many buildings. Maybe it's a warehouse area."

"But the tracker is there, right?"

"Yeah." His voice sounded dry. Cecil reached for a hotel bottle of water, cracked the cap, and drained it in three gulps. "Where are my Cheetos?"

"Shut up and get back to work."

After ten minutes, Cecil blew out a lungful of air. "Sorry. Can't get much more at this time."

When room service brought the Cheetos, he ripped open the top and munched on a handful. His voice muffled, he asked, "Now what do we do?"

Albert stepped to the window and looked out on the park, one of the largest in Cape Town. Women walked in pairs. Black women were dressed in *dashikis* in vivid colors of yellow, emerald, and crimson. Their hair was wrapped in the same colors and stacked a few feet above their heads. They moved at a regal pace.

He spun around to face Cecil. "Since one of the trackers is stable, we should go after the one that has been moving—before we lose it. Besides, trapping the smugglers is more important than seizing the entire shipment. We can always come back and scoop that later."

"Brilliant idea." Cecil smiled.

"Is the car here?" Albert packed one of the laptops in a thin case. From the leather satchel, he pulled out two Plastico Sudafricano pistols, lightweight but deadly at close range. He straightened and looked at Cecil. "Are you prepared to go all the way with this mission?"

"Of course."

"Because whatever it takes, I'm not going to fail."

Cecil brushed his hands against one another, leaving orange snow on his keyboard. "Hey, Albert. We got trouble. The bogie's moving again." He pointed to his screen, where the blue teardrop in Stellenbosch moved to the south, following city streets.

They raced out of the hotel, picked up the rental car, and sped out of the city on Highway 1. The traffic was sparse going east, so they made good time as they passed the towns of Boston and then Kraai-fontein. The freeway rolled amongst low hills. Their slopes were covered with grapevines that surround the hills like green skirts. In the valleys, oak trees and South African pines grouped together, topped in round green bunches.

Albert drove so Cecil could navigate using the computer.

"Stay to the right. Get off at R101 and follow it to Elsenberg," Cecil instructed.

"Now it's back where it started on Kromme Rhee Road."

Albert turned off the freeway and entered a narrow, two-lane road that split a row of shops down the middle. Two-story Tudor buildings sat close to the edge of the road. Small leaded-glass windows watched the traffic sail by. It seemed like there was a wine shop on every corner. "The Pinotage Grape" read a sign hanging out from a shop that offered one of the region's best wine types.

"Has the tracker moved?" Albert asked. He raced the engine.

"No. Turn left at the next corner. Don't you think we should wait until dark?"

Albert jerked his head toward Cecil. "And let them get away?"

Cecil looked out the window and didn't respond. They drove along a stand of eucalyptus trees, their mottled trunks twisting up to the canopy that arched over the road. He told Albert, "Uh, I really don't have much training with firearms."

"How much?"

"Maybe none."

"Don't worry. Usually the sight of a drawn weapon is enough to get people to obey. Where are we?"

Cecil looked at the map. "Take a right here and stop by a white house. Big jacaranda tree in the front yard."

Albert slowed the car and crawled past the one-story colonial. A freshly painted wooden fence hid a garden of pink Madonna lilies. The glare of the sun on the windows concealed the interior. Near the front door, a jacaranda tree shaded the entrance. During high season, the blooming flowers made the trees look like enormous lavender clouds. This one looked stressed.

"We'll reconnoiter the back side also." Albert passed the house. He turned at the corner and found an alley that ran behind the suspect's house. Albert turned into it and drove at a normal speed. "We'll confirm the takedown soon."

Behind the house, they spotted a Chery Tiggo SUV parked at an angle near the back door. There wasn't any free-standing garage. A yellow glow shone from two windows, but they couldn't see anyone inside. Albert continued his steady drive down the alley until he reached the street. He turned and stopped at the curb.

"Something's not right," Albert said. His face was moist.

"Looks totally normal."

"No, I mean the shipment. Where is it? Even if they split it from the other half, that's a big load."

"Hidden in the house?"

Albert nodded as he leaned forward to watch the street. "Can you tell exactly where the tracker is located?"

"No, can't get that precise. It's somewhere around that house."

"Time for action."

"Uh, should we wait for backup?"

"Cecil, you watch too many crime shows. Since no law enforcement agencies know what we're doing, we are our own backup. Besides, I don't need help. I thought you wanted combat action." A smile creased Albert's lips.

"Sure, but what about the interior minister? He could give us a team, and of course, you know how he is about the procedural rules. If we fuck this up, he'll be furious."

"You're right, but I'm doing this on my own—with your help." Albert raised both his palms into the air. "Do you ever read history?"

"Sure."

"Then you know the Bolsheviks would never have accomplished the Russian revolution if they'd followed the rules. This is our own revolution."

"I suppose you're right." Cecil paused between each word.

"I'll post you in the front. Whenever a house is raided, the bogies always bail toward their best escape opportunities. In this case, it'll be that car. I'll station myself there. You're going to cause them to run."

Air escaped from Cecil's chest. "Okay." He folded the laptop and wedged it between the front seats. He took a long drink of bottled water. "Uh, Albert, what if they come out my way?"

"You blow the front door and jump 'em. The weapon of surprise plus the sight of the gun will get them running to the back. Afterward, we search the premises."

"But you said the American had military experience in the Middle East."

"So what?"

"Well—"

"Cecil, it's simple. Never, never get close enough for him to be able to grab you. In the alternative, shoot the bloke."

Albert got out of the car. He looked back and forth across the street, glanced at his watch, and opened the back door to the car. He reached into the leather satchel and removed the two weapons. He checked that they were loaded and ready to fire, then came back into the driver's seat and handed one of the guns to Cecil. "You can do this." Albert started the car and turned right around the corner and coasted to a stop in front of the suspect's house.

"I want you deployed in a crouch behind that fence. Give me ten minutes to get around the block and in position. Then you will go to the front door, ID yourself, flash the weapon, and force your way inside. When they bail out the back door—I'll drop them. Once they are in my custody, we can retrieve the shipment."

"Then what?"

"Then I'll interrogate them to find out who they're working for. We expose the poaching ring, and I get credit for it. My plan takes off."

Cecil cleared his throat and turned over the gun in his hands. He looked up at Albert. With his fingers spread in a V-sign, Cecil pointed them toward his own eyes, then pointed them toward Albert. "Got your back, dude."

"Cecil, you're stupid."

Chapter Sixteen

Janette had picked up Pete at the hotel early in the morning and driven to her suburb of Stellenbosch. Her neighborhood looked much like one in Minneapolis: quiet, tree-lined, suburban houses on their own lots and clean sidewalks. A few SUVs drove along the street. A dark sedan pulled to a stop at the curb, halfway between Janette's house and the neighbor's house.

The mild, honey smell of the jacaranda tree by the front door came through the open windows and settled across the living room. Pete was entranced and kept walking out there to smell it. It looked like a lavender cloud hovering between the branches.

Pete reluctantly left the living room and walked back into the kitchen to resume drinking his cooling coffee. Janette came in from outside, where she had parked the car. The back door squeaked when she tried to shut it.

"Beautiful tree in front, but it's lost some leaves," Pete told Janette.

"I know. I's sick. If I ever had time, there's a treatment, a spray that would bring it back."

"Anything to eat?"

Janette laughed. "I'm not a very good cook. Don't watch enough shows on the telly, I guess."

He put the coffee in the microwave, hit the button, and the lights blinked out in the kitchen.

"Oh, sorry," Janette said. "Small electrical problem. I'll tickle the breaker." She disappeared down a narrow hallway, and the lights went back on.

"What about your kids?" Pete asked.

"I have two. Arthur lives with his father in Rye, England. My daughter, Jane, lives here."

Pete looked around the kitchen. "In this house? Where is she?"

"Usually she's here, but you see, Jane's disabled. It's school holiday this time of year, and she prefers to stay there."

"That must be hard on you."

Janette nodded. "There's a series of operations—expensive—that will correct the problem, but I can't afford it yet."

"Just sell one of the tusks," Pete interrupted with a grin. When she didn't laugh at his joke, he said, "Your ex-husband won't help?"

"Can't. He's a loafer and not worth chasing for money."

"You seem tense. Is it your daughter's injury?"

"Oh, of course, but I've also been kicked around a lot, and what I've seen doesn't give me much hope. Like this poaching syndicate we've stumbled into."

"Hope about what?"

"Well— It's a long story." Her eyes focused somewhere toward the ceiling.

"Tell me."

Janette stepped around the corner of the island. She hesitated, sipped her tea, put the cup back on the saucer, and finally said, "Post-apartheid in South Africa is not going well."

"You supported apartheid?"

"No, of course not. You see, it wasn't just anti-black, racial laws, it was an entire system of repression through laws—against everyone—to support a dictatorial government. After my divorce, I dated a lot of black men. Probably to prove how progressive I was as much as any attraction I had for them."

"So, what's not going well?"

"The entire country. We're ruled by corrupt governments, worse than before. Inequality is worse now. The employment laws require employers to hire a percentage from each group in the country."

"Affirmative action, we call it."

"Yes, same thing. We have corporations saying that ten percent of their costs go to worthless employees who know they must be given a job. Nelson Mandela's party, the African National Congress, which I supported, promised to bring the education standards up to the rest of the world. Now most kids are in decrepit schools. Two kids fell into the 'stew' at the bottom of the outdoor latrines when the seats broke."

Pete said, "That sounds terrible." He watched Janette's shoulders stiffen. "But there's something more than politics that's bothering you." He thought of the phone call in the tea shop and how upset she'd become.

Janette sniffed. "I don't know why I should tell— Six years ago, Jane was in a car accident. She became paralyzed from the waist down. It led to her father, Rodney, and I divorcing and a lot of pain for everyone. Now Jane's in a wheelchair with a smashed-up back."

"And you and Rodney still fight over it?"

Janette grinned briefly. "You are a good investigator. Yes. He's an ass. Blames me for the problem." Gripping each hand, she twisted her fingers.

Pete had the good sense to keep quiet for a moment. Steam twisted up from his hot coffee. He sipped it again. "And now—?"

Janette looked up at him, her eyes focused. "I'd do anything I could to help Jane get those operations. I'd even break the law—like we did to get the tusks."

"What does that mean?"

She shrugged. "I'm not sure at this point. But I'm thinking. We may have some leverage with the tusks—"

Pete's phone rang.

Martin Graves spoke crisply. "Pete, it's worse than I thought. Washington dug into Donahue's recent financials, and all hell broke loose. The office was deep in the red. Ian may have been doing some shady things to make up the deficit. As a consequence, all eyes are looking at me as if it's my fault."

"It's not."

"Of course. But that's the way the bureaucrats see the world. What have you found out?"

Pete hesitated because they really hadn't discovered much of anything. "I happened to get ahold of Ian's personal computer. I'm going through it now. I'll let you know what I find." Pete told Graves about the shipment and the items they'd found in Donahue's office.

"What about the murder at the reserve?"

"I'm working with the investigator Ian hired. We're just about to leave for the reserve."

"Work your magic, Pete. I need a miracle." Graves hung up.

Pete walked out to Janette's car and retrieved Donahue's laptop. Back in the kitchen, Pete booted it up while skimming through Ian's password notebook. It enabled Pete to open the financial records for the bank, including the loans to the Sirilima Game Reserve.

There was a knock on the front door. They ignored it as Janette continued, "The pain I feel for Jane is unbearable at times. I need a lot of money for the medical procedures. The specialists are in London."

"National insurance won't cover it?" Pete asked as he scrolled through the data.

"Some of it, but since it's considered experimental, I have to pay a big portion." Janette sighed. "If I had the money, I'd fly her to London as soon as possible."

They stood without talking, each of them pulling into their separate thoughts.

Pete compared the paper file with the financial records in the computer. One set matched; another set of financials was different. Clearly, the first set was the official reports Ian was required to send to Washington. They showed a healthy cash position. The second set revealed the opposite---which was what Graves must be talking about. Pete kept searching through more pages. On page fourteen, there were several extra cash payments made to the game reserve. Unusual. Once funds were lent by the bank, there would not be separate cash payments made in addition.

Pete stepped back from the countertop. He looked at Janette and saw a deflated replica of the strong person he'd met at the harbor. Pete walked to her and slid his arm behind her back. She turned to him. Her hips flattened along his side, and he felt her breasts push into his arm. It was more than he expected but didn't discourage him.

"Sometimes, we all need a hug," she said and squeezed Pete with her arm. She lifted her head and shook out her hair with a hand. "Better."

Pete waited a few more minutes. He explained what he'd found on the computer. "So, we need a plan."

Janette straightened and stepped away from him. "What was Isaac doing when he was shot? Was he fighting with someone? We'll get up to Sirilima as soon as possible."

"In the meantime, the Border Patrol people want that ivory. If they're the ones who put the tracker in the tusk, it won't take them long to find us here," said Pete. "Maybe we should get rid of the tusks. Then we go to the game reserve and investigate the murder. Try to determine if there's any connection to Donahue's death."

Janette said, "If we get rid of the tusks, we'll never figure out what's going on. It's the only bargaining chip we have. I have to admit, Donahue fooled me. I would never have imagined he was implicated like this, but it looks like he was."

"But they'll find us," Pete insisted.

Janette grinned, coloring her cheeks and the bridge of her nose. "If we leave for Sirilima now, I think we can evade them. They may chase us, but we're small fish to them, which means they won't use all their resources against us."

Someone knocked on the door.

Pete said, "I'll get it."

Janette stopped him. "Could be the Border Patrol. Be careful."

He didn't need to be warned, but Pete nodded and slowed his steps to the front door. There wasn't a peephole in the door, but if he leaned to the left, Pete could get a slight angle on the outside. He saw a tall, thin black man. Young. No uniform, so he probably wasn't with the Border Patrol. He shifted from one leg to the other. And there was something clownish about him: his lips were tinted orange.

Still, from all his training, Pete prepared for anything that might happen. He sheltered himself behind the door, opened it just a crack, and jammed his shoe behind it. The man on the other side yelled, "Hey, dude, I know you got the ivory."

Pete tried to push the door closed, but the man ran at the door, and his momentum overwhelmed Pete's foot. Pete jumped back to give himself space to work. His taekwondo training kicked in. He locked into a crouch, drawing back his left leg, until he saw the man pull out a small gun. It looked like it was plastic. But even plastic guns can shoot bullets.

"Janette," Pete yelled into the kitchen. He heard shoes shuffle on the tile, the scrape of a drawer, and Janette shouting.

At that moment, the man lunged through the door with the gun pointed out in front of his chest, two hands gripping it like he'd undoubtedly seen on TV cop shows. Wrong move.

It exposed the forearms of the man and the gun. Perfect target for the basic front kick. Pete had his left knee up in the air and rotated his standing foot. Remembering to swing the hips into the move to generate power, he shifted his left hip forward. The final snap of his leg brought the toe of his shoe into the clasped hands—all within a second.

The man screamed and the weapon flew toward the fireplace. "Shit!"

Pete turned his body and executed a side kick. By raising his leg waist high, he gained maximum power when his foot crashed into the man's chest. He folded in half, flopped over the arm of a chair, and lay still on the floor.

Pete was about to run back to Janette when he thought to grab the gun. A Plastico Sudafricano. Not too accurate, but at least it was a weapon. He grabbed it from under the table and lunged for the kitchen.

When he got there, Janette started for the back door. Pete yelled at her to stop. She did and turned to question him.

"Oldest trick in the book. The guy out front didn't come alone. So, where's his backup?"

"Right."

"Waiting to ambush us." Pete watched Janette dart into a back bedroom and return with a 9mm automatic. "I've got a better idea. We get the others to come in here."

"No," Janette said. "We don't know how many are out there."

"I don't intend to fight them. I want to distract them." He motioned Janette to stand on the far side of the door. "We wait," he said.

Five minutes passed. A cardinal called from the backyard: *skew* . . . *we, we, we, we, we.* The wind hummed around the corner of the roof. Otherwise, silence.

Three minutes passed. Pete peeked out the window. A lone black man, tall and fit, edged from behind the hibiscus bush. The color of his beret matched the red flowers near his head. He swayed from side to side as if trying to get a glimpse into the house. The partner, Pete thought. Were there more? He waited but saw no one else.

Janette had seen the man also. She looked at Pete. He raised a finger to his lips.

The man in the backyard came forward, slow steps, heel on ground, roll to the ball of each foot. He moved past Janette's car, touching it lightly as if for balance. He pulled out a plastic gun from the small of his back, stopped and went into a crouch. His head twitched as if he were smelling the wind, like an animal.

Then, silence.

Pete motioned for Janette to stay behind the door and whispered in her ear what to do. Then he scurried around the island in the middle of the room and ducked down behind it.

Four more minutes. After the knob on the back door clicked, it squeaked open with a puff like a breeze coming into the room. No one moved. The black man leaped through the door and jerked to the right with his gun drawn.

At that moment, Pete stood from behind the island with his gun pointed at the man. "Stop!"

When the man shifted to the right, Janette slammed the door shut and put the muzzle of her 9 mm on his neck. "Stop!"

The man lowered his arm with the gun and pulled back his shoulders. Head up. Clothes tight on his body. Shoulders bulging.

"Who are you? Border Patrol?" Pete asked as he stepped from around the island. He took the gun from the man's hand.

His eyes narrowed as he glared at Pete.

"Answer me."

"It doesn't have anything to do with you." He smiled with large white teeth. "You don't know what you're doing. Go home."

Something bothered Pete. Why didn't the man say anything about the escape from the police station? Maybe he wasn't with the Border Patrol. "How many others are out there?"

"I'm not talking."

"Okay, let's put you with your partner." Pete tipped his head toward the living room. He told Janette, "Watch out the back and let me know if anyone else comes up." The man walked ahead of Pete into the next room. When he saw the first man on the floor, he glanced back at Pete.

"He wasn't very good," Pete explained. "Get down on your stomach next to him."

The man knelt on his knees, then flattened out on the carpeting. The first man shook his head, turned it to the side, and said, "Albert. Sorry, I screwed up."

Pete called for Janette to get more duct tape from the kitchen. When she returned, he said, "Okay, Albert, hands behind the back." Pete wrapped his wrists together, then bound his ankles as he had done with the first man. They looked like two shrimp curled backward on a grill, ready to be cooked.

His words muffled in the carpeting, Albert shouted, "You are a small bump in my road. When I find you, I'll squash you."

Pete didn't like the guy's attitude. He raised his foot and stomped on Albert's lower back. He screamed in pain. "Don't underestimate us," Pete yelled and gave him another hit. Finally, Janette pulled him away.

Back in the kitchen, they gathered water and the weapons, then peered outside. They moved to several different windows to get a full view. No one. They hurried out the door and got into Janette's SUV. She backed into the alley, straightened, and raced to the end. Once there, she turned the corner toward the front of her house.

"We'll get all your belongings from the hotel and beat these guys out of town." She grinned, eyes flashing at Pete, and shifted into first. The tires squealed on the pavement as they lurched forward.

Chapter Seventeen

The township of Langa, on the edge of Cape Town, was one of the oldest black communities in the region. Under apartheid, coloreds and blacks were forced into ghettos of wretched conditions. After apartheid fell, many people assumed the communities would be abandoned. Instead, the residents stayed, improved the neighborhoods, and retained their pride in the old cities. Langa had even begun work on attracting tourists by offering guided tours of the township.

Matimba had flown from Pretoria earlier in the morning. Now he drove his Mercedes into Langa on Harlem Street past Mzansi Restaurant, one of his favorites, turned into N'Dabenit Street, and crossed through the township. The home he shared with Abimbola was on Winnie Mandela Street in an area called Beverly Hills. Most of the doctors, lawyers, teachers, and engineers lived in one-story brick houses painted in bright colors of lime, peach, blue, and golden maize.

Matimba was scheduled to meet with Freddy and another man, whom Matimba had never met. He was anxious because the operation seemed to be ripping apart like an impala being butchered by predators—something Matimba must prevent at all costs.

He pulled into the short driveway of his home and felt immediate peace. Even though he enjoyed a good job and position with the government in Pretoria, Matimba felt more comfortable back in the township with "his" people, meaning people of his extended tribe. To an outsider, Langa didn't appear beautiful in any way; to a resident, the people gave it immense beauty.

Except for the tourists, everyone was black. Most people dressed in Western-style clothing, but many women still wore *dashikis*, the long wrap-around dresses. They topped them with matching head scarves wound in high stacks above their heads. Whatever a person chose to wear, there was only one rule: it must be colorful.

When Matimba walked into the house, he went into the kitchen. No one was home. Abimbola must have taken Susan, their daughter, to the art center after school. The South African government subsidized many art centers in the townships in an effort to give local artists an outlet to sell their work. Susan liked to make sand paintings, where tiny bits of colored sand were glued onto a canvas to create images of animals like zebras or giraffes. When finished, they looked like hand-painted masterpieces.

Matimba called out *"Molo,"* hello. No one answered. Good. Under the impending crisis, he didn't have much time for his family. Draped across a chair on the far side of the room was part of his ceremonial garb. When he had a chance, Matimba would look in the garage for the remaining articles.

He opened the refrigerator and smiled when he saw that Abimbola had saved him some Chibuku Shake Shake. It was tribal beer called *umgombothi,* made from sorghum and corn. Matimba shook it, then drank the dark brown beer from the container. It had a vinegar, yeasty aftertaste that reminded him of his childhood, when he was allowed to sip the beer, always served warm, during ritual celebrations.

Matimba looked at the clock on the wall. Freddy was late. Storming out the front door, Matimba looked up and down the street. The sun poured down to give everything a bright blaze. Normally, he accepted the fact of "African time," where everyone ignored clocks. But today Matimba faced a crisis.

The neighbor across the street, Norman, waved to Matimba and yelled, *"Molo.* How are you and your family?"

Matimba answered, of course, but was too upset to engage in the usual long conversations between neighbors in Langa. He marched down the street toward the corner to watch for Freddy. Winnie Mandela Street was paved, but the side streets were pounded hard dirt.

Across the road a line of shipping containers, brought from the Cape Town harbor, were spaced at regular intervals. Residents had cut windows into the sides, turning the containers into solid houses. Clothes, flapping in the wind, hung on lines between the homes.

Cars passed, people walked by, and kids skipped to music in their heads. A Volkswagen Polo leaned to the side as it careened around the corner. In a burst of dust, Freddy slid to a halt before Matimba. *"Molo,"* Freddy called from the open window.

Matimba scowled and nodded toward his house. Freddy obeyed and pulled into the driveway, parking behind Matimba's car. He jumped out to intercept Matimba before he ambled back.

"I'm thirsty. Do you have something to drink?" Freddy asked, his buck teeth showing.

"No. We don't have time." Matimba straightened his body and looked down on Freddy. It had the effect Matimba hoped it would. Freddy cringed. "Where is our man?" Matimba demanded.

Freddy pointed to the right. "Follow me." He loped between two houses while Matimba followed.

Although the streets of the township were squares, the back roads meandered through the neighborhoods, following old dirt walking paths. They passed through a section of two-story apartment buildings. Painted yellow, they had open windows and sprouted white dishes from the exterior walls to bring satellite connections to the residents. Women were in the streets, washing clothing in big tubs. They waved and smiled and said "*Molo*" to the two men.

"What do you expect this man will tell us?" Matimba asked.

"He has news about the shipment."

"Were they able to intercept it?"

"I don't know."

Matimba stopped and clapped his hand on Freddy's shoulder. "I'm not happy about this."

Freddy took a deep breath but said nothing.

Matimba scowled again and, turning a corner, they found a group of children. Some of the boys sat on concrete steps with overturned plastic pails in front of them. They drummed rhythms that rolled and bubbled with energy while the rest of the group danced and sang tribal songs. The hems of the girls' colorful dresses bounced around their legs. In the reflection of bright sun off the walls, their faces were so dark it was impossible to distinguish between black hair and skin.

"Almost there," Freddy said. "We'll meet him by the 'smileys.'"

They hurried beside some one-story retail stores: barber shops, shoe stores, restaurants, a health clinic. One had a black-and-white painting on the side of a wall of an African chief.

They smelled the food before they reached it. Smoke from a barbeque drifted around them. They crossed the street, dipped through a shallow gully, and stood before the outdoor restaurant. On a grill the size of a picnic table, the severed heads of six sheep roasted over the coals. A woman in a pea-green turban used tongs to shift the food. These were an African delicacy, called "smileys" because as they cooked, the sheep's mouths curled up into a "smile."

Matimba came to a stop next to the grill. He breathed heavily and said, "Okay, where the hell is he?"

"He's African, remember?"

The barbeque smell made Matimba's stomach rumble. He realized how little he'd eaten in order to get back to Cape Town as soon as possible. It all added to his frustration and fear. He yelled at Freddy, "Go find the son of a bitch. Is he from my tribe?"

"No."

"Don't trust him already."

Freddy looked around but didn't move. "He'll be here."

In ten minutes, a thin man popped through the crowd gathered around the restaurant. He came to Freddy and smiled. "*Molo.*" He had short hair, wore a long cape, and spoke in his tribal language. Many of the sounds clicked as the man talked. Although it was different than Matimba's language, he could understand most of the dialects in Southern Africa. Matimba shifted from one side to the other, anxious to get the report.

Finally, Freddy and the man turned to him. Freddy started the introductions by saying his name was Zoya. As was common in Africa, the process took three to five minutes. It was necessary to establish trust, or "provenance," using the old rituals. Zoya began talking to Matimba by recounting the name of his tribe, clan, and the names of six generations of his fathers. When he finished, Matimba countered with his own lineage.

Finally, Matimba said, "Did you recover the shipment as I ordered?"

Zoya glanced around the crowded area. His eyes flicked to the side. "Come. Follow me."

Matimba wanted an answer but understood the necessity for secrecy. He followed the other two as they moved down the street. They passed piles of lumber laid out along the walls of buildings and men sitting on wooden crates, and they heard music through the thin walls of the homes they passed. Some buildings were shacks; others were more substantial. Some needed paint; others were maintained in bright colors.

They came out toward Settlers Way, a major street with traffic and bus service. A tour bus had stopped at the far corner. A line of white people with sunburned faces stepped down from the bus, looking around in the bright sunshine.

"Over here." Zoya led Matimba and Freddy along the sidewalk for several blocks.

Matimba did all he could to control himself. They reached an open field filled with wild rosemary bushes. Next to it was a high wooden fence that ran parallel to the field for several blocks. Matimba couldn't take it anymore. He jumped ahead of the other two, grabbed Zoya by the shirt, and slammed him against the fence. "Stop and tell me what the fuck is going on. Did we get the shipment?"

Zoya's eyes looked up and down at Matimba. He took his time answering. "Yes."

That caused Matimba to release his grip.

"I want to go inside the protected area. No one will overhear us," Zoya insisted.

Matimba stepped back and let him walk to the door in the fence. It enclosed a large area that had never been cleared or settled with homes. It contained trees, dense brush, grass, and rocky hills. Its purpose was for an ancient ritual experience in the initiation of young men into adulthood, called *ulwaluko*.

During the initiation, young men would be sent to the mountains to live in the wilderness for many weeks. They sought visions, blessings, and the ability to survive on their own to prove their manhood. In modern times, it was impossible to go to the mountains, so the wild area inside the fence was used instead. A young man entered the enclosure for up to three weeks with only food and water.

No one used the area otherwise, so when Matimba and the two men walked in, it was deserted.

Zoya turned to Matimba. "You must learn patience, my friend."

"And you must learn who is the chief here. Tell me what happened."

"We were able to assemble a small team and discovered where the local police on Albertus Street held the shipment. As you ordered, we told them the Border Patrol was taking jurisdiction of the shipment. We moved quickly, but we discovered a small problem."

"Where is it now?"

"Well, we didn't get—"

"Where the hell is the crate?" Matimba stood on his toes, towering over Zoya.

"Uh, it's missing. But we have a small clue."

"What?"

The wind blew the prickly smell of rosemary over them.

"We think another party has the shipment."

"What the fuck do you mean?"

"When we arrived, the crate was gone. The local police didn't seem to know anything about it. When we investigated, we found two people that we suspect stole the shipment."

"Who did this?"

"We got lucky. The two strangers came back into the station. We surrounded and arrested them, of course. The only reason they could be there was to search for more."

"Who were they?"

"I'm getting to that. We interviewed the police who had seized the crate off a ship in the harbor—"

"I know all that," Matimba shouted. "Who the hell do you think ordered it onto the ship for export?"

"Yes. Well, during the investigation at the harbor, apparently, two strangers became involved in the incident. There had also been a shooting—"

"Get to the point."

"They went into the ship and were present when the crate was opened."

"Who let that happen? I'll kill 'em."

"I don't know. But the crate was transported back to the police station, and then the same two people entered the station, snooping around for the crate."

"What happened?"

Zoya turned around as if he were checking the security in the enclosure. When he faced Matimba and Freddy, his face was pinched. "We arrested them, identified them, and proceeded to interrogate them."

"And?" Matimba leaned forward.

"Well, uh, they escaped before we could find out anything critical."

Matimba's face darkened, and he bent down to pick up a large rock. Winding his arm behind him, Matimba pitched the rock at Zoya's head. He ducked, but the rock still glanced off the side of his head. He fell to the ground.

Freddy jumped between the two men. "Matimba! Control your anger. Zoya works for you; he's only trying to help."

"Zoya has failed me," Matimba shouted. He stood above Zoya. "What you're telling me is two things: you didn't recover the shipment, and the suspects escaped."

"Uh—" Zoya rolled off to the side and groaned. He rose up on his hands and knees. He peeked to see if Matimba was going to strike him. Then Zoya stood up. He wobbled for a moment.

Matimba turned his face to the sky. Through gathering clouds, the sun still warmed his skin. He tried to stay calm, to think.

Freddy interrupted, "Matimba, if we can find the suspects—"

Matimba dropped his head and counted to ten. He was surrounded by idiots. He spoke the words slowly. "The two dogs probably have our shipment. What will they do?"

Freddy swallowed hard. "Maybe alert the government inspectors?"

"Although you have missing pieces from your brain, you finally get it. They could alert others who are not in business with us, or they could sell it out away from us. If either of those things happen, both you and Zoya will lose your careers, because our buyers will not receive what they paid for, and they will kill all of us." Matimba relaxed his shoulders. "Have you ever seen how an elephant kills? How it knocks down its prey and crushes it to death with feet as large as suitcases?" The other two glanced at each other. "Because if you fuck this up any more, I will stomp each of you to death."

No one said a word. Faint music carried on the wind from the township—American rap. The sky clouded over in thin gray bands that ran across the horizon to the west, toward the ocean.

"Do you have anything positive to tell me?" Matimba said.

Zoya smiled quickly, then let it go. "While we had the suspects in custody, we were able to identify them. A bloke from the U.S., Pete Chandler, works for the U.S. Export/Import bank in Minnesota. The other woman is more troubling. Janette Koos. A private investigator."

Matimba's head jerked up. He chased Zoya out of the enclosure. Zoya was thinner and faster, but Matimba closed the gap easily with a burst of speed like a panther. He crashed into Zoya, knocking him onto the sidewalk. Zoya's head thunked on the concrete like the sound of hitting a ripe melon. "You stupid piece of cattle dung!" Matimba screamed at him.

Freddy jumped in and pulled Matimba off the other man. "Don't kill him! We need him to help us find the shipment."

Matimba rolled off into the dust and got up. He brushed his pants legs and shook his head. "You're all fired!"

People from the neighborhood gathered to watch a new drama. A row of women in green, blue, and cinnamon *dashikis* tilted their hips to one side or the other in order to balance the pile of silk wrapped high around their hair. They watched but stood far away from the men.

Freddy whispered, "Since Zoya identified them, we can apprehend them. They parked a car at the back door of the station. We obtained the license number, traced it, and know where Koos lives. You've been so mad, we weren't able to tell all of this to you. At your order, we can set up a dragnet for the car and also raid the house. We'll get a SWAT team. Either way, we've got them."

Matimba thought about that. "And the missing shipment?"

"Koos must have it hidden somewhere."

"You're not sure?"

Neither Freddie nor Zoya answered.

"You fools! What are they going to do?" Angry, he slapped Zoya's face to the side, the crack echoing off the wall of the enclosure. The village watched, but nothing moved except the pieces of laundry, slapping against each other on sagging clotheslines.

Zoya lay on the sidewalk, his body twitching. He opened his eyes and tried to focus. In five minutes, he was able to sit up.

Matimba knelt next to him. "Sorry. My anger was out of control. I won't fire you."

Zoya's bloodshot eyes rose to meet Matimba's. Zoya said, "You should be more careful, Matimba. Treat me like a dog and you will not have my loyalty for long."

Rain clouds lowered across the sky.

"I am not as stupid as you think. When we found the car at the back door, we didn't have time to search it thoroughly, but we did our own trick. We will catch them," Zoya continued.

Matimba's face split into a huge, white grin. A tooth on the left side was missing, but the smile still conveyed his pleasure. He lifted Zoya onto his knees and steadied him as he planted first one foot and then the other onto the ground, stood, and wobbled on his legs.

Matimba said, "First we will set up a dragnet at all major points here. Across the country."

"Yes, sir."

Thunder rumbled from the west. Fat drops of rain slapped the ground, causing volcanoes of dust to erupt.

Zoya stood. "I suggest you go personally to take jurisdiction of the case."

"We will take back our property and then get rid of them." Matimba breathed more slowly. He could fix this problem, after all. He looked from one man to the other. "What the hell are we waiting for? You know where this woman lives. Let's grab her as soon as we can."

Chapter Eighteen

Janette headed south on Highway 7 through Bloubergstrand toward downtown Cape Town. They were headed for the Pilgrim Hotel so Pete could get all his things. She pushed the little SUV hard. Since they were traveling the opposite direction from the rush-hour traffic, they made good time.

Occasionally, she rested her hand on Pete's thigh. He liked the feel of it and didn't discourage her. It was the loneliness. All the loss and death that weighed on him. It had been a long time since he'd been close to a woman. He remembered the smell of Janette's hair, like shampoo, when she had pressed her head into his chest. Nothing permanent could happen with Janette, but he imagined what might happen between them now.

From the direction of the ocean, black clouds rolled over Table Mountain, threatening to tumble onto the city. Pete checked the weather forecast on his cell phone.

"Major storms headed this way." He looked at Janette. "And it's getting dark."

"The freeways out of town are good. We should be able to make it, depending on how much time it takes to get your gear from the hotel."

"Fast."

"Sometimes the storms are really brutal because the cold air from the ocean crashes into the hot air over the city." She gave the car more gas, and they raced forward.

In twenty minutes, they came into the south side of Cape Town. Janette had to slow down because of the weather. Rain started to fall, glistening across the roads. In late afternoon, the air glowed a pearl color that made seeing the traffic difficult. They jammed into the afternoon rush hour traffic and came to a stop.

"How much farther?" Pete asked.

"We must get to the central city, then over to the harbor. You handled those thugs back at my house," Janette said to Pete. "Impressive."

"Lots of practice."

"Did you learn that in the Army?"

"I was assigned to criminal investigation. Spent a lot of time in the Middle East."

"But where did you learn some of those moves? You looked like a superhero from a movie."

Pete grinned. "Just a few taekwondo stances. I was trained years ago but still practice it regularly to keep in shape." He patted his stomach. "I need it more than ever."

"After your performance in the police station, I had my concerns."

"I know. Sometimes my temper gets the best of me." The traffic moved, and Janette flowed into an open lane. Pete's anger had gotten him in lots of trouble over the years. He knew exactly where it came from, starting with his father's treatment of him and his father's lies about the woman—Pete's mother—in San Francisco. When Pete got the chance, he would go out there and finally uncover the mystery.

"Dammit," Janette swore. "Look at this mess." She waved her hand toward the windshield.

"I've been wondering who those guys at your house were. Not the same agency that captured us at the police station."

"I don't know. But suddenly, we are very popular. Which reminds me. What are we looking for at the game reserve?" Janette pressed on the brakes to avoid a stopped car in front of them.

"There's not much of a connection, I admit. There's Donahue, the sniper, the crate of illegal ivory, tusks with embedded trackers, and the death in the park. For me, it's more of a gut feeling. I think we should follow normal procedure. Interview witnesses, look at the crime scene, check out the forensic work."

"Isaac worked as a ranger in the reserve for years."

Pete nodded.

"Rangers are highly trained professionals. Isaac attended the Southern African Wildlife College."

"Do they have female rangers?"

Janette frowned. "Not many. There's one group called the Black Mambas in Kruger National Park in eastern South Africa. It's an all-female anti-poaching force."

"So, what happened to Isaac?" Pete asked.

"I'm told he was out in the field inspecting the perimeter when he was shot."

"And no one was caught?"

Janette shook her head. The windshield wipers flapped uselessly against the deluge. She stopped in traffic again. "But there was something else strange about the whole incident. Isaac wasn't at the perimeter. There was no explanation for what he was doing out there."

"And the nuclear waste in his backpack?"

"Yes. The connection between the waste products, poaching, and local terrorists is well established."

"How does that work?"

The left lane opened, and Janette gunned the car. "This exit ramp leads to your hotel." She followed the ramp down and turned left. The car wallowed for a moment in the deep water puddled at the bottom of the ramp.

Janette replied, "South Africa is a stable country, and so is Botswana to the north. Beyond that, many of our neighbors are a mess. The worst is the Democratic Republic of the Congo—a misnomer since there's nothing democratic about it. Many armed groups are jockeying for power."

"What does that have to do with Isaac?"

"It's simple. The militias need money in order to buy weapons. Poached animal parts can be sold for weapons or nuclear waste products. They also kidnap women and children to hold them for ransom. There's—"

"But you said Isaac had cesium-137 on him."

"That is used in two ways. It can be traded for money, but it can also be used to make nuclear weapons."

"Ugh," Pete grunted. "Not pretty. The small amount of cesium found on Isaac probably wouldn't be enough to make a nuclear weapon like we think of one. But if they packed it with high explosives, they could make a dirty bomb. Do you have any suspicions that Isaac was a terrorist?"

"It certainly looks like he was involved in some kind of smuggling operation with the militias farther north."

"Is cesium-137 common around here?" Pete asked. "If it isn't, maybe we could trace where Isaac got it."

"Five years ago, we never saw any of it in South Africa. Now it surfaces occasionally. It's all underground, of course. But there's so much corruption in South Africa now, who knows where it might be found or who is trafficking it?"

They inched along Buitengracht Street until Janette could turn right onto Port Road, which would lead to the harbor area and the Pilgrim Hotel. Pete couldn't see beyond the car in front of them. He was glad she knew the way because even with GPS, it would be hard to navigate.

In forty minutes, they reached the courtyard of the hotel. Janette turned into it, pulled as close to the door as she could, and shut off the engine. She sighed and let her shoulders collapse. "Didn't know if we'd make it."

It was dusk when they left the car and ran for the lobby. The air smelled fresh and electric. Inside, they huddled by the door, drenched from the downpour. Pete looked at Janette. Blonde hair was matted over her forehead, but she smiled at their arrival in a dry place. Her eyes held his for a moment, sharing the happiness that occurs after coming through even a minor crisis.

The concierge warned them the storm was predicted to worsen.

"Can we get out of the city if we hurry?" Janette said.

"No, ma'am. The M1 motorway is flooded and closed until further notice. You could take the M2 and then cut north to R300, but it's the same with those roads. And, of course, the cars and lorries are already crowded everywhere."

She turned to Pete. "Now what?"

"Get out of this wet clothing," he said.

The concierge volunteered a porter to retrieve Janette's suitcase from her car. Luckily, there were a few rooms still available and Janette booked one.

They changed clothing and met in the hotel bar. Janette recommended local red wine, but Pete chose a martini. "Tell me more about the game parks in South Africa."

"The bigger, public parks are better known. Kruger National and Chobi National Park in Botswana, just across our northern border, are more touristed."

"Is Sirilima different?"

"Sirilima is big, but its purpose is to maintain a protected environment for a wide variety of species. For instance, cheetahs are endangered and quite rare. I'm sure Sirilima has a coalition of them, usually male, as the females prefer solitary life. If you went to Kruger, you probably wouldn't see any cheetahs. The bigger parks don't manage the animals in any way. They only want to protect the existing ones."

"Why would the cheetahs go to Sirilima?"

"They may be in the area naturally, or the lodge would import them to balance the population. They carefully monitor each species so if they become too large, they are culled in order to preserve the balance."

"It sounds like an African type of zoo for the tourists."

"Oh, no. Once imported, the animals are released into the wild and survive on their own—or not. Tourism plays a big part, of course. It brings in lots of money. But a legitimate park like Sirilima also wants to preserve the largest variety of species as possible. The tourism helps pay for that goal, and you and I get to see some extraordinary African game. What's wrong with that?" Janette leaned forward as if to challenge Pete.

"Well. . . When we get our work done at Sirilima, Karen and I can take our time viewing game." He asked Janette, "They give guided safaris, don't they?"

"Of course. That's one of the things Isaac did."

"I want to go farther north to Chobi National Park. What's that like?"

"At the intersection of Botswana, South Africa, and Zimbabwe, you have two of the greatest rivers in Africa, the Chobi and the Zambezi. Those rivers draw millions of animals. If you get a chance, you should go up there."

"If we're lucky, we may get to see a Western black rhino."

Janette chuckled. "Afraid not, Pete. They're extinct."

"Maybe—" Pete said.

"As you Americans say, 'go knock yourself out.'" Janette threw back her head and laughed, covering her mouth.

As she did so, Pete noticed her breasts press against her t-shirt. His partner, Barbara, used to wear t-shirts all the time, and he remembered the sight of her breasts. Barbara had been more polished, more sophisticated than Janette, but there were definite similarities.

Janette's dismissal of his goal to find the rhino irritated him as many others' dismissals in South Africa had irritated him. They all thought he was crazy. But Pete's dream was to find one of the rhinos. After he finished Isaac's murder investigation, he'd focus on that.

"I can tell you want to get together with your daughter again."

"Sure, but she can be challenging at times."

"Tell me. My daughter's medical issues are much more challenging. And the emotional stuff that goes with it is overwhelming."

"That's why you're so anxious to get the operations done."

"Yes, but—" She paused. "I'm working on something else."

"What do you mean?"

Janette put down her glass and looked around the room. No one else was near. She lowered her head and whispered to Pete. "What if we pretend to have the shipment?"

"Huh?"

"We pretend to have it and hold it out for ransom to the smugglers."

Pete leaned back, waving his hands. "No. No way—"

"I know it sounds dicey, but maybe we could do it. A 'sting,' as you Americans call it."

"But we only have a few tusks. What happens when we get the cash and then have to produce the shipment?"

Janette nodded. "That's the tight spot."

"And how do we find the smugglers?"

Her glass was empty. Pete stood and offered to get another. She nodded, and he walked to the small bar in the corner. A black man in a crisp white shirt with a blue bow tie smiled. He took the order and said, "Yes, *ma baas*." Pete felt slightly uneasy being called a boss but let it pass.

Back at the couch, he commented on it to Janette.

"Hangover from the old days. Many of the young blacks reject all of that. Of course, I never supported apartheid; I don't know anyone who did. But now we have a backlash with chaos. I certainly wouldn't go backward, but I'm not happy with the present system. Especially if you're white."

"We have our racial issues—"

Janette's eyes blazed. "You live in a white majority. This is a black majority. Totally different environment—if you're white."

"Okay, point taken."

"You must understand how racial separation started here. When the British pushed the Dutch out of Cape Town, the *boers*, as those farmers were called, began the Great Trek to the interior. Beyond freedom from the British, they were also on a holy mission to create a Christian, racially pure colony, free of the black natives. Over the years, that twisted into apartheid."

"But that's changed. What about the Truth and Reconciliation Commission? Our cab driver told us Bishop Desmond Tutu began it."

Janette looked out the front window. "That was the high point."

"Oh?"

"Let me tell you a story. Amy Biehl was a twenty-six-year-old California woman who came to South Africa to fight against apartheid. While driving some black friends home, she was attacked by another group of blacks who stabbed and stoned her to death—because she was white. All four men were caught and convicted. One died in prison, but the remaining three appeared before the commission, which released them, with the agreement of Amy's parents. Today, two of the men work for the Amy Biehl Foundation, which still tries to empower young men and educate them."

Pete felt his throat tighten. He couldn't speak for a moment. But he didn't want to get into an argument over race relations. Not now. "You said you have a degree in animal biology?"

"Yes. From the University of Stellenbosch. Not far from where I live now." She shrugged. "Odd. I always thought I'd be studying elephant mating patterns in Southern Africa. Instead, here I am investigating murder. How'd that happen?"

"Life always turns the opposite way."

"Black people are very proud of this heritage, and to be active in the tribal culture is to remind them of the greatness they had before the Dutch, Portuguese, and British tried to destroy that culture."

"Sounds impressive."

"Sometimes it's ludicrous. The president of our country often consults with the king of his tribe before making decisions of state."

"I'd like to see more of the tribal culture."

"We will have an opportunity to see the bush as we travel into the interior. Ancient medical practices, herbal medicines, ritual dancing and singing, and even some old-fashioned magic."

"Great."

Outside the hotel, thunder rumbled up from the ocean. It was black beyond the windows. He and Janette were alone in the bar. Lamps set along the walls glowed golden and made the hotel seem old —just like Africa.

She shifted on the couch to sit next to Pete, touching along their legs. "Tell me about yourself."

Pete shrugged. "Been to lots of places around the world. I'm good at what I do, but not so good when it comes to the family part. As you can probably detect."

"I am an investigator," she said with a sarcastic edge to the words. "Married?"

"Uh, no. A few almost happened." He looked up and across the deserted lobby. The talk was coming too close to him now. Besides, he didn't want to seem like he was complaining about his life if he told her about the lost women, some who had died, his jerk of a father, and the surprise he'd learned about his real mother. Some things were called secrets for a good reason.

Pete could feel Janette's warmth next to him and the electricity in her words and the looks she gave him. Desire built and pushed into his chest. Should he accept it, give in, and enjoy the natural progression? He turned back to look at the line of her jaw and how it angled down toward her full lips. Temptation. But wouldn't it complicate all the work they had yet to do? Of course, but now Pete's face warmed uncomfortably.

"So, why did you come here?" she asked.

"In my position with the bank, I often get sent to our different banks in different parts of the world. This assignment is all about solving Isaac's death. Of course, that now seems to be the tip of a dirty iceberg."

"Do you like the work?"

He tilted his head from one side to the other, ambivalent. "I guess I like it. I like the travel."

"Then what's in this for you?"

Pete's eyebrows rose over his forehead. Thoughtful. How much should he reveal? "When I was a kid in high school, I watched a local bully beat up a defenseless kid, and I stood there like everyone else. I did nothing. So now, I want to stop people who prey on others."

"Better pick your battles or you'll be exhausted."

He drank the last of his martini. The sharp taste of gin mixed with olives. "Walk you up to your room?"

"Sure, I'd like that." Janette set her unfinished glass on the table, stood in one athletic motion, and walked toward the elevator. They rode up to the third floor, got off, and walked down the quiet hall. Her fingers intertwined in his.

At her door, she turned to face Pete. "Storm should blow out by tomorrow morning. You're in for a fantastic drive through mountains and up to the highlands."

"I can't wait. Africa has affected me more than I imagined it would."

"I'm still thinking through my idea of a sting. Imagine the money we could—"

"No. Too dangerous."

"If we do it, you have to trust me."

He shook his head back and forth.

"Besides, Pete, you're too anxious. This is Africa; things move slowly in rhythms that are ancient and can't be forced." Janette's arms rose. She draped them over his shoulders and drew him closer. Eyes fixed on his. Assuring. She pressed her chest against his and lifted her face to kiss him on the lips for a long time.

Pete's insides went slightly liquid. "Your room?" he mumbled.

"We're here at my door, aren't we?"

Chapter Nineteen

Albert laughed when he looked over at Cecil. He resembled a dead cockroach with thin legs and arms tangled around his back. The humiliation was unacceptable. Albert knew he would kill Chandler at some point. The revolution—the new South Africa—needed blood to stain the earth and bring new growth.

But first, he had to get free and find the ivory.

Once free, Albert and Cecil would search the house. If they didn't find it, Albert calculated the two would have about an hour lead, carrying whatever part of the shipment they had grabbed. If he and Cecil could get on the road, it might still be possible to catch them. He rocked back and forth on his stomach in order to twist to the right. He looked around the room. Cecil was jammed under a coffee table but was near the far wall and a fireplace. Matches? Burn off the duct tape?

Albert surveyed the left side of the room. Plants, chairs, a couch with two end tables and lamps. Nothing helpful.

He strained his neck to look right again. Next to the fireplace was a set of andirons, the black ends covered in soot. An old set of bellows hung from a hook in the brick wall. Albert jockeyed himself closer. The end of the bellows had a long metal funnel that concentrated the air. He rolled his head to get a better look. The end of the metal funnel was old and, more importantly, sharp.

Duct tape was impossible to break—unless you were able to get even the smallest cut along the edge. Then the tape ripped easily. The funnel on the bellows might be sharp enough to create such a cut.

Albert called to Cecil, "Can you get closer to the fireplace?"

"Huh?" Cecil tried to look at Albert. "I don't think so." Cecil grunted as his head dropped onto the carpeting.

"Think of this as 'Mission Impossible.' You have to get the gadget that will free us."

"Okay, yeah, I get it. Mission Impossible." His face convulsed with a renewed effort to wiggle toward the fireplace.

"See those bellows? Can you get them down?"

Cecil grunted again while he inched closer. He managed to get next to the fireplace. When he arched his back, his head came close to the bellows. "Can't. Can't even see anything."

"You don't have to. I'll watch for you. Raise your head and knock the bellows off the hook."

Cecil jerked his head upward several times. Each time he missed. He dropped his forehead on the carpet, breathing heavily. "Won't work."

"You're Tom Cruise. Keep trying."

Cecil took a deep breath and heaved upward. With a slight twist of his head, he connected with the bellows. They rose, hung for a moment, and crashed down onto Cecil. "Shit! That hurt." The bellows lay on the floor between them.

"Good work. I'll give you ten bags of Cheetos," Albert said. "Now comes the hard part. I'm going to grab the bellows in my hands and try to put a cut into the tape holding your hands." He rolled onto his side and explored the carpeting with his fingers, like a spider trying to escape. Nothing. Albert shifted his hips closer to Cecil and repeated the exploration. This time, he touched the bellows. Closer. He reached out again. His fingers wrapped around one of the handles. Patience. He walked his fingers down the side of the bellows, dropped them at one point, found them again, and finally came to the pointed end. He gripped it while letting his body rest. Sweat covered his forehead, and he blinked to keep it from streaming into his eyes.

"Okay, Cecil. I got it. You roll over with your back toward me."

He moved and they both worked their hips closer to each other. When Cecil bumped against him, Albert used his fingers again to find Cecil's hands. It was difficult since Albert had to maintain a grip on the bellows at the same time. He found Cecil's hands and the intersection where the tape met his wrists.

Albert breathed hard. He concentrated on the stretch of tape. Back and forth, back and forth. He sawed the edge of the metal funnel against the edge. Since Albert's own hands were taped together, he could only move about an inch each way. It would take a long time.

"Ouch! Hey, you cut me," Cecil yelled. "Be careful."

"Shut up. You want to get into military training? Well, this is your first lesson."

After a while, Albert stopped to rest. He explored the tape with his fingers and found a slight cut. With renewed energy, he dropped the bellows and gripped the tape between his fingers. "I'm going to tear this. You help by trying to separate your arms."

Albert pulled in two directions. His fingers, damp with sweat, slipped and he started over. Little jerks on the corner. Cecil strained to pull his arms apart. It was tedious, difficult work. Finally, Cecil gave a grunt and his arms snapped free of each other.

He rolled over to work on Albert's tape. When he was free, both men flopped onto their backs, exhausted.

"Get up," Albert ordered. "We have to search the house. Fast."

Cecil propped himself on one knee and breathed hard. "Give me a minute—"

"No. Get up." Albert led him throughout the house and into the basement. They didn't find any part of the shipment or the tracking device. It must be in Koos' car. Albert searched for the pistols. Gone. Chandler had grabbed them. "Come on, Cecil."

Albert bounded out the front door and crossed the lawn in a gallop. Rain fell lightly, carried on a strong wind blowing from over the ocean. At the car, Cecil jerked open the door. Albert got into the driver's seat.

"Can we keep tracking them?"

Cecil collapsed into the seat. His face compressed. "Sure. The Google maps I can do on my phone. The apps for the tracker and that data are larger, but I could use the laptop."

"What the hell are you waiting for?"

Cecil paused and raised his head to look out the windshield. The rain fell harder until a waterfall curled over the roof to blind his view. "More Cheetos?"

"Shut up."

"Got you." He laughed with the crazy abandon of someone who's come through a very stressful experience. Sliding his thumb across the screen of the phone, Cecil keyed up the app. "Okay. It's downloading, but this rain doesn't help. Signal's sketchy."

"What about the map?"

"Look for yourself." Cecil held out the phone to show Albert the swirling gray lump on the screen. They couldn't make out anything.

Albert leaned back in his seat. He'd never accepted defeat. There was always a way around a problem. Most humans took what came to them without working to change it. That was why Albert would be successful in the revolution. A new South Africa needed a leader like him. *Carpe diem.*

But how to do that now? Sitting in the pouring rain while the last two years of hard work escaped with a couple of professionals? He couldn't bear to sit still. "And we haven't gotten any more intel from the Captain." He listened to the drumming on the roof. "Cecil, tell me where they went."

"Uh, don't know."

"You're worthless."

"Sorry, but who knows what they planned to do?" His face reddened.

As usual, Albert was alone with his thoughts. If Koos and Chandler were as capable as they had demonstrated, Albert could actually think through the scenario. It was amateurs that were difficult to predict. Where would they go with the shipment? Although much of the trafficking of illegal game parts went north through Zambia to the Democratic Republic of the Congo, much of it shipped out of Cape Town. Shipping to Hong Kong and Asia would be the most efficient from there.

Although the thugs and terrorists in central Africa paid, it was nothing compared to what the billionaires in China or Vietnam would pay. It made rational sense that Chandler and Koos would head for Cape Town.

Albert wondered: Why had these people gotten involved? What was their mission? A legitimate investigation for the bank, or had they decided to jump into the supply chain to scavenge it for themselves?

He leaned forward and started the engine. It roared.

"Hey?"

"We're going back to Cape Town."

"Sure. I've got all the backup equipment at the hotel." Cecil looked out the window again. "Uh, I don't know how far we're going. We may end up sleeping in the car."

"We'll catch those dogs. After we seize the tracker and the shipment, I'll finish with Chandler."

Cecil nodded in agreement. "Shit, yes. I'll help you." He looked over at Albert. "What're we gonna do? Waterboard him?"

"Shut up, Cecil. You're stupid."

Chapter Twenty

Sun flooded into Pete's bedroom the following morning. Gulls called from the nearby harbor as if to wake him. He climbed out of bed and cracked open the window. The cool air smelled like salt water. And it had stopped raining. Pete hadn't experienced a downpour like that since he'd been in Southeast Asia.

He thought about Janette. It had been a long time since he'd had sex; it had felt great and made him feel alive again. He thought back to the half-light of the evening in her bed. How they had explored each other's bodies with increasing excitement until she'd rolled on top of him with her own need.

This morning, he was still in a dreamy condition. Satisfied. But there was a part of him that felt hollow. It hadn't been sex like the sex with Barbara. Or a few others he had loved.

Pete walked to the shower. Still, their lovemaking complicated the investigation. Something Pete usually didn't do, but it had felt so good and he'd needed it so badly, he had given in. Part of him regretted his weakness. He'd make a point to keep it separate from the work they must do now.

Then he remembered yesterday and the tusks hidden in Janette's car. They had to get out of Cape Town as fast as possible.

His smartphone beeped, and Pete saw the call from Karen.

"Hey, I'm loving it out here!"

"Have you been looking at animals?"

"Awesome rhinos, wildebeest, lots of gazelles and my favorite—the warthogs. They're so ugly they're cute, always scuffling around like they're very busy and determined."

"We're leaving this morning. I'm sure Janette will push it to get there as soon as we can."

"What's the rush?

"Anxious to see you again."

Karen paused, then said, "I'm getting to be really good friends with Frimby. Such a nice man. Handsome. We had dinner at the lodge last night. He told me some things—"

"I told you not to go snooping around. You don't know what else has developed in the case."

"Oh, Dad. Frimby says he doesn't believe his brother was involved in any crimes."

"But the cesium in the backpack sure makes Isaac look guilty."

"Frimby says someone must have planted it on him."

"Maybe he's right."

"And Frimby says Isaac had turned off his radio to the main control station. That would be unusual, so Frimby thinks Isaac was going there for some other purpose than checking the perimeter."

"Yes, I agree. Apparently, when his body was found, it wasn't anywhere near the perimeter."

"I'll get more secret stuff for you."

"No! I'll be there in a day or so."

"Bye, Dad—"

* * *

Just before he walked into the shower, the hotel phone rang. "How are you?" Janette put a lot more feeling into those words than they normally warranted.

"I'm great. Thanks for last night. It was special."

"Yeah, for me, too."

"I normally don't mix business and pleasure, but—"

"Don't say it. I know. Let's not make this into too much right now."

"Right. Besides, we need to talk about our plans."

"Mmm."

"See you in the dining room."

"My beauty routine takes a while; I need a lot of work, you know." She laughed with a light edge to her voice.

In a half hour, Pete had his luggage in the lobby. He walked into the dining room to wait for Janette.

"Morning." Janette had her hair pulled back in a ponytail. Her face glowed with pink highlights across her cheeks as if she'd just come in from a day in the sun and wind. She ordered the local tea, rooibos. It came in a pot, and Janette poured a stream of red liquid into her cup. When she noticed Pete staring at her, she said, "It's made from the leaves of a local bush. You should try it. It can cure headaches, insomnia, bone weakness, hypertension, and—here's one for you—premature aging."

He frowned. "How do you—?"

"Oh, it's on the back of the tea bag."

Pete finished his coffee. "Let's grab a couple rolls and get going."

"Yes." Janette gulped her tea.

"What's the plan?"

"We race our way to Sirilima."

"Of course. With the tusks and the tracker?"

She tilted her head. "Why not?"

Pete's chest tightened. "For one thing, the bad guys are still chasing us. While you sit here having your morning tea, they could be right outside. Let's get rid of that fucking tracker."

"All right, stop it." Janette chopped the air between them with her hand. "I live here, and I know those bastards. I've tried to explain this to you previously. Of course they want the tusks. But right now, it's like we're witnesses to a murder. In order to get away with the crime, they must eliminate us—unless we have a bargaining tool. The tusks."

Pete grudgingly admitted she was right.

"So, the only question is: can we keep ahead of them before they catch us?" Janette looked from one side to the other as if the other diners might be watching them. "I think we can. The rain would've stopped them also. Now we have to get moving."

"How long will it take to get to Sirilima?" Pete asked.

"If we get out now, less than two days."

It took some effort to fit all the bags into her SUV. They had to squeeze them around the curved tusks. Janette managed to fit one underneath the seats in the spare tire compartment. Pete climbed in next to Janette. She keyed the address of Sirilima into the GPS and shifted into first gear.

Janette picked her way through the city streets, avoiding debris and downed trees lying across the roads. "We'll take the national route to the east, M1. It's the best road available."

"Scenic?" Pete asked.

She nodded. "Yes. The Val de Vie Winelands are beautiful. Rolling hills covered in green. Looks like moss growing on the land. Then we go up into the Hawequas Mountain Catchment area. There's a pass through the peaks. Stunning."

In forty-five minutes, Cape Town thinned out and they passed through Kraaifontein. Small houses that reminded Pete of the English countryside dotted the low hills, the sky arching over them like the skies of the American southwest. He looked straight up into an endless blue expanse.

Once out of the urban area, Pete was surprised at the open and unpopulated country. They passed farms of lemon and orange citrus groves and apple trees. Between them, fields of bright green sugar cane waved in the wind.

The freeway curved to the northeast and started to rise. After a stop for coffee, bathrooms, and gas, they came into a higher country. The wind blew harder and carried the smell of dry grass. It became warmer.

"This is called the veld," Janette explained. "We're coming to the mountains soon."

The M1 freeway took them higher until Pete saw some gray saw-toothed peaks in the distance. Rows of grapes, trellised above the soil, stretched out in straight lines as if pointing the way to the Hawequas Mountains. Bursts of sun shone on the flanks to color them purple for a moment until the light moved on and the mountains returned to gray rock.

All around Pete, life thrust itself up. Relentless and eternal, it grew in the fields, in the masses of people, the tribes, the trees, the tawny grasses, and the animals. Janette drove up into the pass through the mountains and came out to another high plain. Out here, with the massive presence of nature all around them, Pete felt small. The thought of any danger seemed remote. Hawks soared on thermals in lazy circles. They dipped and climbed endlessly, but always hunting.

Janette drove off the freeway for gas and a rest. She pulled into a Shell station and stopped under the roof by the pump. Pete got out and arched his back. The air was hot and dry. Wind blew the smell of dust across the concrete pad.

"Want to take over driving for me?" she asked Pete.

"Sure. Is it legal?"

"Yes. Just remember you're driving on the left side. Since we're on the motorway, it shouldn't be a problem."

"Got it." Pete slid behind the wheel.

They passed a tribal village. People walked among modern houses and thatched huts. While some of the women wore colorful dresses with matching turbans, most others wore Western clothing. They filed through a gate in a thorn bush fence, smiling and waving to the passing car. "Interesting," Pete said. "I'd like to see one of the villages."

"Maybe we'll have time when we get near the game reserve. South Africa has dozens of tribes, each of them with their own language and culture. That *kraal*, or village, is probably the Sotho tribe. All the tribes are black, but that's like saying all Europeans are white—there are still huge differences between them all."

As they drove, the sun curved over and began to descend behind them. Long shadows raced alongside the car to point the way to the northeast. The immensity of the land drew them forward, but when they reached a landmark, the country still rolled away to disappear on the horizon. Janette leaned her head against the window and dozed.

The GPS beeped. Pete looked at it and realized they were only a few miles from entering the suburbs of Johannesburg, the largest city in South Africa. "Janette, you should take over."

"Right. Pull off when you can."

They switched drivers. Janette drove faster than Pete, and they began to see small clumps of homes among the fields. More roads intersected the freeway. Retail stores offered car repairs, electronic products, and fast food: Nando Chicken, McDonald's, and Kentucky Fried Chicken. Buses, delivery trucks, cars, and motorcycles surrounded them.

In the distance, an upside-down bowl of dust and pollution covered the central city. Glass office towers poked through the top side of the bowl, glowing golden in the setting sun. "Downtown Jo-burg," Janette said.

"Hey, I saw a sign back there," Pete said. "Soweto. Isn't that the worst township?"

"I don't know if you can say 'the worst.' They were all bad. It is one of the largest in South Africa. We'll go through a corner of it in a few miles. They were created because the white elites took the good areas to live in and pushed the blacks and colored into slums on the edges, called townships."

The GPS routed them around the southwest side of the city. Soweto meant "southwest township."

Pete asked, "Isn't that where the protests against apartheid started?"

"Yes. Nelson Mandela lived there with his family and practiced law. It was mostly black, very poor, and very violent. Some of the earliest organizers against apartheid started there. In fact, Mandela was arrested for his protest organizing and went to prison as a result."

The road tapered from four lanes to two, swinging around to the west and then to the north to run between the township and Jo-burg.

Janette continued, "Many of the South African leaders came from the townships. Also great food. Some of the most progressive chefs go there to take advantage of the melting pot of culture and tastes. When Paul Simon came here to record his album *Graceland,* he pulled lots of his band from the townships."

In ten minutes, Janette pointed to the left. "There. Not the prettiest sight."

Pete looked out the window. In contrast to the gleaming glass towers of downtown, he saw narrow dirt trails dip down into an endless sea of one-story shacks. All had flat roofs, some had corrugated steel walls, some were made of plywood, and many were painted in bright colors: peach and sky blue or green like the grass in the veld. Most were drab, dust-colored lean-tos. A fat woman walked in the middle of one of the roads.

There were dozens of cars left along the sides of the dirt streets, with wheels off, hoods open, and worn upholstery with cuts that coughed out white stuffing like popcorn. "What's with all the wrecks?" Pete asked Janette.

"Many people can't afford to buy a car, but they can pay for a junker. Over the years, as they get some money, they find parts and repair them. Hopefully, in a few years the car is finished and the family will be able to use it."

"Are they that poor?" Pete said.

"Most are, but not everyone. You're seeing just the edge of the township. There are nicer areas as you go deeper into it. That's what I meant when I told you earlier that the government is so corrupt. Many of these people live as they did under apartheid—while the elected officials pocket the money meant to help these people."

Pete saw more houses squeezed at angles next to each other so close only a child could walk between them. Several of the roofs were rusted, while many had tires piled on them to hold the flimsy roofs in place. He'd seen poverty in many parts of the world, but this was overwhelming. A few trees bulged over the roofs in the distance. No grass grew anywhere, and he spotted a group of boys shooting baskets on a concrete slab next to a wooden animal corral. It held a goat that watched the game with indifference.

"It used to be worse," Janette said. "Under apartheid, there were no cinemas, hotels, shopping centers, or even electricity in many parts. It was designed as a giant labor camp. The thought was if the blacks became miserable enough, they'd leave South Africa."

Pete jerked and shouted, "Look. Up ahead." He squinted into the dust and saw four squad cars parked on both sides of the road. "What is it?"

"Don't know," Janette said. "Looks like a roadblock. We can't chance going through."

"Can we go a different way?"

"No. This is the main *deurpad*, freeway, to the north. We've got to ditch the ivory." Janette slowed to turn onto a side street. This one was paved and led to a more affluent area. She stopped and worked on her phone. "I'll see if I can find a storage facility nearby. We'll go through the roadblock now after we stash the ivory. Maybe by tonight they'll have found what they were looking for and we can come back safely." Her phone indicated a facility three miles away. Janette shifted the car and bumped up onto the tar road to go ahead.

They found a storage warehouse next to a Sasol service station. She drove through a dusty yard into the back. The corner of the car bounced as it dipped into holes on the surface. At the far end, Janette stopped. A one-story row of storage boxes stretched in both directions. Rust streaked across the corrugated steel door.

Janette and Pete got out of the car and went to the padlock on the door. He lifted the lock to slip in the key. The lock was scarred with cuts where someone had used a bolt cutter, unsuccessfully, to try and break it. From across the yard, through dust blowing waist-high, the setting sun caused the broken glass on the ground to shine like diamonds.

In a few minutes they had stacked the three tusks against the back corner and covered them with a stained blanket Janette carried in the trunk of her car.

She re-routed up the tar road and turned onto the main north/south road. The police cars were still there. Slowing as she came near the roadblock, Janette said, "It's lucky we saw this earlier." A line of cars was stopped ahead of them.

Janette rolled to a halt when the officer waved her down. Two other officers stepped forward. One carried a long pole with a mirror and some kind of gadget on the end. She lowered her window.

"Stay in the car. We're checking all vehicles." The officer spoke with an Afrikaans accent. He straightened and stepped back.

"Routine check? That's okay," Pete said. He watched as the man with the pole placed the mirror under the car in front of the tire. The other two officers stood without moving.

"Something's wrong," Janette said.

"Huh?"

"These aren't the local police from Jo-burg. See, look at their shoulder patches. Damn, they're Border Patrol."

The man with the pole worked his way down the side of the car and rounded the back end while the two officers waited.

"Relax. Probably looking for a bomb or drugs. We're clear."

Janette's eyes shot back and forth as she tried to see what was going on. "And they're not even opening the boot. That's not right."

The officer on her side jumped away from the car and shouted, "Everyone out."

Pete and Janette got out, stood next to their doors, and finally followed the officer's directions to move away from the car. Janette walked to within a few inches of the officer. "What are you doing?" She stared at him.

His eyes remained half-closed. He waited before answering. The officer with the pole handed the first one a plastic baggy. Something was inside. He reached down to grab the pole and raised it in front of Janette. "This is a Geiger counter. A Soeks 01M. Very sensitive and very accurate." Holding the baggy up in front of Janette, the officer said, "Now I have my own question: what are you doing with this?"

Janette frowned and her head jerked backward.

"Whatever is inside this box is radioactive. Highly illegal. It's probably uranium, plutonium, or cesium. It will be tested. In the meantime, go into custody with Officer Van der Merwe. You are both under arrest."

Chapter Twenty-One

Albert uncurled from the front seat of the rental and stood outside to stretch. He'd lowered the back rest, but the night had been painful just the same. The rain had stopped sometime in the early morning. He'd slept badly and was irritable. He looked over at Cecil, who snored, still sleeping, his bird-like legs jammed against the dashboard. A slight smile crossed his face.

With a punch to his shoulder, Albert woke him up. "Get up, you fool."

Cecil stirred, stretched his arms above his head, and yawned with his mouth wide open. "Yeah. How'd you sleep?"

"Shitty. Get up and get working."

"I need to pee. Like right now." Cecil looked around to see if there was a bush or fence he could hide behind. "I'll go in the house."

"No. We'll go after we get moving." Albert straightened his clothing and sat in the driver's seat. Cecil climbed out and took long strides to Janette's house. The front door was still unlocked.

Albert waited. He looked at his watch. Started the car. Waited. Finally, Cecil made his way back and settled into his seat. Albert said, "You are so damn slow. That's going to change if you want to get into Special Forces."

Cecil shrugged. "It's African time."

"That's the fucking problem," Albert shouted. "It's this lackadaisical attitude toward time and punctuality that is holding back our country from development. If we don't start doing something about it, nothing will ever change here."

Cecil blinked but didn't respond. "I'm hungry."

Albert stomped on the gas. The car shot forward. He squealed around the corner while ordering Cecil to recover the tracker's location again.

As they headed back to Cape Town, Cecil worked on his phone. "I'm not getting good reception here. Wish I had the laptop." He swiped his finger across the screen several times. "Got it. Finally found it."

"Where?"

"Uh, you won't like this."

"Where the hell is it?"

"It's going in the opposite direction. They're going east."

"What the hell?"

Cecil squinted at the screen. "Hard to see the Google map with this device. I'd estimate they're about two hundred kilometers out."

"That means we're not far behind."

Albert drove fast to get back to their hotel. In two hours, they pulled up in front of the hotel across from the De Waal Park. The park glistened with raindrops from the bright sun as if it were covered in ice. The car rocked to a halt, and Albert jumped out. Cecil bobbed after him.

In the room, Albert ordered Cecil to get his computers up and running.

"I need a shower," Cecil said.

"Do you think you can stop everything in combat and take a damn shower?"

"I thought you said you were never in combat."

"Well— That doesn't make any difference. Get those computers up."

Cecil shuffled over to the desk and powered up two laptops. While they booted, he rummaged through the papers and loose files next to them. He found a crumpled bag of Cheetos and ate a mouthful. Crunching, he said, "Coffee?"

"Oh, all right. You keep working, and I'll call room service for some food."

Cecil sat down and played with his equipment. In a few minutes, he had a clear picture on the screen. He called Albert over and traced the progress of the tracker with his finger. "Here it is. Looks close to Bloemfontein."

Albert leaned closer to the screen and studied it for a while. "They've gotten farther than I thought they would. Must be on M1. What is their ultimate destination? If we knew that, we could cut them off."

"I would guess they're going to Jo-burg. Which is good for us since we can fly back right away and intercept them when they arrive."

Albert nodded as he thought about the strategy. "Yes, that should work. I want you to get the flight manifest prepared for us to return. Tell them it is high priority."

Cecil nodded and started to work on the scheduling.

On his screen, Cecil had an emoji of a green crocodile. His tribe, the Venda, had a special relationship with crocodiles and the water they lived in. The tribe believed the spirits of ancestors lived under the water, especially waterfalls. Luckily for their tribe, during apartheid, they had been given a homeland in the eastern part of South Africa and were relatively unaffected during that time.

Like all black Africans, Cecil lived in two worlds—part of him in the modern world and part still living in the tribal one. Every day he felt as if he stepped through a waterfall and exposed only half of himself on either side.

A knock on the door brought two trays of breakfast. They ate a traditional English breakfast: runny eggs, blood sausage, grilled tomatoes, and a puddle of brown beans. A pot of coffee accompanied the food. While Cecil worked on getting a plane out of Cape Town, they both finished all of the food quickly.

Albert got up from the desk and darted back and forth across the room. "When can we get the plane?"

"They're working on it."

"Working on it! Didn't you tell them it was important?"

"Of course. But there's a delay."

"What?"

"They won't tell me. Something big."

"There's more than one plane available for government use. I'm going to call the interior minister." He grabbed his phone from the desk. Of course, the minister was unavailable. Albert left a terse message with an adjutant and hung up.

The African concept of time made Albert furious. Across southern Africa there had been several campaigns to change the attitude and become more punctual. Studies had shown how missed meetings, appointments, and even late buses cut productivity. Everyone seemed to agree, and then—nothing changed. Some critics even said to be punctual was to be on "Mr. White Man's Time." When the revolution happened, Albert would ram through rules about punctuality and people would have to obey.

He walked back to Cecil. "When are we leaving?"

Cecil shook his head. "Delays."

"Damn government bureaucrats!"

"I have been informed that the Minister of International Relations and Cooperation is scheduled to fly to Botswana to hold high-level talks about diamond mining."

"So what? They have other planes."

"For security reasons, everyone else is grounded until he leaves."

Albert threw his coffee cup against the far wall. It crashed to the floor and left a brown streak on the wallpaper. He took several deep breaths. "When is the asshole supposed to leave?"

"Hopefully, within two hours."

"Okay." Albert turned in a circle. "Okay. Let's make use of the time. Have we heard anything from our informant?"

"The Captain? No."

"Can you research more about our bogies? Chandler, Koos?"

"Sure." Cecil slid his chair to the right until he faced the second computer screen. His fingers tapped on the keyboard.

In twenty minutes, he looked over at Albert. "Got something for you," Cecil said. Albert came beside him and looked at the screen.

Cecil pointed out that Janette Koos was an accomplished investigator who had done a lot of work for financial institutions. Most recently, she had been employed by the U.S. Export/Import Bank in Cape Town. The intelligence didn't say what she was doing for the bank. The director, Ian Donahue, had been killed a few days earlier in a restaurant at the harbor. During that investigation, Koos and the others had discovered the special shipment.

"I don't like the sound of this. She's a pro."

"Here's something. Divorced, but she was into something illegal with the ex-husband. Looks like he was working at the University of Stellenbosch, where she was a student. Together, they cooked up a scam to steal money from the school. They were caught, but not prosecuted because of their young age, and they gave back the money."

"How about Chandler?"

"He's from a state called Minnesota. The data suggests he came here originally for a vacation with his daughter. But then I found information that revealed his work with the same bank as Koos. He was also present with Donahue when he was shot."

"That's not coincidental."

Cecil reviewed Chandler's military service, his work for a congressional committee in Washington, D.C, and his affair with a congresswoman who had committed suicide after a scandal broke about her.

"So, he's got connections in Washington, D.C.? Not good, Cecil."

"Since then, Chandler's been on several dangerous assignments for the bank to Southeast Asia, Ecuador, and Peru. He's had many disciplinary problems with previous employers but managed to keep his job." Cecil scrolled down through several pages. "Can't find much more. He's kind of a mystery."

"Damn. That's a threat multiplier."

"Huh?"

"Besides getting the tracker and the ivory, we have to determine why they're involved in this. And stop them."

"Should I scramble the team back home?"

"No. We don't want our mission compromised by too many people. There could be leaks."

"Of course." Cecil groaned. "But I remember how that dude trashed me. You didn't see the moves he put on me in the house."

Albert laughed. "That's why you need some combat training."

"Okay, but I don't have it, and this dude is tough. We should have backup."

Albert stopped laughing. "I can handle him. He's an older guy, probably slowing down. And you said his daughter was with him?"

"They arrived in South Africa together. Don't know where she is now."

"We'll grab her; she could be our leverage."

"Are you serious?"

Albert walked up to Cecil and stared into his eyes. "You don't get it, do you? I planned this mission for months. I won't fail, and I won't let these vultures stop me either." He spun on his heel and marched away.

In three hours, Cecil announced they'd been cleared for the flight to Johannesburg, leaving in thirty minutes.

They threw the equipment into bags and raced out to the car. At the international airport, the gate was open to the private section for government and military flights. Albert drove through it and came to a stop next to a small administrative building. With markings of the South Africa Air Force on its fuselage, a C-130 Hercules transport plane lumbered into position for takeoff. Its four propellers spun faster. Seeing the fat belly of the plane reminded Albert of a hippo trying to become airborne.

"Wait." Cecil tried to catch up.

"Meet me at the gate. I'll start the check-in."

They passed through the security gate and lugged their bags across the hot asphalt and climbed the steel ramp into the Dassault Falcon 900 jet. It held six people. By the time they got into the cabin, all seats had been taken except for two in the rear. Sweating, Cecil flopped into the starboard side. Albert sat on the opposite side, his face dry but tinged darker than usual. He removed his red beret.

The flight attendant closed the door and sealed it, and the air conditioning started to hum. In a few minutes, the pilot rotated the plane to face into the wind, the jets whining at a higher pitch, but the Dassault remained on the runway.

They waited for twenty minutes. Finally, the plane turned back toward the terminal. The pilot announced an unexpected delay—with no explanation.

Chapter Twenty-Two

The rain had come across the township fast and hard, so that by the time Matimba got back to his house, he was drenched. Abimbola greeted him at the door. She hugged him tightly and kissed him several times.

"The kids?" he asked as they parted.

She grinned. "With my sister for the night. I have you all alone."

Matimba walked with her into the kitchen. He missed the children and loved to play with them when he was able to be at this home. Matimba noticed his tribal regalia still sat on the chair. He knew what was coming. He waited for it.

"Matimba, do you know where—?"

"Yes," he lied. "I have it stored in two boxes in the garage." He wasn't sure where it was exactly, but he would find it when he had more time. He slumped into the open chair, tired and worried. If his operation was exposed or failed, all of his families would suffer. His own honor would be destroyed. The tribal regalia was a minor problem at this point, although he understood Abimbola's concern. Her tribal lineage went back farther than his. Her great-great-grandfather had been a famous and powerful chief. Abimbola had inherited some of his regalia, which Matimba now used. Therefore, it gave her pride and respect in the community.

Darkness descended on the house as the rain came harder. It drummed on the corrugated tin roof over the outdoor kitchen in the back. While Matimba waited for his men to carry out his orders, he could relax.

"Are you hungry?" she asked.

Matimba hadn't thought about food all day. Now he realized he was starving. "Yes."

"Good. I bought fresh springbok today." She smiled and walked behind the counter. She removed ingredients from the refrigerator and asked him to start the grill.

In a half hour, they sat at the small kitchen table. The springbok meat was like gazelle but tastier. Matimba had grilled it rare, almost bleeding, as they liked it. Abimbola had prepared African stewed potatoes, which included onions, garlic, smoked paprika, and white pepper. She boiled green beans and set two Carling Black Label beers out to drink.

They took a long time eating as Matimba listened to news of the family and their friends.

After dinner, the rain continued, blocking any view through the windows. Abimbola lit several candles around the living room. She put on a CD of Gina Jeanz, a female vocalist from Cape Town. Her soulful voice complemented the rock beat behind her singing.

In spite of his size, Matimba padded quietly into the room. He relaxed in the only comfortable chair and drank more beer. Abimbola stood before him and slowly dropped her *dashiki*. She danced to the music and turned in circles before him.

Matimba always liked the full curves of her bottom. He'd watch it while Abimbola walked ahead of him through the market, and now he watched it move as she danced. From her head, she unwrapped a silk headdress that was the color of lemon sorbet. It fell around her shoulders and across her bare breasts. She turned and the material curved around her body.

Abimbola danced faster, her hips shifting from side to side, and a sheen of sweat appeared on her lower back. The scarf looked cool against her heated body. With a hand above her head, Abimbola twitched the silk back up.

The candlelight reflected off her skin. It reminded Matimba of the color of the first darkness of night in the African bush. The time when, after resting from the heat of the day, the animals came to life and played, hunted, and mated with noisy abandon.

Later, she climbed on top of Matimba, who lay on his back in the bed. As she looked into his eyes, she grinned and lowered herself onto him. From the first time he met her, Matimba had liked that her appetite for sex matched his own. Gina Jeanz sang to them as they settled into a rhythm that lasted long into the night.

The next morning, Matimba got up early, kissed Abimbola goodbye, and raced back into Cape Town. Since the rain had passed, the hand-selected units could finally move again. Matimba ordered Janette Koos' house in Stellenbosch to be surrounded. The first step was simply surveillance. Command decisions would be made depending upon the results of the stakeout. Probably an invasion.

He had to be careful. Even with his authority as commander of a South African National Defense Force division, he must be very cautious in his actions toward the civilian population.

His immediate perimeter security consisted of three unmarked vehicles within less than a block from the target. Two other teams were stationed as backup four blocks away to avoid suspicion or alerting the suspects. These units had gathered quickly with assist from the Stellenbosch police SWAT team. Matimba hoped these men would not be needed since he wanted to keep anything about the shipment of ivory and rhino horns secret.

He squirmed in the front seat of the Tahoe SUV. He had a direct sightline to the Koos house. All units waited for his orders. The difficulty in any operation like this was keeping the lid on the men. Once in position, they wanted to perform the duties they'd been trained to do—whether that was wise, legal, or they weren't qualified.

They were like so many of the younger black people. They didn't appreciate the hard work Matimba and his generation had done. The lives they'd given. The sorrows suffered. Under the new government's affirmative action employment rules, even the police force must mirror exactly the percentage of colors in the population. The black kids knew they were guaranteed a job, so they didn't give a shit—while Matimba still worked hard in so many ways. He was sure about half of the officers out here were incompetent.

His radio crackled. It was Matimba's lieutenant in the lead vehicle. "Should we go?"

"Wait."

"I cannot see any activity inside. I can drive through the alley behind the house."

"Good idea. Let me know what you find."

IVORY LUST

In ten minutes, the lieutenant reported, "Nothing there. Her car is not present."

"What?" Matimba sat up in the seat.

"The house appears deserted."

Matimba got out of the SUV. He stood next to it and felt hot sun burning across his shoulders. The air smelled grassy and pungent like the new den of an animal. His breathing came hard. He'd lost them.

The second reconnaissance vehicle pulled up. Freddy jumped out. "What should we do?"

Matimba glared at him.

"Remember Zoya said they prepared a trick? They obtained more cesium-137 from our contacts at the power plant. Then Zoya hid the cesium under the back bumper of Koos' car." Freddy's buck teeth poked out through his smile.

Matimba smiled in return. "Pull back the men," Matimba shouted from over his shoulder and walked down the street. He stood under a sycamore tree. He told Freddy, "There will be questions. I want this closed down completely, as if it never happened."

"Yes, sir." Freddy slid into his car and squealed into a U-turn on the street.

Matimba settled back in the Tahoe and told the driver to return to Cape Town. The potential problems unspooled in his mind. Throughout his checkered career, Matimba had always been able to avert disaster. Would his luck continue? On his mother's side in the tribe, her relatives had always been lucky. At his last visit with a *sangoma*, Matimba had prayed to his ancestors for help. So maybe the roadblocks he'd set up would snag the trio. Matimba decided to wait in Cape Town.

The Motorola CP200 series radio came alive. They'd been installed in the Border Patrol vehicles only a month earlier. As usual, they didn't work as the government contractors had promised. The driver answered but couldn't get a signal until it rang again. He handed it to Matimba. "Might want to add some gain to the volume."

"Sir, Officer Regis. Johannesburg Border Patrol. We're liaising with SAPS in Province 23. We have arrested the two civilians you were looking for and are holding them in custody, waiting for your orders."

"Did you find any contraband?"

"Affirmative. Suspected cesium-137, hidden under the bumper."

Matimba's face split in a huge smile. "Good work, Officer. Hold them until I am able to get there." He started to hang up but instead shouted into the radio, "And don't fuck this up."

He told the driver to alter course for the airport. In an hour, they drove along the outer fence of the international airport at Cape Town. The driver continued until they came to the private section, reserved for government and military.

Stopping in front of the departure gate, the driver walked inside to get a flight for Matimba back to Johannesburg. Matimba waited in the car. The sun warmed the car, and he looked at his watch. None of his officers who had caravanned behind him had arrived yet.

The driver trooped down the steps until he reached Matimba's window. "Problem, sir. They tell me there are no flights out for at least three hours. The deputy president is scheduled to leave for Zanzibar; however, he is late."

"God dammit! Get back in there and tell those hyenas who I am."

In ten minutes, the driver returned. He stared at his feet as he came up to the Tahoe. "No change. Even after I told them about you."

Every minute he delayed was risky. He didn't know the Border Patrol people in Precinct 23 and didn't trust them. From years of experience, he knew the bureaucrats inside would not budge. They were trained not to budge. Matimba climbed out of the Tahoe. He looked around. "Where the hell is Freddy? Get him on the phone."

Thirty minutes later, Freddy's car rocked to a halt before the departure gate. He popped out and ran up to Matimba. "You need me?"

Matimba explained the apprehension of the targets. "I also want to know what happened to the snitch after the sniper missed."

Freddy nodded several times. When Matimba finished, Freddy went back to the trunk of his car, pulled out a small suitcase, and walked inside the gate.

When he came out, Freddy waved his hand. Matimba rose in a fluid motion and followed him inside. Neither of them had any luggage.

Matimba asked, "How much this time?"

"It went up to 37,000 rand. About 3,000 dollars—because we had to pay off an extra man this time. Another new hire." He followed Matimba out on the tarmac toward the waiting jet.

"What's this country coming to?" Matimba sighed. "I'm glad it's not my money."

Chapter Twenty-Three

The soldiers from the Border Patrol were gentle. They led Janette by the hand and opened a space for her to walk. Pete followed behind. Maybe the drawn Vektor R4 assault rifles substituted for any need of force. He looked back to see what they did with the car. It remained where Janette had parked it.

The officers' behavior had been odd. After they'd found the suspected radioactive material, they didn't search anywhere else in the car. Luggage, purse, back seat, or passports. They did take the keys. What was the reason for the roadblock? Typically, it would be guns or drugs. Maybe in South Africa, smuggling of animal parts or the payment for them was more critical.

Pete watched Janette walk ahead of him. Her back was straight and head erect. He liked her defiance and attitude. It matched his. Sometimes, simple *chutzpah* won the day.

In other tight situations Pete had been in around the world, the most brutal police were usually the most inept. These men, joined by the local police, were quietly efficient and professional. That worried Pete. He counted the officers, surveyed the terrain they moved through, and decided the odds of him fighting his way out were slim. This situation might take more than simple *chutzpah* to get away.

The group walked through the cramped street of the township. The road was pounded dirt, and one officer pointed out a broken piece of concrete so Janette avoided tripping on it. Local people stood with bored looks on their faces as the police moved the group along. Maybe the people had seen so many arrests this was nothing unusual.

They worked their way deeper into the township. Pete tried to remember each turn, a signpost, or landmarks. They turned west, and the setting sun skimmed over the tin roofs to blind them at times.

His anger focused on Janette instead of the police. Why was she carrying the radioactive contraband? Was it part of her plan for a "sting"? Whatever she was doing, it put them at risk. Pete didn't mind facing risks—had done it all his life—but he always wanted to know ahead of time what those risks were. This time, he'd been blindsided.

The level of trust he'd developed for her evaporated. That hurt because he was attracted to Janette. How could she have put them in this kind of a situation? Or was there an explanation? His mind turned over the various possibilities, but he couldn't settle on one that seemed most likely.

The group turned another corner and stopped. Ahead of them was a one-story, dirty white building. A chain-link fence circled the front lawn. In this case, "lawn" meant a flat dirt space that contained a teeter-totter with a broken handle in one corner. Two guards stood outside the front door. A new sign above it read "South African Police Force, Province 23."

Without a word, the officers led them inside. At the lobby, hallways split in three directions. The group turned to the left and marched down that one. A row of rusted lockers lined one side; it must have been a school at one time.

They walked deeper into the building. This area was quieter. All the doors were closed. A faint smell of Lysol drifted around them, as if the floors had recently been cleaned.

Pete caught up with Janette. She had her head down and plodded ahead. He felt for her hand, found it, and grasped it tightly. She didn't pull away. "We'll be okay," Pete whispered. "I'll get us out."

"Uh huh." Janette didn't raise her head.

The officers stopped before a door. The word "Humanities" was stenciled into the door. Below that, "SAPS Room 14." The man with a ring of keys stepped forward, unlocked the door, and moved back as they were herded into the room. It smelled stale, closed up. On the far side was a double-hung wooden window, closed with a steel bar across the bottom section.

A table filled one corner, two sofas sagged along the wall to the right, and several stuffed chairs beckoned them to sit and relax. One was a Barcalounger covered in bright orange material. He walked toward it and noticed the footrest had two stains running parallel up and down the front side. About the size of someone's calves. They looked darker than would be caused by normal wear. Heavy sweating might leave stains like these. The front end of each armrest had been torn to expose off-white padding that bulged out as if it were trying to escape.

As Pete turned around, one of the officers said, "You will wait here until the constable is available. There is some bottled water in the cooler under the table." He turned to leave. The remaining officers followed him out and locked the door.

Janette started to explore the room. He sat back on the couch. There was a long history of him losing women in his life. A sharp image of Barbara snapped into his mind. Gone now. After her death, he'd realized all the things he wanted to tell her, apologize for, and plan for the future.

And there was Julie, the congresswoman from Wisconsin. When Pete had worked for the congressional committee, he'd fallen in love with her. But the very scandal his investigative work had exposed ultimately caused her to commit suicide. Gone now.

Would it also be too late for him and Janette? Karen?

Pete had thought by coming to South Africa, he could find peace of mind and some final end of the pain, but here he was, trapped in a police station—again. He was determined to get out and start over with Karen.

Janette finished her sweep of the room. She glanced at Pete to invite him to come beside her. He walked to the table. Janette leaned against him and rested her head on his chest. He could feel her shaking. That surprised him. Janette had seemed so strong. He paused before confronting her about the stuff under the car.

She tipped her head up, kissed him on the cheek, and pulled back while still hugging. "I'll be okay. Just a quick dip into feeling sorry for myself." Janette sniffed and unwrapped from Pete. Her eyes focused. "Okay. We're in a bit of a jam here." A thin smile creased her face, and she wiped her hand across it.

"Jam?"

"A big, shitty jam. I don't understand why both the Border Patrol and local police are here."

"Joint exercise?" Pete studied her face, searching for an opening to ask her. It made him feel bad, but she'd done it and now they were in danger.

"Janette, why don't we sit." He guided her into the chair next to the table. From the metal cooler, Pete took out two bottles of Aquabella. He drank almost all of one bottle. He paused and looked into her eyes. "What were you doing?"

"Huh?"

"The stuff in the back of the car?" His voice rose in volume.

Janette frowned.

"The radioactive shit they found. What the hell do you think I'm talking about?"

"Wait a minute—"

"Paying for smuggled ivory?"

"What the hell are you talking about?"

"Have you lied to me all along? Are you part of some smuggling ring?"

Janette pushed out of the chair. "Stop this."

"Was our time at the hotel a lie also? Something to get me distracted?"

"You're a fool. You seem smart, but then you say and do stupid things. This is one of them."

Pete got up. "Stupid? It's simple: car stopped, only a specific area of the car searched, radioactive crap found hidden under the car. They didn't touch anything else inside. What am I supposed to deduce from that?"

"Oh, my God. So you think I—" Janette turned and paced toward the wall with the window. "Let's follow your clever investigative analysis. I hide the junk in the car, knowing if I was stopped it would be found easily."

"You didn't know there would be a roadblock."

"No, but have you forgotten we were carrying the ivory with a tracker embedded in it? A tracker than would lead whoever planted it right to us? Would it make sense for me to jeopardize everything by adding some radioactive stuff?"

She had a point. Pete thought about it. He wanted to believe her. But his freedom hung on what she had done—or not. "If I believe you, how—?"

"Someone planted it. I don't know when. Probably by the same blokes who are smuggling the ivory and rhino horns. They know we have something, and this way, they can add pressure on us to reveal everything—then get rid of us."

"It's illegal to possess that stuff?"

"Highly illegal."

"Like how illegal?"

Janette shrugged. "Well, they don't execute people by firing squad anymore, but it's a long prison sentence." She came back to Pete again and grabbed his arms. "But these are prisons left over from the apartheid regimes."

Enough said. She'd scared the shit out of Pete.

They both jerked when the door flew open. Five men entered. Four of them fanned out to either side while the middle officer stepped up to them. He had light black skin, a scraggly beard, and one eye that focused somewhere off to the side. He didn't say anything but circled around them, tipping his head to one side and then the other.

The man stopped in front of Pete. "Who are you?"

"Who are you?" Pete glared at him.

The man waited for a moment, then moved to the side. Another officer came forward. Pete knew what was coming and he braced for it, determined not to let any pain show at this point. The baton came out from behind the second man like a thin torpedo, jamming into Pete's gut. Pain streaked through him. He grunted and staggered but didn't fall.

The first man resumed his position. "Who did you say you are?"

"Pete Chandler. I'm a U.S. citizen."

"Who is your friend?"

Pete told him, then asked, "What are we being held for?"

"I am Constable O'Brien. I am in charge of this investigation right now. We are waiting for more personnel from the Border Patrol in Cape Town. They should be here soon. In the meantime, it would be very good for my career if I wrapped up the case before they arrived." He tipped his head to the right and continued to stare at Pete with one eye. "I will be easier to work with. You don't want to wait for those, uh, psychopaths. Understand?" He pushed his face close to Pete's.

Pete nodded and smelled heavy cologne on O'Brien.

"To encourage you, I have the authority to charge all of you with aiding and abetting a terroristic act against the Republic of South Africa. Carrying the radioactive material is a serious felony, and terrorism carries a life sentence in prison."

"Terrorism? But I'm a U.S. citizen—"

O'Brien barked a short laugh. "But what if no one tells your embassy that you are here? However, if you tell me who you are working for, you will avoid more harsh treatment."

Janette shouted, "He didn't know anything. The material was planted in my car."

"Planted?" O'Brien squinted at Janette.

"Yes. I didn't know anything about it. You have my personal papers; you know I'm a licensed investigator. Why would I risk my license and career by doing something so stupid?"

"Why indeed? That is what we will discover—before the others arrive." He walked to the door and talked quietly with one of the officers, who left afterward. O'Brien hurried back to the center of the room. "We don't have much time."

Through the window, Pete could see the sun had set. The remaining light was pearl gray, while brown shadows crept higher along the far wall.

"We will start questioning the woman."

The two men on either side of Janette pinned her into the Barcalounger chair. When Pete started to help her, the man with the baton shot it into the back of Pete's legs. He crumpled onto the floor.

One of the officers asked, "Tape on the mouth?"

O'Brien shook his head. "I rather like the sound of the human voice in pain. It's so expressive."

"Wait a minute," Janette yelled. "What do you want to know?"

"Not yet. I doubt it would be the truth anyway. After some persuasion, I will be happy to listen to the truth," O'Brien said. He walked in a tight circle around the room. The door opened and an officer came in with a curling iron used by women for their hair. The black cord flopped between his legs as he hurried forward.

"I didn't have time to clean it," the man said as he handed it to the constable.

When Janette saw it, she twisted back and forth on the chair. The two officers pressed harder on her arms. "I don't know a fucking thing," she screamed.

Pete tried to rise, but one of the officers pressed a boot into Pete's back, pinning him to the floor.

O'Brien took the curling iron in one hand and slapped the metal end into the open palm of his other hand. His eyes grew larger. "We think it's cesium-137. What are you doing with it?" He walked next to the chair, bent down, and plugged the iron into an outlet beneath the window. The smell of the iron heating up filled the room.

Janette's pallid face glistened with sweat. She jerked to one side and then the other, but she wasn't able to get free. Janette yelled, "Wait! Wait, I'll tell you."

Pete's mind blurred. At that moment, it sounded like Janette knew about the cesium and had risked getting them into this nightmare. He hated her for that.

One of the radios attached to an officer's shoulder beeped. He spoke something into it and called to O'Brien. The door opened and someone in a new uniform entered. From the floor, Pete couldn't see any identification. The new man whispered in O'Brien's ear and left.

The constable stood still. His posture deflated like a balloon losing air. Without a word, he jerked the cord of the curling iron from the socket. He sighed. "We have received orders to wait. The Border Patrol has arrived at the airport and will be here to take jurisdiction of the case." His eyebrows rose. "You will no longer be under my protection. They won't waste time with you," he promised and left the room. All the others followed him out.

Pete got up and ran to Janette. She was shaking uncontrollably. Her skin was wet and cold. Pete lifted her into his arms and hugged her, rocking her back and forth.

This was the second time they had been in a police station, faced with violence. Pete promised himself it would never happen again—after they escaped. But right now, he was immobilized. He didn't know what to do. Could he believe Janette?

IVORY LUST

"Come on. We have to get out of here." Janette put a hand on each of the armrests and struggled to stand. She followed Pete over to the table, took a cold bottle of water from him, and drank all of it. He did the same.

"Better." Pete's vision cleared, and the pain in his body receded.

Janette worked her way around the room and tried the door handle. Locked. She peered at the hinges to see if there was any way to pry them loose. "Nothing here," she announced. "Can you check the ceiling?"

Pete stood on the sofa and poked his hands against the plaster. "Old style. This isn't a drop ceiling. It's solid." He bounced down onto the floor.

Janette looked at the far side of the room at the window and pointed. "That's the only way out."

"How?" Pete said. "There's a steel bar."

"The table? Throw the table against it."

"It's too heavy to lift. Besides, it would make so much noise those thugs would be back in here in a second."

They stood still, thinking. "The cooler," Pete said. He dragged the metal cooler out from under the table. He tipped it over while water and ice gushed across the floor.

Janette understood.

With a hand on each side, Pete lifted it and walked to the window. He took a breath and smashed the cooler against the bar. It clanged and echoed around the room. He stopped to see if the noise would bring the cops back. When nothing happened after a few minutes, Pete slammed it again. And again. After several blows, the rod bent. Pete set down the cooler and wrestled the rod with his hands, trying to pull one end from the wall. Janette came beside him and grabbed it also. Together, they pulled until the left side popped free. Both of them rested against the wall.

Pete lifted the window, Janette picked up more bottles of water, and they squeezed out through the opening.

It was higher than they had anticipated, and they fell onto the ground in a tangled heap. To the left, the building blocked their way, but to the right a narrow alley led into the darkness. They stumbled toward it, feeling their way along the stucco siding of the wall.

"Do you remember how to get back?" Janette asked Pete.

"I think so. I tried to keep track of where they took us. I learned a way to memorize things like that in the Middle East."

"Hope it works this time."

Pete grasped Janette's hand and led her forward. The alley ran for several blocks until it opened onto a dimly lit street. A dog wandered on the far sidewalk. Somewhere nearby, another one barked. It seemed like they had reached a corner of the police station. If Pete could orient himself to the front, he was sure he could get back to the car.

"How are you going to start the car? They took your keys," he asked Janette.

She smiled. "I always have a spare hidden in a hubcap."

"Like you hid the cesium?"

"You know I was faking it back there, don't you? I was prepared to say anything to save us."

Pete looked into her eyes, but in the dim light it was impossible to tell if she was being honest. Right now, they had to escape. When they reached the street, Pete didn't know which way to turn. He guessed to the right. They hugged the shadows along the sidewalk and hurried without running. In three blocks, he spied the front of the station. It looked quiet. Two squad cars were parked at the entrance.

Janette said. "Which way?"

Pete pointed across the street. "We'll get over there, then follow it to the first corner. I have to remember everything in reverse." He led them to the other side. As they started for the corner, yellow lights inside the police station flashed on.

They started running. Pete led them around more corners, past a closed spice market, in front of a barber shop, and down the dirt road. He stopped and looked around. "Wrong road. We have to backtrack." They reversed course.

As they got closer to the paved road, more street lights made it easier to find their way.

"There! Over there," Janette shouted as she peeled off toward her car. Beside it, she dropped to her knees at the front wheel and looked around on the ground. "Need something to get the hubcap off."

Pete found a long flat stone and handed it to her. She jammed it into the edge and pried it backward. The stone popped out. Janette tried it again. It didn't work.

Pete kneeled beside her and took the stone. "Stronger hands," he said and pushed the stone into the edge of the rim. He grunted and the hubcap popped off. A set of keys tinkled onto the ground. Janette snatched them and jumped up.

They clambered into the car. Nothing had been disturbed inside.

Without turning on the lights, Janette made a U-turn and bumped up onto the paved road. She drove slowly in the opposite direction from which they'd come earlier. The roadblocks had been removed, and there were no squad cars. A long line of poles with power lines sagging between them pointed the way out.

When she was a mile away, Janette said, "It's safe to turn on the lamps." With the light, she sped up. "We'll grab the ivory and get out of town."

Back at the storage locker, they loaded the ivory quickly, covered it in the trunk as best as they could, and Janette drove off, the tires spewing gravel and dirt. She drove north, got back on the paved road, and went past the place of the previous roadblock. Police sirens wailed somewhere to their right, but they didn't encounter any squad cars. Janette raced through sparse traffic.

In ten miles, the outskirts of Johannesburg thinned and the sky opened above them. With a bright luminescence, the stars arched over the land. An occasional farmhouse dotted the horizon, barely visible in the glow from the stars. The high plateau around them stretched out flat and as far as they could see.

They drove in silence for a long time. Finally, Janette spoke. "That convinced me."

"What?"

"The Border Patrol definitely does not have the shipment—but they want it badly. That's how I'll work the sting."

"What the hell are you talking about?"

She looked over at him, and her eyes bored into his. "It's for Jane. Our only chance."

Pete sighed. "I don't want to have anything more to do with those guys. I want to finish this and get back to Karen." He didn't know if he could trust Janette.

Janette pointed through the windshield. "Look. Up there ahead of us."

Pete dropped his head and looked out the windshield. "Billions of stars. Impressive, but so what?"

"The Southern Cross. It's a cluster of five stars, with four of them positioned at each end of a giant cross." She pointed into the sky just above the horizon.

Pete shifted his eyes back and forth, trying to find it. Then it jumped out at him, bright and obvious now, even though the cross beam was slightly askew. He sat back and let Janette follow the constellation to the north that led into the deepening darkness.

Chapter Twenty-Four

Matimba, Zoya, and Freddy landed at the O.R. Tambo International Airport in Kempton Park, a suburb of Johannesburg but also close to Pretoria. Matimba used his bulk to force his way ahead of the other passengers. The other two hurried to catch up.

He stormed through the check-in gates and into the terminal. Large concrete posts, with spreading beams that resembled a baobab tree, supported the roof.

An official car waited at the outside curb for the men. Matimba squeezed into the back seat of the Mercedes sedan while the others found a place. "Get going," Matimba shouted. The car rocked backward as the driver stomped on the gas. They were headed for the Soweto Township on the southwest corner of Jo-burg.

Matimba was worried. He didn't know the two BP officers and had no idea how reliable they were. The local police were notoriously corrupt. Could the Americans buy them off? It wouldn't be the first time. All the Americans Matimba had met had money. Lots of it. His stomach rumbled.

The sun fell lower behind them as they threaded their way through the dense traffic. The last of rush hour. One of the benefits of the economic progress of South Africa was another first-world problem—traffic jams. The dust and pollution around the car glowed in a golden haze, like sailing through a royal cloud designed for a chief like Matimba.

The driver swerved into the left turn lane and stopped. He looked back and forth, then squealed into a U-turn to go in the opposite direction. He glanced up into the rear-view mirror. "Sorry, sir. Wrong turn."

"God dammit," Matimba shouted. "Am I surrounded by idiots?"

It was dark by the time they found the lone paved freeway that hugged the west side of the township. The traffic had thinned, and the driver made good progress. "Almost there," he announced.

But they weren't almost there. It took another forty-five minutes to find the dirt road that turned off to the provincial station.

Although Matimba had never lived in Soweto, it was the largest black city in Africa. In the center were several churches, a golf course, and hospitals. Every road wrapped in concentric circles around the center —like an African village in the bush.

Most casual visitors saw only the outskirts of shanties and dirt roads, with colorful laundry flapping in the hot wind. But Matimba knew of the deep cultural history that permeated the city. The Oppenheimer botanical gardens, a new soccer stadium, the Kiptown Open Air Museum, and the Mandela House museum, where Nelson Mandela had lived and launched the fight against apartheid. It still had bullet holes where an assassination attempt was made on his life.

"Maybe they'll have something to eat," Zoya said.

"Shut up." Freddy hit him on the shoulder. "Don't piss him off." He nodded toward the front seat.

The driver careened off the pavement onto the dirt road. The car dipped and rolled through potholes and puddles of stagnant brown water. They slowed to avoid hitting a long line of women coming back from washing clothes at a laundromat. The women waved, walked slowly, and sang a tribal song. They all sang in harmony while the last woman in line tapped a stick against a hollow wooden box. The sound echoed off the stucco walls surrounding them.

Matimba loved this music and was proud of its African heritage. He remembered a proverb his grandfather had taught him: *Birds sing— not because they have answers, but because they have songs.* The women took their time dancing across the street. In spite of his anxiety, Matimba waited. He thought of his grandfather—one of the last of the Tswana tribe who could actually track animals. It was a skill that all males in the tribe used to have, but now only the professional trackers and guides in the game parks could do it expertly.

Finally, the driver moved forward and the car continued its jarring ride.

A sparse scattering of light poles shone yellow in the dark when they reached the station. Two squad cars blocked the front door. Matimba was out before the Mercedes stopped moving. In three strides he was through the door. It was dimly lit inside. Two policemen sat on short stools in the corner, watching a soccer game on a TV that sprouted a bent coat hanger for an antenna.

"Hey!" Matimba bellowed. He looked and sounded like a Cape buffalo.

One of the men fell off his stool. The other stood, smoothed out his uniform, and saluted.

"Where are they?"

"Who?"

"The people arrested at the roadblock." Matimba's breathing came faster.

"Uh—" The man who had fallen off the stool came forward. The muscles at the corners of his jaw twitched. "I'm not sure, sir. You will have to talk with the National Defense Force officers. I mean, your officers. You know. What I mean is— Back there." He cocked his head to the door leading into a dark hall. "I will call for them right now." He moved to the counter and dialed a rotary phone.

"Who is in charge?"

"Let me check." The officer jumped over to a desk. There was a paper log on it that contained the names of all law enforcement who had checked in. "It looks like Officer O'Brien."

Matimba glared at him for a moment until he was convinced this man was *chipi*, worthless. Pushing him aside, Matimba stormed behind the counter into the hallway beyond. Freddy and Zoya followed.

The phone in Matimba's pocket buzzed. He ignored it until the third ring. "What?" he barked into the phone.

"My little *katsana*, kitten," Dakini purred into his ear. "When are you coming home?"

Matimba curved his arm behind his shoulder, prepared to pitch the phone against the wall. He thought a second time and put it back to his ear. "I am in the middle of official business. I cannot talk."

"But you promised to come home. My clothes will become rags if I don't get some new ones. Would you want your wife to be seen around the village looking like a beggar?"

Listening to her, Matimba thought of her name. In Africa, unlike Europe, most names were exotic and beautiful and always connected to a meaning. They often came from a mix of cultural backgrounds. Dakini came from an Indian name that meant *demon*. He loved her—especially their physical relationship—but Dakini's parents had named her well. "I cannot come now. I have a huge problem." He didn't add that failure to get the shipment assembled and off to Hong Kong would mean Dakini wouldn't get *any* new clothing.

"*Sala sentle*, good bye." His thumb started to press the off icon.

"When are you coming to see the children?"

Matimba stopped. He felt a stitch in his chest. "Soon."

"How long?"

"Uh, I will be there in two days." He had no idea how that would happen if he didn't fix the problem immediately. But the promise placated Dakini for now. Matimba clicked off.

The hall he stood in split in three directions, each one long and dimly lit. The three men stopped, unsure of which one to take. A female officer walked past them. Matimba asked her for O'Brien.

She stopped and said, "I think they're that way." She pointed to the hall running away to the left. "In Room 14. That room is reserved for special assignments." Her eyes opened wider. "Got it, *Bra*?"

Matimba scowled. He didn't like the informality of these provincial stations. Broken discipline always meant trouble. The three turned to the left. It took them a few minutes of wrong turns to finally reach a short hallway with a door marked "SAPS Room 14." Matimba opened the door. Inside, the room was empty. It smelled stale and sweaty. On the far side of the room, a steel bar, one end still attached to the wall, bent toward the floor. Two screws hung at angles from the loose end. The wall beside the window had a crater where the sheetrock had been ripped out. The window was open.

Matimba teetered on his feet, hiding his anxiety from the others. The open window. A familiar sensation rose from his groin up through his chest. Pressure. He breathed faster. He counted each intake of air, let the anxiety of failure settle down, and replaced it instead with pure anger. But he must control that. Matimba was capable of tearing apart Zoya or Freddy like a lion feeding on a kill. They weren't to blame.

He spun on his foot and marched out of the room. Matimba was determined to kill O'Brien in a small, private room similar to Room 14. Just the two of them.

As the three headed to the lobby, a group of officers came running toward them. In the lead was a slight man. His name badge said "Officer P. O'Brien." He stopped about four feet from Matimba. "Sir!" O'Brien shouted.

Matimba inched closer to him and stared into his eyes—or eye, as one drifted off to look up into the air to the right.

O'Brien tilted his head to one side. "There seems to be a problem—"

"Shut up."

"Yes, sir."

It would be so easy, Matimba knew. He could wrap his immense arm around O'Brien's throat, kink his fucking head to one side, and then Matimba would smash his palm against the head, snapping the spinal cord in a satisfying crack. Once accomplished, the body would flop to the floor like a dead fish. Then Matimba smelled O'Brien's cologne—something floral. Pity seeped into Matimba's senses, replacing the anger. Such a worthless dog.

Fighting to control himself, Matimba leaned back. He channeled his thoughts away from violence and into something resembling logical strategy.

"We seized the contraband." O'Brien smiled. "Preliminary tests show it's cesium-137. We've got them on possession and terrorism charges."

"*We've got them?* But we don't have them."

"I can explain. Just a momentary lapse."

Fatigue swept over Matimba. Dealing with incompetence all around him was tiring. He waved his hand. He instructed Freddy to record the name and rank of everyone in the Border Patrol who had participated in this fuck-up. "There will be consequences—later. Right now, I want those people. It could not be more simple than that."

"Of course."

"Where are they?"

O'Brien tilted his head to the other side. He looked from one of his lieutenants to the other. "They're not here, sir."

"I know that. Where do you think they went?"

"Well, the roadblock was on N1, near Devland. They were headed north. I think we can assume they kept their plans and are going north."

"How much time do they have on us?"

The man next to O'Brien pulled out a cell phone and began calculating time, speed limits, and distances. In a few minutes, he looked up. "Can't be too far, sir. They would have had to walk back to their car first. Since it's night, they probably aren't going flat out on the motorway." He came forward and held up his phone for Matimba to see. The officer pointed at a map on the phone. "I estimate they are somewhere between this point and the one to the north. Not far."

"More roadblocks?" O'Brien asked.

Matimba shook his head. "They'll know it's us and avoid it somehow."

"Brilliant idea, sir." Freddy leaned forward. His teeth stuck out when he smiled. "Now what?"

"We go back to Pretoria. I want to assemble a small strike force of our most dependable men who won't talk and are not afraid to kill if necessary." Matimba led them away from the incompetent officers.

Freddy waited until they had moved back to the lobby. In a corner, he whispered to Matimba, "I just received intel from the northern border. Our stations there report a possible intrusion by the Lord's Resistance Army."

"I don't give a shit. They're not a threat to our operations."

"But what if our targets and the shipment fall into the hands of the army before we find them? What if their plans are to sell it to the army?"

Matimba's head jerked up. His eyes narrowed. "All the more reason to act as fast as we can."

"Should I recruit the sniper?"

"Who?"

Freddy said, "The Afrikaner. Swart is his name."

"Sure. I may need him."

"Why don't we requisition a chopper from the army? We might spot them easily."

Matimba glared at him. "You idiot! What is the first thing they would ask us?"

"Why do we need a helicopter?"

"Exactly. I don't want anything leaked about our operation. Not to anyone. Instead, I want them to think they've gotten away. That will cause them to drop their guard."

"But how will we find them?"

"Ground surveillance. I want the Border Patrol outposts notified to watch for their car—but not to interfere with it. Report back to me. When contact is confirmed, we will mobilize the strike force for the attack, which I will personally command. And we will finish this."

Zoya added, "Charge them with terrorism?"

Matimba almost smashed in his buck teeth. "No, you fool. I don't have time for that. When we capture them, we'll get our ivory and I'll kill them."

Chapter Twenty-Five

When the Dassault Falcon 900 jet reached Johannesburg, it skidded to a halt at the airport. Albert and Cecil hurried out. They raced back to their compound in the warehouse district. Some of the city's newest cutting-edge restaurants populated the corners formerly occupied by abandoned storefronts.

Albert urged the cab driver to hurry in spite of the darkness.

Cecil opened the window and took a deep breath. "I love Johannesburg after a rain. It smells fresh for a change, and the buildings finally look washed and clean."

The cab they rode in turned the last block and drove through a narrow tunnel of gray buildings without windows. As they passed a restaurant called the Gazelle, Cecil looked at it. "I'm hungry. I love that place." He turned back to Albert. "We got time?"

"You're worthless, Cecil. There are a few bags of Cheetos in the office." He pointed his finger at Cecil the same way Albert's father had pointed at Albert. "What the hell do you think we're doing? Having a *braai?*"

"So I like barbeque. Why can't we get some at the Gazelle?"

Albert blew out a lungful of air. "We've lost the bogies, remember?"

"But I was able to get the signal in the plane and found the tracker. Here in Jo-burg."

"I appreciate your hard work. But we don't have time for food now."

In ten minutes they came through the metal door in the front of their building, it clanked shut behind them, and Cecil went directly to his stool before the bank of computer screens. His fingers ticked along the keys. Images flickered in front of him.

The only light in the room came from the screens. They reflected blue, green, and sometimes pink off of Cecil's face as he worked. From a tiny speaker on the wall, the lazy rhythms of the South African group Ladysmith Black Mambazo calmed him.

While they were in the plane, the tracker had been stationary near the Soweto township. But now, as Cecil coordinated the data, he saw the bogies were moving again, to the north. He superimposed Google Maps on the tracking program and saw they were on the N1 freeway. He decided to call in Albert.

"Good work, Cecil. When we've smashed the trafficker's operation, I'll recommend your promotion."

Cecil traced the screen with his finger. "Look. N1 heads north. If they continue on that, they'll get to Botswana."

"Or they could be going to Zimbabwe or Zambia; all the countries' borders come together there. That's the point for trafficking ivory and horns. The border crossing there is totally porous."

"Would the bogies make contact there?"

Albert leaned back on the stool and looked up at the shadowed ceiling. "Maybe you're right. The ivory they have now could be a sample of the entire shipment that disappeared from the police station in Cape Town. They show the sample to the terrorists to convince them of the authenticity of the contraband." He stood up, excited. "That leads to a mega-sale of the entire shipment."

"Right there?"

Albert sat again and leaned closer to the screen. "Zoom in," he ordered.

Cecil toggled the cursor, and the map exploded into detail. A wide river curved like a Cape cobra between flat expanses of green foliage. Looking tiny against the endless green, a narrow bridge crossed the river. On either side of the bridge, trucks lined up for miles, idled along the road.

"That's the Limpopo River, the border between the countries. See, there's only one way to get across, so the trucks are stalled for miles. They wait for days to get over. Most of the drivers sleep in the cabs, so food vendors supply them. And their other needs are supplied by a herd of prostitutes."

"Not much law enforcement?"

"No. Perfect place to make the deal." Albert pushed the cursor up, and the map flowed to the north. "N1 goes up here through Zambia and then cuts along the southern edge of the Democratic Republic of the Congo—the headquarters of the Lord's Resistance Army. They can take the motorway, grab the contraband, and get back into the cover of the DRC quickly."

"I remember my dad telling me about the N1 freeway. The road from 'Cape Town to Cairo,' it was called. The British were going to build it to unite their colonies. I loved the names of the cities it would travel through: Pretoria, Harare, Nairobi, Khartoum, and Cairo."

"Cecil—"

"When that didn't work, a British airline decided to capitalize on the plan. Imperial Airways, remember? Flew passengers in the 1930s from Cairo along the same route as the highway, with an added stop at Lake Victoria in Tanganyika. What a romantic time to have been living in Africa."

"Shut up, Cecil." Albert slapped him lightly across the head. "We've got work to do now. We're not living in the 1930s."

"Of course. What should we do?"

Albert lifted his hand to his hair. Fingers disappeared into his thick Afro as he scratched, thinking. "The safe strategy would be to tag behind them, waiting. But the aggressive plan would be to head them off. We could be present when they make the deal with the terrorists. Catch 'em in the act. Perfect."

"That's what they're going to do?"

"What else could it be? If they were dealing with the Chinese, they would have stayed in Cape Town or headed east on the motorway, N4, toward Mozambique. Here." Albert had moved the map to the southeast. "A totally lawless wreck of a country if I ever saw one. But it has access to the Indian Ocean. They could ship the product to Hong Kong from the port city, Maputo."

"Or Hanoi." Cecil blinked. "Shit, Albert. This is bigger than we thought. Once the sale goes down, it's like geographic malware."

"I don't give a shit about that. We have a vision. 'The ends justify the means.' Pure Marxism." Albert turned his head and stared into the dark corner. A grin broke out across his face.

"So, should we call in help?"

"No." He spun back to face Cecil. "This is my operation." Albert clasped his hands on either side of Cecil's face. "You dream about the old Africa. I dream about the new one. A new generation of leaders.

Better than Mandela, better than Tutu or Kathrada. They didn't have the staying power. We will, God dammit."

"Sure."

"And you, Cecil, will have a significant role in our new regime—if you help me break this down."

"Of course."

Albert popped off the stool, took four steps to reach the wall, and came back again. "We have to 'war-game' this to the last detail. No fuck-ups. You're right to this extent: we could use the local police or border patrol in Botswana. They'd help us capture the bogies but wouldn't get any credit in South Africa for doing it. I would get full credit." He sat on the stool and, with a kick of his boot, scooted closer to the screens. "Where could we land?" He searched over Google maps.

"Land?"

Albert didn't answer, intent on what he saw on the map. His head came up. "Right here. At the border crossing. There's a shitty little building, a few chain-link fences, but at least there's a flat, open space nearby. I think we could squeeze the chopper in there."

"Wouldn't we tip off the smugglers?"

"You idiot! We'd come in ahead of the bogies and their ivory samples. Get the perimeter established prior to the take-down."

"Oh, yeah."

"I want you to contact the interior minister. No—I better do that. He's not going to be happy when I tell him we need a chopper. Of course, I'll figure out something to justify the expense. He's always distracted. His wife is unfaithful. I want you to make contact with our assets up there. Tell them to scramble their best men for our arrival."

"Our assets?"

"The database, you cow."

"I'm all over it." Cecil bent to his work, pecking at the keyboard. At the sound of a soft bell, signaling that a new image had appeared on the closed-circuit TV, Cecil looked up at the monitor. "Finally—" He jumped off the stool, knocking it backward. "Albert, he's here."

"Who?"

"The Captain's coming up to the back door."

"Where the hell has he been?"

In a few minutes, a white man entered the room, dressed in a white shirt that bulged around the middle. Thin gray hair combed backward emphasized a large forehead that fell down further to brown eyes. Eyes that never went to sleep. "Don't bother me," he said to head off Albert's sure questions. A smoldering stub of a cigarette hung from the corner of the Captain's mouth.

It felt crowded in the room. "No thanks to you, we've got a location for the bogies," Albert told him.

When the Captain and Albert had settled on the undercover work, Koekemoer had set his fee. Albert had said yes to everything, but insisted he pay the Captain in bitcoin. He never did fully understand the new cryptocurrency. That was the first problem he'd come into the lab to fix.

"Bottom line, Frikkie, what's the intel?" Albert demanded.

"I'm more interested in getting paid right now."

"You are getting paid."

"I don't trust bitcoin. I want cash."

Albert shook his head in short strokes from side to side. "You're too old to get it. Bitcoin is the 'currency of the Internet.'"

"But it's just bits of code on the computer. How can you be sure it'll be there when you need it?"

"It's called 'blockchain.' I haven't got time to go over this again. Totally transparent to all the world. Who could cheat us?" Albert threw up his hands in the air.

"What's that again?"

"Here's the real reason I use it. Anonymity. All the identification I have on the exchanges is a number. No names, no credit scores, mortgage payments, and dues at the local strip club. When you move cash, you attract lots of negative attention. Crypto-currencies allow us to stay in the dark from everyone. Get it, Mr. Kokomo?"

Koekemoer nodded. "I need more."

"Why?"

"I was the one who took all the risks to plant the fake tusks with the trackers in the shipment. And I'd say getting targeted for a hit on the ship justifies it." He scowled. "Besides, I had to dress in those filthy overalls."

"The bloke missed."

"They know who I am, you ass—but I don't know who they are. At least not yet, and I don't have enough proof to expose them."

"Where does this lead?"

The Captain took a deep breath, as if to tell a long story. In fact, it was brief. "It's a cell within the National Defense Force—"

"—run by Jackie Chan. Everyone knows the Border Patrol is full of holes. I pay you to tell me specifically where and who."

"Pretoria."

Albert's eyes opened wider. "Pretoria? Not in the field offices at the border crossings?" He smiled wider. "That could only mean the cell is directed from the top levels." He spun in a circle. Then he stopped. "Who?"

"Humph. Not sure yet. I've got my own snitches."

"I need to know right now. The mission is unfolding faster than I planned. And with better outcome programming. Are you in contact with your people?"

"Of course," Koekemoer barked. "I'm meeting a black man at a *boeremusick*."

"That concertina music crap you Afrikaners like?"

"Can you imagine a black man coming to one? That tells me he has something important to sell." He laughed weakly. "I'm trying to get him to 'come in from the cold' as soon as possible."

"What's his name?"

"I know him only as Zoya."

Chapter Twenty-Six

"Looks like we missed sundowners." Janette laughed.

"What are you talking about?" Pete listened inattentively while he gazed out the window. Even though it was night, the stars created such light it seemed like late afternoon.

"It's a term for taking drinks after work."

"Like a happy hour."

"I guess so." She looked over and saw Pete in a pale glow. Janette slowed the car as they approached a bubble of yellow light beside the road. "We need petrol."

A Shell Ultra City gas station sat in the middle of the pool of light. Next to it, a darkened market with a tin roof looked like it was abandoned. She swerved into the station and stopped beside a pump. Pete volunteered to pump it while Janette went inside to look for something to eat.

He had such confused feelings about Janette. He knew that loneliness and grief had helped push him into bed with her. It had seemed simple at the time. Of course, it seldom was. But now, with the discovery of the cesium-137 under the car, Pete wondered.

What was she really doing? Had she hidden it there herself? Or had it been planted, as she insisted? And now that she was talking about working some kind of a sting on the poachers, Janette seemed even more unstable.

He wanted to trust her. After all, she would help him with the investigation. And he'd come to appreciate many things about her.

The pump clicked off, and Pete walked inside to the restaurant. Loud music startled him. It was the music of the American band War, with a song from the '70s called "The Cisco Kid Was a Friend of Mine." But the African version substituted a different title and words: "Vasco da Gama Was No Friend of Mine." It was a historical reference to the Portuguese explorer who first rounded the Cape of Good Hope—and brought all the Europeans in his wake.

"What do you recommend?" Pete looped his leg over a plastic chair. Back home, he rarely ate fast food. Here in Africa, he looked forward to it.

"Try the *boerewors*. South African sausage." Janette laughed. "This isn't California cuisine with lots of vegetables. This is Africa, and this is meat."

Pete got up to order one.

Back at the table, Janette ate timidly, picking at her sausage. "What's wrong?" he asked.

Her eyes became unfocused. "I don't know. I don't know what to do about Jane. I need the money for the operations." Janette sighed. "I have to do the sting. I hope it'll work."

"How will you do it?"

"I have some contacts with the senior Border Patrol people in Pretoria. I'll start there."

"And then?"

"Make contact and dangle the shipment in front of them. Depending on how they respond, I've got a plan."

Pete shook his head.

"That's why I need you."

"No." Pete bit into his *boerewors* sausage.

"I don't care what happens to me. But if there's a way to score some money, I'll try it. You'd do the same for your daughter."

Of course he would. He thought of Karen, Barbara, other women he'd lost in his life. How could he have been so short-sighted? He could have spent more time, done more with each of them. He looked at Janette as she pushed away her meal. He didn't doubt that she'd give up her life for Jane. At that moment, he flipped. He would help.

After eating, they walked outside. Warm, moist air hugged him—in contrast to the air conditioning inside. Stretching his arms over his head, Pete looked up at the dome of stars above. Endless, eternal. It made him seem small and transient.

In the driver's seat, Janette asked, "Ready? I can take you to one of the finest hotels in deep Africa." She swung out her arm in a gesture of offering. "From here, we're heading into the 'true Africa.' The land of tribes and indigenous people. Some have been on this land for thousands of years. In many ways, not much has changed for them."

In an hour, Janette slowed and bumped onto the gravel shoulder. She stopped the car.

"We're going to sleep here?" Pete looked around at the exposed spot.

"No. I need your help."

He followed her out of the car and walked to the rear end. Janette opened the trunk lid. Flipping aside the blanket, she tugged at the first tusk. "Take the heavy end, will you?"

Pete cupped his hands beneath it, felt the cool weight, and levered it over the edge of the trunk. She caught the tip, and together they backed down into the ditch beside the road.

"In fifty meters, there's a drop-off that's hidden from sight. We're going to toss the tusks down there for now."

"What—?"

"Hurry. I want this done."

When they had finished carrying all the tusks to the drop-off and rolled them over the edge to thud somewhere below in the dark, Pete stopped her. He could see her damp face in the light from the headlamps. Hair stuck around the edges. Janette flashed a brief smile and shook her head back as if to clear her face of the wet hair. "So, what's going on?" he asked.

"I'm sure we'll be searched at the game reserve. Don't want them to find these."

"Wait a minute. For days you insisted those were our 'bargaining chips.' Our only hope to assure our safety."

She looked up at Pete. "From here on, we must be very careful. We're headed into the dangerous part."

Chapter Twenty-Seven

Even with headphones on, it was difficult to hear Albert trying to talk over the roar of the engines powering the Atlas Oryx transport helicopter. Cecil sat next to the hull, felt the shaking, and hoped it had been serviced recently. When he had climbed into the South African military transport, it looked like a very angry grasshopper. Same blunt nose, same body shape, with camo shielding over the side wheels that resembled powerful hind legs. The four-rotor blade package was so large, the tips drooped toward the ground until the pilot fired the engines and they began to spin.

Cecil had joked with one of the pilots. "Hope the engine doesn't fail."

"Don't worry, sir. We have two, and if one goes down, the computer management system automatically advances the power setting on the remaining engine. This bird hardly needs a crew."

As they approached the border where three countries came together —South Africa, Botswana, and Zimbabwe—Albert had been screaming something in the headphones, so excited he couldn't help himself.

As for Cecil, he gazed out the open hatch on the opposite side and saw the sun cresting the horizon. The sky above was dark blue, but it spread out in the distance in gold, salmon, and orange streaks. People who hadn't been to Africa assumed it was all jungle. But most of South Africa was dry. The plains below Cecil stretched out like a yellow blanket as far as he could see. Roof acacia trees, baobab, and even an occasional jacaranda, probably transplanted by seeds in the wind, grew in clumps across the surface.

He bent closer to the opening and spotted game. Four elephants, including a baby, surrounded an acacia tree, trunks tugging on the branches for the succulent leaves. Three giraffes bobbed forward in their accentuated gait. Game was everywhere in Africa. Cecil marveled at the immensity of the land, how fertile it was, and how much life it nurtured. It made him feel proud to be part of a mission to save this country.

The engines throbbed at a different speed. Cecil checked the webbed shoulder harness. The last thing he needed was to fall out of the open hatch just before they touched ground again.

Albert motioned to position the goggles over his eyes. Cecil didn't need the reminder.

The pilot banked sharply to the left. Like a roller coaster cresting the top incline, the Atlas slid toward the ground at a scary speed. Outside, Albert and Cecil saw the winding Limpopo River, brown, smooth, and wide. A rusty boat churned upriver. They spotted the bridge spanning the river between Botswana and Zimbabwe with miles of trucks lined up on either side.

Albert yelled orders about landing placement to the pilots, who ignored him.

At one mile out, the Atlas leveled off and raced toward the border station. The roar of the engines bounced off the ground, and the rotor blades churned up dust that rolled out in all directions.

They flew over a tall fence that marked the border between South Africa and Botswana. Made of steel mesh, it had a wide gate directly below them, and there were small brick buildings on either side of the border.

When the pilots reached the landing site, they hovered for a moment. Dust billowed in through the hatch. Even with their goggles, Albert and Cecil ducked their heads. The struts on the Atlas bounced once on the ground before it settled down. The engines whined to a halt. The two men worked their way out through the dust. Albert tore off his headset and goggles.

Around them, the land was dull brown, flat, and had been stripped of all vegetation for security reasons. Three one-story brick buildings stood in a row in front of the steel fence. Both of the weighted vehicle barriers were open. Under the roof in the shade, a line of people leaned against a wall of the first building. They all stared at the helicopter and the men who emerged from it. Since it was normally quiet here, the landing was a fascinating occurrence.

Albert loped toward the building. Dressed in full uniform with his red beret, he stopped long enough to brush the dust off of it. "Who's in charge?" he called. No one answered.

Four green Toyota trucks were parked at an angle on the shady side of the building. The beds of the trucks were open, with three rows of seating permanently fastened into the box for tourists on safari.

While Albert charged ahead, Cecil worked with the pilots to unload their gear. Along with the computers and technical equipment, they had brought small arms. Four Beretta Px4 automatic handguns rested on the top layer of a Styrofoam-padded carrying case. Below those were two Milkor MK-4 rifles with a grenade launcher attached underneath each barrel. He felt comfortable with the handguns but worried about the rifles. They were essentially machine guns with the added firepower of a grenade launcher. Cecil had never fired one before. What the hell would a grenade do to the three civilians? he wondered.

Cecil believed in the revolution, but when he touched the oily metal gun barrel, the ugly realities of the operation struck him. After assuring himself all the gear was accounted for, he closed the hard case.

When Cecil reached Albert at the customs building, the Atlas roared into life. Dust billowed out from the chopper as if a grenade had been detonated beneath it. The noise faded a few minutes after it left.

Albert tapped him on the arm. "Here's the checkpoint. The bogies will come from over there." He pointed to a narrow, brown road that led farther into a brown landscape. Two palm trees offered the only shade for as far as they could see.

Four men in uniform approached them. The uniforms were pale green, the color of sage, and tan. Patches on their chests and shoulders read "Botswana Defense Force." The letters curved over the logo of a lion's head. Below that, another patch read "Military Band."

Albert studied them closely. He took a deep breath.

"Major Noonan?" the first man said.

"Yes." Albert looked behind the men. "Is this all you've got?"

"Uh, yes, sir. We've been detached from our command to assist you in any way we can."

"Do you have any idea how serious this op is? International terrorists?"

The first man looked over to the second one. They both shrugged.

"Well, God dammit, we won't be playing Mozart at some music concert. This is a war."

"Of course, sir."

"What have you got for firepower? We anticipate members of the Lord's Resistance Army."

"We have our standard issue sidearms."

"That's all?" Albert slapped his forehead and turned away. He stomped for a few steps, then returned to the group. "Okay. How about your Air Support Branch? Can we scramble them quickly? If the terrorists manage to escape from us, they'll be headed toward the DRC. Air support can knock them out."

"We don't have the authority to activate them. I could make a call—"

Albert blew out a lungful of air. "Not now. Let me think about our strategy." He stepped out into the sun and walked a small circle in the dirt next to the building. The line of people hadn't moved, but they followed Albert's path with their eyes.

Cecil waited and brushed away flies that circled his head.

In a few minutes, Albert came back. "Here's the plan. How many vehicles do you have?"

"Three Jeeps, sir."

"Good. I want one hidden behind each of these buildings. Do you have communication among yourselves?"

The officer held up an old Midland two-way radio. "These work pretty good."

Albert's jaw tightened. "The bogey will come north in an SUV. We anticipate it will rendezvous with terrorists for the exchange of illegal ivory. It is at that precise moment that we will attack. We must catch them in the act in order to obtain the necessary evidence. After we arrest the suspects, I will take custody of the prisoners and transport them back to South Africa for further proceedings."

"What do we do?" the officer asked.

"You will station your men behind the buildings. On my command, you will execute a classic pincer movement to trap them between our vehicles. If they try to escape, you are authorized to use force—but they must not be killed. I need to interrogate them."

The first officer shifted from one leg to the other. He removed a cloth hat and wiped his forearm across his face. He brushed away some flies. "Yes, sir."

Albert turned to Cecil. "You accounted for the grenade launchers?"

Cecil nodded.

"The trick is not to actually hit them with a grenade, but to drop it in front of their vehicle, forcing them to halt. It's like shooting sand grouse. You have to lead them a little before firing."

"Of course."

Two dogs with sagging backs loped by the group. In the distance, a blurred line of trucks slept in the sun. The stiff wind did little to reduce the temperature, which was probably over one hundred degrees.

Cecil asked, "Want me to power up the computers?"

"Later." Albert looked at his watch. "By my calculations, they should be here in two hours." He turned to the Botswana police. "At ease, men. Take this time to prepare yourselves. Also, we need the area cleared of all civilians. We don't want collateral damage." Albert walked away.

He led Cecil back to the equipment piled in the shade next to the tourist vehicles. "Think of it, Cecil. It's all come down to this moment of truth. Of course, these suspects are only the mules, but they will lead us to the ringleaders. That's the prize. Eyes on the prize, Cecil." Albert straightened his shoulders.

They all waited.

Three hours later, the wind died, the sun dipped lower, and the temperature fell with it. Albert paced and stopped to look down the N1 freeway. Two tourist buses and a truck carrying sheets of copper sulfate had lumbered through the checkpoint. At the border crossing, the armed guards from the truck stopped at the vending machine next to the building to buy Cokes.

Albert questioned them. "See anyone else out there? A small SUV?"

One guard was a large black man with a bandana wrapped around his head, discolored from sweat. He smacked his lips after a long drink of Coke. "No. Couple of scooters and some local farmers."

Albert walked back to Cecil. "Any minute now. I'm sure."

"We got a call from the minister's office."

"What do those baboons want?" Albert snapped.

"They reminded us the ministry is getting billed by the Botswana Defense Force for five men—"

"There are only four!"

"I know. Anyway, the office wants to know what the hell we're doing out here."

"Did you tell 'em?"

"Sort of."

"You didn't reveal anything classified—"

"Of course not. But the thing is, if we don't get something done here, the chopper will be back to extract us early."

"Damn! Why don't they trust me? When we take over, that ministry will be the first to get a shake-up." Albert looked back and forth. The four Botswana police had disappeared behind the buildings. "Come on." He led Cecil back to the equipment.

Together, they carried the computer and power units into the building. An office in the back had a wooden desk with one chair squeezed in front of it, so close that no one could really sit in it. But the room was air conditioned. Albert commandeered it and instructed Cecil to get the computers booted up and find the tracker.

Cecil squeezed into the space behind the desk with his knees jammed so high it looked like he was squatting. In spite of the air conditioning, his face gleamed with moisture. He looked up at Albert.

"What? What is it?" Albert hopped across the room in one step to look over Cecil's shoulder at the screen. He squinted. "What's that mean?"

Cecil cleared his throat. "It means the tracker is stationary."

"What?"

"It's not moving. They must have stopped."

"Where?"

"Here." Cecil pointed at the map superimposed over the tracker's history, which was recorded in a string of red dots until the string ended. "Right there. Looks like they're about seventy kilometers north of Jo-burg."

"God dammit!" Albert staggered backward through the door. He came back to stand behind Cecil. "Show me."

Cecil zoomed in on the map. The setting sun cast long shadows that streaked across the ground. He toggled the joystick to get a view from different angles. Finally, Cecil said, "Looks like the middle of nowhere. All I can make out is a steep cliff here. The tusks must be hidden somewhere in the bush."

Albert clamped a hand on Cecil's shoulder. "Where is it?"

"I told you, I can't see the tusks."

"No, I meant, where is the car?"

Cecil frowned and bent over the monitor screen. He rotated the view 360 degrees. No car.

Albert's breathing came faster. "Where did they go, Cecil?"

Chapter Twenty-Eight

At first light, Matimba waited at his house in Pretoria. He had come home late, argued briefly with Sabella about sports equipment for the kids, and flopped into bed for a few hours' sleep. He'd promised to have the money in a few days.

From the living room of his Tudor-style home, Matimba watched for Freddy. Matimba would never admit to anyone, not even to one of his wives, about his fear. The kind of fear that starts as a nagging thought, then grows into anxiousness, worry, and then blooms into gut-twisting fear. Freddy, Zoya, and the others thought this was just another shipment, like dozens of previous shipments of illegal ivory and rhino horns.

Matimba had handled problems in the past. But he also knew how easy it would be for the operation to come apart, to be discovered. One loose end, one string coming undone, would bring down his entire world. Not only would the lucrative stream of money disappear, but so would his career and his role as a chief, along with the respect it carried.

Never before had something like this happened—three amateurs stealing a shipment. Were they trying to eliminate him? Could he stop them? Had the Chinese secretly recruited them as competition to Matimba's operation?

In times of stress in the past, Matimba had always retreated to his tribal village. It was the place that made him feel closest to the earth, felt peaceful, and was surrounded by his kin—those alive and those in the spirit world. He hoped it would work this time.

The Mercedes glided to a stop in the street outside. Matimba carried an expensive leather briefcase. He fit into the back seat and ordered Freddy to get going. "Where is Zoya?"

"Not sure. He told me he had something important to do." Freddy pulled into the traffic, still sparse at this early hour.

"What information do we have?"

"No reports yet."

"They probably stopped for the night. Put all spotters on high alert."

"Yes, sir."

Matimba sighed. He didn't like to wait for events. Especially now, when time and containment were so critical. But until the three dogs were located, there wasn't much that could be done. His village was north of the city, in the same vicinity where the targets were probably headed. He spoke quickly. "Freddy, drive to the village. It's near Mafikeng."

Within a mile, Freddy turned north. Jacaranda trees lined the freeway. The Limpopo region stretched before them, bordering Botswana to the northwest and Zimbabwe to the northeast. It was a wild area with few established Western-style cities. Instead, tribal villages, with histories going back for hundreds of years, dotted the landscape. Wild game roamed freely, although there were several game parks nestled into remote corners of the area.

As they drove the land rose in more dramatic outlines, with steep mountains, valleys, dry plains, and small farms. Gravel roads twisted off the main road to be lost behind dense growths of vegetation. Matimba spotted two elephants ambling along a stream bank.

As the sun rose, more traffic came from the north: buses with workers going to Pretoria, small cars, pickups, and the lumbering flatbed trucks weighted with sheets of copper sulfate—a valuable load.

Matimba managed to doze in the back seat. He dreamt of Abimbola. Of all his wives, she was his favorite. Besides, he didn't want to think of the youngest of them—Dakini, who would be waiting at the *shamba*, or farm, for him. She was the smartest—and most demanding at times—but her youth always gave him energy.

In two hours, Freddy turned onto a gravel road. The car bumped over ruts in the road as they threaded their way into the deep bush. This was tribal area. Although it was technically under the jurisdiction of the South African government, most administrations left it alone.

Different tribes occupied different areas, as they had for hundreds of years. The Zulu and Xhosa were the largest. Each had their own culture and language. The Xhosa were cattle breeders. The Zulu descended from warriors, although today the warrior aspect was mostly symbolic. They carried spears and colorful shields whose markings told stories of ancient victories. Matimba's tribe, the Tswana, were known for their complicated legal system of courts and mediation practices.

As the Mercedes plowed deeper into the grassland, dust billowed around it, causing Matimba to raise the window. Freddy swerved to avoid striking a line of Zulu men walking in single file. They wore traditional cowhides over bright, printed cloth shirts. On their backs, each man carried a ceremonial shield. "Must be lost," Freddy joked.

They turned the last corner, and he saw his village. This sight always made his heart stop for a moment. So peaceful and so comforting. It made him think back to his boyhood, when he would stay for a month at a time with his grandfather and participate in the training for future chiefs. Matimba remembered that young boy, trim and athletic, who could run over the grasslands for hours without fatigue.

The village sat on a wide plain of yellow grass between two mountain ranges. Beehive-shaped huts with conical caps for roofs lined up in a row to form the edge of the community. Between them, stick fences made from dried thorn branches separated each yard from the neighbor's. A pack of friendly dogs loped out from the corner of a hut to greet Matimba as he grunted and got out of the car.

With Freddy following, Matimba walked across the dusty field and came closer to the homes. A group of children ran out to surround the two men. The kids yelled and jumped up and down with the arrival of guests.

Matimba led the group through a narrow gap in the fence that opened to the central plaza that tied all the huts into a circular pattern. An ancient sycamore tree dominated the open area. Around it, flowering lavender bushes and Madonna lilies grew, tended daily by the young girls of the tribe. Each hut had a grass mat before the low, open front door.

Dakini's home was on the far side. He made his way toward it but was slowed by all the people who came out to greet him. Smiles and laughter and singing surrounded him in welcome. Three men from the adjacent fields dropped their tools and stepped over the cobbled rows of dirt to come back and say hello. To deal with the heat of the day, most of the men didn't wear shirts, only a pair of shorts. Some wore cowhide sandals while a few wore flip-flops, their black feet dusted tan. Women wore colorful headbands and necklaces of shells or gems or gold.

Matimba's chest swelled and he began to relax. The outside world didn't exist here. After all, this tribe had lived and farmed and hunted here long before the Europeans had intruded into South Africa. Surely the tribe would outlast them all. Besides, they all subscribed to the idea of *ubuntu,* which meant "I am, because we are." Starting with the family and radiating out to all of humanity, all were dependent on each other for survival—and that gave them their ultimate strength.

For the first time in weeks, he could hope for a respite from his fears. A woman he'd known since childhood came out of her hut with a cup of *umgombothi,* corn beer. He tipped it up and drank deeply while a stream spilled over the edge to dribble down the front of his shirt.

The village practiced a careful balancing act: to preserve the ancient ways and culture while accommodating modern life. For instance, the village had electric power. Most villagers had smartphones, and many had at least one car for the family's use. Some worked as farmers and sold produce. Others made items to sell to tourists. Many people had day jobs in town but lived in the village.

Matimba reveled in the attention but knew he must see Dakini. She would not come out to meet him, but would wait in her home.

He pushed his way through the crowd and circled the open space to the familiar hut at the end. It stood next to a thorn branch enclosure that held four chickens. He stopped, listening to the bees humming from behind the hut in the hives. Two stick fences guarded the hut in the front, with a wide opening that invited guests to ignore the fence. Thanks to the money Matimba gave to her, Dakini had expanded it from a hut to a more permanent structure. The outside was whitewashed and had geometric designs—circles and triangles—painted over the base color.

Matimba looked to the left down into the valley, which was green because of the river that churned through it. His eyes rose and fell with the terrain until they became lost in the clear blue sky beyond. He turned and ducked his head and entered his home.

Dakini was a large woman, strong and busty, with a wide smile. She had been educated in Jo-burg but chose to come back to the village and raise their children. Her skin was lighter than most of the tribe's, and that had led over the years to jokes about who her "real" father might have been. She came out from behind a hanging blanket that acted as a wall, her arms raised. Grabbing Matimba around his neck, she rose on tiptoes to kiss him for a long time.

She wore a short skirt and a red cotton bra strapped across her chest. Matimba ran his hands from her hips up toward her back. Her skin felt warm, and her middle was still thin in spite of childbirth.

She stood back and looked him up and down. "I cannot call you my 'little panther cub' anymore. You are much too big." She laughed and patted his bulging stomach.

Matimba agreed. "I'm so busy working at my job, I don't have time to work on my diet."

She bounced on her feet. "Come. Let us take a walk down to the river. It is a beautiful day. And my husband has returned home to me. I am happy now."

She led him by the hand outside, and they walked to the left. He could smell someone grilling impala in preparation for the evening meal. They passed through another stick fence and started downhill. The yellow grass changed to green as they descended toward the river.

"The *sangoma* visited again last night. The eldest one. He went into his trance and communicated with my ancestors. When he came out of the trance, he announced our child, Jabari, is also a *sangoma*."

Matimba stopped and looked at her. "That is wonderful news. But it will be a great responsibility for him. I'm proud."

"I knew he was the incarnation of my great grandfather."

"You only guessed. But now you know for certain." Matimba smiled at their good luck.

"How is your work?" Dakini asked

Matimba sighed. "Especially difficult."

His phone chirped. Matimba continued to look out in front of him. The valley cut a deep gash between the mountains—sharp edges of rock, but permanent and peaceful. He knew what the text would say. Reluctantly, he gave in and looked at it.

It was from Hong Kong. His buyer. They warned if Matimba didn't get the full shipment to them by Friday, the contract was void. And they had people who would find Matimba to make certain the problem would never happen again.

His shoulders slumped. Today was Sunday.

Dakini noticed. "Something is wrong. I will comfort you."

"I know. You always do. I'm anxious to see the children."

"They will be back from school this afternoon." She pointed toward his phone. "What's the problem?"

"Same things." He hesitated to upset her about the disaster with the shipment, although she had a way of coaxing things out of him. "There is always the pressure to stop the animal losses. The U.N. is sending yet another committee to study the problem."

Dakini stopped walking. Her voice pitched higher. "I hate all these western baboons who try to stop Africans from doing what Africans want to do. It's still colonialism."

"Yes—"

"Disguised as a campaign to save African game. Ban hunting! Stop poachers!" she screeched. "None of them have seen a leopard take a child from our village like I have. It's pure hypocrisy. Westerners talk about South African self-determination after apartheid but then squeeze us about how we deal with our own resources."

"You're right."

Dakini waved her arms. "I read about Americans killing wolves that prey on their cattle. But when Africans try to protect their cattle from elephants or leopards, that is a moral outrage to the West."

He nodded in agreement.

She dropped her arms. "But you have to admit that game viewing tourism brings in millions for South Africa—and pays your salary."

"Of course, but wildlife conservation is becoming a luxury for all of Africa. Even here, the unemployment, housing, health care, and education demand all our resources. Who gets priority? The animals or our people?"

"Matimba, I have pleaded with you many times to quit your job and come back here to live and fight for our people."

He searched her face. It was a tempting offer. "I have many responsibilities: families, children, my tribe. I'm a chief. Unfortunately, to support all of those people, I need money—more than you can imagine." He shrugged. "It's a job."

She lowered her head and looked up at him from under her eyelashes. "Speaking of money—"

"I know, I know. I'm working on another deal. But some crooks stole the latest shipment. I can't find them yet. When I do, the deal will go through, and I'll get an ox cart full of cash."

Dakini led him deeper into the valley. To the left, far up in the valley, rain clouds coalesced and came toward them. The grass was still wet from the morning dew, and it dampened their bare feet. Dakini slipped her arm under his. "Come to the river." She pulled him forward.

Wind brought the first drops of rain. It felt refreshing. The path twisted down the slope to take them past a small brick building. A sign on the squat steeple read "Apostolic African Methodist Church." Christian missionaries had established these churches in the 19th century on the edges of tribal areas. Many Africans chose to follow various aspects of the Christian faith while holding onto ancient tribal religions and even a belief in magic.

As they descended and came closer to the river, Dakini pointed to a group of people in white robes. "Must be a baptism."

Matimba nodded. They stopped at the river's edge. About twenty people, men and women, stood in the water up to their knees along the river bank. The minister was in mid-stream with a young girl. He held a leopard-skin-covered Bible in one hand and the girl's head in the other. The crowd chanted and sang a hymn while two young boys beat a rhythm on the bottoms of plastic buckets.

"By the power of Jesus our Lord, you will be baptized with water made holy by His presence," the minister shouted. "In His name, I command you shall be washed clean of your sins and all your fears." With a practiced movement, he ducked the girl's head into the water. She popped up quickly. Together they came out of the stream and stood in the grass on the bank. Water drained down from their muddy robes and pooled at their feet.

The rain fell harder. Matimba lifted his face to feel it cool and gentle on him. Hand in hand with Dakini, they waded into the water. It always surprised him. The current was strong, and the water felt cold and clear. He thought of the ancient cycle: the rain fell, cleansed the land, and washed into the river, which then carried everything out to the sea to merge forever with the infinite oceans.

Chapter Twenty-Nine

Karen texted her father: "frimby taking me on first game viewing today so excited!! Can't wait for u to get here come soon"

Frimby picked Karen up at the main lodge. She'd had a typical British breakfast: runny eggs, beans, and bloody sausage. She'd eaten quickly and drunk lots of rooibos tea. At the front door to the lodge, Frimby hopped off the side of the Toyota Land Rover. It was a long pickup truck fitted with three rows of seats for tourists. The cab was open, with a windscreen that could be folded forward over the bonnet.

Karen smiled when he came over to shake her hand. If there hadn't been lodge staff behind her, Karen would have given him a tight hug. He was dark and handsome with a wide smile. And such a humble man. Nothing like the smug millennials she knew at home.

"Good morning, ma'am." Frimby spoke with a clipped British accent.

"I told you to call me Karen."

"Okay, Karen it will be all day." He grinned and asked if she was ready. "Do you have a wide hat, water, and sunscreen?"

"Aye, aye, Captain." She placed a boot on the first rung of a short ladder leading into the passenger section. "Anyone else coming with us?"

"Not today. We're in between tourist groups, so I was able to get the Landy for us alone." He directed her to the cab and helped her climb up into it.

Karen settled into the leather seat and pulled her hat down firmly on her head. Butterflies danced in her stomach. He swung in beside her and started the engine.

They bumped up onto the road leading out of the game lodge and into the reserve. The road tunneled through a thick pine forest. It shone bright green, with the night's dew still glistening on thousands of needles.

Frimby drove through an area of tall grass, also green with dew. He slowed to point out two baboons squatting beside the road. The female had a front pouch from which a wrinkled face poked out to watch the big vehicle pass. The mother made coughing sounds and circled the ground on all fours, exposing a bright red butt. The male sat still but noticed everything. Two vervet monkeys descended from the tree branches nearby. Both were males and had turquoise scrotums, which they scratched as they eavesdropped on the baboons.

"What's the most common animal here?" Karen asked him.

"Elephants. Although we also have endangered species like cheetahs. That's because the park encompasses four biomes: aquatic, forest, desert, and grassland. Different species and flora live in each one and are adapted to it. The one animal that will cross all boundaries at will is the elephant."

"How long can they live?"

"The African bush elephant here can live to seventy years. They are the biggest in the world and can weigh up to 13,000 pounds, as you Americans measure things."

"I never realized how big they were until we got next to those four on the way into the park."

Frimby laughed. "They're not afraid of anything—except man. But in the reserve, they're used to smelling our Land Rovers. To them, we are petrol, rubber, and canvas—nothing that would normally pose a threat to them. But when we get close to them, they will sense people inside the Landy long before the humans spot the animals."

"How do they know?"

"Elephants can smell water up to six feet under the ground. I think they can smell you."

"My stinky self?" Karen wrinkled her nose.

"They also communicate with stomach rumblings, called intrasound vibrations. They're too low for humans to hear, but the sounds carry for hundreds of miles."

"They must be able to hear well with those big ears."

"Correct, and some researchers think they can hear sounds through their feet. It's also thought that they communicate with other prides, who in turn communicate with others over hundreds of miles. The elephants may have a network that spreads all over Southern Africa, talking to each other about their environments, availability of food and water, threats, and, maybe, what the local gossip is all about."

"That's amazing." Karen leaned back to enjoy the ride.

Before them, a mountain range stretched to both sides for as far as she could see. Frimby steered for a gap formed by a narrow canyon of tumbled-down rocks. Eucalyptus trees and pines marched the other direction, up the canyon toward the summit.

"Do you have a family, Frimby?"

"Yes. Two daughters. Unfortunately, my wife died a few years ago. Malaria. That makes two deaths including Isaac's. Right now, I am saving money to buy my oldest daughter a bicycle."

Karen frowned. "Your kids don't have bikes?"

"Not in Zimbabwe. My girl walks four miles one way to school. If she had a bicycle, she could make it in much less time. The boys have bikes, but not the girls."

Karen turned to look out her side. So typical the world over. Women treated as second-class. She shouldn't be surprised. Frimby seemed to accept the fate of his daughters but wanted to improve their chances. She looked back at his face and saw determination in the set of his forehead and eyes. Handsome.

She was attracted to him in an unusual way. There was something elemental about him, simple yet proud and competent. Or was it caused by her loneliness and grief? In the past months, she had lost almost all the significant people in her life and failed at her dreamed-for business. Karen recognized her vulnerability, but she didn't care. Out here in the wild of nature with Frimby, she felt renewed and free of her past. She reached over and ran her hand along Frimby's shoulder. He turned and grinned at her.

The road narrowed to not much wider than the Landy. Frimby down-shifted and eased up the slope. To their right, the granite formed an impenetrable wall several hundred feet high. To the left, the edge of the road dropped steeply into the rugged canyon. If they met a vehicle coming down the mountain, one would have to back up the entire way. Karen was glad Frimby was driving. One accidental jerk of the wheel would cause the outer tire to drop over the edge.

Karen felt the temperature cool in the canyon. Plant life grew all around them in rich profusion, creating a green tunnel for them to pass through. Partially hidden behind the shining leaves, monkeys continued to heckle them with screams and barks.

After a half hour, the Toyota crested the mountain and entered an open plateau. From this height they could look backward out across the endless plain. Shadows from retreating clouds left dark stains on the grasslands below.

Frimby gained speed and followed a red sand road. Above them the sky arched across and looked transparent. For a moment Karen forgot about her loneliness, her losses, her failures, and let herself be carried through this expanse of land and sky.

"Can you smell the sweet sage?" Frimby interrupted her thoughts.

The earth exuded the odor. As they wound their way over the immense plateau, Karen spotted a bubble mountain off to the right. This one looked like the shaved head of a Buddhist monk sitting on the ground with his back toward her. When they reached it, she saw etched squares on the sides from a million years ago, which the wind and sun were now pulling down. Karen had a sense of why Africans thought these mountains were magical.

At the far edge of the plateau, the land dried to reveal expanses of sand, scrub bushes, and tawny grasses. To the left a lone reedbuck stood still and watched their progress with large, unblinking eyes. Standing behind her, a large herd of zebra chewed on the grasses.

As Frimby gained speed, the Landy bucked up and down. Karen grabbed hold of the top of the door. When they took a left turn that led down into a depression in the land, Frimby stopped suddenly and pointed out over the bonnet of the truck.

Filling the entire road, a gray rhino blocked their way forward. Twice as large as the Toyota, it lumbered ahead in careful steps, like it was nearsighted. Its short legs seemed unable to support the bulk above them that shook from side to side. The head lowered to the ground as if the straight, three-foot horn was too heavy to lift. A tiny eye watched the intruders approach.

"Is it a Western black rhino?" Karen asked, thinking of her father.

"No. Those are extinct. This is a white rhino."

The male moved off the road to expose a female and a calf standing behind him. The calf constantly stuck his nose under the female's belly, trying to nurse. Her horn was curved, and she moved away from the male. The male followed her and lifted his head to nuzzle her back end.

"He wants to make babies." Frimby laughed. "We will see if she wants to mate or not."

"So, this is kind of like a pickup bar out here? That big dude reminds me of a couple of drunken football boys back home."

"It is mating season, but females can be picky."

"They should be. I can say from my own experience."

The female twisted around with surprising agility and swiped her horn at the male. He backed off, waited a few minutes, and resumed pushing his snout into her behind.

Frimby said, "See how the female gets between the male and her baby? She's worried the male could trample the calf. The males don't care who gets in the way." He inched the Landy closer to the performance in order to get a better view.

"I'm not comfortable with this, Frimby."

"Don't worry. I've got it in reverse."

"So, if she wants it, the guy will mount her from behind?" Karen shook her head. "They're so big, I can't imagine that happening."

The wind shifted to blow from behind them. The minute it did, the male's head twitched, and he snorted several times. Frimby sat up and jiggled the gearshift to make sure he was in reverse. The rhino turned toward the truck. It lowered its head, snorted louder, then charged.

"Frimby!" Karen screamed. "I told you not to go too close—"

At 3,000 pounds, the rhino could easily turn over the Land Rover. He built up speed. Frimby hit the gas and the truck jerked backwards. He accelerated as fast as he could, churning dust from the road.

Within fifty yards, the rhino got what he wanted: uninterrupted pursuit of his girlfriend. Frimby stayed out of range. He explained, "Animals are peaceful unless provoked. Then they all give a warning. If you don't back off, the next step is a false charge, then the real charge. That's dangerous. That male could easily tip us over and use his horn on us."

"Then why did you get closer? That's not too responsible."

Frimby said, "I guess I was trying to impress you. I shouldn't have taken the risk."

They waited, but the courtship didn't succeed. Frimby swung wide, out into the grass to avoid the group. He turned back to the road and kept driving while the bubble mountain looked down on them from the right.

The Toyota lurched over the ancient rocks in the road. Frimby drove carefully, and their seat belts held them in place. He pointed to a plant with pencil-thin green stalks and red flowers on the top. "Fire-sticks. A type of cactus. Most of Africa is quite dry, so the plants and animals adapt to the conditions. Look at the trees, for instance. Many have small leaves to limit evaporation."

Karen felt the sun burning down around them, felt it through her shoulders and along the skin of her bare legs below her shorts. She thought of her father. Away from him, things seemed to work better. She still shuddered at the thought of the shooting in the restaurant. But she also had seen her father at work. He had remained calm and took care of her from the first moment. His job was more difficult than Karen had imagined. And in his cryptic way, he obviously loved her. She found herself looking forward to his arrival.

Chapter Thirty

Pete and Janette had already passed through the small town of Bela Bela when the call from Martin Graves came at ten in the morning. That meant he was calling Pete from Minneapolis at two in the morning.

Graves' voice came through clearly. "Pete, where are you now?"

"Heading toward Sirilima." Pete saw rain clouds massing in the western sky.

"Stop. I'm ordering you to stop right now."

"What are you talking about?"

"The State Department has issued new warnings about that area. Increased activity by the SPLM and the LRA. Both are connected to a long chain of poaching, illegal trade, and terrorism with para-military organizational support."

"Who?"

"Oh, yeah, the Sudan People's Liberation Movement and the Lord's Resistance Army. These are not some guys who grab a gazelle here and there and escape on foot."

"What's your evidence?"

"It's all here in a classified communication from Washington for people at the E-17 rank and above. I can't send you that, of course, but bottom line: don't go there. Our people are convinced there's going to be a massed assault on the game parks."

"But the murder investigation . . . Donahue . . . your career. We can't let his murder go unsolved."

"I know, but your safety comes first. Go back to Cape Town. You and Karen enjoy the city."

"Uh, Karen is already at Sirilima. When will these forces reach the area?"

"It's Monday there, isn't it?"

"Right."

"In four days. Satellite tracking has them moving south at a rapid pace to reach your area on Friday morning."

"Okay. Thanks for the warning. I'll be in touch." Pete hung up. He watched the clouds descend until they merged with the horizon. He didn't say anything to Janette for several miles, then told her about the warning.

Janette glanced at Pete several times as she drove. "We have those two plastic pistols."

He laughed. "Worthless against an army."

"The security forces at Sirilima are available."

"Against poachers, not an army."

Janette said, "We can still do our investigation and follow my plan. We've got three days before they get here."

Pete couldn't risk another encounter between Karen and any law enforcement. Could they make it in and out in three days? The game viewing was the purpose for everything—including his own healing. If he was ever to have a chance to spot a Western black rhino, now was the time. "Okay, let's give it a shot."

"It'll be dicey."

A four-lane paved road ran among farms and slipped through small towns as if the road was a foreign visitor trying to get through quickly and not disturb the ancient settlements. They passed through Polokwane and Mookgophong.

Janette pointed out the sights. "There's a baobab tree. It's a *young* one—at 115 years old." The tree had a fat, smooth trunk supporting the branches that flattened out in all directions like short, deformed arms. "The design enables the tree to conserve water since the branches are so small."

Opening his laptop, Pete decided to search Donahue's secret docs. Maybe there was something that could help them. He scrolled through the accounts receivable. Although Pete wasn't an accountant, he could understand most of the entries. He didn't find anything that looked suspicious. He switched to the accounts payable. Rent, utilities, legal services, salaries. It was all in order. Pete almost switched to a new screen when he spotted a strange name: Matimba Phatudi. The payment was large: 600,000 rand. Almost $40,000. Under the name was an email address. He told Janette.

Without moving her head, she shifted her eyes toward Pete. "Where does he work?"

"Doesn't say who he is."

"Let's follow up on that guy."

Each town they drove through was crowded with vehicles and dozens of people mingling on the road in front of small shops. Since the surrounding villages didn't have refrigeration, people came into town daily for supplies and to socialize. The barber shop consisted of a tin box with no front or back. A barber chair barely fit in the space and was occupied by a man whose shoulders were draped in a white sheet. Janette wedged between trucks, scooters, ox carts, and a pile of elephant dung the size of a basketball to get through the town.

Later, Pete saw a funny mountain to the right. Its sides rose straight up to a rounded top instead of the usual craggy peak so that it resembled a mushroom. He asked Janette about them.

"They're called 'bubble mountains.' Originally, an old volcanic eruption pushed up the rock. Then the tops eroded to leave that rounded shape. Local people think they're haunted by spirits and are holy. *Sangomas*, or faith healers, go up into the caves and offer healing to people. I think they're all frauds."

After two more hours of driving, Janette announced, "Here we are." She turned left onto a two-lane paved road next to the sign that read "Sirilima Game Reserve."

"What's the name mean?" Pete asked.

"It's a Swahili word for 'mountains of mystery.'" She pulled over to the side of the road and stopped. Taking her phone out, she said, "I've got a suspicion the man's name you found works for the government. I'll find out who he is." Janette bent her head and swiped the screen several times. She keyed in words and waited. Her head popped up, and she turned to Pete. "You won't believe it."

"What?"

"He's head of a division in the South Africa National Defense Force, the border patrol." Her eyes, large, rose to meet Pete's eyes.

His back tingled. "Okay," he said slowly. "Let's contact him from Ian's computer. That will really get his attention since Ian is dead." He grinned at his own cleverness.

"Give it to me." Janette used a hot spot on her phone for wi-fi access, composed a message, and sent it. "Everything seems to point to Sirilima, so that's where I think we should work my plan. Let's see how he responds."

"He's powerful?"

Pressing her lips together, Janette nodded. "But remember, he'll see Donahue's email; he won't know who we are."

When she pulled onto the road, a line of mountains appeared before them with an escarpment that ran below the peaks for as far as they could see. These peaks had fantastical shapes. Some were jagged, and one looked like the dorsal fin of a shark slicing through the clouds that hung over the escarpment.

No other cars passed them. Sheltered by the mountain range, the air was silent. Full sun bleached out the land, stripping it of color and leaving only a bright haze that gave Pete a slight headache.

Janette pointed out the window. "Look, over there. A giraffe."

Pete turned to see two more off to the right. They loped beside the car, seemingly unafraid of the humans. Such tall and gangly creatures; their bodies moved with ripples but without any hurry. In an instant, they all pivoted away from the road and used their muscled legs to find shade and food under an acacia tree.

"We'll be there in fifteen minutes," Janette said. "I'll introduce you around, and then we'll drive up onto a high plateau behind the mountains to reach the lodge. I could use a shower and a drink."

"After we start the investigation of Isaac's death."

Chapter Thirty-One

Janette drove through a stone arch and followed a gravel road for a half mile to reach the main entrance of the game lodge. When they arrived, Pete thought it looked like a conference center. The low sand-colored buildings had long windows that looked out onto the game park. Janette stopped at a steel gate, which was closed between the legs of another immense arch.

A soldier stepped out from behind the leg of the arch. He was fully uniformed in desert camo and armed with a Ruger American .45 caliber pistol on his hip. The only thing to mar the perfect outfit was the elliptical sweat stain over his chest. His black face shone in the sun, and he smiled but wouldn't let Janette move. She gave him her identification and reminded him of the call she'd made earlier to alert the officials about Pete.

In a few minutes, he stepped back and saluted. "Welcome to Sirilima Game Reserve, Miss Koos."

She drove into the spacious courtyard and parked near a double door. On the far side of the lot, a dozen Toyota Land Rovers cooled in the shade. The roofs had been removed from the cabs, and the cargo areas were fitted with three rows of seats anchored to the floor.

Pete and Janette got out. A tourist minivan pulled to a stop next to them. Six passengers climbed down through the door. They blinked and looked around. They all wore hiking boots, and some had safari vests with red kerchiefs tied around their necks. Several of their new "Indiana Jones" hats had REI logos on the bands.

The double doors of the building opened and a white man approached Janette. He opened his arms and reached forward to shake her hand.

She turned him toward Pete. "This is the chief administrator, Ranger Trevor Smith."

They shook hands. A man with chocolate-colored skin came through the doors. Smith introduced him as Frimby, his first assistant. Smith said, "I'm sure you're thirsty. Let's get out of the heat."

While Smith led them inside, Pete said hello to Frimby. "Thanks for taking good care of my daughter, Karen. She's been impressed with the game viewing."

Frimby smiled broadly. "A lovely young woman. Very intelligent."

Smith's and Frimby's boots clumped on the polished wooden floor. Pete commented on how beautiful it looked.

"African teak." Smith stopped to answer. "Of course, we have to protect them from those little guys out there." He pulled them to a wide window. In the distance, a red mound of earth about six feet high rose to a point. It looked like a piece of the Grand Canyon had broken off. "Termites. The part you see is only ten percent of the colony. It's a constant fight with them to protect our wooden structures. Do you know those critters are so smart they can control the temperature of the mound by opening and closing windows on the sides?"

The group resumed the march down the hall.

Janette whispered to Pete, "You'll find these men are all passionate about the wildlife here—*all* of the wildlife."

They came to a conference room crammed with the usual table, chairs, coffee makers, and whiteboard. When Pete turned into it, he was startled by the high-tech equipment at the far end.

"Have a seat," Smith offered. "I've got tea, South African wine, coffee, or water." He removed his camo-colored hat and sat before the group. Crossing his legs, he exposed a pair of Merrell hiking boots. "I understand you are here to investigate Isaac's murder. It's been tough on all of us. He was Frimby's brother." Smith glanced at his assistant.

Pete said, "We're also investigating the death of a bank employee in Cape Town that we're convinced is tied to Isaac's death. But we only have a few days to get the work done. Can we start right away?"

Smith's eyes shifted from one person to the other. Finally he said, "What's the hurry?"

"We have intelligence that two terrorist groups are headed this way to attack the park. They'll get here by Friday."

Smith's laugh trailed off. "Those rumors float through here all the time. Don't worry." He faced Pete, but Smith's eyes shot over to Frimby's for a few seconds.

Pete didn't like the answer, and he frowned. "Everyone in South Africa tells me 'don't worry,' but what we've experienced so far makes me worry—a lot. It's not going to happen again."

"We have everything under control—"

"To stop a few poachers. I'm talking about a terrorist army headed this way."

Janette interrupted, "Trevor, could you show Pete some of your defenses here?"

No one moved for a few minutes. Smith grunted and stood up. He walked to the whiteboard and picked up a blue marker. "We've experienced surges in poaching activity here in Africa over the years."

Frimby stood and moved to the other side of the board.

"But then, the price of ivory and rhino horn exploded. That got the interest of organized crime for what they saw as a huge profit center. We can tell they're at work because of the scaling up of the trade. A bust in Hong Kong found over twelve hundred tusks in one shipment. That's two tons of ivory, which represents six hundred dead elephants," Smith explained.

Pete took a deep breath.

"Now the trade has moved to 'khaki-colored criminals.' It's a new breed of poacher. Many come from the wildlife industry or government. They're more educated, better funded, and deadly efficient. They can afford to use equipment like an R44 helicopter. It allows them to find a remote, inaccessible area, drop down from the sky, and shoot rhinos or elephants. They use 'wildcat' cartridges up to calibers of .500. One shot drops even a bull elephant. If they have a platform like a chopper, they can mount heavier weapons, like a fifty-caliber machine gun."

"After the kill," Frimby continued, "they land and use chainsaws to hack off the tusks or horns. Back into the chopper and they disappear. Total time elapsed from intrusion—the shot—to evacuation is less than ten minutes." His British accent added to the seriousness of his words.

Smith coughed. "Let me show you a chart of their organizations. It's like the Mafia." He used a blue marker to draw on the whiteboard. "At the low level, we have the poachers on the ground—or from the air, as Frimby just said." Smith drew several circles on the board to represent the poachers.

"Next you have the transporters. They move the contraband across borders by road or chartered air." He drew a few circles above the first ones. "Above them are a tiny group called the exclusive middlemen, because they sell to the world markets. These are dangerous, ruthless men who have impenetrable linkages to corrupt government officials in critical positions. They have no hesitation to use their networks and power to kill anyone who resembles a threat to the operation."

"Where do the terrorists come in?" Pete remembered the LRA terrorists heading for the park.

Smith tapped the two circles he'd drawn representing the middlemen. "They are here, but instead of just pocketing the riches, they use the money from ivory and rhino horn to buy weapons or radioactive material to make bombs."

"Like cesium-137?" Pete said.

Smith and Frimby nodded.

Janette stepped forward. "Besides the decimation in the numbers, the new level of poaching has disrupted the social structure and sex ratios of the elephant herds. Since the bulls with the largest tusks are becoming so rare, the poachers target the females and younger animals. That leaves lots of orphaned elephants. They are as socially cohesive as humans, if not more so. The orphans become disoriented, causing a further decline in numbers—even without shooting any of them."

It made Pete furious. "So, what are you doing?"

Smith's forehead wrinkled. "Come over here. I'll show you why we're safe from any terrorist army," he sneered.

They all followed him to the far end of the room, where the electronic equipment occupied an entire wall. Several computer stations with monitors lined the curved desk that ran from one side to the other.

Frimby stood in front of a terminal and began to key. Edging Frimby aside, Smith continued opening the program on the computer.

Frimby said, "We upgraded to a low-cost technology—UAVs. Those are unarmed aerial vehicles."

"Drones," Smith said. "But the poachers shot them out of the sky."

"What kind of weapons do they have?" Pete asked.

Smith tilted his head. "All over the place. Some of it's military-grade firearms with an occasional RPG. Air cover for spotting and harvesting the contraband is available to them. But they'll also use low tech. For instance, they can start a fire to divert us from our defensive perimeter to fight the fire."

"So, it sounds like you're losing the battle," Pete said.

Frimby smiled as if he were waiting for that kind of accusation. "Not anymore. Look at this." He took a few steps to the left and stopped in front of another terminal. "Normally, it's a constant battle of technology between us and the bad guys. But right now, we're ahead of them."

Smith interrupted and keyed in some passwords. "And thanks to lending from your bank, we were able to acquire this."

Pete came closer to the monitor. It flickered, and an image coalesced on the screen. It was a topographical map. In the middle an irregular-shaped piece stood out in white while the background area was gray.

"Here's the perimeter of our property." Smith pointed at the screen. "Look at the right side."

He scrolled down through a list: rhino vehicle, fence attendant, Muyumbu motorbike, community vehicle, RB682 Jado, boat 3, RAC 23B4U.

Smith smiled in the reflected glow from the screen. "Here's a good example. RB682 Jado is one of our small elephants. I'll key in on her." His fingers tapped the keys, and the screen shifted to another list. "Latitude -1.56344485, Longitude 30.72723770, mph 4.75, Course 113 degrees. This shows where she is and where she's going. If I move here—" he dropped to a lower part of the screen "—you can see this graph labeled *History*. The yellow line shows where she's been in the past twenty-four hours. It's called situational analysis." He clicked more keys. "Here is a heat sensor map. Each color represents a herd of our animals. We can also use a timeline analysis to track where the herd has moved in the past twenty-four hours."

So far, it looked impressive to Pete. But he'd been in enough war zones around the world to understand that tech superiority was only part of the war. "Will the heat analysis target human infiltration?"

"Yes."

"Why can't you use GPS tracking and Google maps?" Janette asked.

Frimby poked his finger at her. "We've already tried that. But that's easy to hack." He looked at Pete. "We aren't as stupid as you think."

"I didn't mean—"

"That's right," Smith added. "We've installed a 'smart park' system, developed by a Dutch conservation organization. It's called a Long-Range Wide-Area Network, or LoRaWAN. It offers us low-power networking technology that can blanket our entire park at a relatively low cost."

"Can it be hacked?" Janette said.

"No. It's much tougher because the signals are sent across frequencies that constantly change, and the data sent across it is encrypted. It's so simple it's foolproof."

Pete asked, "How do you set it up?"

"We start with twelve gateway towers that we assembled at high-elevation points around the park," Frimby said. "They send constant signals to the gateways, which are then relayed to our central control room right here." He swept his arm around the curved desk. "Our people can monitor the location of tourist vehicles, park staff, and animals, or check on the integrity of electric fences and see if intruders are entering the grid. It's all in real time, twenty-four hours a day. We could monitor every data bird in the park."

Pete backed away from the group. "But this is just like Jurassic Park. Don't you see that?"

Laughing, Smith nodded his head. "Of course. But this isn't a movie. It's real. We can keep the bad guys out and the *dinosaurs* inside. Well, the rhino, zebras, and hippos, that is."

"If you can monitor the perimeter, why was Isaac out there to inspect the perimeter?" Pete asked.

"Uh, his assignment was to check fences. I'll address that later," Smith said.

"I came here to investigate his death."

"And we will assist you in every way we can. It's too late today to get started on your investigation."

It all sounded great, but Pete had his doubts. No system was foolproof. What also struck him about Smith was his apparent lack of interest in Isaac's death. Why was Smith delaying?

Smith led the group back to the lobby. "I've got to 'squeeze a kidney.' I'll meet you outside." He left in the direction of the bathrooms.

Janette pulled off to the side of the hall. She made a call on her phone. In ten minutes, she returned. "That was Jane. I couldn't tell her everything about the sting in case I fail. So she's upset with me. I told her to prepare with the arrangements."

He thought of Karen and took a deep breath. He was anxious to see her again.

Pete and Janette walked out through the double doors. A soldier guarded the door, dressed in full camo with a camo-colored balaclava over his head. An automatic rifle hung from a shoulder strap across his chest. The air had cooled and smelled metallic. Rain was coming. Small tornadoes of dust danced over the parking lot to live for a few seconds before being blown away through the palm trees.

Trevor Smith crunched on the gravel behind them as he called, "I say, you two. I'll show you to your vehicle."

They stopped. Pete asked Smith, "What about Janette's car?"

"We'll take custody of it for the time you are our guests." A smile flicked across his mouth.

Frimby approached them from the opposite side. He stood before them. "I am offering to drive you during your stay, as your personal guide. Please climb in." He pointed toward the Toyota Land Rover's cut-out door with a steel hand grip mounted next to it.

Pete hitched his foot to the short stepladder and boosted into the first row of seats. Janette followed and sat next to him with an unencumbered view. Pete's feet rested on the front end of the spare tire that was strapped to the floor.

The engine rumbled like an animal, and Frimby shifted into gear. "I have enjoyed showing your daughter our resources."

"She's texted me about what an excellent guide you are," Pete replied.

Janette whispered to Pete, "Aren't you glad we dumped the tusks?"

He glanced at her but didn't say anything. The cesium under her car and Janette's sudden shift to get rid of the tusks bothered him. Pete had thought he'd put those worries to rest. Instead, they were back.

Frimby turned out of the reception center and followed a gravel road that led toward the escarpment of indigo mountains. In fifteen minutes, he took a narrow road to the right. The surface changed to soft sand, and Frimby geared down to prevent the "Landy" from wallowing in the tracks. The road snaked over the land with sharp turns.

Janette shouted above the noise of the wind from the mountains, "Over there!"

Pete looked to see a small herd of wildebeest feeding. Heads down, jaws chomping, they didn't react to the Toyota passing. Frimby stopped but didn't look. He said, "Wildebeest are herding animals. They always stick together. When threatened, they mass closer and run over everything in a huge scrum."

Pete pulled out a Lumix digital camera. When they'd finished their photos, Frimby started forward. At the next turn, more giraffes poked above the stink trees. They cocked their heads one way, then the other.

They approached a wide stream with yellow reeds growing along the banks. Frimby slowed before crossing a bridge. "Might be hippos here." A burst of wind blew spray off the surface toward them. They searched both sides of the stream but didn't spot any hippos. Frimby bumped over the wooden slats of the bridge as tall reeds slapped against the sides of the Landy.

At a sharp right turn, he stopped again and pointed to the front. Two dozen Cape bushbacks mingled on a green patch of ground. They reminded Pete of deer in Minnesota, except the bushbacks had arched backs of light brown fur with white dots spilled across the sides. Somehow, impossibly thin legs supported them. When thunder rolled out of the mountains and the herd moved as one, they resembled water moving in the stream.

The canopy above the passengers rattled as the wind picked up. Frimby responded by driving faster. As they crossed an open plain, Janette pointed to the edge of the plain, where acacia trees clumped together. Pete couldn't hear her words but followed the line of her finger. Rain was falling over there, and the dark gray shadows under the trees might have been a pride of elephants, but he couldn't be certain.

Frimby stopped and searched the bush beside them. "There." He pointed.

At first, all Pete could see was a stand of bushes that trembled with something behind them. Four elephants stepped from around the right side. "Oh, my God," Pete whispered as the immense animals lumbered toward the Landy.

Frimby shifted into gear but didn't move the truck.

Three adults and one baby came closer. The baby scampered between its mother's legs so quickly, Pete thought he might be trampled. But somehow, the adult avoided any dangerous steps.

The three humans paused, feeling a little fear and awe at the same time. The herd moved slowly and with complete confidence that nothing could stop them. They came within about twenty-five feet of the Landy and stopped. Two adults raised their trunks and wrapped them around the acacia leaves above their heads. One jerk from a trunk caused the entire tree to shudder.

Small eyes scanned over the truck while their immense ears flapped back and forth. Their gray skin was wrinkled as if it was hundreds of years old. Perched on the backs of two elephants, white egrets scanned the ground for prey flushed out by the elephant's feet.

Pete had seen game in other parts of the world, but this was his first encounter with elephants. He was stunned at the size and majesty of the group before him. After watching them chew for several minutes, he relaxed. A sense of peace overcame him. The elephants must be curious, but they weren't aggressive. No one spoke.

Behind the truck, black clouds descended from the mountains. They were moving fast. Pete heard a deep fertile rumble, and the air quivered all around him. The rain hit a few minutes later, driven into the Toyota from the side and drenching the passengers as if they'd fallen into the sea. Frimby flipped an old blanket toward them. "Use this," he shouted. "We have to get out of here."

Pete and Janette huddled together and wrapped the blanket over their shoulders and across their chests. Pete lowered the brim of his hat against the rain. The clouds finally arrived and brought dusk to the entire land so that he could hardly see anything.

Frimby, up front in the driver's seat, disappeared into the silver rain. Somehow, he maneuvered the vehicle through the mud to reach a higher edge of the plain. The road narrowed but turned to a firm surface. He stopped, partially sheltered by the immense trunk of a fig tree.

Pete couldn't see Frimby but heard him yell, "Welcome to Sirilima."

Chapter Thirty-Two

Albert had finally admitted to a miscalculation in their planning. By early evening, the chopper had extracted them. After a short night of fitful sleep, the two men met in their office.

Cecil slumped in a chair and rolled himself into the far corner under a computer screen. "It's all over, Albert. This mission is dead." He'd even refused Albert's offer of a breakfast bag of Cheetos.

"No. I can't fail. Everything's riding on this."

"If we ever get in power," Cecil said, his chest swelling as he took a deep breath, "why don't we just stop all this cowshit?"

Albert stopped moving around the room.

Cecil said, "It's an old, old story that has always turned out the same way. Killing animals was made illegal. That led to poaching. That leads to corruption in government, because they support some level of poaching for the easy money. Then we get tasked to stop the corruption to stop the poachers to stop the killing of our resources."

"Why talk about this again?"

"It's the same story we have seen in the United States. Prohibition. An utter failure. The demand for alcohol remained high while it was made illegal to possess. All it led to was crime and corruption and black markets."

"We have a mission. It's why we're here at this precise moment in South Africa's progress."

Cecil waved his hand in the air. "Then the U.S. started their 'war on drugs.' After years of trying to suppress the trade in drugs by every means possible, the drug trade is still going on." He stood up. "But we have a solution. If we make animal harvesting legal in prescribed, sustainable levels, we can end the cycle."

"I suppose you're going to add, 'we can tax it.'"

Cecil's face darkened. "What the hell don't you understand? Okay. Here's another idea that's already being tried. It is possible to remove the horn of a rhino without hurting the animal. Their horns are like fingernails, and they grow back. If poachers come after the rhinos but they don't have any horns, there's no reason for the poachers to kill them. Simple solution."

"Try that and the animal rights people from all over the world will come down on us."

"So what? These are our resources. Do we tell Europe how to grow their wine? Tell the Americans how to mine their coal and pollute their environment? Slaughter their forests for cheap wood?"

"Forget it, Cecil. Won't work."

"After we take over—"

"Besides, everything I've worked for, everything I've trained for and prepared has been to aggressively suppress the trade. Don't you see the trajectory I'm on right now?"

"But after you're in power—"

"Even my tribe is protecting the game. King Goodwill Zwelithini spoke yesterday to my people and told them they must be the last line of defense to protect the rhinos. So change the subject," Albert ordered.

Cecil returned to the corner. He ripped open a bag of Cheetos and pecked at them.

"It doesn't make any sense." Albert resumed pacing. "Why would they dump the contraband? What will they show the buyers?" Albert crossed the room, thinking. He stopped. Sweeping his arm around the area behind Cecil, Albert shouted, "We don't need any of this."

"What?"

"This." Albert poked his finger at the terminals and screens. "We utilized technology with excellent execution, but we're forgetting our essential skills." Turning to face Cecil, Albert tapped the side of his head. "Brains. We've got brains."

"Yeah, right."

"Scientific research shows that humans only use ten percent of their brain power. I'm trained to use twenty percent."

"Okay." Orange powder covered his lips. "Now what?"

"Think, Cecil, think." Albert clapped him on the shoulder.

"What about the Captain? He's meeting with an informant named Zoya."

"Right. Zoya works with the Border Patrol. He should have some valuable intel for us." Albert swept his hand toward Cecil's computer. "Get ahold of the Captain as soon as you can," he ordered.

Cecil revolved in his chair and tapped on a keyboard, leaving a message for the Captain. Then he waited for the Google map to form on the screen. When it did, he zoomed in to the area around Johannesburg. "We know they left Jo-burg, heading north." The red cursor pointed to a spot not far from the N1 freeway. "Here's where they dumped the stuff."

"So, let's get up there and pick up the contraband."

"And do what with it? We want the targets, not the ivory."

"Then where did they go?"

Cecil used the cursor to trace a route north along the freeway. "See, there are few roads that leave the freeway to either the east or west. If they continued north, they'd have to follow the freeway."

"How do we know they went north? Maybe they came back to Jo-burg."

Cecil rolled back from the terminal. "Don't think so. They could have ditched those tusks anywhere, even in the city. No, they were going north for a reason, and for some other reason, they decided to leave the ivory. So, let's see what's up here." He pulled closer to the map. He explored rugged terrain that would, if he were on the ground, take months to cover. Albert watched the screen.

"There isn't much out here by way of cities. But lots of tribal villages. Tswana, Zulu, Xhosa. Here's a big village near Mafikeng. We know they didn't reach the border." Cecil chuckled until he saw Albert's face contort. "Well, that means they're still somewhere in this area." He ran his finger in a circle over the screen.

Albert's phone rang. He stepped back to answer it. In a few minutes he said, "That was the ministry. We're in deep shit. They are angry about our expenses. I'll deal with those snakes." He made a call of his own and while talking, Albert left the room.

Cecil studied the area in greater detail. Like an archeologist, he drew imaginary cross-hatches on the Google map and explored each one methodically. His mind drifted back to the anger he felt toward the Western governments and NGOs—nongovernmental organizations.

IVORY LUST

They all had a solution to the animal crisis in Africa—but none of them lived here. It was a form of neo-colonialism. The Western powers still dictated how Africans should use their own resources. The money the West offered—always with strings attached—had led to much of the corruption in the government and a huge black market.

Albert had offered a way for Cecil to act on these frustrations: a new generation of young South Africans dedicated to cleaning up the government and running it for the benefit of Africans—not foreigners.

His eyes swept from left to right, then stopped and came back to a fold in the land. A long stretch of mountains pushed up from the plains to run from east to west. The map showed a green, lush landscape. A few rivers gushed through crevices in the mountains to water a dry plain of grasslands below the mountains.

But what really drew his attention was the name: Sirilima. A game reserve.

Albert stormed back into the room. "God damn bureaucrats! I'm going to sack every one of them. Fools!"

"Albert—"

"They don't appreciate the work I'm doing. Those assholes give me a mission, demand results from the undercover work, and then cut me off at the knees."

"But Albert—"

"Cecil, shut up. We're in trouble."

"What?"

"They've cut off funding. Don't you listen to me, stupid?"

"What does that mean?"

"They want to wrap up this mission. Stop it. That will be the end of my career."

"But all the work we've done. We're so close to breaking open the case."

"Right." Albert chopped the air with his fist. "This also tells me there is someone very powerful operating in the system that wants to shut us down. Well, I'm not going down. Never." He looked up at Cecil with a broad smile. "We've got one slim chance."

"What?"

"Funding won't be cut off until the end of the billing cycle. We have, let's see, four days left before we're closed down. Friday. Our cash accounts won't be frozen until then, and we still have our official identification badges and positions."

Cecil said, "Come here. I know where the targets went."

Chapter Thirty-Three

Frimby waited twenty minutes. The storm roared over the plain, reeds and trees bending before its fury, and then it moved on. Everything in nature straightened up. Above the Toyota, in the fig tree, whydah birds called out, *her-reet, her-reet, her-reet.*

"Ready to go?" Frimby asked.

Clouds followed on the heels of the rain. But these were different: tall, mighty columns of white that sailed on the wind. The sky cleared and painted the far hills a fresh deep blue.

Pete unwrapped the blanket from around them and hung it over the seat in front. It hadn't provided much protection, and he was mostly wet. It didn't matter. The air warmed quickly. Besides, he was tired and wanted to get to the lodge for a drink, dinner, and to spend time with Karen—although he wasn't sure what would happen.

The sun began to set over the peak of the far mountain. Shadows poked at the Toyota as Frimby climbed higher along the side of a new mountain. After ten minutes, he turned left and followed the level road. They reached a section of steel fence with an open gate.

"Don't worry. We only lock this at night to prevent unauthorized vehicles from entering the area of the lodge," he assured them.

Pete smelled pine, and it reminded him of northern Minnesota. At this elevation the air became crisp, cooler. He had to admit that the rough ride and the stiff seats they sat on made the thought of a modern lodge attractive.

Frimby drove past some vegetable gardens, then some outbuildings that sheltered a backhoe and a small tractor. He made a tight U-turn in front of a swimming pool, stopping before the main entrance. A huge cone-shaped thatched roof protected the front door from sun and rain.

They all climbed down from the Landy. Two men came out carrying trays of bubbly drinks in champagne glasses. "Welcome to Sirilima Game Reserve," one of them said as he offered a drink. They all stood under a flamboyant tree that had dropped dozens of orange petals to cover the ground like a welcome mat.

Pete sipped one of the drinks and found it was a mimosa: orange juice and champagne.

Inside, the lobby was paneled in darkened iron ebony wood, polished until it gleamed with reflected light from the lamps around the room. Wooden poles supported the peak of the A-frame roof. Two black women in tan uniforms came from behind the concierge desk. They moved among the guests, welcoming them, while grass mats on the wooden floor muffled the sound of their shoes.

Karen came out of the dining room and gave her father a quick hug. "So glad to see you, Dad." She unwrapped her arms from him and dropped her backpack on the table in the middle of the room. Her backpack looked out of place, something manufactured and modern in a room full of old wood, handmade art hanging from the walls, and a variety of woven grass baskets displayed on the end tables.

Outside, dusk settled quickly. In the lobby, more lamps came on, glowing golden with warmth and light.

A thin man came from the hall to the left. "I am Carl. I will be your host for your stay with us. I imagine you are hungry? First I'll show you to your cabins, where you can dry off and change."

They returned in twenty minutes. Carl met them again and walked them toward the dining room. They passed through a hall of more polished wooden floors and walls. Three steps down led them into a spacious room with many tables. A black iron fireplace took up fifteen feet of the back wall. Two types of meat cooked over the flames: warthog and kudu. Along the adjacent wall, rooibos tea and Nescafé coffee were offered.

The smell of grilling meat made Pete's stomach rumble. He didn't realize how hungry he'd become.

Carl offered, "Dinner will be served in a short time. The bar is over there."

Pete followed his pointing hand and walked down three more steps into a small room with windows that looked out on a lake. On the far side, across the lake and up on a hill, stood the crumbling bubble mountain they'd seen on the way in, reflected across the water. He ordered three gin and tonics.

IVORY LUST

He sat next to Karen and looked outside over the small lake. They didn't say anything but enjoyed the nearness of each other.

Janette came into the room. "We made it, finally." Pete stood, and she leaned into his open arms. "But we don't have much time—"

"Don't think about it. Isn't it peaceful here?"

"Yes."

Their drinks were served to them as they sat next to a fireplace. He re-introduced the two women.

Karen nodded and said, "I'm starving; I'll check on dinner."

After Karen left, Janette said, "Do you believe me about the car?"

Pete hesitated. His emotions conflicted with his common sense. "So, you really didn't know the cesium was stashed under the back?"

"No, of course not. Think about it: would that make any sense for me to do? We were trying to *avoid* trouble." Her eyes opened wide.

He wanted to believe her. After all, to a great extent, his life and Karen's were in Janette's hands. Pete was the tourist in her country. Janette's argument made sense to him, and he had made the decision to trust her when he'd agreed to help with the sting.

He led Janette to a couch that faced the window and sat next to her. Together, they watched night descend outside as the lake and mountains disappeared into darkness.

Carl came into the room. "I've already talked to Karen about this. I must caution you two also. After dinner, you may go to your rooms by the lake. Please follow the covered sidewalk to reach your room. Do not wander off it. That is because there are hippos that come up from the lake at night. You would not want to stumble into one by leaving the path. In addition, please remain in your rooms for the night. Often, elephants come onto the property to play in the swimming pool. Again, you do not want to encounter one in the dark."

"Thanks, but I'm too tired to do anything but sleep," Pete said.

"Good. You will find our lodge is a peaceful and quiet refuge. Well, quiet except for all the animals. But that is Africa. We have shared our land for centuries with many animals and plant life."

"Are you from a tribe here?"

"I am Zulu. My family came from what used to be called Rhodesia. Now it is called Zimbabwe, although many of my tribe also lived farther north in Zambia."

"What kind of work did they do?"

"Mostly cattle farming. Many people worked in the gold mines that, even today, still produce. But my people resisted the lure of money to remain on the land." He smiled with pride. Then he announced that dinner was ready and led them up into the dining room.

Pete and Janette found Karen and sat beside her. Karen had combed her hair, and her face relaxed as she ate.

"Normally, I don't eat much meat, but this is so perfect," Karen said as she cut her grilled kudu into small pieces. Corn and green beans filled the rest of her plate. "This is wonderful," Karen said. She smiled at Pete. "Finally, we're on vacation. The animals I saw with Frimby were beautiful."

"Janette and I have a little work to do. But as for us, yeah, we're free to have fun."

Karen set down her fork and looked closely at Pete. "I missed you."

"And I missed you, too."

"I guess I never knew what your job was really like. It's not easy."

"Sometimes."

"I wish Mom could have experienced this. I feel so carefree here. I watched all those animals out there—" she swung her hand toward the lake "—and none of them keep time, or worry about making payroll for their restaurants, or struggle to pay for their Beamers. We could learn a lot from them."

Pete nodded.

"When you see them up close, Dad, it's like a spiritual awakening. I felt so thankful for the opportunity to experience this. I can't wait to show it all to you."

Hungry and tired, they all ate quickly. Karen said she was going to her room.

After she left, Pete removed Donahue's computer from the travel bag he carried. He booted it up. "Let's see." The screen flickered and colored, and he went to the emails. His throat tightened. Matimba had responded: *who are you and what do you want?*

Janette pulled the laptop around to face her and keyed an answer. She took a deep breath and pushed back her chair. "I think we've got him hooked. Now things get dicey."

"What are we going to do?"

She leaned closer to him and laid out the plan in precise steps.

They took decaf Nescafé coffee out to the deck that overlooked the lake. Weak lights from the lodge lit the area enough for them to find a bench on the far side. Across the lake, a full moon rose in the blackness. Pete hadn't experienced darkness so deep since he'd been in the desert in the Middle East—no wonder the tribes believed in magic. The warmth of the day paused to remain around them. As the moon lifted, a white shaft of light streaked across the lake and revealed the bubble mountain beyond. Hippos grunted at the lake's edge although they were invisible in the darkness far below.

Pete tried to relax. Right now, things were okay. His daughter was safe. Hopefully, he could spend enough time with Karen. He was anxious to see the wildlife, especially a Western black rhino if he could find one. Then they'd get out and go back to Cape Town.

He worried about Janette. How would she get out? What about her daughter's safety if the Border Patrol ever caught Janette? Pete realized that he couldn't leave South Africa until he knew Janette was safe.

She curled next to Pete, under his arm. A breeze puffed up from the lake. "Rather lovely, isn't it?" she said.

"Yes."

They gazed out over the lake, silent in their own thoughts. For Pete, a question hung unanswered—what about the two of them? He certainly hadn't intended to meet someone like Janette and get involved with her, but now that he had, what would happen next? Usually, making decisions was easy for him. But in human relationships, it was never decisive and easy.

Janette said, "I'll ask Trevor or Frimby to take us to the scene of Isaac's death."

"Yeah, first thing tomorrow."

She curled back into his arms. Damp air puddled around their feet and ankles. "I'm tired."

Pete agreed, and they walked, hand in hand, back through the deserted dining room and out to the covered walkways of the lodge. Animal sounds surrounded them. More than simple rustlings and bird calls, these were deep grunts, barks, calls, and even a crying sound like a human in distress. It unnerved him, and he hurried Janette along the path.

A globe of weak yellow light indicated the door to her room. They stopped before it and turned to each other, hesitating. Pete leaned forward and kissed her. A short peck turned into a long, passionate embrace. She smelled faintly of floral perfume, jasmine.

Janette reached behind her and opened the door while pulling Pete inside with her. The lights were off, but the moonlight illuminated the room in a bone-colored haze. A white tent of mosquito netting hung from the ceiling around the bed. She stood beside it and began to undress. Her clothing puddled around her bare feet as she waited for Pete to do the same.

Her breasts were larger than he remembered and her waist a little thicker, and her skin was smoother than he'd thought it was. He studied her face, loving the shape of her nose, and he thought the way her mouth moved when she smiled was the most sensuous thing he'd seen in a long time.

He came forward and placed his hands on her waist, ran them down behind over her butt, and returned the same way he'd come. Her skin was smooth and felt warm in spite of the slight chill in the air. With his left hand, he parted the gauze of the net and opened a gap for them to climb into the bed. He found her, and she moaned with anticipation as they joined together. They explored and teased and pleasured each other as their excitement rose to the breaking point. Pete's last thought before giving in to his passion was how primeval the act of sex was—as old as Africa around him.

Chapter Thirty-Four

Pulling Albert to the computer screen, Cecil pointed at a small name: *Sirilima*.

"So what?" Albert backed away.

"So, that's where they are."

"How the hell do you know?"

Cecil grinned. "I'm using twenty-one percent of my brain." One percent more than Albert claimed. "We know they're involved in smuggling animal parts. Why would they be in the area unless they're going to a place where animals are congregated?"

Albert nodded as he processed the information.

"I'll try to hack into SANParks' website. They have jurisdiction over all the game parks, so I hope to sneak in the back door of Sirilima's system through them."

"Good idea." Albert frowned. "Why?"

"It's obvious."

"Of course."

Cecil scooted back to the screen and began keying. Hacking into the South African parks system would be risky, especially if the site had tracers that would attach to Cecil's probes. The exposure of his and Albert's clandestine work would destroy everything.

The South African National Parks (SANParks) website was huge. Some parts were well designed, and others looked as if high school classes had worked on them for extra credit. The site covered all national parks, such as Kruger National in eastern South Africa, Mountain Zebra, and the Karoo park that resembled the Grand Canyon in the U.S. A total of nineteen parks in all. There were also dozens of other private parks in South Africa. Most were not included in the official website of the national parks, but some were.

Cecil hoped to wedge his way into a program that might give him access to Sirilima. It was a shot in the dark, but it was all he had right now. It would require Cecil to succeed in three separate steps—each one almost impossible.

Albert suspected how difficult it would be and supplied Cecil with coffee and Cheetos. He marveled at the junk food Cecil could ingest and asked him, "How can you do it?"

Crunching on a mouthful, Cecil said, "Ever read the biography of Bill Gates? Know what he lived on while he was on a programming jag?"

"I don't care."

"When Bill was young and started coding, he could go for as long as thirty-six hours. He'd crash for a few minutes with his head on the keyboard. Didn't shower, didn't leave his post. He subsisted on Tang and occasionally proteined with pizza."

"What the hell is Tang?"

"It was a pure sugar drink sold in the U.S. He would sprinkle the powder in his palm and lick it to keep powered up." Cecil turned and smiled to create a large orange slice in his face. "And, by the way, Tang was orange." He turned back to his work.

"Okay, dude. But hurry."

"Like an impala."

While Cecil worked, Albert talked to his back. "I'll develop a plan for our armament requirements, in case they don't cooperate and give us what we need." He ran his hand through his Afro cut. "Even if we're shut down, Cecil, I can get a report with the inculpatory information to the new candidate for prime minister. He can't ignore it, especially now that we know how high this conspiracy goes in the government."

"And you trust him?"

Albert stopped pacing. "Absolutely. It would give him a campaign issue, and we need the positive exposure. Besides, he's my mother's cousin."

Cecil said, "What about Koekemoer?"

"Forgot." He called on his phone and finally reached him.

"Zoya's proving to be elusive," the Captain said.

"We don't have time."

"Should get a meet in a couple days. Trying to get together with that *manspersoon* is like a snake and a mongoose—back and forth." He cleared his throat. "He promised me his intel was dynamite, but he must be really scared."

"Anything less than three days is worthless to me," Albert said and hung up. He barked at Cecil, "What are you doing?"

No answer. Cecil bent over his work, his skin damp and clammy.

Even with the poor sections of the website, he knew the chances of success were low. He bridged across to those sections of the site, the ones probably created by high school kids—dumb ones at that. But he'd left a long trail and therefore was exposed. He doubted the government operators ran regular penetration checks on every node. Still, it would be tough to break in. His only hope was that the kids didn't understand how to create adequate firewalls.

They didn't.

He sent the worms—vulnerability scanners looking for a weakness in the system like bees darting from one flower to another, probing each one for nectar. But, in this case, thousands of them per second.

It took longer than expected. After fifteen minutes, Cecil began to worry. He was too exposed, even for this shitty software. He stood up, bobbed around, looked at the security cameras in the ceiling—as if he could see through their lenses—and dumped himself on the stool again. Time ticked by. Still, the worms hadn't been successful. Cecil spun back to the keyboard. He'd have to abort.

A *ping* sounded from the computer screen above him. He looked at it. The screen blossomed in graphics, scrolling numbers and symbols, and then another ping. Two more. Cecil broke into a wide grin. "Yeah!" he shouted and pumped the air with a closed fist.

He followed up by keying as fast as his fingers would go. It might be a small window that could be closed quickly. Certainly, the breach would be detected. The worm scooped the data and sent it to Cecil's computer instantly. But he needed to kill the worm to prevent the malware from identifying him. Faster. Any remaining worms had self-destructed when Cecil started the abort.

Then the computer screen bonged like a soft bell.

Cecil stopped. He'd been intercepted. Malware had picked up the worm and was checking its identity even as he tried to kill it. The bell chimed again.

Albert came over. "Progress?"

Cecil waved him away. "I'm being chased by their security."

"Like a lion after a zebra?"

"Of course not. It's over the networks, shutting them down. I've got to stay anonymous." It was probably cheap malware, which meant it would be predictable, to an extent. Cecil thought through the actions the defenses would execute. The bell chimed twice more. "Okay, here we go," Cecil said. His fingers blurred over the keyboard. After a few minutes, he sat back, his face wet, and waited.

"What's the problem?"

"Trying to escape without getting detected."

"Why?"

"You'll see."

In five minutes, Cecil relaxed. He had extracted the data he needed, killed the worm, and beaten their defenses. He leaned forward to work on the second goal. The website held data about all the public national parks, and some of the private ones also. Would he find Sirilima on the site? Cecil searched through the complicated data.

He found Kapama, Thornybush, and Sabi Sabi private game parks. Some of them offered safari-like excursions priced at thousands of dollars a week, with gourmet meals and wine. One park claimed they put their customers on the exact spot where Ernest Hemingway had slept. The main reason to include private parks on the site was the advertising potential. Cecil scrolled further.

He found Sirilima. Not much on the site, but at least something to work with. Cecil had no idea how much data he could mine, but he hoped it would be enough to accomplish the third goal—how could they penetrate the park? Most of the private ones had enough money and technology to defend themselves from intruders and poachers. They ran like military operations, and even their armament was up to military standards—all concealed from the tourists, of course.

Cecil looked at the photos. Sirilima was a beautiful park that covered many types of ecological biomes and offered varying terrain. Some of the parks, particularly in central Africa, were flat plains, which made it difficult to enter them without being spotted. Sirilima had mountains, plateaus, and rivers. Any one of them might give cover to a penetration. But the biggest problem still existed.

Cecil knew their perimeters would be heavily fortified with personnel and weaponry. And unless he had a clue to what those defenses were, he and Albert might as well walk in the front door wearing pink bathing suits as if they were on the beach eating at a barby.

"Haven't you finished yet?"

"Don't fucking push me, Albert." Of course, no park would reveal its security. But if a person knew how to interpret their website data, there might be clues.

He spent a half hour roaming over the site. The buildings resembled a lodge from the 1930s, perched on a bluff that overlooked a lake. Beautiful woodwork adorned the walls, and the floors were made of both gleaming wood and sand-colored stone. Next to an outdoor dining area, the owners had built a circular fence of thornbush sticks like a *shamba* in a tribal village. The fence hid some heating ducts. Very authentic touch. A patio sat next to the bar, which had floor-to-ceiling glass doors opening onto the patio.

As he read through the menu about the site, there wasn't anything mentioned about security except to assure tourists the lodge was perfectly safe—causing Cecil to chuckle. When surrounded by huge wild animals, none of the tourists were perfectly safe. Unpredictable behavior was always a threat.

He'd read every word but hadn't found anything of help. Cecil finished and decided to look at the blogs posted by the director of the park, Trevor Smith.

Smith spent a lot of time on elephants. He described how the herd forms a circle with young in the middle, surrounded next by aunties and mothers, and protected by younger males. The oldest and largest female always leads the herd. Scientists are impressed by how intelligent elephants are, and they may communicate through the use of special temple pulsation lobes. Noises in ranges that humans are unable to hear can be heard over miles and probably even penetrate the bodies of other animals and humans. This means that elephants can "read" their interior make-up or even emotional states.

His next blog talked about how elephants "mourn" their dead. If a matriarch has died, the herd will come back to the carcass and bones several times. They use their trunks (which are extended noses) to sniff the remains. They parade by with their young as if to teach them about their ancestors. Smith included a short video of a "funeral." The adult elephants actually looked sad and moved slowly, like humans did while mourning.

But he also warned tourists that even though elephants seemed benign, the African ones have never been domesticated like their relatives in Asia and India. Young African bulls could be aggressive and territorial—you didn't want to be in front of a 10,000-pound teenager with a hormone problem when it charged you.

There was nothing about the functioning of the park itself. Cecil stopped reading, discouraged. He and Albert could go up there and try to figure out a way, on the spot, to sneak in. Really dangerous.

"Mate, we're running out of time. Anything for me?" Albert asked.

Cecil shook his head. One more blog post to finish.

It was an interview with the *Daily Sun* newspaper about anti-poaching efforts. Smith bragged about their new system to track everyone and everything coming into the park, called LoRaWAN. "It's far less expensive than satellite-based tracking, offering an extra advantage to us. We implemented a 'smart park' that's impenetrable to unwanted guests. We make everything in the park measurable so we can predict where trouble might be happening and deploy resources to that point to protect our animals."

Cecil shoved back and smiled. Here was the key he'd been looking for. He was aware of the LoRaWAN system; it was used at parks in Tanzania, India, and even in cities like Amsterdam. Contrary to what Smith bragged about, the system could be compromised. And Cecil had an idea how to do it.

Chapter Thirty-Five

Matimba's phone chirped at seven in the morning on Tuesday. He had just awoken beside Dakini. He learned Koos' car had been spotted going through Bela Bela. "When?" he demanded.

"Yesterday."

Matimba shouted so loudly his children awoke in the room next to the one he shared with Dakini. "Dammit! Why didn't you hyenas let me know immediately?" The youngest child began to cry. Matimba wanted to smash his fist through the wall. If the man on the phone had been present, Matimba would have smashed his face through the wall also. And then beaten him.

Dakini ran her hands across his broad back, calming him.

Matimba took several breaths. "Where were they headed?"

"North."

"Any spotters pick them up at the border? They would have arrived there by now."

"No, sir."

"Then where are they?"

"We suspect they are in the bush between here and the border. As you know, there are many villages where they could hide."

"White people in a black village? They can't hide." Matimba thought of the strange email he'd received from Donahue's computer. Someone had claimed to have the shipment and wanted to exchange it for cash. They even had an exact number: seven million rand, or about 500,000 in U.S. dollars. The gears in his mind clicked into place. Could the email have been sent by the three dogs he was chasing? But how did they get Donahue's computer?

Their demands angered Matimba. How dare they try to bargain with him? On the one hand, he thought of simply capturing and torturing them until they told him the location. Or he could go along with the exchange—that would certainly be easier and faster. Seven million rand was a fraction of what the Chinese buyers had agreed to pay. He rolled over and used his phone to return the email, agreeing to an exchange. Where and when?

He smiled and felt a warmth flow through his belly. After making the exchange, he'd kill them anyway.

Matimba leaned back into Dakini's arms. She hugged him for a few minutes but then left for the crying child. Matimba knew exactly where the three were headed. Sirilima. How stupid of him to not see the connections sooner. The pieces certainly fit. And it worried him, because Matimba still needed to get the shipment by Friday to complete the sale to his buyer—and contain the problem before his operation was discovered.

Dakini came back into the darkened bedroom carrying the newest born. Matimba couldn't help but smile at the sight of her. The previous night, they'd eaten outdoors with the kids in the setting sun. His stomach full and his movements slow, Matimba had still been able to play with them past their bedtimes. Then, after the children were tucked in, Dakini had insisted the two of them play also. Sex had lasted late into the night. Matimba finally fell asleep with the sweet smell of the dried grass around the hut and Dakini's lovely skin.

Now he brushed her aside. He made a new call and barked orders into the phone. "Get the strike force assembled." He stopped and thought about things. "No, cancel that. I'll put together my own team. A small one that I can trust to get the job done. And I want the sniper again."

"Yes, sir," Freddy said.

"Where is that worthless Zoya?"

"He promised to return by tomorrow."

"Dammit! Did everyone think today is a vacation?" Matimba explained about the Sirilima Game Reserve.

"Of course. The dead ranger. We thought it was going to be a minor problem."

"We were wrong, but I think they've made contact with me and want to exchange the shipment. I'm going to agree in order to finish this. Bring the truck, because we'll have to get the bodies out of there." He started to hang up. "I'll expect you here before I get dressed."

"Yes, sir."

In twenty minutes, Matimba had eaten and dressed. Dakini hung her arms around his neck. "Don't leave, my little panther cub."

"I must fix this problem."

"Then you'll come back with money?"

Matimba grunted, "If I don't fix it, there won't be any money—ever again." He turned and walked out through the wide gate. It still seemed like a fair trade: she gave him wonderful children and unlimited sex for supporting her. Maybe Dakini even loved him.

The sun crested the mountains behind him, promising to warm the chilly air. It smelled fresh. But the loose, confident feeling from the night before dissipated quickly, replaced by rage and worry.

He hurried through the village, quiet now as people and animals awoke slowly. A few fires still smoldered. In the distance, the grasses lay on their sides as if to absorb more of the sun that burned them the color of new gold. Just as he stepped around the thornbush fence, Matimba looked out to see a long cone of dust along the road. A red Ford F-150 truck broke out of the dust and skidded to a halt in front of him. Freddy sat at the wheel but didn't look at Matimba.

"How soon can the sniper get here?" Matimba asked as he climbed up into the air-conditioned cab.

"Tomorrow. He's in Zambia on a job but can fly to Jo-burg and get a ride up here."

"Sooner. No more fucking around."

"I'll contact him again."

"The rest of the team?"

Freddy looked sideways at his boss to judge his mood. "Tomorrow?"

"Dammit!" Matimba yelled. "Now!"

"They're moving as we speak."

"Not good enough." He told Freddy about the enticing emails. "I'll go along with them and even set up a trade. But we need a force to take them out. I don't plan to lose seven million rand."

"Should I call up heavy support?"

Matimba shook his head. "That will attract too much attention. We'll do this quietly so not even the game reserve people suspect what's happening. After all, we've paid them more than enough already."

"Of course."

"So, get moving," Matimba yelled.

Freddy gunned the big engine and the truck leaped forward, leaving three of the village's boys staring in fascination. He churned through the sand road on his way to the expressway that led to Sirilima.

"Wait," Matimba shouted. "We can't go in naked. We need the team."

"Do you want to stay here at the village?"

"No. I've had enough of Dakini for now." He laughed.

Freddy pulled off the road into the shade underneath a sausage tree whose long, blood-red flowers hung down on rope-like stalks. He didn't get too close since the smell of the flowers attracted bats, not humans. "I would recommend we convene at the office. It's not more than three hours to the game reserve from there."

"Okay." Matimba sighed. "In the meantime, I'll set up the exchange for our advantage."

Freddy put his hand on Matimba's arm and said, "Don't worry, boss. It's only Tuesday; we have time."

Matimba agreed. His discouragement lightened when he thought of what it would be like to kill the three thieves. There was a looseness in his lower belly, similar to what he felt before having sex. A weapon would be the easiest, but in this case Matimba decided it would be more satisfying to do it with his own hands.

Chapter Thirty-Six

On Tuesday morning, Pete finished the last of the strong African tea. Normally, he preferred black coffee, but in Africa coffee was always Nescafé. So he'd adopted the local tea as his morning drink. He had brought Ian Donahue's computer with him to breakfast in order to complete searching the files. Pete didn't open it. Instead, he watched Karen drizzle her breakfast steak with Wellington's sweet chile sauce and eat more food than she ever had eaten before. A good sign. Janette came back from the lobby to tell them Frimby and Smith would arrive shortly.

Karen looked up. "How long will the investigation take?"

"We'll work as fast as we can," Pete said.

She lowered her head and spoke softly. "Frimby's told me more things. After Isaac was killed, that area of the reserves was declared a 'no go' zone. No one was allowed to go up there."

"What about the local police? The crime scene?"

"Frimby says they are not to be trusted and can be bought off easily. He's mad they didn't do much to solve his brother's murder."

"Well, tell him we're going up there. I must see the crime scene—even this long after the shooting."

"I'm going with you."

"No need for that. Maybe Frimby could take you out to see more game while we look at the crime scene," Pete said. "We could meet up later. Here at the lodge." He thought of all the work he and Janette needed to get done before the fake exchange could happen. He didn't want Karen in any possible danger.

"Perfect. But we must go out together. There's so much I want to show you." Karen went back to finishing her breakfast.

Normally, Pete loved the details of an investigation and took his time. But now he was anxious to finish and get back to Karen.

In twenty minutes, Trevor Smith strode through the dining room followed by Frimby. He came directly to Pete's table. "It's a beautiful morning in Africa. What is your pleasure?"

Pete looked from Smith to Frimby. "The investigation."

"Of course."

"I want to see some more animals," Karen said. "Can you take me, Frimby?"

He glanced at Smith, who nodded. Frimby said, "Sure. Two cheetahs were spotted earlier this morning down by the river in the deep grass. Maybe we can still find them. They're extremely rare."

"I can be ready in ten minutes." She stood up from the table, picked up her backpack, and started for the lobby. After a few steps, Karen returned to the table and leaned down to give Pete a hug. "Have a great day, Dad." She kissed his cheek.

"Uh—sure. Yeah, same to you. We'll meet you back here later this afternoon." He could feel his face flush with surprise and pleasure.

Frimby said, "I'll get the truck ready." He followed Karen out to the lobby.

Scraping a chair back, Trevor Smith sat down. He raised his head to get a waiter and ordered tea. "I know how concerned you are about Isaac's death. We all are—"

Pete cut him off. "We suspect Ian Donahue's death is connected also. We want to view everything you've developed in your investigation."

"The municipal police have jurisdiction in these small administrative divisions. Although the police have been here several times, unfortunately they have limited resources, as you can imagine. We have done our own work, of course."

"Witnesses?" Pete asked.

Smith shook his head.

"Was the crime scene preserved? What evidence did you find?" Janette asked.

"We did the best we could. Isaac left headquarters at oh-six fifty-four to check on the perimeter in the northeast quadrant. Some of our animals perforated the border there. As always, he was in radio contact with dispatch."

"He went alone?" Janette asked.

"Yes. Standard operating procedure for something routine. When he didn't return in time, dispatch tried to raise him on the two-way. No response, so we sent a team to investigate and found Isaac dead in a field with only his backpack. He'd left his radio in the truck approximately three hundred meters from where he was shot."

"With the cesium-137 in his backpack?" Pete said.

Smith nodded. "I'm afraid Isaac was in on a conspiracy to sell it to someone. Clearly, none of us would be carrying anything like that."

"Could you tell how he was shot?" Janette asked.

"We searched the immediate area for footprints, tire tracks, any signs of human presence. Nothing. To the north of where he stood, there is a pile of rocks. Good cover for the sniper."

She looked at Pete, then back to Smith. "Did you find him?"

Smith grimaced. "We tried, but he was long gone. The local doctor who did the autopsy stated that death was caused by the impact of a high-velocity bullet that pretty much obliterated Isaac's skull. Only a hunting rifle or something like it could have caused that damage. Hence, a sniper."

Pete pushed back from the table. The same sniper who'd shot Ian? "Can we see the forensic evidence?"

"Sure. There's not much, but it's all under lock at the municipal police station, and the labs are down in Jo-burg."

"I want to talk with the police who searched the area. But right now, let's get going to the crime scene."

Smith cleared his throat and took another drink of his tea. "Uh, normally we could. But today, we have a problem." When Pete glared at him, Smith continued, "The male elephants are in *musth*—when their testosterone levels shoot up. They become dangerous, unpredictable. A group of teenage males could be fighting or playing, but either way, it's dangerous for the tourists. So, we've temporarily closed off that section of the park until things settle down." Smith grinned.

"But if you drove, we'd be safe, wouldn't we?"

"I'm good, but not that good. You don't ever take on an elephant. Tourists always think they're so Zen and peaceful, and the majority of the time, that's true. But then—" He sat up. "Recently, in the Okavango Delta at a bush camp with tourists who pay four thousand dollars a day for the lodge, one elephant turned on a bloke and crushed him to death for no reason."

Pete twisted sideways in his chair. If they couldn't view the crime scene, if the local police had all the forensic evidence, and if Smith wasn't very cooperative, what the hell could be accomplished? "So, when can we get access to the murder scene?"

"Maybe tomorrow. Elephants are territorial, but their territory is huge. If they move off the spot, we can get in. I'll keep you informed." Smith crossed his arms over his chest.

For all his talk, Smith hadn't really been helpful at all. Pete had an idea. "Okay. In the meantime, I want some things from town. Janette and I will need her car to make the round trip."

"Of course. Carl goes back to the main gate several times a day. You could probably hitch a ride with him."

After Smith left, Pete opened Donahue's computer and resumed searching the files. It took a half hour, but Pete found the evidence of what he'd suspected from the start. Isaac wasn't guilty of any conspiracy to sell the cesium-137. The problems ran far deeper than him. He started to detail it all to Janette, but she cut him off.

"We must get moving."

He closed the laptop and brought his gear into the lobby while they waited for Carl. Pete asked Janette, "Any more contact with the government guy about the exchange?"

She lowered her voice. "He asked me where to meet."

"Great. Tell him we insist on the high plateau we crossed before we reached the lodge. But hold off on the final details until just before the meet. We don't want to give them the location and time to set up their sniper again."

"Okay. Tomorrow is the deadline."

"Yes. If we're lucky, the LRA will run into the Border Patrol guys —after we've left. That should be interesting."

Janette lifted her head to stare outside at the sun glistening on the lawn. "I don't know if I can do—"

"Think of Jane."

She remained still.

Carl came through the front door, smiling. "Ready to go?" He escorted them outside and dropped them off at Janette's car at the administrative center.

IVORY LUST

Pete and Janette drove back into Mookgophong. They parked in the street and walked through the people and dust as they assembled the supplies they needed. It took four ATM machines until they could put together enough cash between the two of them. A new set of clothing for each of them. A pair of field glasses. An air horn like the one Pete used on his boat when cruising through fog, and a two-way radio set. They also added some fruit, power bars, and several sections of *boerewors*.

Finished, they met at the car. Janette said, "I just realized, we must avoid leaving South Africa through the airports."

"What are you talking about?" Pete said.

"The National Defense Force controls all of the egress points in the country. Where are we going to get out?"

Pete understood. He added, "We need the tusks."

Janette's face pinched tightly.

"We have to take the risk. The rangers at Sirilima already searched your car. They probably won't do it again. After all, what will we show to the smugglers to convince them we have everything?"

"Ah, yes. The bargaining chip I kept talking about." She smiled at her own joke, now macabre. Janette backed out of the parking slot and headed south to find the hidden tusks beside the road.

In two hours they arrived back at the main gate to Sirilima. Easily admitted, Janette parked the car in a remote spot in the lot. They locked the doors and, this time, kept the keys.

The sun burned straight down on them, reflecting off the sand so strongly it hurt Pete's eyes. At this time of the day, few of the personnel were present. "I need something to drink," Pete said and went indoors. He found the place deserted except for two technicians in the control room that Smith and Frimby had shown them earlier.

Outside, Janette looked at him. "What? What's that look on your face?"

Pete glanced to both sides but saw no one. "I've got an idea. If Smith won't show us the crime scene, we'll go by ourselves."

Janette frowned.

"The keys are in the truck over there." He nodded toward two Toyotas cooling under the shade of a mimosa tree. Pete straightened his back and walked to the first one. He tilted his head to see the keys in the ignition. The fragrance of the tree settled around them as both decided what to do.

It was a five-speed—which Pete could drive—-but the wheel was on the right side—something harder to get used to. "Get in your car and bring it over here, but park it on the side away from the office."

Janette moved her car. Once she had it hidden beside the Toyota, Pete came around the back end and proceeded to transfer their supplies from the car to the truck, including the tusks. Back into the truck, they turned out of the main gate and churned up the road toward the game park. Hidden by a maroon poncho, all their supplies rested on the back floor under the row seats.

When they reached the river, Pete crossed the bridge they'd been on with Frimby. But this time, he turned left to parallel the river. He stopped on a wide sand beach. "Look at the map."

Janette used her hand to shield the phone. In a few minutes, she had the satellite map pulled up. "Okay, there's a road along the river that forks to the right. Looks like it goes up to the high ridge. From there we get access to the northeast quadrant." She looked up at Pete. "We can do it."

Pete nodded and downshifted to get through the sand. She was obviously afraid—but so was he. He hoped his bravado would give her the motivation to finish the job.

By the time they reached the northeast quadrant, the sun had settled in the sky, coloring the land in bronze shades. On her phone, Janette zoomed into the map. She looked up and pointed over the hood of the truck. "Just over there, Pete. See that open moor?"

He spun the wheel and bounced across the field toward the spot. It took them fifteen minutes to reach the edge of a depression, although to the eye, the distance had seemed closer. On the far ridge, Pete could see a line of trees—probably where Isaac had stood when he was shot. Pete sat back on the leather and started down into the depression.

The smell hit him immediately. Fetid, rotting, the sweet stink of something dead.

"Stop," Janette shouted as she wrapped her scarf around her face.

Pete looked for a place to turn around when he noticed the gray humps scattered across the depression immediately in front of the Toyota. He inched farther ahead.

Bloated like a giant larva, the carcass of a rhino lay on its side. As Pete came closer, a hyena jumped back from where he had been eating the guts of the rhino. The hyena bared its red teeth, and from where Pete sat, it looked like the animal was smiling. He loped off to the right.

"Oh, my God," Janette whispered. She stood up in the cab and hung onto the windscreen before her.

Pete drove slowly past the first dead rhino, then came alongside the second one, avoiding striking its mate lying next to the first one's head. From each snout, the horn had been removed, sawed off to leave a reddened disc. Dozens of animals, Pete estimated. It looked like they had been systematically shot in the head. Hundreds of green bottle flies buzzed over their feast, while the breeze swirling into the depression sounded hollow.

He backed out and curved around the high right side to reach the stand of trees. Both he and Janette stepped out of the truck. His knees felt wobbly, and he grabbed for the side-view mirror to steady himself.

"Oh, my God," she said again. "Did you see—?"

Pete nodded. He wondered if one of the rhinos had been a black Western. His stomach flipped, but he controlled things. The grass up here smelled like the sun. He breathed deeply.

In ten minutes, they had calmed enough to do a search. A broken strand of yellow perimeter police tape attached to a tree flapped in the breeze. A few footprints of deteriorating value still remained in the mud underneath the tree. Pete looked up to see a craggy mound of rocks directly ahead and across the field. The sniper's nest. So easy. "Smith fucking lied to us—the rogue elephants' threat, can't go there. He knew what we'd find, which means he's in on this somehow."

"Let's go over to the sniper's nest. Nothing here."

Janette tilted her head to look up at the sun. "Getting late. We have time?"

"Sure. I'll drive fast."

But Pete couldn't drive fast. He considered it a field, but Janette had called it a moor—and she was right. Rocks, holes, uneven terrain, and a partial road that hadn't been used since ancient people lived in the area. In an hour they stopped at the back side of the mound of rocks. After they had beat their way across the open moor, the shadows behind the rocks felt cool to Pete. They got out and searched over the ground.

Janette shouted, "I found something way out here."

He ran to her. She had wrapped a tissue around a cartridge casing. It glowed bronze where the low sun struck the cylindrical side. Pete took it and tipped it up to read the base. "Can't tell for sure, but it looks like the same caliber as the Tech automatic the cops found at the harbor. God dammit. It's the same killer."

"I found it so far from the rocks, he must have tried to carry out the evidence but dropped this one."

"It's all connected. I finished a search of Donahue's computer files. The horns in the shipment are probably from these rhinos." He explained the evidence Donahue had been gathering.

She looked behind her. "Pete, we don't have much light left."

"Yeah, yeah. Let's get out of here."

The drive back to the main entrance to the park by the river took them two hours. Pete turned left at the bridge and struggled to keep the truck moving through the sand without running off the road. They'd be stuck for the night in the darkness.

The headlights swished back and forth over gray tree trunks. Shapes skittered away from the glow, and pairs of red dots poked out of the darkness beside them. Howler monkeys warned the neighborhood by screeching while they jumped from tree to tree, the pads on their palms silencing them along the branches.

"Can you move bloomin' faster?" Janette said. "Those are bats flying across the bonnet."

Pete tried to go faster, but the conditions were too dangerous. The road lifted as they climbed into the canyon that split a route up to the ridge. It felt claustrophobic to Pete. A foot to the right side, the rocks stood straight up all the way to the top. On the left, he had about two feet of road before the edge dropped off into the steep canyon. Eucalyptus trees marched up the edges of the canyon—maybe they'd break the truck's fall if they went over. He knew how to handle the fear. *Relax. Imagine you're driving on an interstate freeway in the U.S. Lots of room.*

Pete downshifted to handle the steeper grade. The engine grumbled as it worked to get them up the mountain. Now that the sun was down, the air cooled quickly, but a breeze drained the warm air from the ridge above them down into the canyon like a silk shawl.

Janette gripped his arm tightly. "Slow, slow," she cautioned.

Foot by foot, they got closer to the top, where the road opened onto the plateau. At some points, the rocks came so close he could barely fit the truck through. Luckily, there weren't many turns.

Pete stopped to rest himself and the engine. He said, "Almost there."

"*Loop kak*! You don't know for sure."

"Huh?"

"Oh, that means 'shit'! Smell that? Something gamey. Animals."

Pete stopped the Toyota and listened. Other than the clicking of insects, nothing sounded. He felt the great silence of Africa all around them.

"I can smell it on the wind coming down."

"So can I. Leopard? They hunt at night."

"Maybe. Keep going."

He inched the Landy forward, found the solid ruts, and gained what speed he could going uphill. The headlights cast yellow cones in front of them. That helped a little as Pete strained to see the road before them. Out of the corner of his eye, movement in the canyon startled him. He looked but didn't see anything, nor did he hear anything. A few minutes later, he looked again and saw an enormous bull elephant step into the edge of the cone of light, then disappear. "Over there," he whispered to Janette.

She turned her head and gasped. "I saw his eye looking at us."

"So, we should relax?"

The elephant broke the silence. Pete heard crunching sounds and branches breaking as the animal tramped upward. Nothing stopped its progress. "What—?"

"Keep driving. Usually, elephants aren't interested in these trucks."

Pete felt vulnerable in the open cab. The canopy wouldn't provide any additional protection, of course, but it seemed like a little help. He hoped Karen had returned to the lodge and was safe.

The old male kept pace with the Landy as they both climbed the canyon. Pete looked as far forward as he could see and noticed a lighter tint to the sky above the road. The edge of the plateau? He hoped. Once up there, he could go faster and might be able to outrun the elephant if it followed.

"They're mostly curious," Janette said in a quiet voice, trying to reassure both of them.

Pete glanced to the side. The bull flopped his trunk up and down while he ambled along. Then he raised it and bellowed. It was so loud and close, Pete could feel the sound penetrate his body. He gave the truck more gas, and it chugged forward.

The road dipped then rose again, and the headlights jumped upward as the truck came up out of the dip. Pete stomped on the brakes.

Spread across the road, directly in front of them, three elephants stood shoulder to shoulder. They looked pale gray in the light and twisted their heads back and forth as if the light bothered them.

"Shut them off!" Janette screamed.

The elephants' massive heads bumped each other. They bellowed back and forth and struggled to push ahead of one another.

Pete extinguished the lights. The moon must have come up, because from behind the elephants, a faint glow silhouetted the three. They fought with each other and started to come down the narrow road.

"Back up," Janette said.

Pete looked behind them and realized that was impossible. He couldn't see anything and could easily fall off the edge of the canyon. "Are they angry?"

"Can't tell." Her voice croaked. "Maybe playing?"

"I don't want to be in the way even if they're playing." He gripped her arm. "Should we bail out and run?"

"We can't outrun an elephant. Besides, there's the big one to our left in the canyon. We're probably safer in the truck. Remember, they're basically peaceful. Since they don't have any natural predators, they fear nothing—which means they don't have to attack."

"The only predator they have is humans—which is why they may attack us." Pete could hear the *humpf, humpf* as their feet fell on the road.

When they got closer, they snuffed and grunted. Their odor, like raw honey, flowed on the downdraft.

"Don't say a word," Janette said, emphasizing each syllable. "Quiet. There's nothing we can do now except buckle in with our seat belts."

The elephants reached the front of the Toyota and split to walk around both sides. Pete's blood pounded in his ears. The canopy on the truck was high off the ground, but when the elephant reached the side door, Pete was shocked at how tall even this young male stood. It stopped.

Pete couldn't get his breath. He forced himself to take in air, but it came in short, shallow gasps. It felt like he might suffocate. He peeked to his left and saw the head filling his vision. Surprisingly, there were white, stiff hairs that stuck out all over its head. Small eye. The skin looked rugged, old, and folded over on itself in many places, like a dusty old British tent. Then the elephant curled his trunk to reach into the cab.

Janette stiffened and squeezed against Pete.

The trunk was larger than Pete's arm and came forward like a fat snake, searching for something. A yellowed tusk clanked against the door while the elephant pushed further. One curl of the trunk around Pete's arm or head would be the end. This elephant was capable of yanking him out in a second. Pete must have stopped breathing, because he saw flashes of red before him.

Then the trunk slid backwards, out of the cab. Janette groaned and began to cry quietly. Pete's lungs clawed for air. He looked at her, wanting to comfort her with an arm around her shoulders.

Then the other two elephants hit the front end of the Landy.

With only one blow, the vehicle lifted off the ground and crashed back down to bounce a few times. The other elephant bellowed and gave the truck another hit. Even though Pete had the brakes on, they skidded backward with each slam of an elephant's head. He didn't know if they were angry about the humans or were just teenagers having a good time—not realizing their strength.

It was like the elephants were playing with them—teasing them in some way. First one butted his head into the truck, then another took over and gave it another hit. The Toyota inched backward toward the edge of the canyon.

That's when Pete understood what they were doing—driving the alien truck to its doom. "We've gotta get out. Run!" he screamed at Janette.

"No. Look at them. We wouldn't get ten feet." She clung to the steel roll bar over the cab.

"I'm not—"

The back wheel fell over the edge with a sickening drop like cresting the top of a roller coaster. As the metal undercarriage scraped over the rock, it screamed in pain. The front end tilted up in the air, balanced for a moment.

"Pete—!"

The elephants surrounded the wounded Toyota and battered at the sides. Sensing victory, they bellowed to each other. They moved faster and kept hitting. The Landy teetered on the edge, and the closest animal raised his trunk to push against the uplifted wheel. Since its trunk had 150,000 muscles bundled inside and could lift up to 700,000 pounds, it only took a slight shove. The Landy tumbled down into the canyon.

The Toyota rolled over and over along its side as it crashed through trees. It finally stopped at the bottom full of soft dirt. Luckily, it didn't burst into flames. When the noise stopped and the dust dissipated, one elephant padded to the edge of the road. He looked over and saw the wreck but didn't see any other movement.

Chapter Thirty-Seven

After reading Trevor Smith's interview with the *Daily Sun,* Cecil knew how to beat their system and get access to the park. Excited, he stood quickly and felt dizzy. All the diet Cokes he'd drunk had finally hit his brain. "We'll need more—" He folded back onto his stool. It was Tuesday, late morning, and Cecil knew they'd have to act fast.

"More what?"

"Equipment. Three detonation charges, plastic tie-offs, duct tape, stun guns."

Albert frowned. "What the hell are we doing? Attacking Government House?"

"No. We're going to find our three friends. But you remember what the military dude was like. We need more firepower in order to subdue him."

"You sure about the location?"

"Even with Google maps, I can't spot them. But I know that's where they went."

Albert sighed. "We don't have much of a plan beyond that, so, okay. The SUV should be at the back loading dock. Let's get the gear assembled." He started for the door. "We'll lift off in twenty minutes."

"No. Because of their security system, we have to wait until dark. And we need a large panel van, not the SUV." When Albert hesitated, Cecil added, "Just in case."

Albert shouted, "Don't start giving me orders."

By five o'clock that afternoon, they had provisioned a large, unmarked van. After changing to camouflage clothing, Albert grabbed his red beret. They stopped long enough for a fast food dinner of burgers at a chain restaurant called Steers. Cecil drove north out of town on N1. It was a relief to leave Jo-burg, where low clouds covered the city in a heavy, steamy blanket. The small towns passed quickly: Bela Bela, Polokwane, Mookgophong.

In three hours, they reached a turnoff from the expressway. A large sign on the right side announced Sirilima Game Reserve. Cecil slowed and made the turn. A two-lane asphalt road led straight into the fading halo on the horizon.

On either side of the road, they began to notice big game even before they entered the reserve. An eland stood in a field with an upraised head crowned by two black, twisted horns, like a cow. And a small herd of Thomson's gazelles turned like a flock of birds on the ground, either to avoid the van or just because they enjoyed the freedom to run and jump.

After ten more miles of driving, dusk settled around them. The brown land that had been studded with green trees now looked monochromatic. The temperature dropped. Cecil pulled off the road and stopped the engine. "We wait for a while."

They switched seats. "Which way should we go in?" Albert asked.

Cecil lifted his laptop from behind the passenger seat and opened it on his knees. He booted it up and went to Google Maps again. He studied the perimeter of the park.

"How can you see anything in the dark?"

"I recorded these in daylight." He smiled at Albert. "What we're looking for won't move. For instance, here is the lodge with some outbuildings. It's set next to a lake. That's where our targets will be. More importantly, we need to attack at least two of the towers. Question is, which ones?"

Albert leaned over from his seat. He watched as Cecil moved the cursor over the map. "Are you going to hack into their security system?"

Cecil shook his head. "That's the beauty of their system—it's so low-tech there's nothing to hack into. Before we can capture the three, we have to accomplish two goals. One is to assume the identity of one of their vehicles in order to get access to the park. Once inside, we must dismantle at least two towers to knock down their tracking system. Of course, they will respond with deadly force, so we have to be prepared to move quickly, grab our targets, and get out with them."

"Right. The stun guns, restraints, weapons."

"Just the dude. The ladies will be easy for you."

"Of course. I may charm them into coming with me." Albert cocked his head at an angle and smiled.

"Yes, well— We should blow towers that are close to the lodge so we have time to make our grab. Let's see." The screen glowed green against his face. "It's hard to make out what's a road and what's a game trail. All the roads are dirt. And the trees obscure some of them. Damn. We may have to improvise on the ground."

"I've done that all my life."

"Here." Cecil put his finger on the screen. "Here's where we go in."

"Why?"

"I took some time-lapse shots of the park earlier. If I lay them on a spreadsheet, you can see patterns emerge. Mostly, patterns of the vehicles or animals that cross the area. This herd of elephants moves in a circular pattern over a radius of about two miles. Big herd. And here's a vehicle I've watched that moves about every two hours on a schedule. We want to be in that one when it crosses into the park next."

"Why did you choose that vehicle?"

"Because this one occasionally goes deeper into the park. Remember, we need stealth to help us. We can't fight their security by ourselves. So, we sneak in and use their equipment to avoid alerting their tracking system with an alien vehicle like our van."

"Good work. So we can reach the bogies at the lodge."

"—without causing their tracking system to note a discrepancy. I've identified the approximate times one of the vehicles moves. I call it 'Vehicle A,' so we must be there in time to intersect with it. If our timing is off, we're fucked."

"We still must attack the towers?"

Cecil's voice took on an edge. "We have to get back out, remember? Two reasons for the tactical plan. One is to create a diversion away from any problems we may have obtaining the targets. Two, it's such a low-tech system, the only way to dismantle it is also low-tech."

Albert leaned back in his seat and smiled. "I've trained you well, Cecil."

Cecil didn't answer. Even a month ago, he'd been anxious to take on more combat roles. But after seeing the weapons they'd brought to the border and after the way he'd been taken down by the American guy, maybe it was better for experts like Albert to handle that work. Cecil would pretend to be a committed warrior. But he couldn't cross the line into violence no matter how much he wanted their final mission to succeed.

When he thought ahead to the interrogation of the three targets, Cecil began to worry. If they wouldn't talk quickly, what would Albert want Cecil to do? Albert was fully capable of killing, torture even, without hesitation. He was a true believer in the cause. As Albert had quoted the Bolsheviks and Lenin so often: "The shedding of much blood purifies the cause and, therefore, is necessary."

"Which towers?"

"Huh?" Cecil blinked and looked through the windshield into the darkness before them. He went back to the screen and moved the cursor until he found the outer perimeter of the park's defense system. "These two. They're the closest to each other."

Albert's voice pitched lower. "This is what I was trained for. Everything's coming together, just in time." He traded places with Cecil and started the van. "Let's move out!"

"Their vehicles move during normal working hours. If the tracking system spots someone moving at an odd time, we're in big trouble." Cecil studied the map again. "Okay. Go forward and take the first right. It looks like a sand road."

Albert headed into the gloom of the bush. He dropped off the pavement onto the road while the van wallowed from side to side as the tires fought to gain traction in the sand. He down-shifted, the engine groaning with the effort. But they continued forward. His face glistened in the reflected light from the dash. "Can't you use the fucking GPS?"

"Of course. I input the lodge's location, but these back trails aren't like driving around Pretoria in the daylight."

They followed the twisting road deeper into the bush. At times, driving was easier on the straight portions. Albert shifted and braked constantly as conditions changed. The worst thing would be to get stuck. "How's the time?" he called over to Cecil.

"If we can maintain this same velocity, we'll be okay. Vehicle A will be at a crossing point about nine fifteen."

"Shit. This is tough going."

Since they were outside the light pollution from a city, the bush was totally black. Up through the trees, they could see stars coming out. To the sides of the van, dozens of red eyes watched their slow progress. At night in Africa, the animals take over. Their acute senses of smell, hearing, and even taste give them an immense advantage over humans, who wallow around with weak eyes and little ability to smell anything.

The feeble cone of the headlamps before the van occasionally illuminated bounding animals. Antelope? Zebra? Impala? Albert made a sharp turn under an ebony tree. Calling down from the branches, howler monkeys taunted them.

The road straightened out and began to climb. That made Cecil relax since they had to get over the mountain escarpment to reach the high plateau that stretched around the lodge to the far side of the property. He looked at his watch. Eight thirty-six.

The forest closed around them. Dense. The heavy smell of humidity came in the open windows. Cecil knew the plant kingdom was even more prolific than the animal one—which was immense in Africa. The trees and vines and scented bushes could all sense the presence of humans. They probably even communicated with each other over this fact. After all, plants had preceded humans on earth by millions of years. Wouldn't they survive long after humans were gone?

By eight forty-seven they broke out onto a wide plateau. By now, the stars were fully out and provided a bone-white glow to the land before them. The road widened, and Albert was able to gain speed.

As they left the forest for the clearing ahead, they heard the barking of baboons echoing off the rocks below. At first, it sounded like the bark of a seal in a zoo. But then, the pitch of the sound changed and resembled a human crying for help.

To the left, a plateau stretched for as far as Cecil could see in the feeble light. Above, he could make out thin clouds moving swiftly. To the east, a full moon rose, and its light flooded the plateau as if morning had come early.

They drove along the far side of the plateau into dense forest again. The road snaked up and around high hills, dipped into the valleys, and challenged Albert the entire way.

"We're almost there," Cecil announced.

"Good."

The van bumped over the edge of an asphalt road. Albert stopped. "Which way?"

Cecil pointed to the left. "Slow." Two trucks passed them going the other way. "Technically, we're still outside the park."

"Time?"

"Uh, nine twelve."

"Shit." Albert gave it more gas, and they shot down the road.

When Cecil yelled at him to pull off into an opening beside the road, Albert tilted the van far to the left in order to make the turn. Tires squealed. He slammed to a halt once inside the spot.

"Way to be stealthy."

"Shut up. What the fuck are we doing?"

"Pull under that wattle tree. Turn off the engine and wait. The park vehicle stops here and radios ahead to the gate." He looked at his watch. Nine eighteen. "Too late."

"Why don't we just infiltrate ourselves? I've done it before. Lot easier than taking a truck into the place."

"Albert, we're screwed." He started to fold his laptop when the park vehicle stopped near them. Cecil hammered Albert on the arm and pointed to the park van. "We're in luck; he's late," Cecil whispered.

"That's them?" Albert looked back and forth. "Let's take 'em down."

They slipped out of their van, both armed with official weapons this time: Browning Black Label Pros, thirty-eight caliber. Albert also had a Taser X26 strapped on his belt. One of the most powerful of stun guns, it was only available to law enforcement. He took the lead. They edged along the tree line to come up behind the park van. Inside, two men laughed about something.

"I'll flank right and take out the passenger. The driver's easier since he's pinned in by the wheel." He pointed to the right side of the van as if Cecil didn't know directions. "On my command."

"Oh, come on, Albert. It's just us."

Albert scowled and moved forward.

Cecil hung back for a second to let Albert lead. When Cecil heard the door open and Albert shouting, Cecil did the same on the driver's side. The passenger squinted in the dim light from the overhead in the cab. Albert got the big gun in his face as soon as the door cracked open.

"Get out! Get out!" Albert screamed. When the passenger hesitated, maybe confused, Albert slapped him on the neck with the Taser. The man's body jerked into a convulsive spasm and stiffened like a plank of wood.

The driver slid out quietly. "Don't hurt me."

Using the Browning, Cecil waved him toward the back. When they rounded the van, Albert was dragging the passenger toward their own van. Cecil marched the driver behind them. The two park men didn't resist the wrist ties, ankle ties, and duct tape across their mouths. Cecil transferred their equipment to the park van. Then Albert reached down and heaved each man up into the back end of the rented van and closed the door.

"Let's go," Cecil said, glad there hadn't been any more violence. "They were late, so we have to make up the time. I hope to God they got entrance permission before we showed up."

Albert drove fast. In a few minutes, they reached a checkpoint. There was a row of steel fencing on either side of the road, but it ended fifty feet away. Two guards stood at a shack that didn't have any windows.

Albert slowed the van and drove with one hand. In his other, he carried the Browning.

When the guards saw the familiar van, they waved and went back to lighting cigarettes.

Cecil flopped back in the seat. "Goal one accomplished. The rest of them get harder."

"I can handle it, partner."

Opening his laptop, Cecil found the location of the two towers he'd selected. "Turn right in two hundred meters."

The road narrowed, and the forest closed in tightly around them. With all the leaves above them, the moonlight didn't penetrate. The headlamps worked but were feeble in the immense space of nature around them.

Vines and branches brushed the side of the van. Albert had to slow down.

"Their security will give this van some leeway in its movements before the red lights start going on at headquarters. We've got to get the tower down as soon as we can."

"I'm trying. Look at this mess. How can we get through?"

The road forked, and Cecil told him to turn to the right. They drove for fifteen minutes before Cecil said, "Might be the wrong way."

"Might be?" Albert mocked him. "I'm getting sick of your orders. I'm in command. Where is the lodge?"

"I think it's straight ahead, but we've got to blow the towers."

"Fuck it. I'm going for a quick grab of those bastards, then get the hell out!" Albert speeded up, and the van bounced up and down over the road.

"Albert! No. We can't make it out before they detect an anomaly in their system. You have any idea of the firepower these dudes have?"

"I can make it. Watch me."

For another ten minutes, they drove in a downhill route until they broke out of the forest onto a wide plain. Albert stopped at the edge. "This looks familiar—"

Cecil scrolled through his screen. "Let me check GPS. Not sure—" His fingers moved fast. He could smell sweet sage outside the window.

"Naw, this is it. The lodge is over that way." Albert turned his head to search the terrain. A road led off in that direction. He cranked the wheel around and followed the lone road.

"I can't confirm the route," Cecil warned.

Albert slalomed back and forth along the road. Instead of finding the lodge, they came to an escarpment at the edge of the plateau. Albert stopped. "I don't remember this." The headlamps shown out into darkness—there was nothing directly ahead of them. They perched on a cliff. Both of them got out to walk forward in the light of the lamps. The smell of sage was even stronger here.

Cecil reached the edge first. At that angle, he could see the road as it fell down into the darkness with a rock wall on the left and the canyon to the right of the road. Eucalyptus trees grew tall out of the floor of the canyon. He turned to Albert. "Not this way."

"Why not? Remember, we came in behind the lodge. They're next to a mountain and a lake. I say the lake is just over this edge, and the lodge will be waiting for us on the far side." He strode back to the van and got inside.

"I think we're lost." Cecil paused. He couldn't leave Albert; Cecil would be discovered by the security forces, captured, and finished before morning. He walked back to the van. In the darkness behind them, he sensed something. Something alive and large. Noises reached him: snorting, hooves on the dry ground. Cecil reached below the front seat and extracted a powerful flashlight. When he swung it behind the van, he could make out a huge herd of animals. Wildebeest—benign beasts — and he relaxed while climbing into the van.

"Here we go," Albert said as he crept over the edge. "Easy."

The van started downhill. It was so narrow, the van filled the width of the road. If another vehicle came along, someone would have to back up the entire way.

When they'd descended about a hundred feet, Cecil heard crunching among the eucalyptus trees in the canyon, faint but getting louder. He spotted two sets of headlamps at an impossibly steep angle down below them, coming up the same road Cecil and Albert were on. Cecil gripped the handhold on the ceiling of the van. "See those lights?"

Albert rode the brakes as they inched down the incline. "Yes, but we can't turn back now, can we?" He laughed. "They will have to give way to us."

"This is stupid. The only vehicle out at night would be a ranger. Let's get the hell back up."

"You're right. Okay."

Exploding into the light cone, three elephants, each one the size of the van, raised their trunks and bellowed. The sound was so loud, it hurt Cecil's ears. Albert screeched to a halt. The elephants came at them, up the road, on the run. They pushed each other as if they competed to see who could smash the van the quickest. They grunted with the effort.

"Back up! Back up!" Cecil screamed at Albert.

He revved the engine but forgot to put it into reverse. It seemed to infuriate the elephants. They came closer, their heads bucking up and down as their feet fought for uphill traction while their ears flared like sails straining to pull them forward.

Cecil thought of jumping out and running, but he'd heard too many stories of elephants stomping people to death. Better to have the shelter of the van, at least. He crawled into the back. Maybe the seats would provide some protection. A deeper, mature bellow penetrated the thin walls of the van. "Reverse! Put it in reverse!" Cecil screamed above the roar of the engine.

Fear shot a burst of heat through his body. He remembered being with his grandfather when they'd faced an attacking crocodile. But now, there wasn't a body of water from which Cecil could summon his ancestors for help. Cecil closed his eyes and felt as scared as a kid.

Chapter Thirty-Eight

Early Thursday morning, Freddy picked up Matimba from his home in Pretoria.

"You rescued me just in time," Matimba said. "Sabella had awakened and remembered the soccer uniforms I didn't buy."

"Soccer is important."

"The prestige of my children in the community is more important to her than the sport."

Freddy nodded. "Of course. It is so with my wife also. When are you going to get the uniforms?"

"As soon as this damn shipment gets off and the Chinese pay us. I'm getting more pressure from Sabella than those bastards."

Freddy drove from the suburb into the city to one of the poorest areas of Pretoria, called Tshwane. Waiting at a warehouse next to a public park of dried dirt, four men, loyal to Matimba, stood around a large panel truck, smoking cigarettes. Freddy slid to a stop in a swirl of dust. One of the men coughed and threw away his smoke. He jerked his head toward the back end of the truck. When Matimba and Freddy approached, the man opened one side of the tailgate to reveal a forklift to be used to load the shipment of ivory and horns at the exchange.

Freddy drove the Ford F-150 north out of town to reach Sirilima as soon as they could. In the cargo area of the truck, a fitted plastic cover hid a cache of weapons, personal restraining devices, Kevlar vests, and communication equipment for the team behind them.

"Where's the damn sniper?" Matimba asked Freddy.

"Should be here any time." Freddy kept his lips tight to avoid looking like he was smiling at this tense time.

"In the last email, the thieves want to meet on a plateau above the mountain ridge."

"I've been up there."

"They will give us more directions when we get there."

"I don't like it. How can we position Swart? Or the team?"

Matimba grunted. "Fuck, I don't know. But remember, these three are amateurs. We can handle them easily."

"And the shipment?"

"It's heavy. I assume they'll need a truck. So, we look for a truck when we get there."

Freddy nodded.

By mid-morning, they reached the entrance to Sirilima Game Reserve. With their Border Patrol identification, the guard granted them admission, and Freddy followed the curving drive to reach the main office and reception center. Trevor Smith was waiting outside the front door. He bounded off the step and came to the truck.

Before Matimba could get out, Smith welcomed him. Smith looked back and forth across the parking lot and pulled the two quickly through the front door. He led them to a back conference room. It was deserted until Frimby walked around the doorway. He stopped abruptly.

"These are our colleagues from Border Patrol," Smith announced.

Frimby shook hands around, stood still, and didn't leave.

"What do you want?" Smith barked at him.

"Uh, it's one of our vehicles. The Land Rover, license RX CV143. It was here yesterday afternoon; now it's missing."

Smith shook his head. "How could that happen?" He glared at Frimby.

"I accounted for all of them before I went off duty yesterday."

"Well, don't stand there with your finger up your ass; go find it," Smith yelled. "Check on the computer, get out in another vehicle and find it. This doesn't look good for you."

After Frimby left, Smith turned to Matimba. "What the hell are you doing here? If anyone finds out what we're—"

Matimba waved his hand. "Don't worry. We're here on a special mission that doesn't concern you. National security, you know. We're searching for three people—one local woman and an American with his daughter."

Smith's face brightened. "They're here. Staying at the lodge. Do you want me to bring them in for you?"

"No! Tell me what they know about our operation."

"Uh, nothing, really. They're here from the bank to investigate Isaac's death. Wanted to see the crime scene, but I gave them a fake story about how we couldn't take them there. Too dangerous."

"Good work. I want clearance for my vehicles to go into the park."

"Of course, but I'll have to work fast to get you access. Without that, my rangers will interfere with your mission."

"Do it."

"Well, since you didn't tell me you would be arriving, which would have given me time to maintain secrecy, it's going to take a lot of work."

Matimba sighed and turned to Freddy, who stepped forward with a cheap plastic folder sealed by a zipper. The words "Woolworth Department Stores" were printed on the side. He handed the bulging folder to Smith.

"I don't want to hear another God damn word from you." Matimba used his "Cape buffalo" voice and got the response he wanted. "I need a secure space here for my men."

Frimby came back into the room. In spite of the angry look Smith gave him, he reported, "I looked at all the tracking data for the vehicle. It seems to be stationary on the road up to the plateau and the lodge. In the canyon."

Smith frowned. "Not moving? Strange. . . Well, go get it."

Smith led Matimba and Freddy down the hall, past the termite mounds, to a small office in the corner. There were two computer terminals on a counter and a coffee maker on top of a file cabinet. The pot was full of coffee that smelled burned. "What can I help with?"

"Show us a map of the plateau above the mountain ridge," Matimba ordered.

"That's not the kill site."

"I don't care. I want to see how to get up there and look at the terrain."

"Yes, sir." Smith turned to one of the computers. In a few minutes he had a map of the plateau. He pointed out the spot Matimba wanted to reach. "Be careful. To get there, you must drive up a steep, narrow road. Only one vehicle at a time can make it."

"You saw the bigger truck I brought. Can it make it up?"

Smith shook his head. "It'll be tough."

"Okay. Once up there, what's it like?"

"You can see the large herds that graze up here this time of year. Springbok, zebras, wildebeest, and some rhinos." Smith rotated the map for a different view. "Try to avoid this ridge. It runs along the precipice of the mountains. On this side, it drops off all the way down to the valley floor. Roll off into that and your last memory will be of the baboons coming after you. When are you leaving?"

"I'm waiting for a message from someone. I don't know when we'll go. My men would like some coffee and donuts while we wait."

Smith stood up. "Of course. But we've had intel about a possible terrorist attack on Sirilima."

"I know."

"LRA. Tomorrow. I'm sure our security forces can handle them. But there's always more cesium available. Usually, that's all they want."

Matimba took a deep breath. He turned to Freddy. "Tell the men we'll be moving into position as soon as possible."

"But what if we don't have an exact rendezvous site?"

"We move up there anyway and reconnoiter the terrain. Set up as best we can. Is Swart here yet?"

Freddy checked his phone. "He's turning off N1 as we speak."

"Good. I want him in position when we set up."

"Still no message from the three?"

"No."

"Something odd here." Smith interrupted them and ran a hand through his crumpled hair.

Matimba walked over.

"See." Smith pointed at a spot on the computer map. "There's erratic behavior from this vehicle."

"Is it yours?"

"Yes. I've identified it as a small panel truck. It entered the park on schedule last night. But it's in an unauthorized location now. Something's wrong."

"Why tell me about it?" Matimba stepped away from the screen.

Smith looked over at him. "Because it's on the plateau."

Matimba looked back at Freddy, then said to Smith, "Then get that fucking van out of there, now!"

"Of course, sir. I'll scramble a security team to investigate and occupy it, if necessary." Smith hurried toward the door.

"And don't forget to send in the coffee and donuts right away," Matimba shouted after him. He turned to Freddy. "Can you read that map?"

Freddy peered at the computer screen. "Easy." He sat on the stool before it and used the cursor to rotate the map. "I suggest we place Swart over here by the brush. There's one road that goes along the plateau. Right here. Position the men on the quadrants. It will be easy to conceal them behind the rocks." He looked up at Matimba for approval.

Matimba's shoulders bunched. "It should work. At least, it will give us the maximum control of the terrain." He grinned. "It'll be like shooting sheep. Except for the ones I want to do myself."

"I hope the truck can get up there."

"Yes." Matimba looked at his watch. "Get the men fed, and then we leave immediately. Contact Swart and order him to meet us up there."

Chapter Thirty-Nine

Like a kid in a horror movie, Cecil had lowered his head onto his chest and closed his eyes, waiting to be crushed. It never came.

After a few minutes, Albert let up on the gas pedal. The calls of the elephants were muted, fading into the distance. What had happened? Cecil crawled into the front seat, using the light of the moon to help him.

Albert was folded over the steering wheel, his face wet in the glow from the dashboard lights. He breathed heavily. "I don't know—I don't fucking know. I saw them charge, but then, at the last minute, they stopped and went down the road. God damn! That was too close."

Cecil twisted around in the seat. He saw a herd of wildebeest, their hairy backs bobbing as they walked away. "The herd. The elephants didn't want to run up against the herd."

"Maybe. I don't fucking know."

"Albert, we're okay." Cecil laughed in a crazy way, like someone who has seen death pass him by and now tingles with life. He found the water bottle and drank half of it. He stepped out of the van to feel solid ground and walked around in a small circle. Albert did the same.

"Okay, Cecil, back on mission."

Cecil took a deep breath. "Like I told you, we're going the wrong way."

"But where the hell do we go? In the dark, I can't see a thing." He backed the van up onto the plateau.

"Maybe we should try to sleep in the van. Chances are, the security is thin right now and won't pick up on our location. We'll find the lodge in the morning."

*   *   *

Wednesday morning they both awoke, stiff from sleeping on their equipment in the back of the van. They found a power bar, a bag of Cheetos, and several bottles of water for breakfast. While Albert chewed on the honey and raisin bar, he said, "This is good training for you, Cecil.

Live off the land. Rough it on a mission. No coffee out in the bush." He laughed with his mouth full, then climbed out the back end to urinate.

"I can handle this better than you think. We need to get going soon before security identifies this van as being off its assigned route and comes out to investigate. We must blow the towers."

"No. I want to grab the targets first, then blow the towers on our way out of here."

Cecil looked at his watch, calculating the distances and the possibility of how quickly the park's defense system would respond. "Okay. I'll agree under one condition. After the grab, we blow the towers where we came in."

Albert scowled.

"That is the closest point from the lodge for egress. There is a tower to the south about three kilometers. Once it's down, we've got a free pass to get out."

"You're the techie. Just give me the targets and I'll get the information out of them."

Albert swung the van around to face the expanse of the plateau. He gunned the engine, and they bumped over the dirt road toward the bubble mountain they had wound around the previous evening. They spotted small clumps of game spread across the land. As the sun rose, shadows shortened and the land took on a hard shine.

The road wound up and over the land and finally led down again into a dense forest of pine. They rattled over a narrow bridge spanning a creek that still dribbled with a little water left in it. They spotted three giraffes grazing on leaves in the high branches of an acacia tree. With heads tilted to one side at the top of graceful necks, the giraffes watched the progress of the van. Long eyelashes made the animals' faces look feminine.

The road climbed again and turned to the left. They drove through a tunnel of pine trees with an occasional mahogany tree arching over them. Albert slowed when he saw a sign that announced the upcoming entrance to the Sirilima Game Reserve lodge.

"With this van, we shouldn't have any trouble at the lodge," Cecil said.

"Let me do the talking."

In five minutes they reached the main buildings. The gravel road swung wide by an outdoor pool and curved in a circle that ended at the front door. A long, thatched canopy hung out to protect guests from rain as they got out of Land Rovers to enjoy themselves. Albert followed the circle and parked at the end of a line of three Land Rovers. They were all empty.

"What are the chances the staff knows the security people?" Albert asked as he strode toward the front door. His steps were long but fast.

"Small."

They turned into the open door and found a small reception desk made of bamboo. A black woman came from behind a narrow door. She wore a brown uniform with a crisp white collar. She smiled and said, "May I help you?"

Albert stepped forward. "Security. We're looking for three guests. An American man, his daughter, and a South African woman. We have an important message for them from the United States."

The manager raised her eyebrows. "Of course. They checked in and are assigned rooms 102 through 104. Of course, each one is a free-standing building that contains their sleeping quarters, a full bath, and an open veranda for lake viewing. We have full amenities here also."

"Yes, I know; I work here."

The woman laughed. "I am so accustomed to saying that, I forget to drop it. I haven't seen Mr. Chandler or Miss Koos today, but the daughter went out on a game drive earlier this morning. She returned a short time ago. You go to our left, down the hill."

"Thank you." Albert shook her hand.

Cecil wandered into the lobby and looked out over a spread of grass to see a fake *boma*, or cattle stockade made with a circle of sticks. The lodge might have their own livestock but certainly wouldn't keep them next to the dining room. But it added to the ambience of the lodge. He turned to follow Albert out the door.

Albert opened the back doors of the van and removed the Taser and the plastic restraints. He inspected the Smith and Wesson. Reaching into the canvas bag to his left, he removed a silencer, which he screwed onto the weapon. When he looked up, his face glowed. Albert handed a similar weapon to Cecil. "Let's do this," he said, clipping off each word.

It reminded Cecil of too many American cop shows, but he followed Albert's lead. He shut the back doors while Albert jumped into the driver's seat.

Albert crunched over the gravel as he peeled away from the line of Toyotas. As he reached the front door, the manager came out and flagged him to a stop. "Shit," Albert whispered. "Now what? I don't want to shoot her."

"Sir, please wait. I forgot to check with the main office."

"Oh, of course." Albert leaned his head out of the window. "While you do that, I'll deliver the message and stop here again on the way out."

The woman lowered her head and thought for a moment. "Yes, I guess that will work."

With a scatter of gravel, Albert headed downhill toward the rooms. Each one was connected by a wooden walkway covered by a thatched roof. The "cabins" were lovely buildings in the bush style—wattle and daub walls that had been used for centuries in Africa. Vertical wooden stakes were interwoven with branches and all of it covered with clay, except that these buildings were really made with concrete and plaster to resemble the old ones. Beyond the cabins a lake glistened in the sun, while Cecil spotted a fat hippo lying in the mud along the shore.

"We have to work fast, Albert. That woman will discover we're not on an authorized assignment."

"To hell with her. I don't plan to stop on the way out." He slowed the van as they came to Room 102. Albert stopped and looked around. There was no one outside.

They got out and lifted their legs over the low wall to reach the front door of Room 102. The shades were drawn, and there didn't appear to be any lights on inside. "You take the back side to prevent any escape. If you have to shoot, aim for the legs. Nothing fatal until we've gotten our information from them."

Cecil's throat went dry and he croaked a response. "Uh, sure." To himself, he hoped to hell Albert would subdue the person inside immediately. Cecil wasn't sure he could actually shoot anyone. Maybe the American dude who had hit him in the house.

Albert crouched as he approached the front door and revolved his finger in the air in an apparent signal for Cecil to go around to the back side. Cecil left for the back and found himself also crouched under the windows. He didn't hear anything from inside.

When he reached the back door, he stood to the side so anyone breaking out wouldn't see him right away. Cecil waited. In a few minutes he heard Albert shout, "Open up! Park security. Open up now!" There wasn't any response. The front door crashed, and Cecil heard Albert yelling something inside. Cecil waited until the back door popped open. Albert stood there with sweat on his face.

"God damn bogies have escaped. No one here. Let's blow the next one fast."

They approached Room 103 on foot, circled around it like they had the previous room, and Albert shouted again, "Open up!" Once again, when he broke in, the room was vacant. Albert came out in a hurry. Without taking time to crouch into a protective stance, he ran up to the door of Room 104. Before Cecil had time to find the back door, Albert announced "Security" and demanded entrance.

The door opened.

The girl stepped halfway out to answer Albert. "What is it? Is my father okay? He didn't come back last night." She looked up at Albert, then over at Cecil. Her face clouded over.

"Uh—" Albert straightened and hid the weapon behind his right leg. "Uh, we do have information for you. I've been assigned to pick you up and take you to your father. Would you please step into the van?" He stood aside to let her come forward.

"Perfect. Let me get my stuff." The girl retreated into the room, gathered some items, and came outside. She wore REI hiking boots and a safari shirt open in the front to show her tight t-shirt.

Albert paused to stare at her. "Let's get going." He led her to the passenger door of the van and helped her climb up into the seat. Cecil got into the back, and Albert started the engine. "It's not far from here."

"Is he okay? How about Janette?" The girl's voice was shaky.

"Oh, they're fine. They got lost and then their vehicle broke down."

"Lost? They were going to view a crime scene with someone from the reserve. What do you mean?"

"Not sure. We'll get it all sorted out when we meet them."

Albert gunned the engine, and they roared past the main entrance and reception area, back out the gate, and through the long tunnel of mahogany trees.

"This doesn't sound right. What are you talking about?" the girl insisted.

"I told you—I do not know for certain."

"Who are you?" Now the girl's voice had an edge to it. "Stop the van now!"

Albert rocked to a halt. "Here's what I'll do. I'll radio the main office, and you can talk to them." When she nodded, he got out and came around the back end to the passenger door. He flung it open.

"Where's the radio?"

"Right here, you pushy bitch." Albert swung his hand up, with the Taser, toward her neck. He blasted her for a few seconds. Her body shook, straightened, and then went limp. From his back pocket, Albert removed plastic restraint cuffs and fastened her wrist to the inside door handle.

"Albert, what about the other two?"

He grinned. "We got this one; her father will come running to us. Now tell me where that tower is."

Chapter Forty

The smell of fresh elephant dung stabbed Pete's head and woke him up with its pungent stink. He opened his eyes and saw a tan tree trunk standing beside him. Eucalyptus. The light and the air around him were both soft. When he tried to move, he felt pinned down, immobile. Pete raised his right arm. Next, he lifted his head enough to look at his body, pinned between the two front seats, his seat belt still holding tight, the Landy upright but on a steep slope.

His head hurt, along with most of his body. He remembered the elephants, the charge, the Landy rolling over the edge of the canyon, and him tumbling with the vehicle until he lost any more memory of what had happened. Somehow, he'd survived the fall.

Then he noticed pressure along his side. Janette squeezed next to him in the other seat.

He called her name and was surprised at the strange sound of his voice. More of a croak than the normal sound. He tried to move but couldn't budge anything loose from where he was wedged. Sensations came back to him—thirst, pain along his left side, dizziness, and exhaustion.

He looked at Janette. Eyes closed. Clothing covered in dirt.

Pete rested to recoup his strength. He lifted his head and said quietly, "Janette—"

Eyelids fluttered and she opened her eyes, exposing dull brown orbs. She was alive! "Pete— I, I think I'm okay."

After some time, he heard crunching and loose stones clicking against rocks out of sight above him. Not the elephants again! What would they do to him this time? Then he heard the labored breathing of a human. It came closer.

"Mr. Chandler?" A voice with a British accent called down, echoing faintly off the walls around them.

"Frimby! Frimby! Down here. We're down here." Pete tried to shout.

"Stay there. I'm coming."

In a few minutes, Frimby reached Pete and stood beside him, Frimby's legs cocked at an angle. He surveyed the situation and said, "Your seatbelts saved your lives—and the steel roll bar. I'll help you out, starting with Ms. Koos." Frimby reached over to Janette and unbuckled her.

"I'm sore all over, but I don't think anything's broken. Give me a lift," she said.

Pete unfastened his seat belt and pulled himself out onto the ground. He stood on shaky legs, took a tentative step, and almost rolled down the incline until Frimby grabbed him. "Where's your vehicle?"

"Up on the road. You're both lucky." He took a few steps around the scene and leaned down to smell the elephant dung. Pete looped his arm under Janette's arms. They plodded uphill to reach the narrow road and Frimby's Land Rover. Pete limped over to the door and gave Janette a long, tight hug. He felt her body press tightly against his and shiver along with him.

"Ouch, not so tight," she said.

Frimby had water, coffee, juice, and pastries for them. As they ate, Pete explained what had happened. Janette added to the events that Pete forgot.

Frimby shook his head. "If you don't provoke them, the elephants are usually peaceful. I wonder what caused them to charge you? But there was something odd I found down there. The elephants must have come down to where you lay. I found fresh spoor all around you. They probably investigated what happened and may have even tried to revive you. Elephants have an amazing emotional capacity that is similar to humans'—maybe even better."

Pete shook his head. "They didn't look like they were trying to 'bond' with us."

"Sometimes the young bucks get too rough and don't realize how dangerous they can be. In any event, you are extremely lucky. In a way, it was better to roll off the side than take the full brunt of an elephant charge. You probably wouldn't have survived that. Are you able to get in the truck?"

Janette leaned close to Pete and talked in a low voice. "We need the supplies in the Land Rover down there. Now what?" She looked from Pete to Frimby and back again. "Can we trust him?"

"Frimby? No. He works here; they're probably all in on the operation."

"I think Frimby might be different. Besides, we can't do this alone. We need help."

"What if he exposes us? What about Karen?"

Janette laughed. "Expose our crazy scheme? What else can we do?"

She was right. He led her over to the Landy. Frimby finished drinking a cup of hot tea. Pete cleared his throat and started to talk. He told Frimby about what he'd found on Ian Donahue's computer, the shipment in Cape Town, and the planned exchange as soon as the afternoon. "And we think your brother was innocent."

Frimby's eyes opened wider.

"It looks like he became suspicious about the missing rhinos and went out to investigate on his own when he was shot."

"But the cesium-137?"

"We think it was planted on him to make it look like he was running the operation. Sell the 137 to get money to pay for the slaughter of the animals and then sell the horns."

Frimby's head dropped. He took several deep breaths. "I could never believe my brother would do such a thing. My family will welcome this news." He lifted his head. "What can I do to help?"

Janette explained their plan to meet for an exchange, what needed to be done to set it up, and how quickly it all had to happen. Luckily, most of their supplies had been jammed under the rear seats and were still in place. Two tusks had tumbled out, but they found them easily. The three offloaded everything from the smashed truck, carried it up to the road, and loaded it into Frimby's Land Rover.

Janette asked, "You're from Zimbabwe, aren't you?"

Frimby nodded.

"We need a way to escape out of South Africa. All the airports will be covered. Do you know anyone in Zimbabwe who might help?"

"Uh— In my country, everyone has to be very careful."

"When I say *we* have to get out, I also mean Karen."

Frimby frowned. "I have another brother. Robert. I can check with him."

Janette detailed the items they would all need and the timing.

After finishing the food and tea, they climbed into the cab. Frimby started up the road toward the lodge. Warm sun flooded the plateau and made them feel better.

In record time, they returned to the lodge. Frimby dropped them off at their rooms and waited in the road. The first cabin belonged to Janette. As she got to her door, she yelled to Pete. "Come here!"

He rushed over to find her standing back from the door. It stood open. Pete stepped inside, but no one was there. Janette searched her luggage quickly. Nothing was missing.

"Let's check my cabin," Pete said.

They ran to the next room and found the door also open. Pete rushed inside to look for Donahue's laptop. It was still under the mattress on the far side. He looked at his other things and checked the bathroom and the closet. It didn't look like anything was missing. "What the hell?" Pete said. "Maybe the maids forgot to shut them."

"Doubt it. Someone else was in here."

"Why?" Pete looked up suddenly. "Karen!" He ran out the door to her cabin. The door was closed, and he hammered on it. No answer. Locked. He came out to jump into Frimby's Land Rover. Janette followed, and Frimby drove to the main lobby.

The manager smiled at them and asked if they wanted tea.

"Where's my daughter?" Pete shouted.

The woman raised her hands. "The last I saw her, she went to her room." She looked at Frimby. "You dropped her off earlier this morning."

"She's not there."

"Oh, I forgot. Two men from security stopped by and said they had a message about you and Ms. Koos since you hadn't returned last night. They left to give your daughter the message." She frowned. "Come to think of it, they were supposed to stop back here while I checked with the main gate. I didn't recognize them." She looked up at Pete. "But they never stopped back."

Pete charged out of the lobby and back to the truck. They drove to Karen's cabin and used the master key to open the door. Empty. At his cabin, Pete retrieved Donahue's computer. He handed it to Janette. "We've got to assume the worst—these assholes kidnapped my daughter." Pete sat on the edge of the bed. "Janette, set up the exchange. As soon as possible. If they hurt her in any way—"

A knot tightened in his stomach. She'd been so lucky at the restaurant with Ian. But how could he rescue her this time? If anything happened to Karen, Pete knew he'd couldn't go on. Barbara's death and now— It was too painful to even consider.

Janette keyed in an email to the government contact. She dictated the exact location on the edge of the plateau where the exchange should take place and that it should happen at one o'clock. While they waited for a response, Pete paced the room. "Maybe they plan to hold her for ransom in trade for the shipment. Extra leverage for them against us." He found the two plastic pistols he had taken off the clowns who'd broken into Janette's house. They weren't much, but if they were hidden and used only at a critical moment, the effect of surprise might offset the feeble firepower.

Janette got an immediate response. "He's agreed to our terms. They'll meet us at one o'clock."

"That's in forty minutes. We have to leave now."

"I have to check with the bank in London." She scrolled through her phone. "Okay, I've got the numbers."

Frimby offered to drive, but Pete waved him off. "I don't want them to know you've helped us."

"Wait a minute," Janette said to Pete. She walked over to him and whispered into his ear.

"You're right." He turned to Frimby and explained their plan.

Frimby frowned but said, "It could work. And with a few changes, I know how to make sure it works. What else?"

"I'll tell you on the way." Pete looked around the room as if there was something left to do. He delayed for a moment, fearful the plan wouldn't work and worried about Karen. "I changed my mind, Janette. I have to find Karen first. Maybe you could do—"

"I need you."

"But it's my daughter."

"It's my daughter, too."

Pete's mind jumped sideways.

"Chances are, the thugs we're going to meet have her. Our best chance to rescue her is to go to the exchange and get her back."

He felt the guns in his back pockets. "I'll get her out."

"The sting will work, Pete. Then I'll help you with Karen. Let's go," Janette ordered.

The other two followed her outside. They checked the back end of the Land Rover to make sure they had their meager stash of equipment to take on the criminals they would face.

As Frimby started the engine, Pete climbed in behind Janette. She reached for his hand. He held it, and when he looked at Janette's face, he saw it was pale white.

Chapter Forty-One

Matimba and Freddy left just before noon. The big truck trundled after them with the team. They drove along a tar road that led to the sand road and into the park. After crossing a bridge over a stream, Freddy slowed and looked in his rear-view mirror.

Matimba knew the men on the team, knew they were all hardened fighters and loyal to him. Whether the driver could handle the truck was a different question. Freddy waited as the truck lined up and crawled over the bridge. It made it across and pulled up behind Freddy and Matimba.

"Keep going," Matimba grunted.

The sand slowed their progress, which made Matimba angry all over again. They wound through a savannah area. Although he'd been there to help cover up the shooting of Isaac, Freddy had to keep checking the GPS. It made Matimba nervous. Would Freddy find the right location? They came to a row of dark mountains that rose up in an impenetrable wall before them. It stretched from one side to the other as far as Matimba could see.

To calm himself, Matimba watched the game play in the bush. He often thought he would have made a good panther. No, a great panther. The daydream made him feel proud. In a way, he was a panther—bringing home a kill/money to feed his families and protect them.

Freddy stopped at the entrance to a narrow canyon. It seemed to go straight up into the sky as if a deep cut had been made between the gray and blue mountains on either side. A stone road twisted into the canyon. This must be what Smith had cautioned Matimba about—could the heavy truck make it up the grade?

Matimba didn't wait to think it over. He stepped out and waved the truck forward. It groaned as if it knew what lay ahead.

Together, they entered the canyon and started to climb. In ten minutes, Matimba looked behind but didn't see the truck. "Stop," he ordered Freddy. They waited. In a short time, the truck came into view, moving slowly up the road. Its right side scraped the granite wall with a screeching sound every time it touched. Freddy moved forward.

Matimba checked his watch. Twelve-twenty. His phone beeped, and he opened it to find a message from the two thieves: meet at the edge of the plateau at one o'clock. "We got 'em!" he shouted to Freddy. "Get this old baboon moving."

In fifteen minutes, they breached the top of the canyon and came out onto a broad, flat plateau. It rolled off toward the horizon through fields of sage until it bumped against a bubble mountain in the far distance. Freddy stopped the vehicle.

The truck lumbered over the top and also stopped. Everyone got out and looked around.

"Get the sniper," Matimba said to Freddy, who called on his phone.

The team unloaded weapons, field glasses, ammunition, and piles of camouflage clothing, which they spread out on the fragrant ground. The sun was full in the sky and the breeze had died, so the temperature climbed. In spite of that, all the men dressed in the camo and moved off to their assigned positions. Luckily, the map back at the ranger's office had been accurate, and Matimba didn't need to alter much of the planning.

He watched as the men deployed. Two would cover the edge of the ridge behind them. One hiked across the open field to hide behind a red penstemon bush that flamed as if it were on fire this time of year. Perfect cover. The fourth man lay in a low ditch beside the road in case the three dogs tried to escape in their vehicle. Each man in the team carried .45 caliber Colt automatic pistols with speed loaders in pockets on their pants legs. They also had Winchester .308 Predator rifles with scopes, although at this close distance they probably weren't necessary.

A dusty SUV climbed out of the canyon and stopped beside Matimba. A small blonde man emerged and nodded his head. He didn't shake hands. Matimba assumed it was Swart, the sniper. Matimba didn't care to talk with him; snipers were weird people, and they made Matimba uneasy. He didn't feel like they were real warriors. They killed from the comfort of 300 yards away. Freddy introduced them. Matimba glanced at his watch and ordered Swart to hurry to the west end of the field. A scraggly pin oak stood by itself but offered enough cover to hide Swart. He was instructed to set up his nest there and fire only if he received a verbal command from Matimba.

Swart agreed and plugged a bud into his left ear. He retrieved the biggest rifle Matimba had seen outside the military.

"Should I unload the forklift?" Freddy asked.

"Not until we know where they park the crate. Besides, after I'm done, we've got to pick up the bodies." He thought of what it would sound like when the spinal column of the arrogant American snapped in Matimba's hands.

"Smith said all three were at the lodge. Over there." Freddy pointed across the field. "We should see their dust any time now."

In five minutes, everyone was in place and hidden. Matimba turned his face to the sky and felt the warmth of the sun. He thought of all his children and how fun it would be to spoil them with new gifts.

Chapter Forty-Two

The Sirilima van rocked from side to side as Albert sped along the sand road toward the entrance they had breached the previous night. Cecil rode in the back, his laptop open, directing Albert's driving to find the tower.

"It's up on a hill to the left," Cecil said. He looked into the front seat. The girl was still out, slumped against the door. When she woke, he expected a lot of screaming. He looked back at his screen. "Turn left, then keep going."

The van leaned to the side as Albert gave it gas and shot forward on a new road.

"Hey, slow down. It's bouncing so much I can't read the map."

"You said yourself, 'We haven't got much time.'"

The trees closed around them and narrowed the access to the tower. At least it was daylight and they could see, unlike the night before. Whenever Albert slowed, the dust from behind them caught up, covering the windows like a fog.

Twenty minutes later, they still hadn't found the tower.

"God dammit, Cecil. Where the hell is it?"

"I don't know. I think you have to backtrack to the right. The maps are not working here. I'll use the compass."

Karen sat up and her head wobbled from side to side. "Where—?"

"Shut up," Albert yelled at her.

"Where is my father?"

"Oh, you'll see him soon enough. When he finds out we have you, he'll come running—just as we planned." Albert snickered. He shouted over his shoulder, "Cecil, give me the beret. It's important to maintain our identity."

"Oh, you're as worthless as camel shit." Cecil dug around in the equipment behind him until he spotted the red beret hidden in the corner. It was soiled, which Albert wouldn't like, but Cecil handed it forward.

Albert adjusted it over his Afro and snugged it down. "When we get to the tower, how long will it take to set the charges and blow it?"

"About ten minutes. As soon as it goes down, we've got free access anywhere in the park. The easiest way out is the gate we came through originally. That's also close to the tower."

His phone buzzed. Cecil looked and saw it was a message from the Captain. He told Albert.

"Tell him we're a little busy right now."

"He wants to meet us. Has information from his meeting with Zoya. Says it's dynamite."

Albert only grunted.

In thirty minutes, they still hadn't found the tower. Albert stopped the van.

"You're lost, aren't you?" Karen gave a small laugh.

"Shut up!" Albert said.

"When my father finds you, it's all over."

"This time, we're ready for him," Cecil said with a bit more confidence than he really felt.

"You don't have any idea how good he is."

Albert's face became red. He pulled out his handgun and held it up in the air for her to see. "This should give him a reason to respect me. And if he doesn't give me the information I need, I'll use it—on you!" He pointed the barrel toward her head and held it there for a few seconds. "I normally wouldn't kill civilians, but this is for the future of South Africa."

Karen shrunk into the corner of the seat by the door.

Albert leaned into the cargo area of the van. "What do we do now?"

"Uh, the maps are all fucked up. But if we follow the compass, we should get to the gate we came in through. Once we're there, I can work backwards to find the tower. Trick is, we can't be seen at the gate, so we stop before then and make our turns."

Albert sighed. "This better work." He spun the van around in a spray of sand and headed down the road. In five minutes, the road widened. Two signs announced the upcoming gate.

"This is it," Cecil said. "In about a hundred meters, take a sharp left. It should go uphill toward the tower."

Albert slowed, looking for the turn-off. Around the next bend, he hit the brakes. Ahead on the road, two park Jeeps came toward them.

Each one held three rangers and a .50 caliber machine gun mounted where the rear left seat normally was fitted. A man in the lead Jeep spotted the van and pointed.

"Fuck! Albert, get out!"

Albert leaned the van over to one side as he turned around in the road. The equipment in the back slid sideways, and the tires squealed in protest. Even his beret fell off during the maneuver. Albert floored the van and it rocketed forward.

"Where the hell do we go, Cecil?"

Cecil had his head down, pounding on the keyboard of his laptop. "Give me a minute—"

"Where?" Albert yelled.

"Uh, keep going for two hundred meters until you get to a Y in the road. Take the left fork." He crawled to the back window and looked out. "Faster. They're gaining."

Albert kept his foot on the floor while the engine screamed. The temperature gauge on the dash showed the results of the chase—it crept upward. "How the hell do we get out?"

"We have to get back to the plateau. It's open there, and we might be able to gain distance on them. Our only hope is to beat them down the mountain and out the front gate."

"And you don't think they called ahead to that gate? You stupid ass."

"You got any better ideas?"

Albert didn't answer. He swerved to the left at the fork and got back up to maximum speed. The van shuddered with the effort. "Get ready to lay down fire."

"Are you crazy? They'll blow us off the road in one shot."

"We're not going down without a fight."

"Just keep driving." Cecil looked out the back window again. The Jeeps held the same distance. At least they weren't getting closer. There might be a chance.

They entered a thick forest area, and the road rose and fell as it wound through uneven terrain. Albert slowed enough to avoid a rollover. But the van bucked around, tossing their equipment back and forth. At this point, it probably didn't make any difference since the plan to blow the tower was past viability. They needed to escape in any way possible.

The road leveled off, and in a few minutes, they burst out of the forest. Albert gave it more gas, but the van didn't have any more power to give in return. The Jeeps came closer. One of the rangers stood, gripping the windscreen in his hand as he shouted something.

Ahead of the van, Cecil saw the flat fields of the plateau. In the distance, a bubble mountain rose like a bald man sitting to drink his tea. It was very far ahead.

Cecil heard the explosions as the fifty-caliber machine guns on the Jeeps opened up. In controlled bursts of three shots, the guns barked like they were trying to clear their throats. Albert heard them and started to zig-zag to avoid getting hit. The van wasn't designed for that pattern, especially at top speed, so it rolled dangerously from left to right. The girl screamed with each tilt. Cecil clung to whatever hand grip he could find. Luckily, the Jeeps were probably bouncing as much as the van, so the shots were going wild and nothing hit the van.

Until one did.

Over the roar of the engine, Cecil heard a metallic screech behind him. He twisted around to see that a bullet had penetrated the lower left side of the back door. It must have buried itself in their equipment and stopped. He didn't need to tell Albert.

They roared past the bubble mountain and saw vast herds moving across the plain: zebras, giant elands with horns that twisted three feet into the air, springbok, clumps of giraffes, wildebeest, and even a crash of rhinos lumbering among the zebras. The animals played in the warmth from the sun.

Beyond the herds, Cecil saw a faint dust plume trailing a vehicle. Someone was crossing ahead of them, traveling in the same direction. Security? Probably not, since they certainly would have turned around to catch Albert and Cecil.

Although from a distance the plateau looked flat, it actually contained several depressions hidden throughout the area. Cecil hoped if they could get the van into one of those depressions, they might be able to hide long enough to turn onto a different road before the Jeeps knew which way they'd gone. He shouted his plan to Albert, who nodded with understanding.

Trick was, could they make it before being shot?

Cecil looked through the windscreen, searching for the nearest depression to head toward. It was hard to determine until they got right on top of it. The land in Africa was deceptive from a distance. His eyes followed the herds. Four hundred yards ahead, the giant elands spread out like a sand-colored carpet. Cecil let his eyes travel across the backs of the animals until, in the far distance, the herd disappeared —because they stood in a depression and were lost from Cecil's view. "There, over there," he shouted at Albert. "Go to the right and follow the elands."

Albert curved onto another road and raced after the herd.

The Jeeps followed and closed in.

Cecil crawled to the back window. Another advantage they would have was the dust. Billowing in clouds behind them, it would screen their escape.

That's when the shooting started again. Although the van was obscured by dust, the Jeeps must have become desperate and taken their chances at hitting it. Cecil couldn't see the guns firing, but he could hear the barking of the shots. With the sound of metal ripping, a bullet crashed through the upper side of the van and tore through the roof. The shooters had zeroed in on them.

Chapter Forty-Three

Frimby gunned the Toyota and just barely missed hitting the swimming pool on his way out of the lodge. Since he'd driven this way so often, he knew the road well but would switch driving with Janette later. That enabled them to gain time. The sun crossed the middle of the sky as they burst out of the forest onto the open plain.

The Land Rover rattled and bumped through the sage bushes. Pete thought about Karen. Their entire plan depended on timing. At the right moment, he would have to grab her and get away. Although Janette had promised to help, ultimately there would only be time and opportunity for one rescue. If Pete failed, they all failed.

Frimby steered around the small hills and gunned it into the depressions. Each time, he managed to keep the speed up. Herds of peaceful animals drifted around them, searching for sweet treats in the grass.

Within twenty minutes, Pete spotted two cars and a large truck parked near the edge of the ridge. Beyond them, the canyon he'd been pushed into slanted down at a steep angle. The smugglers would be trapped against it if everything went as he hoped. Pete raised the field glasses and scanned the area. He saw two black men standing beside a car. One was older and looked fat and out of shape. Should be easy to take. From the number of vehicles, Pete suspected there were other men, probably hidden in the grass around the site. He told Frimby to stop before they were spotted.

They waited until the dust behind them had settled. Frimby changed places with Janette. She shifted into gear and eased the Landy forward. "I don't think I can do it, Pete."

"You have to. I have to grab Karen."

She glanced at him twice. "I can't—" She stopped and raised her hand, reddened, veins protruding, and pounded the wheel.

"Don't think about it. Creep forward until we can drop off Frimby."

Janette drove at a slow pace. In five minutes they stopped at the predetermined point.

Frimby jumped out and reached for the field glasses to survey the area to his right. Back and forth he swung them until he stopped to focus in front of himself. "As we planned. Coming this way." He handed the glasses to Pete. Frimby climbed up into the back and pulled out the two-way radio and the rest of the equipment he needed. "Channel four," he told Pete. Frimby took a deep drink of water, wiped his mouth off, and looked at both Pete and Janette. "Give me seven before you move again." He nodded with a slight grin and left on a churning run that made him look like a young springbok.

Pete waited for seven minutes and signaled Janette to move. She took off at a slow pace to give Frimby more than enough time to position himself.

In several hundred yards, they reached the exchange site. The same two men stood in the shade of the truck. One came forward to make contact. He had buck teeth that made him look like he was smiling although he certainly wasn't. Janette stopped the Land Rover on the road, facing toward the canyon. She kept the engine running.

The lone man shouted, "You got the shipment?"

"Yes," Pete replied.

"Where the fuck is it? Hidden under you bonnet?" He pointed at the hood of the engine.

"We've got it. But first, I want my daughter."

"What are you talking about?"

"My daughter, you asshole. Where is she?"

"We haven't got anyone. We want the shipment. We got the money, so where is our crate?"

Pete looked from one car to another to the truck. They must be holding her inside one of them. He had to get her out before anything else happened. Without that, it would take too long to locate her. He eased himself down from the Land Rover, leaving the door open. Janette did the same and came around to stand by him. He felt the two pistols in his back pockets.

Pete said, "First I want to see my daughter. I want her released so I can be sure I get her back."

The man looked at Pete and looked back at the fat one. "Don't know what you're talking about."

"I demand to look into your cars."

The fat one shifted his shoulder away from the truck and waved his hand. The man with the buck teeth led Pete and Janette toward the fat man. When they got there, he said, "What's the problem, America?"

"The problem is, I want my daughter before you even see one piece of ivory."

The heavy man pursed his lips and gave a tired laugh. "No games. Where's our stuff?"

"I want to search your vehicles for her."

The man hesitated, then waved a heavy arm toward the truck.

Pete hurried to the back and threw open the door. It was empty except for a diesel forklift. He moved to each car and opened the doors. She wasn't there. He spun around and walked directly to the large man. "Where have you put her?"

"We don't have anyone. All we want is our shipment."

At this point, there wasn't anything more Pete could do. For a moment, time stopped. The sun smelled hot on his shoulders, and he felt defeated. Standing out here, hoping a ludicrous plan would work with only *chutzpah* to support it. Surrounded by lots of hostile firepower. And even then, he worried whether Janette could pull it off. Besides all that, Karen was still missing.

Janette spoke up. "We don't have the entire shipment because we didn't have a truck large enough to transport it. It's back in Cape Town. Safe in a warehouse."

The fat man stepped forward. "I am Matimba," he said and raised his eyebrows as if to question her.

"Koos." She stood in the cab and rested one arm on the windshield, defiant.

Pete woke up. Maybe the plan could work, after all. "We've got some samples in the back of the Land Rover to prove we've got everything else. But first, the money has to be transferred."

"Not so fast, America. We'll do this my way." Matimba waved the second man toward the Land Rover. Janette got out and flipped the plastic off the cargo in the rear end. The man lifted a tusk up and out of the truck. He dragged it over to Matimba. Together, they read the number on the side: *Block 9*. The man scrolled through several screens on his phone. Then he looked at Matimba. "That's ours."

Pete helped the man with the buck teeth carry the other two tusks. When their authenticity had been verified, Pete said, "We need the money, and we'll give you the GPS coordinates for the rest of the shipment. Your men in Cape Town can check it out."

Matimba came forward surprisingly fast for such a large man. He stood two inches taller than Pete and faced him. "You think you can do this shit to me? No shipment when you promised it? I come all the way out here for nothing?" His eyes were edged in red.

"She told you: we don't have a truck."

Matimba thought about it. He looked at the tusks on the ground. "Okay. We'll play it that way for now. But you two aren't leaving until we confirm the shipment's location."

"The money."

The other man stepped up with his phone. "Where do you want it?"

Janette read the account numbers off her phone. "The account is at a London bank." She gave him several passwords and more numbers, which the second man put into his phone. It took a few minutes. Janette watched her screen. She broke into a brief smile when she saw the money move into the account. "Wait," she said and scrambled the passwords before anything else happened. She looked at Pete and nodded.

Matimba moved to Janette and towered above her. "Give it to me."

She read off the coordinates and gave the address in Cape Town also.

"Stay there," Matimba ordered. The second man made several phone calls.

Pete said, "We're going back to the Landy to sit down. It's hot out here."

"You're not going anywhere," Matimba growled.

Pete stared into his eyes. "It's just over there." He looked around the field. "I'm sure you've got plenty of guns out there to stop us. What are you worried about?"

Matimba frowned but didn't stop them from leaving.

At the truck, they climbed in and sat. Pete glanced at his watch. "How much time do you think it will take before they realize the ivory and horns aren't there?"

Scanning the field behind them, Janette said, "Depends on how close his men happen to be to the warehouse. It's a real address, but I have no idea where the rest of the shipment went."

Pete didn't want to move too early. He waited. The second man talked more on his phone. They all waited. The wind blew the smell of animals over them. It smelled fresh, like the sage. An African fish eagle chased two hawks across the sky toward the canyon. The breeze carried the sharp musky odor of animals, stronger now. They waited some more. Then Pete bent down in the cab and picked up the two-way radio from the floor. Hiding from the smugglers, he clicked it on to channel four and told Frimby, "Now!"

Pete sat up and looked at the two men. They had moved back to the shade of their truck. Then Pete heard it clearly—the blast from an air horn off to their right, opposite from the canyon and out on the plain. In a few minutes, a second blast came from an angle to the right, then a third blast soon after that. Always the sound moved parallel to them. More blasts of noise.

Matimba and the other man stood away from the truck. They looked out toward the plain. The second man talked into his phone, shouting this time.

Pete saw a third man stand up along the side of the road, dressed in camo and shouldering a rifle. He side-stepped toward Matimba but kept the rifle pointed at Pete and Janette. None of the three knew what was happening, but they sensed trouble.

Suddenly, Matimba charged toward the Land Rover. He jumped onto the first step up to the cab and grabbed Pete by the shoulders. Matimba wrenched Pete out and threw him onto the ground.

Before Pete could get up, Matimba had kicked him in the side. Pain shot down through Pete's legs, and he curled up for protection until he could get a chance to stand. Matimba delivered two more kicks, working his way around to Pete's back, aiming for the kidneys, which would devastate Pete.

Janette came around the truck and jumped on Matimba's back. He roared and rolled his shoulders to throw her off. Janette spun off him and landed on her back with a grunt. At least she had given Pete some time to get up.

He moved into the classic taekwondo stance in preparation for a deadly kick. Matimba's surprise attack had thrown off Pete. He would try to stall him, but he sensed Matimba was in this to the end. Pete bicycled to his right, moving his legs up and down for balance, looking for an opening, coiled. He studied Matimba and noticed how broad his shoulders were and how big the muscles were as they bunched. Matimba wasn't in any hurry. He, too, waited for the moment to kill.

Pete saw him raise his arms momentarily, so Pete executed a sidekick, pushing off his back leg for maximum speed and power. It was designed to come in under his opponent's raised arms, hit him in the chest, and stop his heart. Pete missed and spun around to recover.

Matimba smiled and kept inching forward.

Pete circled in the opposite direction; sometimes an opponent has a weaker side. Pete moved to the left and unleashed another fast kick. It missed but struck Matimba on the shoulder. It should have knocked him down. Matimba staggered but remained standing.

When Pete spun around to regain his balance, Matimba attacked. He slammed into Pete with his forearms and, like an NFL lineman, lifted his arms to throw Pete backwards. The blow stunned Pete. He fell onto his back, the wind knocked out of him. He gasped to get his lungs working again but knew he had to keep moving, so he rolled to his side.

Anticipating the move, Matimba used his outstretched leg to trap Pete. On his knees, Matimba crawled along Pete's side and flipped him over like a dead animal. Matimba wrapped his hands around Pete's neck and thumped his head onto the ground several times.

Pete's vision blurred, and he kicked his legs uselessly. He felt the roughened fingers crushing his throat and smelled the man's breath—onions—and Pete knew death was stalking him just like a predator on the African plains.

Chapter Forty-Four

The vibrations coursing through the ground helped Pete focus. Irregular pounding sounds surrounded him with a great rush of air. Frimby had succeeded! The sound of the air horns had stirred the large group of wildebeest into action, and their herding instincts had made them charge together in one direction. Frimby had assured Pete and Janette the animals would run mindlessly, shoulder to shoulder, until stopped by a barrier of some kind.

In the meantime, Pete was dying.

Matimba also heard the sound. Without letting up the pressure on Pete's throat, Matimba twisted around to look behind him. He turned back quickly and squeezed harder. Matimba's eyes were fully red now, and he smiled as he bore down on his work. It seemed fun for him.

Pete fought to stay conscious. Starbursts exploded before him. He pried at the hands on his neck but couldn't budge them. Pete realized that by the time the wildebeest reached this spot to scatter Matimba and his men, Pete would be dead. His mind unplugged from the present and he thought of his family, of women he had loved and lost, and of Karen —he had to save her.

He dug deep inside for the strength to get his right hand beneath him and search for the Plastico pistol in his back pocket. His hand inched between the ground and his body, searching. It was gone, probably dislodged during the fight. What about the other one?

He raised his hip on the left side and began another search there. He had to work his hand around Matimba's forearm. The effort used most of the little strength Pete had left, but he found the side of his own body. His hand squeezed underneath him.

The gun was still in his back pocket. Pete's fingers curled around it and he tugged at the gun, hoping he wouldn't drop it. Pete wasn't left-handed, but he managed to get the Plastico out. He raised the gun and tried to work it underneath Matimba's chest. Fighting to stay conscious, Pete was unable to position it in the right spot. The gun slipped in his sweaty hand. The angle was awkward, and he wasn't sure the one bullet in the gun would hit home.

He fired.

Matimba's bulk muffled the sound, and his body shuddered. Rolling his eyes up into his head, Matimba teetered from side to side. He recovered and snarled as he pressed even harder on Pete's neck while thumping his head against the ground to make the kill quicker.

Pete didn't know if the pounding sound was from his head or the herd, but the noise increased to a steady roar. The honking and grunting of the wildebeest carried across the plain. How close were they? Too far. Unable to breathe or move, Pete's mind fought back, but his body gave up. He felt only sadness.

Then Matimba reared up into the air, bawled, and with a convulsive shiver, rolled off and lay still on his back. Although his eyes remained open and staring at the blue canopy of African sky, his heart had stopped, fatally damaged by a small bullet.

Pete couldn't think. All he knew was that the massive pressure was gone. His lungs inflated tentatively, pumping in more air, and his brain clicked back to life. He still couldn't see well, but he felt the earth shake around him.

Janette ran to him. She brought a bottle of water, forced him to drink from it, and helped him sit up. "Come on, we've gotta get out of here," she screamed.

"Karen—"

"We'll find her, but we've got to move!" She tugged at his arms to get him standing.

"Where?"

"Over there. The Landy. Come on."

Pete stumbled alongside Janette, his arm draped over her shoulder. Even though he tried to lift his feet, they dragged through the grass. Besides, the ground shook so much it was hard to keep his balance. Pete's vision was clearing, and he saw the truck. It looked very far away.

Clouds of dust surrounded them, and the sound of the wildebeest charge was so loud Pete couldn't hear anything Janette yelled at him. She pushed him and directed him with hand signals to run for the Land Rover. He tried but stumbled into a heap on the ground. Janette stopped to lift him again. This time, his legs worked and he gained speed.

They reached the Land Rover. The doors were still open and the engine running, as they had planned. Pete settled into the passenger seat and finally was able to breathe deeply. He looked to his right. The chaos must be what a hurricane was like. He saw a wide, dark shape running at them from out on the plain. Within the shape, individual wildebeest appeared, their heads down, horns swinging back and forth and their shaggy backs bucking up and down.

Janette paused just long enough to drink more water and forced Pete to do the same. Pete pointed down toward the canyon, and she nodded.

He looked to the side again. Several men dressed in camo were running just in front of the wildebeest. Intent on their instinctive herding stampede, the animals were oblivious and trampled over everything in their path. Then Pete spotted a lone man perched high in a pin oak tree. He had blonde hair and hung on to the safety of the branches as he looked from side to side at the thundering mass of animals moving below him. Pete saw an unusually long rifle in the man's hands. The sniper. Only a sniper would have such a weapon.

Of course, Matimba had deployed a sniper at the site. Pete and Janette would never have left alive.

The sniper grasped a branch with one hand while cradling the rifle with the other hand. The oak tree began to shake as the wildebeest herd thickened around it. As dust rose above their backs, they ran uncontrollably. Then Pete saw the sniper fall from the tree directly into the churning herd. He flipped upside down so his legs spread in a V shape into the air and then disappeared below the heaving flanks of the animals. In a few minutes, the sniper's body bounced up in the air, off the back of one of the beasts, and fell again to be trampled to death under hundreds of mindless hooves.

"Frimby!" Janette yelled.

"He'll be okay. We don't want him to be seen with us."

As she put the truck in gear, Pete looked back again. Far behind, a van raced along the same road, coming toward them.

Janette glanced also. "They're after us."

IVORY LUST

Pete saw a logo on the side of the van and the words "Sirilima Game Reserve." "Wait. It's not the Border Patrol."

"So what? Let's get the hell out of here."

The leading edge of the wildebeest herd reached the ridge. Some of the animals tumbled down into the canyon, others picked their way through, and many others managed to turn to avoid falling in. It caused the herd to clump together, tighter and more congested than ever.

The van raced along the side of the herd. Weaving to avoid hitting some of the animals, it looked out of control. Then it hit a pothole and flipped onto its side, scouring out a long trough in the dirt as it skidded to a halt. A door came loose and cartwheeled into the air. In spite of the new obstacle, the wildebeest continued to pound forward beside the van.

Janette had started toward the canyon when Pete stopped her. He shouted into her ear, "Go back."

"What?"

"There's something about that van. Go back."

"No."

"It won't take long."

"We'll get run over by the animals." But then she agreed and shifted into reverse. Janette sped backward on the road until they reached the overturned van.

Pete jumped out and ran toward the van. To avoid the herd, he circled to the far side. A black man lay in the dust without moving, but he groaned in pain. Pete slowed enough to recognize him—one of the two who'd broken into Janette's house. The skinny one. He climbed up to the top of the van and looked inside. Karen lay in a heap on the bottom of the lower side, the one lying on the ground. "Karen!"

She stirred and blinked her eyes.

"It's me. Are you able to stand?"

Karen rolled from side to side and sat up. She looked up and screamed when she saw Pete. "Dad! Help me." She got to her knee, wobbled a little, then stood up. She raised her arms toward him. A snapped-off plastic restraint dangled from her wrist.

Pete shifted his body forward over the opening where the door had blown off. He stretched his arms down until his hands grasped

Karen's. "Can you get your feet on top of the seat? Get up there and push." He directed her until she had climbed onto the seat. "Hurry." He spotted a second man lying in the back end of the van. Albert. The one whom Pete had stomped in the back. For a moment, Pete thought of crawling down into the van and finishing what he'd started at Janette's. But the rage caused his arms to shake so badly, he couldn't maneuver himself inside.

Albert uncurled from the door he lay on and stood up. It took him a few moments to comprehend what was happening. His eyes blinked and he grabbed for Karen, catching her ankle.

Pete grunted and heaved her up through the opening. She flopped over on the ground and he followed, curling his arms around her. She cried and shook.

"Please—" she cried. "Dad."

Albert, coming out through the door, had his arms on either side of the frame, elbows bent, as he shoved down and popped his body through the top.

"Come on, we have to get out of here." He helped her to stand, and they hurried to the Landy. Janette watched them, and when they'd climbed in the back row of seats, she gunned the truck and shot forward. Janette swerved off the road to avoid the wildebeest who charged headlong in a circle now that they'd been blocked by the ridge.

Karen leaned against Pete while he wrapped his arms around her. He faced the right side of the Land Rover and could see the herd over Karen's head. Janette began to pull away. Pete watched the wildebeest in a whirling chaos of bumping bodies and rising dust. Then Pete saw three rhinos running among them. The rhinos thundered between the animals, unperturbed by the stampede. They looked like ancient, gray tanks.

Appearing out of the dust, a fourth rhino emerged for an instant. It was darker than the others, almost black, and thrust its long horn toward the sky as if to declare its preeminence.

Chapter Forty-Five

Janette rattled down into the canyon. Her fingers flattened over the wheel, and she pumped the brakes constantly. When the Land Rover got too close to the edge, eucalyptus branches brushed the side to warn Janette.

It took a long time to work through the canyon and come out onto the savannah below. Sun sparkled across the water as Janette rattled over the bridge on the way toward the exit. Delicate-looking antelope scampered alongside the truck. It seemed so peaceful here compared to the chaos and death behind them. African wildflowers carpeted the fields. There was a purple stretch of pretty lady, some fairy elephant's feet, and even African wild potato with broad lime-colored leaves. Songbirds called. Life was still precarious down here, but it pulsed with power and persistence.

"Can we make it?" Karen yelled from the back seat.

"I'm sure all these vehicles have GPS trackers embedded in them. The rangers or the Border Patrol can use it to find us. We have to get as far away as we can before they mount their pursuit."

Pete crawled under the seat to check their supplies. Since they'd left all their belongings at the lodge, the wad of cash hidden underneath the plastic tarp in a leather pouch would be needed more than ever. He worried about the guards at the main gate. Would Janette be able to get past them?

He squeezed between the seats to reach the cab, where he plopped next to Janette. The wind in his face was hot and smelled of dust. "How are you?"

"That was too close up there."

He leaned over to Janette and spoke into her ear. "Thanks. And we got Karen."

"And we got the money. I'll text my daughter in case something happens to me—"

Pete's chest tightened at the thought. And at that moment, he knew this relationship was different from those he'd had with other women before. He admired Janette immensely and was impressed with all her skills. Sex had been wonderful, and now, Pete wondered, how could he continue without her?

Just before they reached the main gate, Janette stopped. "How are we going to play this?"

Pete turned around to look at Karen. There was a nasty cut across her forehead that had dried blood on it. He told her to lie down across the back seat and practice moaning.

Karen's face screwed up, but she agreed and propped herself against the side door, legs outstretched on the seat. "If you think this will get us the hell out of here, okay!"

Janette pulled into the lot by the office and control center. It was quiet. Two guards stood at the main gate. She slowed at the gate and then stopped.

"Where is your ranger?" the first guard demanded.

"Frimby was thrown out when the wildebeest charged," Pete said. "You heard about their stampede?"

The guard dipped his head once. "You can't leave without authorization. Besides, you are driving an official park vehicle."

"I know, but we have a medical emergency." Pete pointed at Karen. She moaned on cue. "We must get to a hospital as soon as possible." Karen begged in the most pathetic voice Pete had ever heard. It worked.

"Okay. I guess so; I know who you are. When do you expect to return?"

"Don't know. Depends on the medical procedures."

The guard raised the gate and waved them through.

Janette shot out onto the road. Far away from the entrance, she laughed. "Great acting, Karen."

"Oh, I did my share of whining when I was a girl."

Pete looked back at her but didn't say anything.

Janette turned onto the N1 freeway and made good time toward Johannesburg. "Text Frimby and see if he can help us at the Zimbabwe border."

"Border?" Karen asked. "Aren't we getting the hell out of here by something called an *airplane*?"

"We can't leave through any South African airports. The Border Patrol will be able to stop us before we could even board. We'll go through Zimbabwe."

"Don't we need passports? Visas?"

"Yes, but Frimby may be able to help. And, when all else is hopeless, bribes work wonders in Zimbabwe. That's why we have so much cash."

"Hope it works," Karen said. "It could only add to the fun I've had in this country."

Pete turned around to catch her expression. This time she smiled, and when she saw him looking at her, she broke into a grin.

"I'm getting to like this life you lead, Dad. Is it always, like, this exciting?"

He closed his eyes and shook his head. "Did you get to see enough game?"

"Perfect. I was surprised by how many animals are all around. It was awesome."

In two hours, they stopped for gas, food, and to make phone contact with Robert, Frimby's brother, on the border. They passed around Johannesburg to avoid the worst traffic and were headed toward Musina, the border crossing between South Africa and Zimbabwe.

Frimby had replied that Robert would meet them in Musina. He would relay directions as the three got closer.

Pete drove instead of Janette. She told them, "Musina is the northernmost town in the Limpopo province, so it's the closest for us."

"Won't there be a border patrol on the Zimbabwe side?" Karen asked.

Janette laughed. "Did you ever see the first *Star Wars* movie? Remember the bar scene where Luke first meets Hans Solo and Chewbacca? Take the characters in that bar and multiply them by hundreds. That's Musina."

"I can't go back to boring Minnesota." Karen laughed.

"I'm worried that we'll look suspicious with the park's Landy," Pete said. "Won't that delay us, or even stop us?"

Janette shrugged. "The border crossing is one of the busiest in the world. That's because of the thousands of people coming into South

Africa every day for jobs. Fifteen thousand of them live in ramshackle camps around the bridge that crosses the Limpopo River." She raised both open palms into the air. "I'm counting on us blending into all that traffic."

"Hope it works," Pete said.

Karen climbed forward from the back row of seats. She swung her arm out to the side. "Hey, this is easy compared to what happened today." Her hair flowed out behind in the wind like a black cape. She smiled. "Now that I survived, Dad, this has been awesome." She reached forward and wrapped her arms around his neck.

"Yeah," he said. "Who were those guys?"

"I don't know. They acted like a government agency, but something secret. The heavier one kept talking about 'the revolution' and the 'new Africa.'"

"Can you go faster?" Janette asked Pete.

Within two hours, they saw signs announcing Musina, the Limpopo River, and the Musina Baobab Reserve. Pete looked at the gas gauge. "We're getting low."

"From Musina, we cross into Beltbridge. To get to the airport at the capital, Harare, takes another two hours. Don't waste time stopping here; we can get gas on the other side."

The sun set in front of them, making it difficult for Pete to see. He slowed down to compensate. In the golden glow, he saw the outlines of a city on the horizon. "There it is," he announced.

The traffic thickened, which slowed them. Pete still felt exposed, driving an open Land Rover, outfitted for safaris with the game reserve signs on both sides. He'd be glad to get over the border.

That's when Pete first heard the airplane. It was a small spotter plane, probably an old Beechcraft Bonanza. Pete glanced up and saw it come in behind them from the north and then center itself over the freeway. At first he thought it might be evaluating the traffic jams, and he didn't pay any more attention.

Later, Janette tapped his arm and pointed to the sky to the left of the Landy. There was the plane again, bright yellow and with the logo of the South Africa National Defense Force stenciled along the fuselage. The pilot was visible as he looked down at them.

"Can we get lost in the traffic?" Karen shouted from the back.

"Not with this vehicle," Pete said. Ahead, he saw low tan buildings, some warehouses, and a line of cars backed up on the road, waiting to cross the border. He pressed forward.

"He can't do anything up there," Karen said while pointing at the plane. "What's he gonna do, shoot us?"

"No, but he's contacting the Border Patrol at the bridge to stop us," Janette said. She phoned Robert for advice and listened as he gave her instructions. "No, we agreed— Okay, okay, you'd better get us over." She hung up. "Wanker! He wants more money."

"Pay it," Pete shouted.

The plane made two shallow dives over the Land Rover and then lifted to fly over Musina. Once there, it banked, turned, and came back to check again.

Pete could see the bridge. The land around it was semiarid and crowded with housing like he'd seen in the townships of Johannesburg: lean-tos with corrugated tin or cardboard roofs. The riverbed, almost full, contained dirty water that tumbled under the bridge.

The traffic stopped again, and Pete was stuck in neutral.

"Can't you move, Dad? We're sitting ducks out here." Karen shifted from side to side on the seats.

Janette's phone rang. She answered and, while still listening, shouted to Pete, "Robert says get in the right lane. Now!"

Pete squeezed the big vehicle through half a dozen cars as he worked to the right. When he got within fifty yards of the checkpoint at the bridge, he saw a group of uniformed men hurrying toward them. In a single line, they ran between the stalled cars. Pete knew who they were. "We have to move," he shouted.

Janette talked fast on her phone. "Got it." She pointed to the shoulder of the road. "Get over there and gas it!"

Pete obeyed. The Land Rover shot forward. He bounced over the uneven ground but kept going forward. Just before reaching the bridge, Pete saw a lone man standing under the bridge on a slope that led to the river. He waved his arms.

"That's him! That's Robert," Janette said. "Follow him."

"Where? He's at the river." Pete drove down the bank toward the water. He looked for a road or smaller bridge. There was none. "He wants me to fucking go through the river?"

"Follow him. It's our only chance."

Robert held up a hand for them to halt at the river's edge. He smiled at Janette and handed a packet to her as she passed a bundle of cash to him. "Thanks, Robert."

He stood aside and waved them forward—into the river.

"Robert?"

"Go! Go! It's not too dangerous this time of year—before the rainy season," Robert shouted.

The team of uniformed men turned from the road and started to descend the bank of the Limpopo River, chasing after the Land Rover. They yelled while two of them waved handguns. Pete looked at them and looked back at the river. Shifting into drive, he hit the gas.

The Land Rover's knobby tires bit into the mud and gained traction easily. The front end wallowed side to side for a moment until there was more momentum, then plowed forward. The river appeared peaceful, but it was still a current of churning water. Pete got as much speed out of the truck as he could when they hit the edge of the water.

For the first twenty feet, the Land Rover dug down into the water. Then the front end bobbed up as it half-floated. It kept moving. Water rose over the front grill and up the sides of the doors. From either side of the Land Rover, a wake of brown waves broke in long curls. Still, they moved forward. They might make it across.

When they reached the middle, the current took over and began to push the front of the truck downstream. Instinctively, Pete turned the wheel, but of course, that was worthless. He couldn't tell if the tires were on the river bottom or they were floating completely off the ground. The tires lost traction, but they kept moving forward.

The headlights went under. Their progress slowed. After driving for years in snowstorms in Minnesota, he knew to let up on the gas. That seemed to help, and the front end straightened out to point toward the far bank.

People had assembled on the bridge and on both banks. With cheers and whistles, they supported the escape.

Pete felt the front end bump into something solid. It must be the submerged river bank on the far side. Finally, they were rising out of the water. The engine kept running. Karen screamed as they got closer. Janette gripped Pete's arm so hard he almost lost the wheel, but he managed to keep control of the Landy. It climbed the bank like a prehistoric beast coming up from deep under the sea. Finally, they were in Zimbabwe and safe.

Chapter Forty-Six

By early evening, Albert and Cecil had been released from the custody of the Sirilima rangers. Trevor Smith was furious but realized there was no reason to hold them except for the minor crime of trespass onto private property. Smith was more concerned about keeping the details of the afternoon's debacle quiet and hidden.

After they had been dropped off at their vehicle, Albert, who was bandaged around the head, told Cecil to drive.

"Okay." Cecil climbed into the driver's seat and settled himself. He wished for some Cheetos to help calm his nerves that still twitched like corn popping in a hot pan. His phone beeped and he answered. It was the Captain.

"Finally got to you," he said. "I've been trying to reach you all day. I met with Zoya and taped his statement, and you'll be damn happy you paid me what I asked for."

"What did you find out?"

The Captain told Cecil the highlights of Zoya's information. When he finished and had hung up, Cecil thumped the dashboard with his fist. "We got 'em, Albert!"

"What?"

Cecil explained Matimba's entire smuggling plot. His network had generated obscene amounts of cash and spread it among themselves and through a web of corrupted government officials in order to get away with everything.

Albert beamed in spite of his pain. "Cecil," he whispered. "I'll get this to the candidate for prime minister as soon as we're back in Jo-burg. We'll also feed it to our press sources. Everything." He squinted into the setting sun as it bathed his face in a golden light. "It's coming, Cecil. The new South Africa. I will accept my responsibilities with humility and grace."

Cecil started to laugh, cut it off, then merely nodded. "Don't forget me."

Albert slapped him on the shoulder. "We're comrades, you and me. I'll never forget that."

IVORY LUST

* * *

At the Robert Gabriel Mugabe International Airport in Harare, Pete, Karen, and Janette waited for their flights. In the new facility the most impressive feature was the tower—built to look like an African hut of gleaming white stone, rising above the runways.

Pete and Karen were going to New York; Janette looked forward to seeing Jane in London and scheduling the operations.

"I feel sorry for Ian," Janette said.

"Yes. A horrible accident. I called my boss with all the evidence in the hope he can avoid a scandal. He was relieved."

"So, Ian knew about the smuggling?" Karen asked.

"Since the park was slaughtering animals for their horns and ivory, they always needed more stock—which costs money. Ian discovered Sirilima had accounting irregularities and was constantly losing money. So, they started selling cesium-137 for more cash to replenish the books."

"Where did the money go?"

"Donahue found payments made to the head of the Border Patrol, Matimba Phatudi, for his help. In turn, Phatudi sold the stuff to the Chinese and paid off enough government officials to keep the operation a secret. But he kept the majority of the profits. I can't even imagine how much money went through his hands."

"And how many innocent animals he slaughtered," Karen said. "Was he the dude you killed, Dad?"

Pete answered softly, "Yes."

"So why didn't Ian tell Washington right away?" Janette asked.

"Don't know." Pete shrugged. "I guess he thought he could solve the problem, expose the network, and become a hero."

"Or help save the animals," Karen suggested.

"Yes, that's possible."

"Too bad; he was a decent man. After all, he hired me to investigate the problem."

"Hey, you two, I've got to recharge my entire electronic life. Be back in a few light-years." Karen left her new backpack on the floor beside them. She almost skipped a little as she walked away. Then she stopped, pulled the buds from her ears, walked back, and asked, "Hey, what happened to that crate full of ivory and horns you told me about?"

Janette stretched her arms across the back of the chair. "Don't know. I can check with my friend in the police station."

"All this trouble," Pete chuckled, "and someone else grabbed it."

Janette turned to him when Karen plugged in her buds and walked away. "What will you do now?"

He decided to tell her about his mother, who had secretly lived in San Francisco for so many years, unknown to Pete. Together, he and Karen would visit her and rebuild their family.

Pete studied how Janette's hair hung to her shoulders and thought of how her hips moved as she walked. He thought of Barbara and the stab of pain came back again, but not as sharp this time. Was it the passage of time that had dulled it? The improvement in his relationship with Karen? Or was it the woman who sat next to him?

Pete turned back to look at her. He'd grown to love all the parts of Janette. And now she was leaving for London—the same story of his life repeated once again. The women he loved always left.

Not this time. She met his eyes with her own. A warm feeling surged through Pete. "Uh, maybe I could come to London to see you? I mean, after the operations. When everything has settled down. If you're not too busy?"

She smiled broadly. "Why wait? I would love to have you with me during the procedures."

"I'd have to talk with my boss about some time off. After all, I do have a job, you know."

Janette laughed again and waved her hand to the side as if to dismiss a minor obstacle.

"Okay. I mean, I'll come over—as soon as I can."

He leaned back in the chair and tried to get comfortable. Thoughts of the past few days coursed through his mind, and he closed his eyes. He felt good. He was surprised at how everything in Africa continually pulsed with new life. There was the female lion he'd watched with three tawny cubs who rolled on top of her, playing like Karen had done as a child with Pete on the ground. He remembered the dark rhino bursting out of the dust cloud from the wildebeest to appear momentarily and raise its head to the sky. Had he seen one? A Western black rhino? Pete would never know for sure—probably not—but as the image lingered in his mind, he was at peace.

Made in the USA
Middletown, DE
24 May 2019